Rodrigo And

THE CONSTRUCTOR

The Constructor by Rodrigo Andolfato

Independently published (Indie book)

This is a work of fiction. Names, characters, places, and incidents are products of the author's imagination or are used fictitiously. Any resemblance to actual events, locales, or persons, living or dead, are entirely coincidental.

This book is an English version of *O Construtor*, the Portuguese original edition, published in Brazil. Copyright © 2024 Rodrigo Andolfato.

All rights reserved. No portion of this book may be reproduced in any form without permission from the publisher, except as permitted by U.S. copyright law. For permissions contact: andolfato77@gmail.com

ISBN: 9798372427570

To my family. They are the ones who always stand by my side, whether in good or bad times. my father, mother, brothers, uncles, nephews, daughters, and wife.

I would also like to express my gratitude to all the relatives, friends, and co-workers who, upon hearing the initial idea for this book, consistently showed excitement and encouraged me to write and publish this work.

The way of life can be free and beautiful, but we have lost the way. Greed has poisoned men's souls, has barricaded the world with hate, has goose-stepped us into misery and bloodshed. We have developed speed, but we have shut ourselves in. Machinery that gives abundance has left us in want. Our knowledge has made us cynical. Our cleverness, hard and unkind. We think too much and feel too little. More than machinery we need humanity. More than cleverness we need kindness and gentleness. Without these qualities, life will be violent, and all will be lost...

Charlie Chaplin – Final Speech of the movie "The Great Dictator".

Prologue

It was nearly the end of the day. Zalthor Acri sat on an old wooden bench near the edge of a large cliff, listening to the waves crashing against the rocky wall below him. He gazed out over the ocean of the planet Hubberia, while a cool breeze from the sea provided relief from the heat of the sun.

Positioned on one corner of the bench, Zalthor left enough space for another individual to join him, a clear sign of his anticipation for company. His torso leaned slightly forward, supported by a wooden cane, while his hands rested upon the stick.

Zalthor's appearance revealed a person approaching the end of his life, not solely due to advanced age, but also due to the fragile state of his health. His skin was dry and brittle, and only a few strands of grey hair remained atop his head. His frail body made his clothes hang loosely, as if on a wooden hanger. Around his waist, a liquid bag was tied, and a thin rubber hose extended from it, reaching up to his neck.

Suddenly, he looked up and noticed a small dot moving in the sky. Gradually, the object gained speed and started emitting a sharp noise, revealing itself to be a large aircraft. Within moments, Doctor Axlow's ship hovered above the area.

Zalthor looked up serenely and waved, to which Doctor Axlow responded from the ship's window. Despite being as elderly as his friend, the Doctor appeared to be healthier. The ship moved away and landed a short distance behind the bench. A door opened on the fuselage, and Doctor Axlow descended through a small ramp, approaching Zalthor to sit beside him.

"Hi, Axlow," Zalthor greeted in a low voice.

Observing the near-horizon sun of planet Hubberia, the Doctor remarked, "It is a beautiful spectacle, Zalthor! I understand why you chose to spend these days here."

Also gazing at the horizon, Zalthor responded, "Soon, I will become a part of the soil of this place, Axlow. After they bury me, plant a seed over my grave. Perhaps the tree that grows there will inherit part of my essence.

A brief moment of silence followed. Doctor Axlow studied his friend for a few seconds before smirking and saying, "I believe the soil of this place will have to wait a long time to receive your body, Zalthor. I mean, a really long time."

Without turning to face the Doctor, Zalthor asked, "Were you able to solve the reactor instability problem?"

"I was right all along, my friend. I was the one destined for the task. The reactor instability is no longer an issue. We conducted all the necessary tests. Now, all we need to do is place the first Hubbian inside the Converter Chamber. And that Hubbian will be you!"

Zalthor displayed a gentle smile.

The Doctor continued, "Think about it, Zalthor. With such power, we will finally free our people from Zorts' domination. We will become the most powerful race in the galaxy."

Zalthor contemplated the horizon for a few seconds, his mind filled with new thoughts. Suddenly, everything was different. Just minutes before, he was facing the end of his life, but now he stood on the edge of a new world. Doctor Axlow had dedicated decades to developing the Converter Chamber, but Zalthor had long given up hope that the Doctor would complete the project in time to save his life. He had accepted death as an unavoidable fate.

Zalthor turned his head and looked thoughtfully at the Doctor, who couldn't help but notice a change in his friend's posture. Now Zalthor appeared sturdier. The news had revitalized his ailing body.

"Listen to me, Axlow. Once the news spreads across the galaxy that we possess this power, thousands of planetary systems will come to attack us. Civilizations everywhere will make every effort to steal this technology from us. Are we prepared to fight them? We have never been a warrior people."

"That's the reason why we need to initiate the conversions right away, Zalthor. Tomorrow, I will take you to the underground base and place you in the Converter Chamber. You will become the first converted Hubbian. Every cell in your body will be altered. Upon emerging from the Converter Chamber, you will be more powerful than any other being in the Galaxy. And above all, you will live forever and remain eternally young. In a matter of weeks, thousands of Hubbians will be converted. In a few years, millions of Hubbians will possess the same power as you. We will become an invincible race. Our enemies may have larger and more advanced ships, but we will be able to tear through their fuselage as if they were made of paper. Even if the opposing soldiers outnumber us, they will fall one by one while the Hubbians will stand strong. No weapon will be able to harm us."

Exerting a big effort, Zalthor stood up. Then, moving slowly, he walked toward the edge of the cliff. The Doctor struggled to contain his own pride and remained silent as he watched his friend.

The planet Hubberia's sun now sank below the horizon. Zalthor gazed at the sky, feeling his stomach churn. At that moment, he was unaware of what was causing this sensation, but in the following years, when the planet Hubberia ceased to exist, he would come to understand it as a bad omen.

Zalthor turned to Axlow and asked, "Doesn't immortality scare you, my friend? Living forever! What if our minds were designed to only live for a hundred years and not for eternity? How will that affect us? What if, one day, we wish for death? What will we do?"

Doctor Axlow also got up.

"You think you might desire death just because you're in pain now, Zalthor. Your body is old and weak. You feel miserable all the time and want to end your suffering. I know it's not easy, but tomorrow you will be young again, stronger and healthier than ever. I'm confident that no Hubbian will desire death after being converted, not in a million years."

At that moment, the first stars began to appear in the planet Hubberia sky.

"We won't know that for a million years, will we?" reflected Zalthor.

With conviction, the Doctor stared at his friend.

"The sun that will rise tomorrow, Zalthor, will witness the birth of the most powerful race in the Galaxy. The Zorts or any other race will never be able to enslave us again. We will be free and invincible."

Axlow turned to his ship. A young man with red hair had just stepped out of the vehicle and stood beside the access ramp.

"Jwinxs, come here!"

The young man walked toward the two friends.

"This is my new assistant. He will stay here tonight to ensure that everything goes well for you." Axlow placed his hand on Zalthor's shoulder and continued, "Now rest, my friend.

Tomorrow, you will become the first immortal living being of the Galaxy. From tomorrow onwards, we Hubbians will be gods."

Axlow turned and walked toward his transport ship. Zalthor started coughing loudly. Jwinxs went to him and grabbed his arm, helping him stay on his feet. Axlow looked back, noticing how frail his friend appeared. When the disease first appeared, ten years ago, medical professionals predicted that Zalthor would only live for two more years. It was a miracle he was still alive.

"Be strong, Zalthor. I will instruct my shuttle to pick you up early tomorrow morning so that we don't risk you dying before your conversion. Try to rest tonight," advised the Doctor.

Axlow then turned to his assistant and said, "Take good care of him, Jwinxs."

"I will, Doctor. You can count on me."

Axlow turned and walked up the access ramp to his ship.

Before the vehicle door closed, Zalthor took a deep breath and, with great effort, managed to speak loudly enough for the Doctor to hear him.

"Axlow, are we ready?"

"Ready for what, Zalthor?"

"To become gods. Are we prepared for such power?"

The Doctor smiled but didn't answer. Instead, he waved to his friend and boarded his ship. The access ramp retracted, and the vehicle door closed. The shuttle took off and departed, flying toward the ocean.

Zalthor gazed at the stars, which were now more numerous and brighter. He slowly turned and walked toward a log cabin a few dozen yards away.

Jwinxs gently held Zalthor's arm, providing support.

"I must say, Mr. Zalthor, it's an honor to finally meet you in person. The Doctor always spoke highly of you."

Zalthor looked at Jwinxs and gave a gentle smile. Then he said, "You know, Jwinxs? I'm not sure if I want to be a god."

Before entering the cabin, Zalthor glanced back and watched the Doctor's ship disappear among the sky.

"It seems like too much to me," Zalthor concluded.

One million years later...

Part 1

Mark

Chapter 1

The cell phone rang for nearly two minutes before finally stopping. Detective Mark Randall responded to the persistence of the device and opened his eyes. He gazed at the ceiling, remaining motionless for a few more minutes.

Driven by a tenacious curiosity, Mark picked up the phone and noticed a flashing icon indicating the most recent missed call. The device's screen also displayed that it was nearly two o'clock in the morning.

The detective noticed that the call was made by a registered contact, Oswald, his boss. Now Mark was convinced that something awful had occurred. When the chief called at such an hour, there were bound to be bodies to investigate.

Aware that he wouldn't be able to fall back asleep, Mark decided to rise from his bed. Soon he would begin creating hypotheses about what might have happened, and visions of mangled corpses would inundate his thoughts. Two decades of dedicated service in the police department had profoundly deteriorated his mind.

Mark walked to the bathroom, brushed his teeth, washed his face, and combed his hair. After a few seconds of combing, he inspected the comb bristles and noticed how they were filled with strands. For approximately five minutes, he remained still in front of the mirror, inspecting his own appearance. He recently turned forty-six, and most of his hair was already gray. The receding hairline above his forehead reflected the bathroom lamp's light. However, what troubled him the most were two deep wrinkles on his face. They lay just below his eyes, crossing his cheeks in the middle. Resembling two prominent scars, the wrinkles gave Mark a sinister countenance. He had even grown a beard to attempt to mask the scars, but the graying hair covering his face only made him look older.

Mark opened a small medicine cabinet behind the mirror and picked up a tiny bottle containing a few small pills. He turned the bottle upside down, and three pills fell into the palm of his hand. He then put all three pills into his mouth and swallowed. The bottle bore a label indicating that it was a prescription medication, and Mark was advised that he should not consume more than one pill at a time. Unfortunately, ingesting just a single one no longer produced the desired effect. Now, only two pills remained in the bottle.

Mark left the bathroom and proceeded to open the wardrobe, taking a white shirt, an old suit, and a pair of pants. Sitting on the bed, he began putting on the pants. As he straightened his leg, his left knee emitted a sharp crack. He clenched his facial muscles, suppressing the urge to cry out, and took a two-minute pause, patiently waiting for the pain to subside before continuing to dress.

Searching under the rumpled blanket on the bed, Mark located his cell phone. It took him nearly half an hour to return the missed call.

"Hello, Oswald. Good evening! My apologies for the delay. What happened?"

After carefully listening to the chief, the detective replied, "Understood! I'll be there in twenty minutes. Ensure no one disturbs the crime scene. Has Andrew arrived at the scene yet? Tell him to await my arrival."

Upon ending the call, Mark set his phone aside, stood up, and walked to the kitchen. There, he picked up his wallet from atop the refrigerator and made sure that his Civil Police ID and driver's license were inside.

Leaving the apartment, the detective entered the elevator, sensing the familiar smell of dog urine and hearing the loud and characteristic noise of the device descending to the basement. Nothing out of the ordinary.

Upon arriving at the building's underground parking lot, Mark's attention was immediately drawn to a leak from the ceiling, dripping onto the hood of his car with a distinct sewage odor. Shaking his head in disapproval, he got into the vehicle.

Twenty minutes later, Mark Randall drove through a neighborhood near the city's downtown. He was well aware of the residents who inhabited the area: primarily middle-class families consisting of small business owners and well-paid employees.

Mark arrived on a street filled with a crowd of onlookers. He parked his car and got out of the vehicle. The scene was bustling with at least a hundred people, some still in their pajamas. In the middle of the crowd, there was even a vendor pushing a hot dog cart and offering soft beverages and snacks.

"The people of this city are always eager for any event that breaks their routines, even if it is a tragic one," Mark pondered.

The detective discreetly weaved through the crowd until he reached a yellow tape in front of one of the houses on the street. There, he encountered a uniformed police officer who raised a hand, gesturing for Mark to halt. Responding to the signal, Mark took out his wallet from his pocket and opened it, showing his police ID.

Upon seeing the identification, the officer lifted the tape and said, "Good evening, Detective. You may proceed."

"Thank you," Mark replied. His attention turned to the entrance gate of the property—a wealthy family home that, while not extravagant, radiated an air of prosperity.

"There's another detective already inside the house," the officer informed. "He arrived fifteen minutes ago."

Mark entered the property and found several uniformed police officers chatting in the garden. One of them recognized him and spoke up, "We haven't touched anything."

The detective remained silent and proceeded toward the front door of the house. He noticed that the lock had been destroyed and turned toward the police officers.

"It was made for one of you or was it already in this state when you arrived?" he inquired.

"We did it," the same officer responded.

Mark sighed, expressing his frustration.

The same officer exclaimed, "How else do you expect us to enter a house? Dead people don't answer the door, buddy!"

The other officers laughed. The detective turned his face and proceeded into the house.

As Mark entered the residence, he found his partner standing in the middle of the living room. The two colleagues had been working together for just three months since Andrew transferred from a smaller city to be closer to his fiancée. Andrew was fifteen years younger than Mark and had been interviewed by Police Chief Oswald on his first day at the police station. Impressed by Andrew's calm demeanor during the conversation, the chief deemed him a suitable partner for the older detective.

"Tell me, how many body bags are we going to need today?" Mark asked, skipping the usual greetings.

"We have three victims: a young teenage girl and her parents," Andrew replied.

"Have you determined how the perpetrators entered the house?" Mark inquired.

"They entered through the rear of the house. The kitchen window was broken," Andrew informed.

"Which rooms are the bodies in?"

"The girl is in one of the bedrooms, and the parents are in the kitchen."

"Let's start with the kitchen," the veteran suggested, attempting to delay confronting the sight of a deceased teenager.

The two detectives walked to the rear of the residence. Mark immediately noticed that the kitchen door was closed but unlocked, and the key was left in the inside lock.

Next, they saw the woman lying with her back against the floor. Her body was straight, and her eyes were wide open, directed toward the ceiling. Bruising was evident on her neck.

"I believe someone strangled her. The killer likely stood facing her, using both hands to squeeze her neck until she lost consciousness due to lack of oxygen," Andrew speculated.

Mark took a pair of glasses from his pocket, put them on, and bent down to examine the woman closely.

"And continued squeezing until he was certain she had perished," he added, his voice filled with sorrow.

The older detective turned his attention to the other body, beside the woman. The man was also lying face up, but his face was severely disfigured. His eyes, nose, and mouth were crushed.

"Look at the state of his face. Punches didn't cause that damage. It appears to be the work of a heavy instrument, possibly a large hammer," Mark evaluated. "How is the young woman?"

"She suffered the same fate as her father. Her face has also been crushed," Andrew reported.

"Have you found this hammer?" Mark inquired.

"No, I haven't."

"If the killer used a hammer immediately upon entering the kitchen, it's likely that the weapon already belonged to him. You know what that implies, don't you?" Mark asked.

"That he already planned to use it?" Andrew suggested.

"Exactly! This was a premeditated murder. A hammer is a powerful weapon, capable of killing someone silently. Burglars usually prefer firearms or knives, as they are more intimidating. Those who break into a house for robbery don't typically want to harm their victims, just to scare them," Mark explained as he stood up. "However, anyone who enters an occupied residence in the middle of the night, armed with a hammer, does not carry it for intimidation. How many criminals do you think were involved?"

"Probably two. One likely attacked the man, while the other strangled the woman. The couple must have confronted the intruders after hearing the sound of the broken window, and that's when the burglars turned violent," Andrew deduced.

"Let's examine the girl's room," Mark suggested. "Where is her bedroom?"

"It's down the hallway," Andrew answered.

The two detectives proceeded to one of the bedrooms in the house. There, they found the lifeless body of a girl lying on a bed, her face crushed as described by Andrew. However, there was another bed in the room that was empty but messy, indicating that someone else was present during the time of the crime. Mark looked around, observing the pictures on the walls, and realized that the family consisted of the parents and two teenage daughters.

"It seems that the other daughter was also present at home during the time of the murders. Where is she now?" Mark inquired.

"We haven't found her," Andrew replied. "Perhaps she managed to escape."

Mark sighed, noticing that the bedroom window remained closed.

"She didn't run away. It's likely she was kidnapped," Mark concluded.

"Why do you think that?" Andrew asked.

"She didn't leave through the bedroom window. Otherwise, it would be open. Look at the lock: the window is closed from the inside. Furthermore, the girl didn't exit through the front door, which was also locked when the police arrived."

"Maybe when the intruders entered the house, the girl was in another room," Andrew deduced.

"Are any other windows in the house open?" Mark questioned.

"No," the young detective answered. "Only the one in the kitchen, which was broken."

"A young girl running away from a home invaded by criminals would leave her exit open. The only open exits are the kitchen door and window. The girl wouldn't have escaped through the same path the burglars used to enter the residence. Not without being noticed. The expected behavior in such a situation is that the intruders exit through the same passage they entered. In this case, through the window above the sink. They wouldn't have chosen to leave through the kitchen door unless..."

"They were taking someone with them," Andrew concluded.

Chapter 2

Two hours later, Mark and Andrew were seated inside a restaurant called Café and Grill. It was Mark's go-to place when he worked late at night, as it was one of the few establishments open at that hour and the only one he liked. The two detectives were seated at a table in the corner of the restaurant, right beside a large glass window. Andrew was eating a cheese sandwich and drinking a soda. In front of Mark, there was only a bottle of mineral water. He didn't feel hungry.

"The whole operation was swift. It likely didn't last more than a few minutes," Mark evaluated, gazing out of the window at the empty street outside. "Think about it. No drawers were opened, and valuables weren't taken. I believe the intruders entered the house with a single purpose: to kidnap the eldest daughter. The rest of the family may have tragically lost their lives because they stood in the way of the criminals and the girl."

"Any idea who these criminals might be? Ex-boyfriends, perhaps?" Andrew asked.

"We need to dig into the family's background. Find out if the girl had any unwanted admirers or if there was someone stalking her. We need a suspect, someone who deserves to be investigated," Mark replied.

"It's also possible that the father had enemies," Andrew suggested. "Maybe they targeted him, not the girl."

"But why would they go on to kill the youngest daughter? And why take the eldest? It doesn't make sense," Mark retorted.

"The girls might have awakened when the intruders attacked their parents," Andrew speculated.

"Tomorrow, we'll look into the family's contacts," Mark stated. "But right now, what's more urgent than understanding the motive behind this crime is finding the whereabouts of the missing daughter. I believe she's still alive, but time is running out. At this very moment, she may be suffering a lot."

"May God protect her!" Andrew sighed. As he uttered these words, he noticed a sudden change in his partner's expression, as if he had offended the older detective.

"Of course! Your God will protect her. Just like he protected her parents, right?" Mark retorted with heavy sarcasm. "What nonsense!"

Mark crumpled a napkin he used to wipe his hands and tossed it onto the table, displaying his displeasure. Andrew looked at the crumpled napkin for a moment, contemplating the situation.

"So, I can assume you don't believe in God," Andrew stated.

Mark stared at his partner and responded with a sarcastic smile.

"I outgrew the age of having imaginary friends."

Andrew mimicked his colleague's smile and took a sip of soda. He then put the last piece of sandwich into his mouth and calmly chewed, crumpling the small paper bag that wrapped his meal.

After swallowing the last bite, Andrew spoke, "I can imagine it must be difficult to discuss belief in God after what we witnessed tonight. But I must say one thing: I was raised in a family of skeptics, and my parents always taught me that God was a fantasy. I remember my father saying, 'When you're a child, they make you believe in Santa Claus. Then, when you're an adult, they expect you to believe in God.' As a child, I found it amusing, although I didn't fully grasp its meaning as I do now."

"Your father sounds like a wise man. What's his profession?" Mark inquired.

"He is a biologist," Andrew responded.

"Ah, so he likely has solid reasons for not believing in fairy tales," Mark observed. "Your father understand the principles of evolution and how the structures of all living beings are intricately linked to their environments or their closely related species, rather than being the arbitrary creation of an imaginary artist. Am I correct?"

"Yes, my father says things like that all the time. I know I have many reasons not to believe in God, but when I reflect on my life, the decisions I've made, and their consequences, I can't help but conclude that someone or something is looking out for me."

"Have you ever considered the possibility that you're simply a prudent person?" Mark countered.

Andrew took another sip, shifted in his chair to find a more comfortable position, and began, "Let me share two examples to help you understand my perspective. I have an older brother. Around ten years ago, he started investing in the financial market. Every month, he allocated a significant amount of money into stocks, hoping their prices would rise. Over time, he had a substantial portion of his assets invested in various shares. However, he confided to me that things weren't going well. Every time he bought stocks, their prices went down, but when he sold them, their prices increased. It seemed to him like a curse."

"Perhaps your brother simply lacked skill as a financial analyst," Mark suggested.

Andrew disregarded the comment and continued, "After losing money for three years, my brother finally understood the message God was trying to transmit: He should invest his money in something beneficial to the community and not just chase profits through speculation. With that epiphany, my brother decided to open a school to help children from low- and middle-income families. Today, he owns five schools."

Before Mark could respond, Andrew carried on, "I also have a friend with a very different but equally intriguing story. He noticed something peculiar about his life. Every time something good happened, and he believed he was finally on the path to complete happiness, something unfortunate occurred simultaneously. When he got a good job, his girlfriend broke up with him. When he could afford to buy a new house, his brother fell seriously ill."

Mark interjected, "What did he understand of all that?"

"He understood it as God's plan for him: he would never reach absolute happiness. There would always be something to upset him," Andrew explained.

"And why would God subject someone to that?" Mark inquired.

"My friend doesn't know exactly, but he believes it's God's plan for his life. When he reached this conclusion, he began to feel the presence of God in his life. He claims to have found peace ever since," Andrew concluded.

"I don't agree with that way of thinking," Mark countered. "It leads to complacency. What will you think about God when you face a tragic event? How will you accept the notion that your god has abandoned you?"

"I will believe that my time has come, and I will calmly accept my fate because I believe it's part of God's plan," Andrew responded.

Mark rubbed his chin, chuckled softly, and raised one hand, pointing outside the restaurant.

"Look around you, Andrew. Look at this city. Every day, we witness old criminals preying on the vulnerable youth. Dozens of brutal murders occur here each year, and no one seems to care about it. Otherwise, our police station wouldn't be as neglected as it is. The people in this town have grown accustomed to violence. They think it's tolerable for a murder to happen every week, as long as it doesn't affect them directly. They are like old sheep, aware that the wolves lurk on the other side of the fence, ready to jump into the pasture when they're hungry. And nobody takes action to change this reality. All of this happens before the eyes of your God, who seems to be powerless to intervene," Mark expressed.

The older detective gazed at the desert street in front of the restaurant, thinking about what he had just said. Andrew was silent too.

Suddenly, the emptiness of the street was interrupted by the presence of a young girl standing on the pavement. Her clothes, short and flashy, contrasted with the cold night descending upon the city. She looked uneasy and fearful.

Mark took a small bottle from one of his coat pockets and extracted the last two remaining pills. Still fixated on the street, he continued, "Unlike you, my friend, I don't need to indulge in fantasies to face the realities around me. I prefer to stay connected with the truth, no matter how harsh it may be. That's the only advantage of this job. It reminds me of the true nature of the world." He placed the pills into his mouth, took the bottle of mineral water, had a sip, and swallowed the medication.

"Or perhaps you've found another way to cope with reality," Andrew suggested, pointing to the empty bottle on the table.

Mark remained silent and kept his focus on the girl on the street.

"Do you know that woman?" Andrew asked.

"No, I was just thinking that my daughter would be around her age if..." Mark looked at his partner. "Listen, I can't sleep now. I've decided not to go home. I'm heading to the police station to search for any information about the murdered family on social media. Do you have the victims' names?"

"You? Using social media? I thought you despised that kind of thing."

"I do, but nowadays it's impossible to conduct an investigation without utilizing such tool. You know that," Mark replied.

"That's true," Andrew agreed. He took out a small notebook from his coat pocket, tore out a page with the victims' names written on it, and handed it to Mark. "Here are the names. Are you going to the police station right away? It's already five o'clock. I barely had two hours of sleep before Oswald called me. I'm going home."

"I know it's late, but I'd rather not go to sleep right after seeing dead people, especially when young girls are involved. It will disturb my sleep."

"Why are you still in this job?" Andrew asked. "You don't seem happy."

Mark examined the names written on the sheet given by his partner and replied, "Well, twenty years ago, I applied for various jobs and ended up being accepted at the police academy. It's a tough job, but I think I've gotten used to it. Nowadays, I'm not sure if I could do anything else."

"I hope I never end up in the same situation," said Andrew, standing up and returning his notebook to his pocket. "I'm just curious to see how sleepy you'll be when we meet the boss in the morning."

Chapter 3

Five o'clock in the morning at the Civil Police Station, Detective Mark Randall was sat at his desk. The only illumination in the room emanated from the glow of his computer monitor. The entire floor remained empty, with only a few officers on duty on the lower level.

Mark relished being at his workplace during these unconventional hours. The silence and solitude enveloped him, providing a sense of comfort. In a couple of hours, the building would be teeming with activity as it filled with bustling individuals speaking loudly and scurrying about.

At his workstation, Mark logged into the city's most popular social network. His profile page lacked any friends, save for three pending friend requests. One was from his partner, Andrew, another from his boss, Oswald, and the last request hailed from Lauren, a secretary in the same department.

With the names provided by Andrew, Mark navigated to the profile pages of the murdered family members and discovered that the parents, Humbert and Marie Sinclair, were the owners of a clothing factory specializing in wedding party dresses. The girl who was killed was named Joanna Sinclair, a fourteen-year-old. The eldest daughter, Carol Sinclair, the presumed kidnapped victim, was sixteen years old.

While perusing Humbert Sinclair's profile, a particular photograph captured Mark's attention. It featured Humbert and Marie beside the Mayor and the first lady, Charles and Leticia Andraus. The image was taken during the birthday celebration of Charles' youngest son, a ten-year-old boy. The party took place just two months ago.

Upon catching a glimpse of the Mayor's photo, Mark stared at the image for nearly a minute while absentmindedly rubbing his left knee.

"What have you been up to, Charles?" Mark whispered to himself.

Another picture showed Humbert and his wife standing beside the Mayor, this time in the company of a religious figure—a tall man slightly older than the Mayor, donning a voluminous white choir robe.

Mark investigated further and discovered that the religious figure accompanying the Mayor in the photograph was Euzebius Andraus, Charles' brother-in-law. Euzebius was an influential archbishop of a local church. Despite not having a social media profile, his image was widely featured on major news sites, portraying him as a discreet yet prominent figure. Articles in which he appeared may not have revolved around him directly, but everyone else in the photographs seemed proud to be photographed beside the Archbishop. Mark also found a picture of Euzebius standing alongside the president of the republic.

Shifting his focus to the missing daughter, Mark delved into her active social media profile. Through the girl's pictures, he observed a cheerful young lady surrounded by friends. His attention was drawn to a particular photograph featuring Carol Sinclair embracing Paul Andraus, the Mayor's eldest son. This caught Mark's interest, especially due to Carol's seemingly uncomfortable expression next to Paul. Despite searching for more pictures of the two together, the detective couldn't find any.

Mark was familiar with the stories surrounding Paul Andraus. The young man, in his early twenties, engaged in extreme sports, martial arts, and had a penchant for sports cars. However, Paul tended to get involved in more trouble than other affluent youths. He had been linked to two serious car accidents in the past. Although no fatalities occurred, it was proven that Paul was speeding and driving recklessly. During his college years, he gained a reputation as a feared bully. In one fight he participated in, an opponent was stabbed in the back. However, it was never proven that Paul was the assailant.

These were not the only problems Paul had been involved in. He had also faced allegations of sexual misconduct from some college acquaintances, but these charges were mysteriously dropped without a clear explanation. Rumors circulated that the removal of the accusations came at a hefty bill for his family. Although these cases had largely disappeared from public attention, they remained vivid in Mark's memory.

The detective continued his search for more information about the victims' relatives. On Humbert Sinclair's profile page, he found the businessman's brother, named John Sinclair. John's profile didn't provide much information, only a blurry photo of his face and another where he was seen standing beside the four members of the Sinclair family, occupying the corner of the picture.

Mark leaned back in his chair, gazing at the ceiling as he pondered the case. The aged ceiling had some dark stains that reminded him of the blood spilled beside the lifeless bodies. The haunting images of Humbert and his daughter, Joanna Sinclair, with their faces brutally crushed, as well as Marie Sinclair, with the frozen expression of her death in her eyes, flooded the detective's thoughts. Although he had witnessed worse in his work, nights like these were never easy. Mark yearned to clear his mind but instead found himself reliving scenes of horror. He envisioned the assailants entering the house, the father's heart racing as he realized his entire world was about to crumble. What were his thoughts when the first blow of the hammer struck his face? Is it even possible to think about anything after such an ordeal? Humbert Sinclair, undoubtedly, did not perish instantly with the initial blow. Perhaps he remained alive for a few more agonizing minutes before blood and fragmented flesh obstructed his airway, suffocating him.

Mark's stomach churned with nausea. Fortunately, he hadn't eaten since the beginning of the night. The gruesome events at the Sinclair family home had stolen his appetite entirely. However, fatigue began to weigh heavily upon him. Mark rose from his chair and walked to a couch at the rear of the department. He lay down, without bothering to remove his shoes, and adjusted a small pillow on one of the couch's arms before resting his head and closing his eyes.

Chapter 4

Nine o'clock in the morning at the Civil Police Station, Mark and Andrew were in Chief Oswald's office. Oswald had been working in the police department for over thirty years. He was the kind of boss who might not have had a full understanding of the technical aspects of the job but possessed excellent intuition and knew how to deal with people, particularly those involved in city politics. His expression indicated that last night's crime held greater significance than what they typically encountered.

Seated behind his desk, Oswald drank on a large cup of coffee while conversing with his two subordinates. Andrew stood near the entrance, arms crossed, while Mark slumped in an armchair, facing the boss' desk.

Two chairs in front of Oswald's desk remained unoccupied. In the chief's perspective, the two detectives should have been seated on them.

Oswald noticed Mark's struggle to keep his eyes open.

"Why do you look so tired? Did you stay awake all night?" the boss asked.

"I slept a few hours on the office couch, but I don't think it was enough," Mark replied.

"How's your leg today? Is the knee still bothering you?"

"The knee always bothers me, boss. Sometimes less, sometimes more. But it's been worse lately," Mark answered.

As Oswald took a sip of coffee, Andrew looked at him and inquired, "Do you know if the forensics team found any clues at the Sinclair's house? Any hairs or fingerprints from the criminals?"

"I spoke to an expert earlier this morning. The hairs and fingerprints found in the house all belonged to the Sinclair family. The expert believes it was a short operation," Oswald responded.

"We believe that too. The criminals likely didn't spend more than ten minutes inside the residence," Andrew remarked.

"They entered the house, killed the parents, then the youngest daughter, abducted the eldest one, and exited through the kitchen door," Mark added. "Did the forensics find any traces of the kidnapped girl's blood?"

"No. All the blood found in the house belonged to the father and the youngest daughter," the boss replied.

"This suggests that the girl was taken from the house unharmed," Mark concluded.

"She was likely in shock after witnessing what the criminals did to her family. They must have carried her out of the house," Andrew added.

"That's highly probable," Oswald pondered, rubbing his chin. He then pointed to Andrew and said, "Please close the door."

Andrew extended his arm and obeyed the boss' request.

Oswald signaled for the two detectives to come closer and pointed to the chairs in front of his desk. Mark and Andrew moved toward them, took a seat, and leaned toward the boss.

Speaking in a low voice, almost whispering, the chief said, "An assistant to the Mayor contacted me earlier, even before I arrived here. He wanted to discuss the murdered family. Mayor Charles Andraus has great interest in this case. He was a friend of the murdered family and held Humbert Sinclair in high regard."

"I expected something like this," Mark spoke. "I've seen photos of the Sinclair family with Charles Andraus. The Sinclairs even attended the Mayor's youngest son's last birthday party."

"When did that happen?" Andrew asked.

"Two months ago."

"Listen closely, both of you," Oswald interrupted. He signaled for the detectives to come even closer. Andrew and

Mark rested their elbows on the table, and the boss spoke in an even quieter tone, "The Mayor suspects that these deaths may be connected to him."

"What was the exact nature of the relationship between the Sinclair family and the Mayor? Can we know?" Mark inquired.

"The Mayor had been in talks with Humbert Sinclair to appoint him as the Secretary of Public Transportation. Mr. Sinclair was highly regarded by the local community. The plan was to launch him as a candidate for councilor in the upcoming elections," Oswald explained.

"They killed three people over a councilor candidacy? That can't be true!" Andrew exclaimed.

"I wouldn't doubt it," Mark said, leaning back and yawning, his hand covering his mouth. "It wouldn't be the first time something like this has happened in this city." Mark looked at Oswald. "Do you think the Cacellas could be involved?"

"We must keep this investigation strictly confidential. Vicent Cacella himself called me earlier. He's concerned that the Mayor might try to take advantage of this situation and blame rival politicians for the murders. Mr. Cacella intends to closely follow this investigation. As you can see, this case is a major headache," Oswald stated.

"What about the girl? Why would they take her? Did the Mayor provide any leads?" Mark asked.

"The Mayor believes that the girl's abduction is unrelated to the murders. It's likely that the criminals took her for their own sick amusement," Oswald replied.

"Sick amusement?" Andrew questioned, eyes widening. "What do you mean by that?"

Oswald answered, "She was a young and beautiful girl. You know how these individuals can be. They will use her body until it starts to get too damaged. Then they will kill her because it's easier than giving her a bath. That's typically what happens in such cases."

"That's the most horrifying thing I've ever heard!" Andrew expressed his disgust.

"Welcome to the big city, rookie!" Mark mocked. Then he leaned toward Oswald. "Listen, boss, the murder of an ally of the Mayor is a politically motivated crime. It's often premeditated, and the perpetrators eliminate only the target and any unfortunate witnesses. We can't rule out the possibility that it happened in this case, of course. But kidnapping a teenager to 'use her body'? That's the behavior of a maniac."

"They may have hired a maniac," Oswald replied. "Being deranged is a desirable quality when you're looking for someone to take another person's life."

"And what about the Mayor's eldest son?" Mark asked.

"What does Paul Andraus have to do with this?" the boss questioned.

"You know the Mayor's son been involved in numerous troubles in the past. He's the closest we have to a deranged here. I found a picture of him with the kidnapped girl, and her expression raised suspicions. She looked uncomfortable. I think we should interrogate Paul Andraus."

Oswald took a pen from his desk, shook it for a few seconds while pondering, and then gave Mark a stern gaze.

"Answer me one thing, Mr. Randall: You don't intend to let your anger with the Mayor guide this investigation to his son, do you?"

"It has nothing to do with me, boss. You know how the press is in this town. If I made that connection, the journalists will too. It won't be long before people start discussing it on social media. I should question the Mayor's son. He has a troubled past, and soon many nosy people will ask why we aren't investigating him."

"It won't be easy to convince the Mayor to allow you to question his son without a court order," Oswald cautioned.

"I know you have ways to get in touch with the Mayor's family. Speak to Charles Andraus. Explain that our intention is to assist his family, so we can obtain answers before the press starts spreading conspiracy theories."

"I'll see what I can do, but it won't be easy," the chief replied.

Mark stood up, yawned, and stretched.

"I'm leaving now. I need to make a visit. But first, I need to talk to Lauren. Has she arrived?"

"Yeah, she's at her desk. In her usual bad temper," the boss warned.

"What are you going to do?" Andrew asked Mark.

"I'm going to try speaking with a relative of Humbert Sinclair. Would you like to come with me?"

"Of course, I want."

The two detectives left the chief's office.

Like Mark, Secretary Lauren had been working at the Police Station for approximately twenty years. At that moment, she was at her desk, attempting to organize some papers. Recently turning forty-two, Lauren's appearance could be considered attractive. However, her somber choice of clothes made her look older and unapproachable. Her computer shared desk space with ten potted plants, which seemed a bit excessive for Mark's taste.

Upon noticing her colleagues standing in front of her desk, the secretary grumbled.

"Couldn't you at least wait for me to finish what I'm doing?"

Mark took a seat in front of the desk while Andrew remained standing.

"Good morning to you too, my dear! I need you to find a phone number or address for me."

"I'm not your secretary. Is that clear to you?"

"Yes, but you're the best at finding information in the station, and this is an urgent matter. Have you heard about the family that was murdered last night?"

"Yes, the Sinclair family case. Another dreadful night in this wretched city. Those poor people!"

"Did you hear that the eldest daughter may still be in the hands of the crooks who killed her family?"

Lauren let out a sigh and paused her work.

"What do you want from me, Mark?"

"Can you find me the phone number or address of the girl's uncle? He is Humbert Sinclair's brother, and his name is John Sinclair. I believe he will speak with us, even without a court order."

"Just give me a moment," said Lauren as she focused on her computer screen.

Mark crossed his arms, patiently awaiting the results of the search. In the meantime, he glanced out at the bustling lobby of the police station, filled with numerous journalists likely in search of information about the murder from the previous night.

Suddenly, Mark heard a high-pitched noise coming from above. It resembled the sound of a drill. The detective looked up at the ceiling.

"Is anyone working on building the second floor?" Marcos asked.

"Not that I'm aware of," Lauren replied.

"Are you hearing this?" Mark insisted, pointing upwards. "It sounds like a drill or a circular saw."

"I'm not hearing anything," Andrew replied. "It's probably coming from a neighboring building. You've got good ears, don't you?"

"Or he's hearing things," suggested Lauren mockingly.

"Yeah... that could be the case," Mark replied. "So, what did you find?"

Lauren grabbed a pen and a piece of paper, jotting down some information.

"Here it is! I hope it helps."

"Thanks, Lauren! You're my favorite!" Mark said, taking the paper and standing up.

"I'm sure I am," Lauren responded sarcastically.

Chapter 5

Outside the police station, the two detectives walked down the staircase and headed toward the parking lot.

"The boss seemed worried that this case could harm him in some way," Andrew commented. "What could happen?"

"Both sides have the power to end the chief's career," Mark replied. "Charles Andraus is the Mayor, but his rivals, the Cacellas, have a very strong influence over the city council and the judiciary. If suspicions start to turn against either side, they won't hesitate to threaten Oswald. When one of them does, the other side won't lift a finger to defend him. The boss knows he can't rely on anyone."

As they reached the entrance to the parking lot, Mark stopped and placed his hands on his hips. At the end of the night, when he arrived at the police station, the place was empty, but now it was packed with cars.

While Mark tried to locate his vehicle, he asked his partner, "Do you know how the Cacellas and the Andraus families came to control this city?"

"I heard that the Andraus family were prominent farmers and the Cacellas were influential wholesalers," Andrew answered.

"Bullshit!" Mark retorted with a deliberate air of authority. "The Andraus family were land grabbers, and the Cacellas were militiamen. The grandfather of Charles's wife, George Andraus, was a cold-blooded hitman. In the middle of the last century, George was the most feared gunman in this region. One day, he realized he could make much more money by seizing land from the farmers he was eliminating. Before executing his victims, George forced them to sign documents transferring all their lands to him. He promised not to harm their wives and children if they obeyed. After the victims signed the papers, George killed the men, their families, and anyone else who could claim the inherited of the land. Afterwards, he remained silent for two or three years, keeping a low profile during that time. Then he returned to the properties and evicted anyone living there, presenting the signed documents as proof that the lands belonged to him. He arrived with a group of gunmen, and no one could oppose him. Technically, the city police could have intervened, but they chose not to. It would have cost the lives of many police officers."

Mark raised his eyebrows and pointed to where he parked his car. The two detectives started walking again, and the older one continued, "After a few years, George Andraus began going after even the owners of large plots of land near the city. It no longer mattered whether it was an ordered kill. By the time George reached old age, he owned half of the county's area. Many of his farms have been transformed into gated communities surrounding this city's outskirts."

The two detectives got into the car. As Mark fastened his seatbelt, he continued speaking, "On the other hand, the patriarch of the Cacella family was the leader of a militia group, one of those that exploit poor communities by selling cooking gas and charging for street surveillance. His most profitable idea was to open a warehouse designed to supply small stores. The Cacella family prohibited and threatened any rival who tried to sell to small groceries or local bakeries. These stores could only buy from the Cacellas, who soon established exclusivity in supplying these establishments. Anyone who dared to break this monopoly had their warehouse set on fire or even faced intimidation targeting their loved ones. In the following years, the Cacella family expanded their business to several other cities, and their company became the largest wholesale supplier in the country."

The older detective stopped talking. Andrew noticed that his colleague looked tired.

"Are you sure you want to drive? You look exhausted."

Mark smiled.

"Don't worry about me. I can drive," he responded, handing Andrew the piece of paper Lauren gave him.

"Do you know where this street is?"

"I have no idea," Andrew replied. "Let me check on my cell phone."

The young man typed the address on the device.

"It's on the way to my house. Do you know where the Traditionalist Church Cathedral is?"

"That building that looks like a futuristic medieval castle? How could I not know? That monstrosity has ruined the city's landscape."

"Exactly," Andrew replied. "You need to turn left at the Cathedral, and then just keep going straight for a few miles."

"Understood!" Mark responded. He started the car and maneuvered out of the parking lot.

As the older detective drove, he resumed the conversation.

"Let me share an interesting piece of information with you, Andrew. Did you know that the construction cost of the Traditionalist Cathedral exceeded the combined investments our city made in health and education over the past ten years?"

Andrew sensed the direction the conversation was taking. He responded with a faint "No," barely audible, but it didn't discourage Mark from continuing.

"According to a newspaper article I read, the Cacella and Andraus families are currently responsible for nearly half of the religious donations in our city. However, they support different churches. The Andraus family is linked to the Traditionalist Church, while the Cacellas support the National Church."

The car left the parking lot and merged onto a busy avenue.

"Let me ask you something, Andrew: how much do you tithe to your church?"

"Why do you want to know that?"

"I'm Just curious."

"Well, it depends. In a good month, I can donate up to fifty bucks. But when I'm facing financial difficulties, I give less. In recent months, with the expenses of moving house, I have to admit I haven't donated anything lately."

"Fifty bucks? That's less than one percent of your salary! Isn't it supposed to be ten percent?"

"Today, very few people actually pay that full amount. It's a large sum of money, especially in difficult times like these."

"Isn't it written in your holy book that you should give a tenth of your income?"

"That instruction is written in the first part of the book. However, in the second part, which focuses on the teachings after the coming of the Messiah, the book tells us to donate according to our hearts and financial capacity. In my case, my current circumstances temporarily limit me."

"Or have you simply chosen to adopt the passages from the book that suit your convenience?"

"I believe that if there were any problems, God would have already sent me a sign," Andrew replied, feeling uncomfortable with the conversation. "But, on the contrary, in the last few months, I was hired at a new job and became engaged to a very beautiful woman from a good family. I see these as signs that the Lord judges me to be on the right path."

"Or maybe your life hasn't been so bad thus far," Mark retorted, mockingly.

"It seems you don't hold religion in high regard," Andrew observed.

They halted at a red light. Since Mark stopped the car too close to the traffic light, he needed to lower his head to see above the vehicle. He remained silent, gazing at the lights.

Andrew continued, "I've heard that your attitude toward religion has made you quite unpopular at the police department. Have you ever considered taking it easy a bit?"

"Take it easy on what exactly?"

"You have an evident aversion to religion. Many colleagues in the station have cautioned me to be patient with you. However, until yesterday, I hadn't witnessed it myself."

The traffic light turned green, but Mark didn't press on the accelerator. He continued to stare at Andrew. The vehicle behind them honked its horn and overtook them. The driver yelled profanities at them, but the detectives pretended not to have heard.

Mark resumed driving, but instead of moving forward, he turned the corner and parked at the curb, turning off the car's engine.

The older detective pondered for a minute. Then he looked at his partner and said, "Let me tell you a story, Andrew. Someone at that police station must have mentioned that I had a daughter, right?"

"You mentioned something about it at the restaurant last night."

"Her name was Luana. She passed away when she was only three years old."

"I'm sorry about that," Andrew expressed, lowering his gaze.

"She fell into the pool. I was at work that day. I received a call from a paramedic, or maybe it was a police officer. It doesn't matter. They informed me that Deborah, my wife, was in shock and that I urgently needed to go home." Mark took a deep breath and continued, "We had just bought that house a few days before, and I didn't even like the pool. I didn't agree to purchase the property because of it. I bought the house with the intention of establishing a vegetable garden at the back of the lot. However, I decided to utilize the pool. It was a something new, and my wife seemed very excited to have such a luxury at home. So, I cleaned the pool and filled it up. Deborah asked me not to fill it without putting on a cover first because we had a small child at home. But I assured her not to worry, that I would buy the cover or install a fence around the pool the following week. However, before that, on the first weekend in the house, I filled the pool, and we had a nice barbecue beside it. I invited several colleagues from the station, and it ended up being an amazing weekend—one of the best in my marriage."

Andrew remained silent, keeping his gaze down.

Mark continued, "I had planned to purchase the cover on Tuesday of the following week during my lunch break, but that day I was called to a crime scene and had to postpone the purchase. So, I left it for Thursday."

Mark tightly gripped the steering wheel. Andrew noticed his partner's hands trembling and decided to just keep listening.

"On Wednesday, while my wife was working from home, my daughter fell into the pool. Deborah had left her in the living room, playing on a colorful rug. You know, those rubbery ones for children. She took her eyes off Luana for only a few minutes, which turned out to be enough."

Mark gestured as he spoke. Andrew understood how difficult it was for his colleague to say those words.

"When I arrived home, as soon as Deborah saw me, she began screaming, 'It's all your fault! It's all your fault! You just had to buy a damn cover!' The officers had to restrain her, and the paramedics sedated her. She was devastated. I think if she could, she would have killed me."

Mark took a short pause and looked at Andrew.

"After that, I didn't go to work for a week. Oswald asked me to rest at home for a month, but I couldn't stay there, not with my wife looking at me as if I were a monster. So, I went back to work. I remember vividly the first day back at the office. Everyone seemed to avoid me. It was as if I were carrying a dark cloud over my head or suffering from some contagious illness. It was the longest day I've ever had in that place. By late afternoon, the main lobby was crowded, and there was a lot of chatter. At that moment, amid the voices, I heard the following sentence: 'If he believed in God, this wouldn't have happened to him!' That's what I heard." Mark took another deep breath. "I immediately stood up and searched for the person who uttered those words. All I knew was that it was a man's voice, nothing more. Anger rose within me, and I ended up shouting, 'Where is the scumbag who said that?' Everyone fell silent, staring at me, some with embarrassment, others with pity, but no one confessed to saying that. Some of them didn't even know what I was talking about, but the person who said those words did. He knew what I was reacting to and chose not to reveal himself. I often wonder what I would have done if I had found him, but now I accept that I will never know who he was. He probably doesn't even work at the station anymore."

The older detective started the car again.

"My apologies. I didn't realize your anger originated from that," said Andrew.

"It's from that and other things that are not worth mentioning. Not now," Mark answered, rubbing his left knee.

As the car moved forward, the two detectives maintained a contemplative silence for about ten minutes.

Suddenly, Mark started lightly slapping his own ear.

"That's strange!"

"What's strange?" Andrew asked.

"I'm hearing that sound again, the one I heard at the station. It's like it's coming from above, as if some sort of pneumatic drill is hovering a few feet above the car, following us in mid-air."

"I said you looked too tired to drive. You should go home and try to get some rest."

"I'm starting to think you're right. We'll finish this visit, and then I'm heading home. Maybe I'm not well."

Chapter 6

Upon reaching the address indicated by Lauren, the two detectives, still inside the car, examined the building's exterior. The structure where John Sinclair resided was a dilapidated, aged construction. It was one of those residential buildings with four floors that, by law, were not required to have an elevator.

"It seems this construction is on the brink of collapse," Andrew remarked.

They got out of the vehicle and walked to the entrance of the building. Before pressing the doorbell, Mark provided a briefing to his younger partner.

"Let's approach this with empathy. This man has lost his brother, sister-in-law, and one niece, and another niece is still missing. I'll take the lead in the conversation. Speak only when necessary, especially if it's something we can discuss later. Avoid contradicting me; we need to maintain a professional image. Understood?"

"Yes, sir," Andrew responded, saluting like a military man, but with a mocking smile.

Mark mumbled something unintelligible to his partner and pressed the button on the doorbell corresponding to the apartment number that Lauren indicated.

"I hope this old thing still works," Mark grumbled.

It took a while, but someone answered. A melancholic voice emanated from the doorbell speaker.

"Who is it?"

"We are Detectives from the Police Department. We would like to speak with John Sinclair, brother of Humbert Sinclair."

"It's him."

"Good morning, Mr. Sinclair. We apologize for the interruption, but we are hoping to get any information that could assist us in locating your niece, Carol Sinclair. Could we have a few minutes of your time to talk?"

"Yeah. Alright. You can come up. It's on the top floor."

The sound of a slight click resonated as the building door opened, allowing the detectives to ascend the stairs leading to John's floor. Upon reaching the top floor, Andrew noticed his partner's labored breathing and pained expression.

"Should I call an ambulance, partner?" Andrew jested, trying to conceal genuine concern.

"On some days, it feels like this knee wants to kill me," the older detective responded. "I should have climbed these stairs more slowly."

A tear escaped from Mark's tightly shut eyes, which he quickly tried to hide by wiping his face with the back of his hand. Painstakingly straightening himself, the older detective rang the apartment bell.

"I'm fine now. The pain has subsided," he reassured.

The door opened, revealing John Sinclair, the brother of Humbert Sinclair. John appeared to be around fifty years old, with dark hair but a bald spot on his crown. Despite having an overweight physique, John's puffy eyes did not appear to be the result of a negligent diet, but rather a consequence of excessive alcohol consumption. He looked considerably worse compared to his social media profile picture.

Five minutes later, the three men were inside the apartment's living room. Andrew and Mark took seats pulled from a small dining table, while John settled onto the sole couch in the room. The detectives detected an unpleasant odor permeating the air, indicating that the apartment had not been cleaned in weeks.

"I apologize for the condition of my home. I've been sick. I suffer from diabetes. I've been unemployed for two years and cannot afford a cleaning service," John justified. "I live alone here. My life hasn't been easy lately. And now this happens!"

"We understand, Mr. Sinclair. These are difficult times for everyone," Mark responded.

"May I serve you a glass of water?" John offered.

"We aren't thirsty, Mr. Sinclair. This will be a brief visit. Listen, we don't want to impose anything on you, especially considering your recent losses," Mark clarified.

John nodded, signaling his understanding.

Mark began, "Tell me, how would you describe your relationship with your brother, Humbert Sinclair?"

"Well, I believe we had a good relationship. Humbert had been supporting me financially since I lost my job. Every month, he sent me an allowance," John sighed. "I don't even know what I'm going to do now that he's gone."

"What can you tell me about Humbert's relationship with Mayor Charles Andraus? Are you aware of any connections between them?" Mark asked, making it evident that John's relationship with his brother was not his primary focus.

"I believe they had been developing a friendship in recent months. My brother mentioned it to me a couple of times. He seemed optimistic about the Mayor. He believed that their friendship would bring advantages to our family."

"Do you think there might be a connection between your brother's murder and his friendship with the Mayor?" Mark queried.

"Are you suggesting that the Mayor killed my brother?" John asked, looking frightened.

"No, quite the opposite. It's possible that an enemy of Mayor Charles Andraus orchestrated this crime to harm or intimidate him. We are trying to establish a motive for what occurred last night in your brother's house," Mark explained.

"Was there any business or financial dealings between the Mayor and your brother?" Andrew interjected, receiving a nod of approval from Mark.

"My brother didn't discuss the details, but it was known that he was preparing to enter the political arena, with the

Mayor's support. However, I don't have any details about it. I'm not well-versed in these matters," John admitted.

"Alright," Mark acknowledged. "Let me ask you another question: how did your brother and the Mayor become friends? Do you have any knowledge about this?"

"John was silent for a moment, appearing lost in thought."

"Andrew noticed that his partner was slapping his own ear once again."

"Are you still hearing that noise from earlier?" the young detective asked, placing a hand on his colleague's shoulder.

"Yes," Mark responded, his gaze fixed on the ceiling of the apartment. "The noise has returned, and it seems even closer now."

At that moment, John raised his head, signaling that he had recalled something important. He interrupted Mark and Andrew.

"Yes, indeed. My brother and Charles met at the church. That's where I first saw them together. Humbert initially became friends with the Archbishop Euzebius, and it was through Euzebius that my brother was introduced to the Mayor. Humbert's business was on the verge of collapse, burdened by a huge debt. So, he mentioned to me that he planned to seek help from the Archbishop. Shortly after that, I noticed the Mayor attending church more frequently. It was around that time when Charles' eldest son joined the church choir and became friends with my niece."

"Are you referring to Carol Sinclair, the oldest daughter?" Mark inquired.

"Yes. Carol herself. I used to see Carol and Paul together quite often," John confirmed.

Mark raised an eyebrow and asked, "Tell me, what was the nature of the relationship between Paul Andraus and Carol Sinclair? Did they have a romantic involvement?"

"No, I don't think Carol ever had a boyfriend. She was quite young and fully devoted to her religious duties," John explained.

"Can you inform us if Paul or anyone else displayed a particular interest in her?" Mark probed further.

"I don't know. I wasn't close enough to Carol to be aware of such matters," John admitted.

"Did Carol Sinclair ever express any negative sentiments about Paul Andraus' behavior?" Mark asked.

John thought for a moment before responding, "No, she never confided in me about anything concerning Paul."

Mark noticed a suspicious expression on John's face while answering the last question.

"Was there anyone closer to the couple? Someone who might have more information about the relationship between Paul Andraus and your niece, Carol?" Mark inquired.

"I believe the Archbishop was close to them. I often saw Euzebius chatting with both Paul and Carol before the choir performances," John recalled.

Mark glanced at his partner, Andrew, who recognized the significance of this information.

"Have you ever had a conversation with the Archbishop or the Mayor?" Andrew asked.

"No, I only exchanged greetings with them. During the services, I usually sit at the back of the church," John clarified.

Mark rubbed his chin, pondering for a few moments before asking another question.

"Tell me, what do you know about the Cacellas? Do you know they are rivals of the Mayor's family, don't you?"

"Of course, I'm know that. Who doesn't? However, I've never had any contact with them, and I don't believe Humbert did either. My brother never mentioned anything about the Cacellas. Honestly, I don't think these deaths occurred due to the rivalry between the Mayor and the Cacellas," John explained.

"What do you believe could have been the motive behind this crime?" Andrew inquired.

"I think it was a botched burglary. The criminals intended to rob the house, but they encountered my brother in the kitchen and ended up killing him. Then Marie and Joanna woke up, and they had to kill them too," John speculated.

"And what about Carol Sinclair? Why do you think they didn't kill her?" Mark questioned.

"I don't know," John replied. "Maybe they intend to demand a ransom for her."

A brief silence filled the room. Mark slapped his own ear once again, displaying discomfort. He quickly stood up, with Andrew following suit.

"I believe we have gathered enough information, John," Mark stated. "Thank you for your cooperation. Your assistance has been valuable, especially considering the circumstances today. We apologize for any inconvenience caused."

John also stood up, looking doubtful.

"Do you have any leads on where my niece might be?"

"We're working hard on it, but I'm unable to provide any details at the moment. Sharing information prematurely could hinder the investigation," Mark responded.

"Do you think you'll find my niece?" John inquired.

"We'll do everything within our means to locate her. That's all I can say for now, John," Mark assured him.

Mark walked toward the apartment's exit, shaking his head as if he was trying to get rid of something. John passed by him and opened the apartment door. The two detectives left, and John closed the door.

In the hallway, Andrew turned to Mark and asked, "Are you okay, partner?"

"Yeah, it's just that sound in my ear again. It's getting louder, almost as if I could reach up and grab the source of the noise," Mark explained.

They began descending the stairs.

"I want to speak with the Archbishop," Mark declared.

"Talk to the Archbishop? Are you sure?" Andrew questioned.

"Didn't you hear what the man said? The Archbishop was close to Paul Andraus and Carol Sinclair at the church. The Archbishop may possess information that Humbert's brother hasn't shared with us," the older detective explained.

"You suspect the Mayor's son, don't you?" Andrew inquired. "Do you think Paul Andraus killed the family?"

"For now, I can't suspect anyone, Andrew, especially not the Mayor's son. Oswald doesn't want me to prematurely shift the investigation toward someone so powerful. It could cause him trouble.

When Mark was near the building's exit, he stumbled over his own feet and faltered. It looked like he was on the verge of losing consciousness. Andrew swiftly grabbed his arm, preventing the older detective from falling.

"Listen, partner. I think you better go to the hospital," Andrew suggested.

"Don't worry about me. I'll be fine. I just need a long night of sleep in a proper bed. Here's what we'll do: take me home. I'll rest until lunchtime. Once I wake up, I'll head back to the police station," Mark said, handing his car keys to Andrew.

Chapter 7

Half an hour later, the two detectives were in the parking garage of Mark's building. Andrew had already parked the car in his colleague's space.

Sitting in the driver's seat, Andrew asked, "Do you feel better now? Are you sure you don't prefer going to a hospital?"

"I feel better now, Andrew. The noise stopped. I plan to rest for a while, and I'll be fine after lunch. You can take my car and return to the police station. Later, I'll call a taxi," Mark replied.

"Don't talk nonsense, partner! This car is yours. I'll take a taxi to the station," Andrew insisted as he opened the door on his side. "Do you need help getting up to your apartment?"

Mark also opened the door on his side and responded, "If I needed help getting to my apartment, I would have followed your advice and gone to the hospital. I feel fine. Don't worry."

The two stepped out of the car, and Andrew returned the keys to Mark.

"Andrew, do me a favor: search for information about the Archbishop," Mark asked. "I want to learn more about him."

They walked in opposite directions, Andrew toward the building's exit and Mark toward the elevator.

Once inside his apartment, Mark took off his shoes, unbuttoned his shirt, lay down on the living room couch, and placed his hand on his forehead. He contemplated the Sinclair family case and realized the gravity of attempting to approach the Archbishop. Euzebius Andraus held tremendous influence in the city, possibly even surpassing that of the Mayor and city council president combined. Mark's boss, Oswald, would surely be worried upon being informed that his subordinates planned to interrogate such a high-ranking figure.

Mark gazed at the ceiling. It was eleven in the morning, and the building was likely nearly empty by now. The silence created a peaceful atmosphere inside the apartment, which pleased him. The previously heard strange sound had vanished. Perhaps he no longer even needed to rest.

Mark decided to get up. With a bit of luck, he might find Andrew outside the building, still waiting for the taxi, and the two detectives could return to the police station together.

However, as soon as Mark stood up, he was startled by a loud crash, as if a metallic machine had collided with a rocky wall above him. Suddenly, a sensation of being grasped by the waist overcame him. His vision blurred, and he felt himself being lifted, yet there was no sign of the floor moving away. Instead, he saw the floor approaching his face and instinctively protected himself by placing his arms in front of his body.

Fallen on the floor, Mark's consciousness began to fade. Soon enough, everything succumbed to darkness.

...

When Mark regained consciousness, he found himself trapped inside a deep, shadowy pit. A colossal metallic claw was enveloping his waist, clasping tightly. Suspended above the claw, a peculiar drone hoisted him upwards. The drone ascended through the hole using four wheels, pressed firmly against its walls, gradually accelerating in speed.

Gazing at his hands, Mark noticed they were pale and scrawny, with a dying appearance. Fastened to one of his wrists was a sturdy, silver-colored metal bracelet, displaying a blinking small blue light.

After nearly ten minutes of climbing the walls, the drone finally reached the pit's summit. The machine retracted its wheels and activated four turbines, propelling it into flight. Mark gazed upward and saw a starry sky akin to outer space.

As he looked downward, a distant gray surface rapidly receded from view.

As Mark reached higher altitudes, he realized that he had been extracted from the interior of a colossal rocky sphere. He had been entombed underground on some sort of moon. In the background, behind this moon, he observed a vast red planet.

"What an utterly bizarre dream, yet it feels so vivid!" Mark pondered to himself. His attention was drawn to a bright speck ahead, gradually growing in prominence against the starry dark backdrop. Within seconds, the speck expanded, revealing itself to be a spacecraft. The drone decelerated and headed toward an open hatch in the ship's fuselage.

Inside the spacecraft, the drone gently placed Mark's body onto a stretcher situated in a room resembling a hospital ward. Releasing Mark's waist, the device retreated. The detective attempted to rise, but his body was too weak to move.

The hatch through which Mark entered was now closed. The drone landed in a corner of the room and powered down. On the opposite side, a door opened, and two individuals wearing white clothes entered. The detective couldn't see their faces due to the intense illumination overwhelming his eyes, which were too sensitive to light. Mark discerned that one of them possessed a female voice, while the other spoke in a distinctly male tone.

The woman pointed a device at Mark's face. The object emitted a yellow light and an intermittent beep. Soon, the light turned green, and the beeping ceased.

"Positive identification, Physter," the female declared. "This is Zalthor Acri. We must promptly transfer him to the recovery tank."

"I hadn't imagined Zalthor would appear so frail, Fhastina. I always believed Hubbians to be invincible," remarked Physter.

"Ten thousand years buried tens of miles deep within a desolate moon is a pretty long period, even for a converted

Hubbian, Physter. However, don't worry. We only need to immerse him in the recovery tank. It will only take a couple of days, and Zalthor shall be totally recovered. I will accompany him to the tank. Contact Lintsa and Doctor Axlow, and inform them that we are en route to the Doctor's planet."

"To the Doctor's planet? Shouldn't we be heading to the planet Dolmen? After all, Zalthor is the owner of that planet," inquired Physter.

"Yes, indeed. However, the political climate in Dolmen is currently unstable. It is imperative that the information of Zalthor's rescue remains confidential until he has made a full recovery. Only Lintsa and Doctor Axlow are supposed to know his whereabouts. Zalthor is currently in a vulnerable condition, and if Pheldon's allies launch an attack on this spaceship, we will be unable to protect him."

Abruptly, Physter exclaimed with surprise, "Fhastina, take a look at his wrist. That bracelet! It has this flashing blue light. What could it possibly indicate?"

The woman examined Mark's left wrist and responded, "It appears to be some sort of Hubbian device, but I can't determine its exact nature. Perhaps it's what emitted the signal received by our spaceship. It's best not to touch it. Go to the bridge and send a message to Lintsa. Inform her that Zalthor Acri has been rescued on moon B-23 in the Francia System."

Mark could hear the conversation between these unfamiliar individuals and understand their words, yet he remained utterly confused. Why were they referring to him as Zalthor Acri? Who were Doctor Axlow and Lintsa? And why would these Pheldon's allies be a threat to him?

The stretcher began to move, hovering three feet above the floor, with Fhastina following Mark.

They carried the detective into a spacious chamber. Mark's vision was blurred, preventing him from discerning the unfolding events until he found himself submerged in a tank with thick glass walls. The tank was filled with a warm, transparent liquid tinged with a slight green hue. To Mark's surprise, he didn't experience any sensation of drowning; instead, he felt cozy. Through the tank walls, he caught a glimpse of Fhastina's figure. He noticed that her head resembled that of an eagle, covered in feathers, with a gleaming beak before her face. The female operated a control panel attached to the tank.

"This dream is becoming increasingly bizarre," pondered the detective.

Fhastina turned toward Mark and addressed him, saying, "Greetings, Mr. Zalthor. Just rest now. In a few days, you will be removed from this liquid. I will adjust the sound waves to provide you with a comfortable resting environment. This will help time pass more quickly until Lintsa arrives. Upon hearing of your rescue, she will be eager to meet you."

Fhastina pressed a few more buttons on the control panel, and Mark began to hear a relaxing sound. He gradually fell asleep. Once again, darkness enveloped everything.

...

When Mark opened his eyes, he found himself back in his apartment's living room, lying on the wooden floor. He crawled over to the couch and took a seat, relieved to see that his hands were no longer pale and scrawny.

Attempting to stand up, he became dizzy and sat back down. While waiting for the dizziness to subside, he picked up the television remote control and switched on the TV.

A news program was airing, with a journalist discussing the crime that took place the previous night.

"According to information circulating on social media, the family that was brutally murdered had close ties to Mayor Charles Andraus. This connection has sparked various conspiracy theories within our city. Members of the Cacella family, longstanding rivals of the Andraus, have endured numerous attacks on their social media profiles. Suely Cacella, the wife of the city council president, has even deactivated her profile on some social media platforms due to the aggressive comments and threats she received from many users. On the other hand, this morning, several women gathered outside the city hall, demanding an investigation into the Mayor's son. Paul Andraus has faced previous allegations of sexual misconduct, and the abduction of Humbert Sinclair's eldest daughter has raised suspicions against him. Witnesses also claim that Carol Sinclair and Paul Andraus were frequently seen together during services at the Traditionalist Cathedral."

The television screen switched to display an elderly man, who wore an expression of disgust as he spoke.

" Let me tell you what's going to happen. Once again, the authorities in this town won't find anyone to blame. If by some miracle they manage to arrest a suspect, it will likely be a homeless person or a drug addict. No one in this city dares to confront the Cacellas or the Andraus. And I'll say it loud and clear: I'm certain that the officers from the police department are currently cowering under their desks, doing everything they can to distance themselves from this case. Nothing will come of it unless we, the press, conduct a thorough investigation. These deaths yesterday must be connected to the shady dealings of the Andraus and Cacellas. No one simply enters a house and kills three people for no reason. Mr. Humbert Sinclair, without a doubt, was involved in something dreadful related to the Mayor's family—something we'll probably never know."

Mark turned off the television and headed to the bathroom. He undressed and took a shower.

Chapter 8

Two hours later, Mark was taking another shower, but not in his apartment's bathroom. The hot water flowed over his body as he reached for a bottle of liquid soap, unscrewed the cap, and poured a substantial amount into his palm. He lathered the soap all over his body and rinsed off.

After turning off the shower, Mark grabbed a worn towel hanging near the shower stall and quickly dried himself. As he exited the bathroom, his still-wet body left a trail of water on the floor of a dimly lit and somber room. The only source of illumination was a faint red light penetrating through a small window high on the wall. In one corner of the room, a woman named Millie was getting dressed.

"It's been a while since you last visited me. Rough day?" she asked.

Mark moved to the opposite corner of the room and took a pair of pants lying on a bedside table.

"I should be at the police station right now, but I felt the need to clear my mind before going back there. Work wasn't going easy," he responded. "Have you heard about the family that was murdered last night?"

"Yes, everyone is talking about it. They said the Mayor's son might be involved. He is quite infamous in this part of town. He has a history of assaulting call girls, and he always get away with it. The girls would love to see him finally get arrested," Millie shared.

"Have you ever been with Paul Andraus?" the detective inquired. "Do you know him?"

"He would never be with someone like me. The Mayor's son only hires... you know, more expensive girls. Other girls claim he is like the devil himself, asking them to do things I'd rather not mention. It would ruin your day," she replied.

Mark picked up a shirt hanging near the head of the bed as Millie observed him finishing getting dressed.

"Do you think Paul Andraus killed that family?" she asked.

"Everyone knows the Mayor's son has a questionable behavior, but that alone isn't enough to accuse him of murder. But let's not talk about it any longer. I came here to unwind, not to discuss work." Mark commented. "Tell me, how about you? How's your son doing?"

"His health has improved. The government funded some expensive medication for him. I believe it helped," Millie shared.

"He will recover," the detective responded without showing genuine concern.

As Mark ran a plastic comb through his hair, he attempted to conceal the baldness on his forehead by combing his hair from one side to the other.

For a brief moment, the detective studied his own reflection in a small mirror on the wall.

"How old do you think I am?" he asked Millie.

"You first," she retorted. "How old do I look?"

Mark scrutinized Millie. Despite the poor lighting in the room, she was positioned directly beneath the window, where external light illuminated her figure.

The girl appeared to be around forty, possibly even older. It is common for women in her situation to age prematurely.

"About twenty-five," Mark replied.

"And you look like you're eighteen," Millie mockingly responded.

Mark smiled, took a seat on the bed, slipped on a pair of worn shoes, and gazed at Millie once more. She seemed thinner than before, and the dark circles under her eyes were more pronounced. The girl did not appear to be in good health.

"You look different from the last time I was here. Is everything alright with you?" Mark inquired. "I hope you haven't fallen ill."

"No, I haven't contracted any diseases. Don't worry. I won't pass anything on to you," she bitterly replied.

The detective chose not to delve further into the topic. He wasn't there to discuss anyone's health.

"What about your boyfriend? Is he less hotheaded now?"

"I don't know. I ended things with him two weeks ago. It's not easy to date possessive individuals in my field of work. He was starting to cause problems."

"He won't break down this door and attack me, will he?" Mark asked, pointing toward the entrance of the room.

"Don't worry. He only uses violence against women or children. He wouldn't confront a man of your size."

Millie took a cellphone from her small bag. She turned it on and read some text messages.

"Do you want me to leave now?" Mark inquired.

"No, it's nothing important," the woman responded, placing the device back in her bag. "But what about you? Are you in a relationship?"

"You know I haven't dated since my wife passed away."

"It happened about five years ago, right?"

"Eight."

"I think it's time for you to find a girlfriend, sweetheart. You're not ugly, and you have a job. A man like you would easily find a girlfriend in this city."

"You mean I would get into trouble quickly, right?"

"Why do you think that?"

"What would a middle-aged, low-paid worker with a disability in his left leg find in this town? Probably a divorced woman with so many quirks that no husband could tolerate. Or perhaps a single mother with three children, desperately seeking someone to support her family. With my salary, I can barely support myself. I don't want that for me. I'm happy the way I am."

"Don't think like that, sweetheart. Everyone needs someone. I can see that you're not happy. Having a companion would be good for you."

Mark stood up, took out his wallet from his pocket, pulled out a hundred bill, and held it up, showing it to Millie.

"The best kind of relationship I can have now, Millie, is the one I have with you. I can come here whenever I want, spend an hour, forget about my problems while we're in bed, and then I can walk out that door. At this stage in my life, it's the most honest relationship I can have. Do you know why? Because we both know exactly what the other wants." The detective placed the banknote on the bed.

"In a few years you'll be an old man, darling. You are going to need someone. You don't have children or close relatives. Who will take care of you when you get sick? You'll die alone in your apartment, and the neighbors will only start worrying about you when the smell of your dead body becomes bothersome."

Mark opened his wallet and counted how much money was left. For a few seconds, he thought about tipping Millie but realized he had less cash than expected. He decided to put his wallet back in his pocket without touching the money.

He responded to the girl, "Are you suggesting I find someone to be my caregiver when I'm unable to take care of myself? I don't need that. I don't want to be a burden to anyone. When I can't get out of bed, I want to stay there until I pass away."

"It's horrible to hear, sweetie. Listen to me, you will still find a woman who brings you happiness. Your girl may be closer than you think."

"And who would this girl be? A call girl? Would it be you?" Mark asked, pointing at Millie.

Millie raised her head and replied, "Dear, if one day a call girl asks to be your companion, consider it a remarkable feat. A woman who has been with numerous men, intimately knows them, and chooses you over them all is someone to cherish." Her eyes shone as she spoke.

Mark walked to a refrigerator on the other side of the room, opened the door, and picked up a plastic bottle.

"A woman who chose me? How can I be sure of that? Maybe she offered herself to everyone else before, and I was the only one who accepted," he wondered.

Millie remained silent, her face turned sad, and she lowered her head.

Mark noticed tears in Millie's eyes and regretted what he just said. He realized that he was projecting feelings onto her that had nothing to do with the woman.

The detective opened a cupboard door and took out a glass, but he spotted a small paper package concealed behind some cups. It was about the size of a matchbox. The detective extended his arm and, using his fingertips, picked up the package. Then, with a stern expression, he showed his discovery to Millie.

"This isn't for me! It's for a client," Millie justified.

Mark put the package back and closed the cupboard.

"Listen, girl, you know that if you use one of these stones, it could end your life, right?"

Millie lowered her head and responded, "I told you, it's not for me."

The detective drank his water, walked toward the exit of the room, and gazed at Millie's shadowy figure. He promised himself that he wouldn't return to that place again. However, it wasn't the first time he had made that promise. He left and closed the door without saying goodbye.

Chapter 9

An hour later, sitting behind his desk, Chief Oswald talked to Andrew when Mark entered the office.

"I heard you want to see me," said Mark.

"Please close the door and take a seat," requested Oswald, speaking in a hushed tone.

Oswald ran a hand over his face, revealing his nervousness. "I've been informed that you intend to interrogate the Archbishop. Is that true?"

Mark sat next to Andrew and replied, "What about the Mayor's son? Will we be able to question Paul Andraus?"

"Only with a court order. And no judge is willing to expedite it."

"Isn't there any judge on the Cacella side who is interested in this questioning?"

"We were in discussions with a judge connected to the Cacellas. His name is Robert Brown, but he is hesitant. He claimed that issuing the order without solid reasons might anger the Mayor's family."

"So, until we have solid reasons to question Paul Andraus, let's try to speak with the Archbishop," Mark suggested. "Perhaps he will be more receptive. We spoke to Humbert Sinclair's brother this morning, and he mentioned the close relationship between the Archbishop, Carol Sinclair, and Paul Andraus."

"Why do you think the Archbishop will be more cooperative than the Mayor?" questioned Oswald.

"Listen, boss: I understand that talking to the Archbishop won't be as simple as speaking with Humbert Sinclair's unemployed brother. I know we can't just go to his door, ring the bell, and expect to be granted entry. That's why I need your help. You have more resources to establish contact with the Archbishop. Let him know that our sole purpose is to save Carol Sinclair. He knows the girl, and that might make him more willing to cooperate."

Oswald let out a deep sigh.

"What do you think happened at Humbert Sinclair's house, Detective? Whom do you suspect?"

Mark pondered for a few seconds and replied, "I didn't suspect anyone, boss. I am merely exploring other potential suspects, so we didn't have to approach the Mayor or his son. Carol was a young, beautiful, devout girl. It is possible that some obsessed individual at the church became fixated on her. That's all I wanted to discuss with the Archbishop. It would be sufficient to reduce media speculation. I saw the news before coming here, and I understand that the situation is far from peaceful. I also knew that the image of the Mayor and his son climbing the steps of this police station is not something the Andraus family wants to see on the news. The Archbishop could help us prevent that."

Oswald remained silent, trying to process his subordinate's words. Suddenly, he rose, walked to the door, and opened it a few inches. He peered outside, checking to see who was nearby, and then closed the door again. The chief raised a finger and pointed at Mark.

"Don't try to deceive me, Mark Randall! I knew what you are trying to do, and I knew you are capable of it." He pointed to Andrew. "Just don't involve this guy."

"What am I trying to do?" asked Mark. "Can you enlighten me?"

The chief settled back into his chair and spoke firmly, "I've known you for over twenty years, Mark, and I've witnessed all the shit you've faced. I'm truly sorry for what has happened to you. But if you haven't found the courage to do what your wife did, that's not my fault. If you want to put yourself in harm's way with the Mayor's henchmen, go ahead, but don't drag Andrew into it. If you antagonize these people, Andrew will suffer the consequences too."

"I believe Andrew is mature enough to decide whether he wants to work with me, boss," Mark responded. "I understand you don't want to provoke the Mayor's family, but don't worry, I won't bring you or Andrew any trouble. I've heard the discussions about the case in the news. I'm not the only one suspecting Paul Andraus. And with the entire town turning against him, you won't be able to protect the Mayor's son. If there's anyone who can reduce the tension now, it's Andrew and me. But we need another suspect. The Archbishop might lead us to someone who deserves to be investigated."

"If someone else said it, I might believe it," Oswald replied. "Answer me this: are you still working unarmed?"

"You know I won't carry a gun, boss. That won't change."

"Why don't you carry a gun?" Andrew asked, looking at Mark. "I didn't know that."

"That's not the issue here," Mark retorted, glancing at his partner. He turned to Oswald and asserted, "Call the Archbishop. Let him know we want to help his family. After work, we'll pay him a discreet visit, just Andrew and me."

Oswald took another deep breath.

"Alright, I'll see what I can do, but I'm warning you: if you upset the Archbishop, we'll have a serious conversation tomorrow."

"Don't worry, boss. I'll handle it responsibly," assured Mark. "Right now, the Archbishop may be our best chance at finding a way out of this situation."

"I hope you're right," Oswald pleaded.

Mark rose, and Andrew followed him.

Chapter 10

Early in the evening, the two detectives were in Mark's car, en route to the official residence of Archbishop Euzebius Andraus, the brother of Mayor Charles Andraus. Mark drove while Andrew looked through some papers.

"Do you really believe the Mayor's family is innocent in this case?" Andrew inquired.

"Do you want to know what I think?" Mark responded.

"Yes."

"The Mayor's son has abducted the girl. I don't think he was one of the criminals who broke into the house and killed the family. He is too much of a coward for that. I am certain he paid two thugs to do the job. He will abuse the girl for as long as he can, and then he will dispose of the body."

Andrew's eyes widened.

"Are you serious?"

"The degenerate probably wanted something more than just friendship, and Carol Sinclair must have rejected his advances. He became angry and abducted the poor girl."

"But why didn't he seize her on the street when she was coming home from school? Why did he kill her entire family?"

"I don't know. Maybe it was bad luck. Perhaps the criminals intended to grab the girl from her bedroom while the family was asleep, but the parents woke up first, and the criminals had to improvise. You know how the minds of these people work. At the first sign of trouble, they resort to violence."

"This whole story seems strange to me," Andrew remarked.

"Yes, until we find someone who can tell us what really happened inside that house, we can only speculate. The only ones who can provide answers are the criminals themselves or Sinclair's eldest daughter, if we can locate her."

Andrew remained silent for a long time.

Mark looked at him and noticed the concerned expression on his partner's face.

"Do you think I am looking for trouble? Have you taken Oswald's comment seriously?"

The young man pondered for a moment and retorted, "What did Oswald mean by 'you haven't found the courage to do what your wife did'?"

Mark continued driving as if he hadn't heard the question.

Feeling uncomfortable with Mark's silence, Andrew returned to examining his papers. After a few minutes, he asked, "Do you think the Archbishop can provide any leads on the whereabouts of the girl?"

"That's something we will only find out after speaking to him. Did you carry out the search I requested?"

"Yes, and I discovered some interesting information about the Archbishop."

"Tell me."

Andrew took out his cellphone from his pocket and read the text displayed on the screen, "Euzebius Andraus has always been the top student in his class, demonstrating a talent for public speaking and writing from a young age. His father, Juscelino Andraus, had hoped that young Euzebius would eventually take over the family business. So, it was a great disappointment for Juscelino when his only son decided to pursue a clerical career. This opened the door for Charles Andraus to assume the family business. He had recently married the Archbishop's sister. Euzebius continued studying and graduated in Philosophy from one of the most prestigious universities in the world."

"I thought religious authorities like him usually studied theology," Mark commented.

"He also has a Master's Degree in Theology and another one in Cosmology. I believe you'll find it interesting to engage in discussions about religion with him."

Suddenly, Mark reduced the speed of the vehicle and parked it by the curb.

"Why did you stop? Where are we?" Andrew asked.

"Don't you recognize the street where you live? You'll stay here."

"But why? Is it because of my last comment?"

"You heard what the boss said. I don't want to cause you any trouble. I don't know how my conversation with a religious authority like the Archbishop will unfold, especially regarding a murder that may have involved one of his close relatives. It's a delicate topic. Euzebius Andraus is a powerful man, and if he takes offense at the questions I ask, he can harm us. Stay here for your own safety. I'll share all the details of the visit with you later."

Andrew looked at his partner with a serious expression.

"Are you sure I have nothing to worry about? I suspect you're planning something foolish, as the boss warned."

"Stop dwelling on the nonsense Oswald said," Mark replied. "Now, get out of the car. It's getting late."

"Fine, but call me later and tell me everything that happened."

Andrew got out of the car and Mark headed toward the Archbishop's residence.

Chapter 11

Upon arriving at the Archbishop's address, Mark parked his car in front of the residence and got out of the vehicle, taking a moment to survey the surroundings. He was in the most affluent neighborhood of the city, where houses occupied entire blocks, resulting in a sparsely populated area characterized by clean streets adorned with lush, well-kept trees.

An imposing white wall, standing at least twelve feet tall, surrounded the Archbishop's residence. Mark approached the entrance and pushed the doorbell button.

After a brief pause, a female voice responded, "Good evening, this is the Archbishop's official residence."

"Good evening, Madam. I'm Mark Randall, a detective from the police department. I have a scheduled meeting with the Archbishop," Mark introduced himself.

The voice on the doorbell speaker fell silent, and Mark waited. Noticing a surveillance camera fixed on him, he waved in its direction. Suddenly, a small gate adjacent to the doorbell emitted a sound indicating that it had unlocked. Mark entered the property.

The detective was instantly captivated by a beautifully landscaped garden filled with exotic trees, vibrant flowers, and lush, well-kept grass. Thoughtfully positioned LED lights illuminated the surroundings, exuding a splendor reminiscent of opulent mansions that Mark had only seen on magazine covers.

A woman, dressed in a dark monochromatic outfit, emerged from the residence.

"Welcome to the official residence of Archbishop Euzebius Andraus, Mr. Randall. I am Sister Anne, and I will guide you to His Grace. Please follow me," she greeted him.

Mark recognized Sister Anne's voice as the one that responded to the doorbell. Together, they passed through a side entrance and arrived in the backyard, where floodlights cast a radiant glow upon a large swimming pool adorned with an enchanting waterfall fountain.

Sister Anne pointed to a small table and two chairs positioned near the pool.

"You may have a seat here," Sister Anne offered. "Would you like something to drink?"

"No, thank you," Mark declined politely.

"The Archbishop will join you soon," Sister Anne informed him.

"Very well, I'll wait here," Mark replied.

Sister Anne retired, disappearing through a door at the rear of the residence. Mark was left alone, his gaze fixed upon the beautiful cascade of the fountain, contemplating the mechanics behind its upward flow of water. His attention was then drawn to a luminous glow reflecting on the water's surface. He raised his eyes and realized it was the full moon, casting its radiant light upon the sky, surrounded by a large colored ring resembling a rainbow.

Mark smiled, amazed at the beauty of the spectacle that, at that moment, nature provided him.

Suddenly, a friendly voice interrupted his thoughts.

"Good evening, Detective. It is a pleasure to welcome you to my residence."

Mark turned his face and saw a tall, burly man, looking about fifty years old. The detective immediately recognized the Archbishop Euzebius Andraus. The clergyman wore fine cotton clothes, very light and impeccably clean, whose shine made him look even bigger.

The detective stood up and extended his hand to the Archbishop.

"The pleasure is all mine, Your Grace. Thank you for taking some of your time to answer some questions. I hope I'm not bothering you." Mark looked around. "And I must say: your residence is a stunning place."

"Thanks, Detective, but this property is not mine. I just live in this house. Not even the clothes I'm wearing belong to me. Everything you see here belongs to the Church, or better yet, it belongs to the Lord."

The Archbishop shook Mark's hand firmly, lowering his head slightly during the greeting— an unexpected gesture of humbleness.

The two sat down, and Euzebius began, "You're the police detective Mark Randall, aren't you? I think my brother-in-law mentioned you once. Yes, it was only once, but I have a good memory. You and Charles studied at the same school when you were young."

"I am surprised that your brother-in-law mentioned my name, Your Grace. We weren't that close."

"I remember when he talked about you. It was right after the news of your wife's death. I'm sorry about that."

As soon as the Archbishop mentioned this case, Mark remembered that Charles, still a city councilor at that time, attended his wife's funeral. The guy had a brief relationship with Deborah during high school, before the detective met her, and Charles certainly went to the cemetery only to remind the detective of that.

However, Mark knew that this was not the best time to show resentment, especially against a relative of the Archbishop.

"It's all right, Your Grace. That happened eight years ago. I have already gotten over it."

The Archbishop suspected that Mark was not sincere in his last statement. Instead, he saw a deep sadness in the detective's eyes.

"Yes. Life always moves on, and time is the only remedy for certain pains," stated Euzebius. "But let's get straight to the point. I know what brought you here, Detective. Your superior called me earlier and explained the details of the situation. I must confess, I am shocked by the events that afflicted the Sinclair family last night. What a terrible crime!

Beautiful and honest people, losing their lives in such a violent way. Since I spoke with Oswald, I can't stop thinking about their suffering, especially poor Carol. Unlike the rest of the family, her pain may not be finished. Have you received any communication from the criminals? Any ransom requests?"

"Unfortunately, this is not the kind of abduction that is usually followed by a ransom demand, Your Grace. I'm very sorry."

"I understand, and I'm saddened to hear this, but I hope there will be enlightening results very soon." The Archbishop paused for a moment and continued, " I know that the majority of the press has suggested that this atrocity may have resulted from Humbert Sinclair's relationship with my family. Many believe that my brother-in-law's political enemies may have committed the crime, perhaps seeking revenge or attempting to intimidate Charles. However, earlier today, I watched a television program on a station that belongs to the Cacellas. They were spreading nonsense about my nephew, Paul, suggesting that he may have abducted the girl. Are the Cacellas putting pressure on you? Are the police trying to steer the investigation toward my family?

As far as I know, no delegate from the Cacellas has appeared at the police station to interfere with the investigation, Your Grace."

"But it's in my house where you are now, at this time of night, not in a Cacella house, isn't it, Detective?"

Mark shifted in his chair and answered, "At this moment, Your Grace, my only priority is to save Carol Sinclair. I came here solely because we were informed that Your Grace is one of the few people close to the girl. Humbert's brother mentioned that you frequently spoke to Carol at the church. I hope you can provide us with some information to assist in finding her."

The Archbishop smiled and replied, "I'm here to help, Detective, although I'm uncertain how I can be of assistance."

"Very well. Tell me, did Your Grace recently speak with other members of the Sinclair family? Did you notice any changes in Carol's parents' behavior in the past few weeks? Anything indicating fear or unusual worry?"

"Not at all, Detective. The Sinclair family has been attending church regularly and has shown no recent changes in their behavior. In fact, over the past few months, I would even say they seemed happier and more relaxed than when they first started attending services at the Cathedral."

"What about the girl? Did Your Grace have any conversations with Carol Sinclair in the days leading up to the crime? Did her behavior seem different?"

"Well, Carol Sinclair usually only spoke to me about the songs she sang in the Church Choir or passages from the Holy Book that she didn't fully understand. She seemed to be seeking knowledge and never mentioned anything about her personal life."

"Do you know if she had a boyfriend? Was anyone at the church flirting with her?"

"You would have better luck asking that question to one of the gossiping old ladies at the church than to me, Detective."

Mark smiled and nodded in agreement. He continued, "What about Paul? How was Carol Sinclair's relationship with your nephew, Paul Andraus? John Sinclair mentioned that the two were always seen together at the church. Is that true?"

Before answering, the Archbishop remained silent for a few seconds. Mark scrutinized the religious man's face, searching for any sign of tension, but Euzebius displayed more anger than fear.

"I must say, Detective, I expected you to ask this question."

"I apologize, Your Grace. You expressed your concern about your nephew's situation. However, this question becomes inevitable after John Sinclair's information about the closeness between Paul Andraus and Carol Sinclair, as well as your nephew's previous troubles with the law."

"You are well aware that all charges against Paul were dropped, aren't you, Detective?"

"Yes, Your Grace. I am fully aware, although I must inform you that it is common knowledge in our town that these charges were dropped under obscure circumstances. When such a situation arises, numerous theories emerge."

"They are merely conspiracy theories. Do you believe in conspiracy theories, Detective?"

Mark's expression turned serious, but before he could respond, the Archbishop continued, "Even if these accusations against Paul were true, what were they? A stolen kiss at an inopportune moment, an indiscreet touch after excessive drinking. I believe there is a vast difference between a reckless, spoiled, young man and someone who would commit a heinous crime by killing an entire family, don't you think?"

Mark recalled the accusation of stabbing a classmate but thought it would be better not to mention that and nodded in agreement. However, he leaned toward the Archbishop and lowered his voice, saying, "I understand your concern for your nephew, Your Grace, but the suspicion of Paul's involvement in this crime could cause significant damage to the reputation of your entire family. If your nephew were to be summoned to the police station, it would create a stir in the city and provide ample ammunition to the press associated with the Cacellas. That is precisely what I am trying to avoid by speaking with you at this late hour. Chief Oswald has explicitly instructed us to handle the investigation discreetly. We understand the sensitivity of the case."

"Very well. I am glad to hear that you have this concern."

The detective leaned back and sighed.

"All I want right now, You Grace, is to locate Carol Sinclair, but without any leads, I'm starting to lose hope of finding her before the worst happens."

"Never lose hope, Detective. The Lord is watching over her. I am certain He will protect her," stated the Archbishop, pointing toward the sky. "We must pray for Carol Sinclair, and everything will be fine."

Mark stared at the Archbishop, just as he did with Andrew at the Café and Grill restaurant, but now the detective was careful to convey his thoughts in a different tone than he used with his younger partner.

"I wish I could share your faith, Your Grace. However, I am not a religious man. I consider myself a man of science."

As soon as the Archbishop heard Mark's words, his expression changed. He scrutinized the detective for a few seconds, analyzing him intently.

Euzebius slightly smiled and said, "So, Detective Mark Randall, I would appreciate it if you could explain to me, honestly: why do you consider science superior to religion?"

The Archbishop's confident demeanor intimidated the detective.

"Well, I'm not sure if I shall delve into this topic, Your Grace. I expressed my opinions on religious matters in the past, and it caused me trouble. Speaking my beliefs aloud, especially in the official residence of our city's foremost religious leader, could potentially land me in hot water."

"Why do you believe that, Detective? Do you think I would be offended? And, in response, would harm you? By assuming such ignorance on my part, you manage to offend me. If you fear speaking out due to concerns of retaliation, you are mistaking me for a scoundrel. Is that how you view religious individuals? Do you consider us scoundrels?"

The Archbishop's words unsettled Mark. The detective even looked around, checking if any local security personnel were approaching the table to grab him. His neck arteries pulsed intensely, but he attempted to conceal his state of tension.

"Not at all, Your Grace. It's just that I had other discussions on this subject in the past, and some of them didn't end well."

"You were certainly among ignorant individuals, Detective. I'm sorry for that. I assure you that will not be the case here. I'm simply curious to hear your perspective. If you think I'm incapable of having a civilized conversation about my beliefs, you are mistakenly associating me with those you had trouble in the past."

Realizing there was no other way out, Mark resigned himself.

"I apologize, Your Grace. I regret that my past experiences led me to give the wrong impression."

"Very well, I accept your apology. But now, please share your opinion on religion. Speak without fear and express the worst you think about us. Speak as if you were the authority here. Show me how much you believe I can handle opposing viewpoints."

These words, spoken in a challenging tone, sparked a thought in Mark's mind. Despite having reasons to fear the Archbishop's reaction, he had always been waiting for that moment, perhaps unconsciously. It might be the reason why he came to that house at this late hour. The time had come. Finally, he had the opportunity to convey his opinion about religion to a prominent religious authority in his city, the biggest religious authority in the city.

Mark took a deep breath, flashed a confident smile, and said, "Well then, Your Grace! I will express, without mincing words, what I think: to me, religious leaders are nothing but scammers who exploit ignorant people, preaching in the name of a nonexistent God and shaping this fantasy for their own interests."

After finishing his statement, the detective fell silent, remaining completely paralyzed. He felt like an insurgent captured by oppressive forces, awaiting execution. However, a part of him felt proud of himself.

The Archbishop, contrary to Mark's expectations, remained unfazed and smiled.

"What about science, Detective?" he asked. "Why do you consider it so superior to religion? Tell me."

Noticing Euzebius' apparent serenity, Mark tried to hide his surprise and maintained a confident posture, as displayed in his previous statement.

"It's simple, Your Grace. Science works. Science builds bridges and designs airplanes. Science saves lives with medicines and vaccines. On the other hand, religion is just a fantasy used to extract money from innocent minds."

"Are you absolutely sure about that?" asked the Archbishop.

Starting to feel more at ease with the conversation, Mark responded, "Of course I am. Everything good in this world stems from science. And what has religion done for our civilization? It has brought us only wars, murders, and the exploitation of people. We are aware of priests abusing children and zealots committing massacres inspired by passages from your Holy Book. I apologize, Your Grace, but there is simply no comparison between the benefits of science and technology and the harm caused by religion."

The Archbishop maintained his serene posture and responded, "Yes, I am well aware of the harm caused by many religious individuals in the world, Detective. I cannot deny that we have had pedophile priests and numerous massacres supposedly carried out in the name of the Lord. False prophets are everywhere, manipulating naive minds with misinterpretations of the Holy Book and enriching themselves at the expense of humble people. All of this pains me more than you may think. However, unlike many I have encountered, I do not abandon my faith. I still believe that working for my Church is the best contribution I can make. Do you know why?"

"No, please enlighten me, sir."

"Because all the wrongdoing you mentioned can be found among the followers of my religion, but they can also be found outside the Church, in equal or greater measure. I cannot condemn my faith in the Lord for the mistakes of members of the Church. If an individual commits an act of violence based on passages from the Holy Book, the error lies not in the Book but in that person's behavior, who would find justification for their violence elsewhere."

Mark remained silent, his gaze fixed on the Archbishop.

Euzebius continued, "I am also fully aware of the benefits science has brought to the world, Detective. However, there is something you need to understand: science has accomplished great things, and religion has had its share of evil in this world. But today, it is science that poses a threat to our world, not religion. Churches have sponsored massacres and supported slavery, but the ability to massacre people on a large scale was made possible by technological advancements. Those who developed nuclear weapons and, as a result, became destroyers of worlds were not religious individuals. Scientists have created vaccines that have saved countless lives, but many major epidemics have emerged in heavily industrialized areas. Uncontrolled advancements in cheaper and more durable plastic packaging are killing our oceans. Families have been driven into poverty due to progress in factory automation and artificial intelligence. But you must understand that I am not condemning science. I am simply pointing out that, soulless, science can lead civilization not to the progress you claim, but back to barbarism—the very same barbarism that religion helped us escape from many centuries ago."

"Listen, Your Grace," Mark interrupted. "It is not science that throws plastic packaging into the sea, and it was not scientists who detonated nuclear bombs over civilians. It was done by individuals who did not know how to utilize the benefits of science."

"The same goes for religion," replied the Archbishop. "That's precisely what I wanted to convey, Detective. Contrary to what you may think, science and religion are not enemies and should not exclude each other. They are simply different tools in service of civilization. A hammer is a tool—it can be used to construct a house, but it can also be used to harm people, as I heard it happened to the Sinclair family. Humbert and Joanna were killed by blows from a hammer, weren't they?"

Mark scratched his chin, pondering, and responded, "It is an interesting perspective, Your Grace. I can accept some of your ideas, but religion holds no significance for me because it is based on an imaginary being. The existence of this 'Creator of the Universe' still seems illogical to me."

The Archbishop smiled.

"May I ask why you think that way, Detective?"

"Because the existence of this Creator contradicts all known laws of nature. It is founded solely on people's need to believe in the existence of a higher protective entity. It is a fanciful way to fill a gap that science has not yet been able to explain. Unlike religion, science does not fill these gaps with fairy tales. Science keeps those spaces open until an answer emerges that can be experimentally proven."

The Archbishop raised his hand and slowly rotated his index finger.

"Look around, Detective. Look at the sky now. Behold this beautiful moon with its colorful halo. Can you truly believe that all of this came about without the intervention of an entity far superior to us?"

Mark glanced around briefly, more to fulfill the Archbishop's request than out of genuine interest. He replied, "I cannot believe that a single superior being designed this world, Your Grace. The existence of everything is the result of billions of years of physical and chemical processes. We were created from the aggregation of matter through gravity. This process gave rise to massive stars, which eventually exploded and generated new stars and planets. Oceans and volcanoes emerged on these planets, creating conditions where life could evolve. We exist not because someone decided to create us in their image and likeness, as described in your Holy Book."

The Archbishop contemplated for a few seconds. His expression, always impassive, combined with his superior posture, caused Mark to doubt whether his last argument affected the clergyman.

"So, let me ask you one thing, Detective: if you were to place a billion small plastic balls into a perfectly sterilized chamber and expose them to constant agitation for a hundred billion years, do you believe that, after all that time, these balls would have evolved into some form of living being?"

"They would not evolve into anything, Your Grace. Without the appropriate conditions, they would remain plastic balls indefinitely and never transform into living beings."

"That is exactly my point, Detective: the appropriate conditions! You believe that there is no intelligent design in creation, but you fail to realize that everything in the Universe has a purpose for its existence. Would you like to see an example? Look at the marvel of the carbon atom. It can form chains, generating increasingly complex molecules. However, who orchestrated that these complex molecules, with specific properties, would transform into proteins and then into a DNA structure capable of self-replication and the generation of new beings? It was not randomness that determined an oxygen atom, combined with two hydrogen atoms, would create the essential element for life that we call water, or that this same oxygen would have properties to produce energy for our cells. Your reluctance to comprehend how this creation was accomplished should not lead you to deny the existence of a Creator."

"What I fail to comprehend, Your Grace, is that while you demonstrate such an understanding of the mechanics of this creation, your Sacred Book proclaims that the Universe came into existence a few thousand years ago, within a few days of magic. It seems illogical to me."

Euzebius gazed at Mark with the tenderness of someone speaking to a child. This began to irritate the detective, but he remained silent.

The clergyman continued, "You must understand, Detective: the Holy Book was written thousands of years ago. Through the prophets, the Lord expressed Himself in words that the minds of that time could comprehend. The people of that era would not have understood the nature of electrical energy or even how an internal combustion engine works. If the Holy Book had spoken about atoms, DNA molecules, nuclear fusion, and black holes, no one from that period would have understood it, and the Book would never have reached the wide audience it did. Do not condemn a text because it was written in a way that allows its readers to absorb its content. Unfortunately, the arrogance of those who deny the Holy Book blinds them to its teachings. Instead of seeking its message of love, they search for supposed contradictions and inconsistencies within its pages, solely aiming to discredit its content. You must understand that the leaders of my church are fully aware that the Universe was created billions of years ago. We are not ignorant, as skeptics often label us."

"I acknowledge your eloquence, Your Grace, but I must also state that as persuasive as your argumentation may be, I simply cannot accept it. To do so, I would have to assume that the Creator emerged without any recipe. You propose that the most complex being emerged from nothingness and then created the simpler beings."

"Ah, always the question of who created the Creator! Contrary to what you might think, Detective, I've heard this question throughout my life. But I must admit, I don't know the answer to it. Do you know why? This question will always be beyond my comprehension and will never be answered by your science either. But now I must ask you: if you can't prove the non-existence of the Creator, who is filling the gap with assumptions now? In my opinion, Detective, claiming that this entity does not exist is just one of the many fantasies we can conceive regarding the existence of the Creator. What sets this belief apart from all others is that it seems to be the most fitting for those who find it difficult to accept the existence of a higher intelligence. Perhaps the difference between a skeptic and a person of faith is merely a matter of arrogance and humility. Have you ever considered that?"

"Sorry, Your Grace, but I have encountered countless religious individuals in my life, and I can say that humility is not a usual character trait to find in these people. The religious individuals I know today are so confident in their belief of divine protection that they refuse to behave as your Holy Book teaches. They have forgotten all the lessons on turning the other cheek and forgiveness. They only remember the parts of the Book that place them in a superior position to those who do not share the same faith. This is so true that I could tell you: if your Messiah returned today and attempted to preach the teachings attributed to him in the Holy Book, he would end up being hated not by skeptics or scientists, but by the most fervent followers of the religion he founded.

"Rest assured, Detective. That will not happen. The Messiah's second coming will not be like the first. You would know this if you had more knowledge about the Holy Book. The Messiah will not return as a wanderer, preaching lessons of love in the streets. He has already done that once. His return will be a grand event. He will descend from heaven to announce the end of time. Those who consider themselves his faithful followers but failed to put His teachings into practice will be the first to fall. Only those who have truly embraced the Messiah's message in their hearts will be taken to heaven."

Mark didn't respond. He simply gazed at the Archbishop, who continued, "Tell me, Detective: what do you believe will happen to you when the day of judgment arrives?"

"I don't follow your religion, Your Grace, so I don't believe in such a day," Mark replied.

The Archbishop smiled. "I'm not asking you to believe in my religion, Detective. I simply want to know: what did you think will happen when the day came for you to be judged by the Lord?"

The Archbishop noticed a change in Mark's expression. The detective's eyes now reflected anger.

"When that day arrives, Your Grace, I couldn't care less about any judgment your god might pass on me. If he desires to send me to some sort of hell, it wouldn't be any worse than the life he has already subjected me to."

A moment of silence filled the room.

The Archbishop scrutinized the Mark's faces and spoke, "I'm sorry to hear that life hasn't treated you well, Detective. From your words and your eyes, I can sense the depth of your sorrow."

Wearied by the long conversation, Mark rose and looked at the sky. He fixed his gaze on the moon once more. The halo surrounding the satellite appeared even more radiant than earlier in the evening.

Euzebius noticed that the detective seemed to be trying to get calmer.

"It's a wonderful sight, isn't? This beautiful moon hangs there in the sky, visible to millions of people across the globe, regardless of their wealth or poverty. It is one of the many gifts granted to us by the Lord each day, although most of His children fail to perceive it. Despite your pain, I'm glad you can still behold the beauty in the work of the Lord."

Mark sat down again, and Euzebius noticed his fatigue.

"I believe we lost our focus, Detective. I just recalled that the purpose of your visit here was not to engage in a discussion about the Creation of the Universe with me. Am I correct?" the Archbishop acknowledged in a friendly tone.

"I apologize, Your Grace. I shouldn't have burdened you with inquiries that go against your faith."

"You did not challenge my faith. You simply expressed your thoughts, posed questions, and listened to the answers."

Mark smiled, lifted his head, and said, "It's unfortunate that you can't tell us more information about Carol Sinclair. Sadly, I fear we have little time to save her."

" I will do whatever I can to help you, Detective. I'll speak with my brother-in-law and nephew to find out if they have any information that could assist you. Additionally, I'll instruct the members of the church to contact me directly if they have any information about the Sinclair family." The Archbishop rose. "And if you ever wish to return here and chat about your uncertainties about life, the universe, and anything else, it will a be pleasure to receive you."

Euzebius pushed his chair closer to the table and said, "Let me call Sister Anne. She will accompany you to the exit door."

The Archbishop walked toward the entrance of the house while Mark remained seated, gazing once more at the pool. The detective noticed that the waterfall fountain and the surrounding lights had been turned off, indicating that the people in the house were preparing for going to bed. The place became so quiet that he could hear sounds from the garden: a frog croaking, a cricket chirping.

Suddenly, Mark heard a female voice.

"Hi, Zalthor!"

He turned his head and looked around, searching for Sister Anne, but he didn't see anyone.

"Zalthor, it's me, Lintsa," the voice continued.

The detective stood up and turned around, attempting to locate the source of the words.

"Who's there? Where are you?" he asked. "Please show yourself!"

Suddenly, Mark felt dizzy, and his vision rapidly became blurred. He collapsed to the ground, losing consciousness.

Sister Anne arrived and saw the detective's body lying beside the pool. She rushed to Mark and cried out for help.

Chapter 12

When Mark regained consciousness, he found himself in the same place of his previous dream—a spacious chamber inside the spacecraft that had previously rescued him. His body remained immersed in the large recovery tank, enveloped by a clear, greenish liquid that provided a comforting warmth. Despite the various strands affixed to his skin, he experienced a profound sense of relaxation, feeling as if immersed in a tranquil pool of warm water.

With his vision considerably improved, the detective turned his attention to his own hands, which now appeared less scrawny and wrinkled compared to when he first arrived on the ship. He also noticed that he could move his fingers ever so slightly.

Suddenly, a voice emanated from in front of the tank, addressing Mark by the same name he had heard in his previous dream.

"Hi, Zalthor. It's me, my love, Lintsa."

Raising his eyes, Mark saw a woman of captivating beauty, appearing to be in her early twenties. She surpassed in loveliness any woman he had encountered throughout his life. Simultaneously, the detective felt his heart pounding with such intensity that it seemed on the verge of leaping out of his chest.

In addition to her physical beauty, Lintsa exuded a profound sense of familiarity, as if Mark had known her for countless years. He felt like reuniting with a profound love from his youth, someone he had wished to meet during an extensive period of absence.

The detective attempted to stir within the tank, longing to emerge and draw nearer to the woman before him. However, his current physical state rendered him too weak, limiting his movements to slight arm motions, but enough to loosen a few strands from his sagging skin.

"Don't be afraid, my love! You will recover your strength in a few days," Lintsa assured.

Fhastina appeared beside Lintsa, allowing Mark to perceive her features more clearly. Just as he had initially imagined, Fhastina possessed a bird-like countenance reminiscent of an eagle, completed with a beautifully sculpted yet robust beak. Despite her avian head, Fhastina's body displayed fully humanoid characteristics, with arms and legs very similar in size to Lintsa's.

"I shall increase the intensity of the sonic waves to calm him," Fhastina informed Lintsa, manipulating a series of buttons on the control panel attached to the tank.

Lintsa inquired, "How much longer until Zalthor achieves a complete recovery, Fhastina?"

"He will be fully restored in two days. This recovery tank is our most advanced, and Zalthor will be in perfect condition by the time we reach Dr. Axlow's planet. I will maintain the sedative sound waves, ensuring that he wakes up after arriving on the Doctor's planet. We must avoid any premature attempts to break the tank walls. When he gets stronger, it will be very likable.

At that moment, Physter entered the chamber and stood beside Lintsa. Mark noticed that Fhastina's partner also possessed an eagle-like head very similar to Fhastina's.

Mark pondered to himself, "Why do Physter and Fhastina have this appearance, while Lintsa resembles a woman from my world?"

"Mrs. Lintsa, we have received a communication from Ranson," reported Physter. "He is online on the bridge, and it seems that the situation on the planet Dolmen is becoming more complicated."

"I will speak with Ranson now, Physter," Lintsa replied. "Fhastina, please take care of Zalthor during my absence."

"Yes, Madam. He's in good hands," Fhastina assured.

Lintsa gazed at Mark once more and spoke, "I must go, my love. Unfortunately, our planet is facing difficult times. I can't wait to see you outside of this tank!" She blew a kiss to Mark.

Mark's heart raced as Lintsa addressed him in such a tender manner. Who is this woman? How can she be so beautiful and treat him as a long-lost love? When did they previously meet? His memory failed him.

Furthermore, why did everyone in this dream insist on calling him Zalthor? Who is this Zalthor? Mark had never heard this name before. Additionally, this dream seemed to be a sequence of the previous one he experienced. He had never had such unusual and interconnected dreams before.

Before Lintsa departed, Physter stepped forward and informed, "One more thing, Madam: the ship's computer has completed the analysis of the bracelet attached to Zalthor's arm when we rescued him."

"Very well, Physter. Once I conclude my conversation with Ranson, I will analyze the results of the bracelet assessment."

Lintsa and Physter left the place. Only Fhastina stayed by the recovery tank, attentively monitoring the screen on the equipment control panel.

During this brief moment of silence, Mark remembered that minutes ago, he was chatting with the Archbishop at the clergyman's house. He attempted to recall what took place after the conversation but couldn't remember leaving the house, returning home, or even getting into his car.

"What would have happened?" he pondered.

Suddenly, Mark's memory resurfaced. He recalled sitting by the pool when he heard Lintsa's voice, and then he lost consciousness upon rising from his seat.

How embarrassing! His body must be lying near the pool, causing a commotion and alarming everyone in the house. His boss, Oswald, will surely be furious when he discovers that his subordinate got into such an unpleasant situation at the Archbishop's residence.

Mark directed his attention back to the unfolding of his dream and noticed Fhastina approaching the glass wall of the recovery tank. She took out a small sphere from her pocket and manipulated it for a few moments. Then, a tiny aperture formed on the sphere, and a luminous dot emerged from it, hovering beside Fhastina.

"You may find my actions a little disturbing, Mr. Zalthor, but in due time, you will comprehend their purpose," stated Fhastina.

The luminous dot moved toward the control panel of the recovery tank, disappearing among its colorful buttons.

Fhastina remained silent, keeping her gaze fixed on Mark. Suddenly, a soft knocking sound emanated from the chamber's entrance. Alarmed, she turned her head but saw no one. With a sigh of relief, she returned her attention to Mark.

The luminous dot reappeared, this time submerged in the liquid of the recovery tank, directly in front of Mark. The detective became apprehensive, suspecting that Fhastina might have malicious intentions. He attempted to move and struggled to shake his body, but he lacked the strength even to raise his hand in front of the luminous dot.

"Don't be afraid, Mr. Zalthor. It will not harm you. It is merely a friend who will pay you a visit in your world," explained Fhastina.

The luminous dot moved toward Mark's right eye, and he was unable to avoid its approach. The radiance became so intense that it momentarily blinded the detective. However, the light quickly dissipated, and Mark's vision returned as if nothing had happened. He only felt a faint tingling at the back of his right eye.

Fhastina displayed a light smile of contentment. She proceeded to the control panel and pressed a sequence of buttons. Mark's drowsiness intensified, and he quickly lost consciousness again.

Chapter 13

When Mark opened his eyes once again, he found himself lying on a spacious couch, his head supported by a plush pillow. Feeling quite disoriented, he sat up and rubbed his hands over his face.

Right in front of him stood Sister Anne.

"How are you feeling, sir?" she asked.

"Where am I? What happened?"

Mark glanced to the side and saw the Archbishop seated on an armchair.

" When Sister Anne went to escort you to the exit, she found you lying by the pool. We called in a couple of our staff members to move you onto this sofa," Euzebius explained. "We pondered about calling an ambulance, but Sister Anne is an experienced nurse. She assured us that your vital signs were normal and that you would regain consciousness soon. It seems you simply had a drop in blood pressure and fainted near the pool."

Mark tried to stand up, but he felt dizzy and almost lost his balance.

"You should sit back down," Sister Anne advised. "You don't seem fully recovered yet."

"I'm fine! It's late, and I've already consumed too much of your time." Mark turned to the Archbishop and requested, "Your Grace, I need to ask you a favor: please do not talk about what happened here tonight to anyone."

"Do not worry, Detective. However, promise me that you will seek medical assistance. You may have a health problem," the Archbishop stated.

The detective nodded in agreement.

"I think all I need is some rest. I apologize for all the commotion, Your Grace. Please excuse me and have a good night." Mark bowed slightly, clasping his hands in front of his chest as a sign of respect.

Sister Anne escorted the visitor to the exit of the residence.

Half an hour later, Mark was in his apartment. As soon as he arrived, he hurriedly opened wardrobes and drawers, searching desperately and pulling out a stack of photographs. The dinner table promptly transformed into a chaotic display of images. Mark carefully examined each picture, hoping to catch a glimpse of a face resembling Lintsa's, but he couldn't find any.

Refusing to give up, Mark fired up his old computer, launching a command to the operating system to search its whole hard drive for any image files. The detective meticulously examined each file found, one by one, but he once again couldn't find any pictures resembling Lintsa. Fatigue and frustration overwhelmed him as the endless parade of pictures exhausted his patience.

Sitting down in front of the computer screen, the detective sank into the chair and closed his eyes tightly. He tried hard to conjure up Lintsa's face in his mind. He delved into the recesses of his memory, recalling famous actresses and singers, hoping to find a semblance similar to Lintsa. Perhaps the woman had the appearance of a celebrity who Mark was once platonically in love. Suddenly, a realization gripped his mind. Lintsa embodied the epitome of his ideal woman—the very image that he would materialize if asked to conjure perfection in the form of a woman.

"Yes! She is my embodiment of perfection. That's why my heart nearly burst when I saw her. It feels as though I've encountered her before, and that dream felt so real," the detective pondered.

A hollow growl resonated from Mark's stomach as he glanced at a clock hanging on the living room wall. It was almost two in the morning, and he realized he hadn't had dinner yet. Consumed by the Sinclair family case, he had spent the entire night without eating.

Mark looked for something to eat in the kitchen, but his hopes for a decent meal were dashed as he discovered the absence of satisfactory options. And at this ungodly hour, ordering food would be impossible.

There was only one place where Mark could satisfy his hunger and organize his thoughts.

Chapter 14

Thirty minutes later, Mark was back at the Cafe and Grill restaurant. Despite the late hour, the place was bustling with activity. A lively group of young people, returning from a music concert, engaged in animated conversations as they replenished their energy after the show. Watching them brought back memories of Mark's own youth. This time now felt like a very distant past, as if it belonged to another lifetime.

Seated at his favorite table in the corner of the restaurant, Mark recalled that he had been frequenting the place since his college days. Unlike him, the establishment had changed very little over the past three decades, undergoing only minor improvements such as a fresh coat of paint and the replacement of old wooden windows with large glass panels, providing Mark with a wide view of the street outside.

A waitress approached Mark's table, and he made his order by pointing to a picture on the menu. The waitress informed him that due to the bustling activity, the order might take around forty minutes to get ready. Mark requested some bread accompanied by a portion of butter to appease his hunger while he waited.

After a few minutes, the waitress returned and set a plate on the table containing a warm and soft damper bread, along with a knife and a small bowl of butter. Mark lightly touched the bread, sensing its warmth and texture, and thanked the waitress. As soon as she left, he took the knife, sliced the bread in half, spread the butter onto one piece, and began to eat slowly, relishing each bite.

Mark wished only to focus on his appetizer and ease his mind after a day filled with strange events. However, as he devoured the last piece of bread, he couldn't help but notice the entrance of a distinguished gentleman. The man possessed very white hair, yet his countenance looked youthful. His erect posture accentuated his towering height of six and a half feet. He exuded an air of elegance, dressed in a refined ivory suit, and carried a small electronic device in his hand. However, the gadget didn't seem like a typical cellphone. Its circular shape resembled more of a small compass.

The presence of the stranger caught the attention of the customers in the restaurant, with some girls even expressing admiration for his stylish and distinguished appearance.

The man glanced at the small screen of his device before turning his gaze toward Mark. Moving swiftly, he stopped beside the detective's table, observing him for approximately ten seconds while analyzing the information displayed on his gadget. Satisfied with the information received, the stranger then placed the device into his suit pocket.

"Good evening, sir. May I sit here?" the man politely asked, pointing to the chair directly in front of Mark.

Mark got so surprised by the unexpected request, that he was unable to decline. He simply nodded in agreement.

The man settled into his seat, his face displaying a distinct sense of joy. He gazed around the restaurant, taking in the surroundings for a few moments, clearly admiring everything within his sight.

A flurry of thoughts invaded Mark's mind. "What is this unusual individual doing here at this late hour? And why did he choose to sit right in front of me, just after I departed from the Archbishop's residence?" The detective sensed an imminent danger.

Confidently, the man locked eyes with Mark and politely asked, "I hope I'm not bothering you, sir, but could you tell me your name?"

The detective remained silent, his gaze fixed on the stranger as he tried to conceal his fear.

Undeterred by Mark's lack of response, the man's joyful expression gave way to a look of surprise.

"Did I ask an inappropriate question, sir? I must confess, I am a foreigner here, unfamiliar with the social customs of this world."

Mark glanced around the surroundings as if searching for another presence, perhaps an accomplice of the stranger. He then inquired, "Who sent you here? The Mayor did it?"

"The Mayor? Who is the Mayor?" the man replied, genuinely confused.

Mark didn't reply, and the stranger noticed the detective was firmly gripping the small knife he had used to cut the bread.

The man extended his hand toward Mark.

"My name is Delasher. It's a pleasure to meet you."

Mark looked at the extended hand but chose not to shake hands with the stranger.

"Have I made a mistake, sir? Is this not how people greet one another in this world?" Delasher asked, retracting his hand.

Mark eased the tension in his muscles.

"Delasher? What an odd name! Where does it come from?" he queried.

"It's Zarconian," the man replied.

"Zarconian!?" the detective exclaimed, trying to recall which country or nationality Delasher was referring to. "I've never heard of this nationality before."

"Actually, the Zarconians are a race. Our ancestral home is the planet Zarco, located in the central arm of the Galaxy," the stranger explained. "But my place of origin is not the focus of our discussion right now. I am here to tell you about a matter of utmost importance, and I urge you to pay close attention to what I am about to say."

Mark's expression shifted from fear to a more skeptical one.

"Do you have something important to tell me? Did you find me at three in the morning to deliver a message? How long have you been tracking me?" the detective inquired.

Although surprised that Mark has disregarded the mention of him being from another planet, Delasher responded, "No, sir. I have not been tracking anyone. In fact, it was through this locator that I managed to find you." Delasher took the device out of his pocket, the same gadget he had carried when entering the restaurant and displayed it to Mark.

"I apologize for this late-night encounter. I arrived earlier, but I entered your world at a location much farther away than anticipated. I had not foreseen how vast your world is, nor the multitude of people inhabiting it. I am utterly amazed by this place. I even pondered seeking rest in one of your so-called hotels and finding you in the morning. However, this device indicated that you were still awake and had stopped at this establishment. I felt compelled to come here and talk to you. Therefore, I am grateful that we can chat now."

Mark frowned, showing impatience.

"Man, what you're saying doesn't make any sense. You know that, don't you?"

"I apologize. This is always a complicated moment for those in your situation. I must warn you: there is no way to convey what I'm about to say without provoking some emotional reaction.

The detective leaned back, gripping the knife tightly once again, pointing it forward, and stared transfixed at Delasher.

"Are you here to kill me? Right now? In this public place?"

"No, sir. Absolutely not. Killing you is not the reason I came here. Just listen carefully to what I have to say and answer any questions I ask. Everything will become clear. Can you do that?

Mark began to calm down, but his breathing was heavy.

"Okay, go on," the detective replied, trying to sound more relaxed.

Delasher smiled and began, "Very well, let's proceed. First, tell me your name, sir."

"My name is Mark Randall. I thought you already knew that."

"How old are you, Mark Randall?"

"I'm forty-six years old."

"And what is the average life expectancy for individuals of your race?"

"Of my race? What are you talking about?"

"Just answer the question. All will be explained in due course."

"Fine. If that satisfies you, I believe I will still live for about thirty more years, perhaps a bit longer if I change my diet and get more sleep."

"So, you are a little past half of your life expectancy. Not old enough to have a senile mind, yet not so young as to have difficulty comprehending me," Delasher concluded. "But now, here comes the question that has brought me to you."

The stranger glanced around to check if anyone else was eavesdropping on their conversation.

"Mark Randall, tell me: do you believe your world has a Creator?"

The detective stared at Delasher for a few seconds, his face expressing confusion. Then he exclaimed, "Wait! Now I understand. The Archbishop sent you, didn't he? Is this some kind of test?"

"I must inform you that I have no knowledge of any archbishop, Mark Randall. I only ask you to answer my question. It holds greater importance than you may have realized."

Mark pondered, his face now brimming with suspicion. Delasher noticed this but remained silent.

The detective gazed out of the restaurant, attempting to divert his thoughts from the bewildering situation.

The stranger persisted, "Answer me, Mark Randall: what are your thoughts on the Creator of your world? Have you ever pondered this subject?"

Mark turned to Delasher, wearing an expression of annoyance.

"Listen, man! If you came here to try to convince me that God exists, you're wasting your time. You may win the argument, but no matter what you say, I will never believe in this fantasy, not even in a thousand years."

"If that's what you think, Mark Randall, I must inform you that what I'm about to tell you might shock you profoundly."

Mark chuckled and retorted, "If you want to know, my friend, I had a lengthy discussion on this topic just a few hours ago, and I was almost convinced of the existence of such a Creator. However, even after that, I still believe: if there is a Creator of the Universe, they couldn't care less about this world. He's merely an arrogant egocentric who never does anything for anyone, at least not for those in need or deserving. That's my opinion about this Creator."

Before Mark finished the sentence, he regretted what he had said as he foresaw the exhausting debate that would follow.

Delasher gazed at the detective, pondered for a few seconds, processed the words he heard, and responded, "Let me make sure I got this right. You claim not to believe in the existence of a Creator, yet at the same time hold visible bitterness toward him. That sounds rather contradictory, don't you think? To be angry at someone you believe doesn't exist."

"Allow me to clarify, my friend. I'm trying to convey that there are two possibilities: either this Creator doesn't exist, or he's a callous jerk. Do you understand?"

Delasher scrutinized Mark for a few more moments, then locked eyes with the detective.

"Well, I'm sorry to say, but what I'm about to reveal will likely trouble you even more, Mark Randall." Delasher took a deep breath. "Firstly: that entity you despise so vehemently... Well... he does exist."

Mark sighed and turned his face away, attempting to display complete indifference to the stranger's words.

"Secondly, that callous jerk...," Delasher pointed a finger at Mark, "is you!"

If the situation already seemed strange to Mark, it had now become surreal.

"What?" It was the only response he could muster.

"You are not who you believe yourself to be, Mark Randall. You are the Creator of this universe. You are the one whom, in my world, we refer to as The Constructor."

Mark remained silent. All he could do was look at Delasher, who noticed the colossal chaos unfolding inside the detective's mind.

The stranger continued, "I know that you have been living in this world since the beginning of what you consider to be your only existence, Mark Randall. Naturally, such a situation makes it difficult to comprehend your true reality, even more so at that stage in your life. The concept of existence as an inhabitant of this world must undoubtedly have been deeply ingrained in your mind."

Mark jumped out of his chair.

"Wait a minute! Enough of this nonsense!"

The detective rose, turned toward the restaurant counter, raised his hand, and shouted, "Waitress, please cancel my order. There is a crazy person in the restaurant bothering me. I will leave!"

Without moving, Delasher addressed Mark, "You, Mark Randall, are actually Zalthor Acri, a million-year-old Hubbian—an immortal being from the planet Hubberia. Ten thousand years ago, your ship crashed on a moon in a very isolated planetary system, and you remained buried there until being rescued by a spaceship commanded by Fhastina and Physter. This ship serves Lintsa, your wife, and Doctor Axlow, your childhood friend."

The detective stared at Delasher, transfixed. In that very moment, the waitress appeared from behind the counter and asked, "What did you say, sir?"

Mark turned to the waitress and responded, in a choked voice, "Nothing... I didn't say anything, miss. My apologies."

The detective returned to sit in front of Delasher, his hands shaking. He took a deep breath, like someone who genuinely needed air to speak.

"Listen, friend: I had two strange dreams today. In both dreams, I heard the same names you just mentioned. Zalthor Acri, Lintsa, and Axlow are names I've never heard before, and I'm certain I haven't told anyone about these dreams. So, how do you know all this?"

Delasher leaned closer to Mark and spoke in a low voice, "Do you recall the luminous dot you saw entering the recovery tank? The one Fhastina inserted through the control panel?"

Mark didn't respond immediately. His left shoulder began to spasm.

"Yes, I remember that very clearly, but, I mean, it happened in a dream I had a few hours ago. It wasn't real. And how do you know about it?"

Delasher reclined in his chair, resting against the backrest. He exhibited a serenity that made it seem like he was enjoying that moment.

"Yes, I observed how frightened you were when I approached your right eye. I apologize for that. It wasn't my intention to alarm you. We expected you to be unconscious during my insertion. We had to deal with this unforeseen event. But don't worry, Mark Randall, you weren't harmed. That light contained only a mental projection device. It entered Zalthor's head through the cavity of the right eye and connected to a nerve between the eyes and the brain."

"A mental projection device? What is that?"

"That's what allowed me to be here, in front of you. It permits me to interact with your world as if I were physically present."

"But that woman... the one with the eagle-like face?"

"Are you referring to the female named Fhastina?"

"You two did everything hidden from Lintsa, didn't you? What's going on? What do you want from me?"

"Calm down, Mark Randall! Everything will be explained in due time. But for now, what's most important for you and your world is that you comprehend your role in this reality we are now."

"But then, who am I? Or, more precisely, who do you believe I am? What in the world is this ridiculous story you've just told?" Mark's voice trembled with a mix of bewilderment and disbelief.

Delasher fixed Mark with an intense gaze, resting his elbows on the table and rubbing his fingertips together as he spoke.

" Listen carefully, Mark Randall. I shall reiterate: you are not the person you think you are. You are Zalthor Acri, a Hubbian immortal, born a million years ago on the planet Hubberia. However, ten thousand years ago, as you ventured alone through the depths of space, your spaceship collided with a moon named B-23—a desolate celestial body situated within the remote and uncharted Francia system, a planetary system at the edge of the Galaxy. As no one knew your whereabouts, you remained buried beneath the moon's surface for ten millennia until Physter and Fhastina came to your rescue."

"I don't understand; that's not possible. Zalthor is nothing more than a dream I had. A dream I had twice, by the way. How can I be him?"

"That is exactly what you must comprehend now, Mark Randall. Zalthor is no just a dream you had! He is you in a reality beyond this one. When your spaceship crashed into the moon B-23, it collided at an incredible speed, pulverizing upon impact with the surface of the moon. However, your indestructible body was pushed several kilometers deep into the moon's rocky terrain, unable to move from there and with no means of communicating for help. With your location unknown to all, you were condemned to be trapped forever, crushed beneath countless tons of rock" Delasher perceived Mark's mind was on the edge of collapse, yet he felt compelled to go on. "Buried beneath miles of stone, with no hope of rescue, you knew that you might be imprisoned in that state for an eternity—an immobilized existence until the end of time. Thus, your Hubbian mind took the only path to survival it could."

"What did I do?" Mark whispered; his voice barely audible.

"Within you own mind, you constructed an entire world—a new universe where you could live while buried. It is this very universe in which you currently reside, Mark Randall. You created everything that exists within this world, all that you now perceive. You are the Creator of this universe."

Confusion washed over Mark's face as he stared at Delasher.

"Tell me, if I had been trapped within a rock ten thousand years ago, wouldn't I have realized it sooner? And I am only forty-six years old. How could I have been buried for ten millennia? That is illogical."

"During these ten thousand years, you have experienced countless lives within this very world where you now live. Your initial existence likely dates back to the formation of your civilization, in the early days of your race's first villages. The life you're currently living as Mark Randall is just one among hundreds that you have experienced since you built this universe."

A strong nausea gripped Mark, and Delasher noticed the detective's throat constricting with great intensity.

"Do not panic, Mark Randall. Take deep breaths. I understand that the information I have presented is difficult to digest."

Mark wiped the sweat from his forehead and looked at the people around him. The young customers continued their tranquil conversations, oblivious to him and the enigmatic stranger before him. The detective's gaze landed upon the waitress, who picked up a plate from the kitchen counter—perhaps his order, finally arriving. However, Mark had lost his appetite. He drummed his fingers on the table with increasing speed, attempting to restore his composure. Then, he stared at Delasher.

"I'll tell you something, my friend. I think I understand what's going on here."

Delasher remained silent, simply observing Mark.

The detective continued, "Fifteen years ago, I suffered the devastating loss of my daughter. She was only three years old. It was a tragic accident, and I still blame myself for it."

"I'm sorry to hear that, Mark Randall."

"Let me continue! A few years later, one evening, I returned home exhausted from work and placed the pistol I typically carried at work on the dining table. I went to take a shower, and as the water fell over my body, I heard the sound of a gunshot. Instantly, I knew what had occurred: my wife had chosen to end her own life using my gun."

"This is a tragic story, Mark Randall. I offer my sincerest condolences, though I fail to see the connection to the subject we're discussing."

"Since my wife's passing, my dear Delasher, I've been dreaming of her and my daughter every night. Every time I go to bed, I know I will meet them. In these dreams, I find myself in our old house, surrounded by my family. However, always during the dream, my daughter vanishes, disappearing somewhere behind the house. I hear her voice, pleading for help, but I can never find her. And when her cries finally cease, I hear my wife's anguished screams, blaming me for everything that happened. For the past few years, I have relived the agony of losing my family every night."

Delasher noticed that Mark's eyes had turned red.

"But today... Today I slept twice, and on both occasions, my dreams were different from anything I've experienced before. Firstly, I found myself in outer space, being rescued and lifted by some form of robot. After that, I was submerged in a glass tank filled with green liquid, with numerous strands attached to my body. In the second dream, I met a stunningly beautiful woman, more beautiful than anything I could imagine. Finally, a small dot of light entered the tank where I was submerged. Now, I'm talking with a peculiar man who claims to have entered my mind, traveling inside that dot." Mark anxiously waved his arms as he spoke. "Initially, I couldn't understand what was taking place, but now everything has become clear to me."

""What have you understood? "Mark Randall?" Delasher inquired.

"I've realized that it has finally happened: the day my sanity crumbled, and my fragile grasp of reality was shattered..." He raised their arms. "...and gave birth to you."

Mark got up abruptly and walked quickly toward the restaurant exit. The waitress called out to him, warning that his order was ready, but the detective didn't stop. The customers inside the establishment observed the scene with curiosity, without any idea of what was happening.

Mark ran to his car. The vehicle accelerated around the corner of the block and disappeared from view down the street.

Chapter 15

The next morning, at the police station, Oswald, Andrew, and Mark were inside a large meeting room. Accompanying them was another individual, a tall and slender man who looked to be as old as Mark. Seated beside Oswald at one end of the central table, the man was dressed in aged clothes, his body trembling incessantly. Positioned across from him at the opposite end were the two detectives.

Mark was hugging a coffee thermos tightly, clutching it as if his very existence depended on it, leaving no doubt that he had no intention of sharing the beverage with anyone else. Additionally, he was grasping a cup that had been refilled three times since his arrival in the room. Oswald took notice of his subordinate's precarious state but didn't comment on it. Being in this condition wasn't exactly new to Mark. Instead, the boss took the initiative to start the meeting.

"Gentlemen, allow me to introduce Benjamin. A colleague of yours claims he may possess crucial information connected to the Sinclair family case," Oswald announced.

Mark looked up, twitching his nose in response to an unpleasant scent. The older detective looked at Oswald and inquired, "Is he a homeless?"

Before the boss could respond, Mark pointed toward Benjamin.

"You're one of those addicts who are always on Aurora Street, aren't you?"

Embarrassed, Benjamin lowered his head. Oswald interceded, saying, "Benjamin has faced difficulties in his life, but he is a decent person. He has help us before."

Andrew addressed Benjamin, asking, "What do you have to share with us? Do you have any information regarding the murder of the Sinclair family?"

"Well..." Benjamin looked intimidated by the presence of the detectives.

"Don't worry, Benjamin! You're among friends here," assured Oswald. The chief filled a glass of water and passed it to the man. "These gentlemen are here to listen to you. Any information you provide will be given due attention."

Benjamin took a sip of water and began speaking, "Well, I know a man. He engages in various tasks, especially those of a questionable nature. Lately, he's been talking a lot, sharing countless stories."

Andrew requested, "Please continue."

"This man is quite large and strong. Standing nearly seven feet tall. I heard a rumor that he was once a renowned fighter, having competed in important tournaments."

"I believe I know who you're referring to," Mark interjected. "This fighter is known as Tortoise, am I correct?"

"Yes, how did you know?" Benjamin inquired.

"I've already watched a documentary about him," the oldest detective responded. "Tortoise was a former wrestling champion. He participated in several national mixed martial arts tournaments but failed the doping test twice and ended up being suspended for several years. After that, he disappeared for a considerable period but resurfaced in the news, revealing that he had become homeless."

Benjamin continued speaking, "Tortoise mentioned that wealthy folks sometimes seek him out on Aurora Street. They hire him to beat someone up or collect overdue payments. He even claimed to have killed people."

"Did he mention anything about the Sinclair family's case?" Andrew asked.

"No. That was prior to the incident involving the Sinclair family, but Tortoise did mention killing people. I asked some people on the street if it was true, but they couldn't confirm it. However, they mentioned that Tortoise often boasts about it as if it were something to be proud of."

"It could just be idle talk," Mark observed. "There are people on that street who claim to be the president of the republic."

Oswald shot a disapproving look at his subordinate.

Benjamin continued, "But there's something that caught my attention regarding the Sinclair family's case. I heard that they were killed with a hammer. Is that true?"

Mark and Andrew exchanged glances, and Mark responded, "Yes. Based on the nature of the injuries, two of the victims were indeed killed by blows from a hammer."

"I've often seen Tortoise carrying a hammer on Aurora Street. He has brandished it on a few occasions when other men threatened him. He warned them that if they got closer to him, he would smash their faces with that hammer."

Mark and Andrew exchanged glances once again, now trying to conceal their excitement at the information.

"After the Sinclair family's crime, have you seen Tortoise again?" Andrew asked.

"No. I haven't seen him in three days. I first heard about the crime yesterday morning, and my suspicions immediately fell on Tortoise. I've been asking people on Aurora Street, and everyone told me that they haven't seen Tortoise since news of the crime broke."

"This is intriguing, Benjamin," Mark commented. "Do you know any close friends of Tortoise? Anyone who might know his whereabouts?"

"Tortoise has a girlfriend on the street named Marisa. I saw her earlier today before coming here. She lives in a large, abandoned house in the middle of Aurora Street."

"Can you lead us to this woman?" Mark inquired.

"Yes. We can go there right now if you want. I can show you where Marisa lives."

Mark looked at Oswald.

"What do you think, boss?"

"I believe it's worth investigating," the chief replied. "Listen, Benjamin, wait for us outside. We need to have a brief discussion among ourselves."

Oswald rose and opened the door to the meeting room. He called for Lauren and asked the secretary to give Benjamin something to eat. The homeless individual left the room.

Once Lauren closed the door, the boss exclaimed, "Tortoise?! Can you explain to me what kind of fighter has a nickname like that?"

"He was known for his remarkable resilience. They said he could withstand a lot of blows and never fall because he had a hard body, although he wasn't particularly a very quick fighter. That's how he acquired that nickname," Mark answered.

"That explains why he didn't find much success in the fighting business," Oswald concluded.

Glancing at his cellphone screen, Andrew raised his hand.

"I quickly searched some information. Tortoise's real name is Joseph Assis. He was married and had three children. He has been arrested a few times for public order disturbances and indecent exposure."

"He sometimes got involved in sexual activities right out in the open on Aurora Street. It's not unusual for that place," Mark added.

Oswald sat back down and looked at Mark.

"What about your conversation with the Archbishop? How did it go?"

"Not very productive, boss. The Archbishop didn't provide any answers regarding the relationship between Carol and Paul. Instead, he dismissed the suspicions surrounding his nephew as mere conspiracy theories. He also claimed to be unaware of anyone harassing or stalking the girl."

"Did he mention anything about Humbert Sinclair's connection to the Mayor?"

"Yes. The Archbishop suspects that the Cacellas orchestrated Humbert Sinclair's murder to intimidate his brother-in-law, and now they are attempting to divert media attention toward Paul."

"So, the Archbishop didn't give us any new information that went beyond what we expected," Oswald concluded.

"Did he contact you today to talk about our conversation?" Mark asked.

"I sincerely hope that won't happen, Mr. Randall. Did you upset the Archbishop? Did you utter blasphemies?" Oswald questioned.

"Of course not," Mark responded, trying to conceal his concern that the Archbishop might call Oswald and reveal details of their conversation, or worse, report to the boss that Mark fainted during the visit. That would be extremely embarrassing. "I merely want to know if the Archbishop has acquired any new information about the crime. He mentioned he would speak with some individuals," Mark justified.

"What's the progress regarding the court order to question the Mayor's son?" Andrew inquired, turning his gaze to Oswald.

"We are still working on it with Judge Robert Brown, but he is hesitant. He expressed concerns that the Andraus family might perceive the order as a personal attack. The Cacellas themselves have requested the judge to avoid conflict with the Andraus. They fear that this order could trigger a war between the families. Today, a newspaper published a cartoon depicting the City Hall building and the Council Hall firing cannonballs at each other," Oswald sighed and continued, "It would be a relief if we discovered that this Tortoise acted alone, entering the Sinclair house and killing the family for some unrelated, trivial reason, without any involvement from the Mayor or his son."

Mark reflected on how accurate the old angry man on television was about the city police and reacted, "Didn't you hear the man? Tortoise often carries out contracted services. So, if he was the one who broke into the Sinclair's house, there must have been a client."

Oswald rubbed his hands over his face.

"Yes, but this client could have been a minor criminal. Maybe Humbert Sinclair owed money to some moneylender. They say he was financially ruined, don't they?"

"The only way to uncover what happened inside the Sinclair's house is to question this fighter," Andrew asserted.

Oswald leaned forward, resting on a table, and declared, "Both of you must go to Aurora Street and locate this Tortoise before any journalist gets him talking nonsense that could spark a war in our city."

Mark and Andrew rose from their seats and left the room, with Mark carrying the coffee thermos.

Outside the meeting room, Mark handed his car keys to his partner.

"Andrew, do me a favor: drive today. I didn't get any sleep last night. Given my current state, I might end up crashing the car into a tree or even hitting someone."

"Are you sure you want to go to Aurora Street right now?" Andrew asked. "You look more tired than usual. Wouldn't it be better for you to go home?"

"Maybe what I need most right now is to keep my mind busy, Andrew. I have to stop thinking on certain matters."

"What happened to you? Can you tell me?"

"Let's just say I had some bad nightmares. Worse than usual," Mark replied. "But don't worry about it. Let's head to Aurora Street now. Where's the homeless?"

Chapter 16

Mark and Andrew stood at the beginning of Aurora Street, accompanied by Benjamin, who seemed proud to be with the two detectives. The place resembled more of a sprawling open-air garbage dump than a street. The stench of urine was so strong that Andrew covered his nose. All the residences in the area had been abandoned by their original owners long ago and were now inhabited by homeless people. Almost all the windows were broken, and most entrances had no doors.

In the middle of the street, around five hundred people huddled together. Some sat on the cracked asphalt or curb, sharing a smoking pipe, while others simply slept on what remained of the pavement, wrapped in dirty, threadbare blankets. Mark thought to himself that if someone were to examine each person lying on the ground individually, they would likely discover that some of them were dead.

"What is this place?" Andrew inquired.

"This is where people who have made mistakes in life gather," Benjamin responded. "People like me."

Mark shared his own perspective on the place, "This place is essentially the outcome of shady deals that sustain the fancy lifestyles of powerful individuals in our city. It is the product of corruption and greed within the Andraus and Cacella families. It is fueled by this new drug, which emerged about ten years ago."

The older detective nudged Benjamin on the arm.

"Can you see Tortoise's girlfriend?"

"She lives in a large house in the middle of the street. We can take a detour if you're afraid of crossing through here."

"No, let's walk down the street," Mark replied. "What do you think, Andrew?"

Andrew examined very carefully the crowd and then turned to Benjamin.

"Do you think we might be attacked?"

Before the informant could respond, Mark interjected, "Don't worry, Andrew. These homeless are accustomed to wealthy tourists coming here to witness this tragic spectacle. They will likely ask us for money. Take some change out of your pocket and give it to the first ones who approach. Once others see that you have already given some money, they will leave you alone."

The three men walked down the street, and as foreseen, some homeless people approached the group. However, a few coins were sufficient to safely navigate through the crowd.

During their walk, Mark noticed a particular man among a group of homeless individuals who was dressed in clean and expensive clothes.

"In a few weeks, this elegant man will be like the ragged ones surrounding him," predicted the older detective. He turned to Benjamin. "So, what did you do before ending up in this place?"

"I used to be a professor. I taught philosophy at the state university."

"How long have you been coming to this street?"

"I've been coming here for two years. I came here the first time after being fired when they privatized the university. I was very upset and made the mistake of trying this new drug. Once you smoke one hit, you can't stop anymore."

"You look good for someone who has been in this situation for so long," Mark observed.

"I try to take care of myself and also support other dependents like me, but it's not easy. I take medications that help me cope with the addiction, but on certain days, I wake up feeling worse, and even the medicine doesn't work."

The three arrived at a large house. The construction didn't preserve much more than the brick walls and a ruined roof. Inside the property, they saw a man lying on top of a woman. His pants were down. As the man saw the detectives, he quickly got up, pulled up his pants, and walked out of the house, passing by the three men indifferently.

Benjamin pointed to the woman, who remained lying down. "That's Tortoise's girlfriend," he said. "That's Marisa."

The woman got up slowly, adjusted her garments, and staggered toward the exit of the house.

Andrew observed Marisa and didn't like her aspect. Her hair was dirty and disheveled, covering almost all of her face. She had a ghostly appearance.

The young man turned to his partner. "Do you think we'll get anything useful here?"

"We'll have to try," Mark answered.

Benjamin approached the woman and greeted her, "Hi, Marisa. It's me, Benjamin. How are you?"

Marisa looked at the three men, trying to figure out what was going on. She ran a hand through her hair, pulling it away from her face.

"The same old crap!" she answered.

"Do you know anything about Tortoise? Did you see him today?"

"That bastard? He's missing! And he took all my money with him."

Mark approached Marisa.

"Good morning, ma'am. May I talk to you?"

"Who's the fancy one?" asked the woman, analyzing the detective. "Is he a cop?"

"I'm a friend of Tortoise. I'm here to help him," Mark replied.

"I'm not an idiot. You came to arrest him. I know it!"

"No, ma'am. I just came to talk to him. Tortoise can help us solve a very important case. You may be rewarded if you lead us to him."

The woman laughed.

"I don't buy that."

Mark insisted, "Do you know who Tortoise has been talking to in the last few days? Did you see him with any different friend? Someone who caught your attention?"

"Just the same old rascals," answered Marisa.

"Didn't he mention any particular job? Has he been more nervous than usual these past few days?"

"Tortoise is always nervous. He wakes up nervous, sleeps nervous, shits nervous...."

Andrew approached his partner and spoke close to his ear, "I don't think she will be of much help."

Mark looked around, searching for any ideas. Meanwhile, Marisa remained still by the gate of the house. The detective noticed that her face bore cut marks, and her yellow teeth revealed slight bleeding when she smiled.

In that moment, a large white van entered the street, capturing Mark's attention. The vehicle parked among the crowd of homeless people, and three women dressed in light clothes emerged from its interior, accompanied by four stern-looking men in black suits. The women set up folding tables next to the van and placed large plastic boxes on them.

"Excuse me, I have to go," Marisa spoke, passing by Mark, who instinctively took a step back, avoiding contact with her.

"What's that?" Andrew asked Benjamin, pointing toward the van.

"They are the nuns from the church. They bring food for the people here," Benjamin explained.

Mark carefully scrutinized the nuns near the van and recognized one of them.

"That elderly one is Sister Anne. She works at the Archbishop's residence."

"Are you sure about this?" questioned Andrew.

"Absolutely. She's the one I met yesterday."

Benjamin listened to Mark's comment and said, "Oh, the Archbishop takes great care of us. That man is a blessing. Sometimes he comes here personally to assist with serving food. On Sundays, he sometimes reads stories to us. It brings a sense of calm to everyone. The Archbishop's presence is quite impressive. His tall figure and bright white clothes make him appear as a messenger from heaven."

"Have you ever seen the Archbishop talking to Tortoise?" Mark inquired.

"I don't know. The Archbishop interacts with many people here, but I can't recall seeing him speaking to Tortoise."

"Could you try to bring your friend Marisa here again?" the older detective asked.

"I'll give it a shot," Benjamin responded, walking toward the group of homeless individuals gathered around the van.

Mark noticed that Andrew was very tense. That run-down environment seemed to be scaring him.

"Don't worry, Andrew. You're more likely to encounter trouble on the street in front of your house than in this place."

"I come from a small town, Mark. I'm not used to this kind of atmosphere."

"This is the big city, buddy! This place is where we sweep the dirt under the rug."

The older detective glanced toward the van and noticed that Sister Anne was staring directly at him.

"She saw me!" Mark alerted his partner.

At the same time, Sister Anne turned away.

"Who saw you?" Andrew asked.

"The Archbishop's assistant, Sister Anne. She noticed that I am here."

"Do you think this will have any consequences?"

"I don't know," Mark replied.

"But, after all, how was the conversation with the Archbishop? You weren't very convincing when you said you didn't discuss religious matters with him. You looked nervous when Oswald questioned you about that," said Andrew.

Mark, slightly embarrassed, answered, "The truth is I blurted out an unkind remark, and he insisted that we discuss religion. The next thing I knew, I was stuck in an endless argument."

"I would have loved to witness this."

"It wasn't the clash you're thinking. I must admit that the Archbishop is a wise man. He has a ready answer for everything without using his authority as an argument. I admit he impressed me."

"So, the Archbishop managed to convince you that God exists?"

Mark thought about the question for a while and answered, "Well, right now, if you asked me about the existence of God, I wouldn't know what to say. But I must tell you, it wasn't exactly the Archbishop who put doubts in my mind."

Andrew smiled at Mark, and the two detectives remained silent, just watching the people around the van. Two elderly men, alongside the nuns, stood out among the homeless individuals. They were arguing over the bag of food that one of them carried. The other complained that the meal belonged to him and ended up grabbing the bag. With four hands pulling, the bag tore apart, and the food fell, spreading across the ground. The two men grabbed each other and also fell, rolling in the street.

"I will ask you a question, Andrew," said Mark as he watched the scene. "What would you say if you discovered that God has no power over what happens in this world and that He lives just like one of us, wandering among the people, not even aware of his position as the Creator of this universe, living as vulnerable and lost as anyone else?"

"That doesn't make any sense, Mark."

"I know it doesn't seem to make sense, Andrew," Mark answered. "But look at this place! What does it tell you?"

"Did the Archbishop tell you this story?"

"No, someone else did."

"Yeah, it doesn't sound like something an Archbishop would say. That's not what the Holy Book preaches."

"The Holy Book may have only told what people were ready to hear, Andrew."

Mark's partner got silent for a while. The two detectives noticed that many other homeless people were now also fighting next to the nuns. The women hurried into the van as the men in suits yelled for the homeless to move away from the vehicle. They pulled out wooden batons and started beating everyone around them.

"People already feel helpless enough, even though they believe in the existence of a God protecting them," Andrew observed. "Imagine if they think they are alone."

Benjamin reappeared, grabbing Marisa by the arm. He pushed the woman closer to the detectives.

"These men have one more question to ask, Marisa. It is important."

The woman held the bag of food she had received from the nuns. She kept it close to her chest, as if her life depended on it. She looked eager to leave and have her meal.

"Just a quick question, ma'am," Mark began. "Have you ever seen the Archbishop talking to Tortoise?"

"Who is he? I don't know any archbishop," replied Marisa.

"He's the tall man who visits here on Sundays," explained Benjamin. "He often reads stories to us after giving us food. Do you remember him?"

Marisa nodded her head for a few seconds and said, "Yes, I remember him. He's quite handsome!"

"Have you ever seen the Archbishop talking to your boyfriend?" Mark insisted.

Marisa looked around and replied, "I don't know. Maybe." But she fell silent, turned, and ran into the interior of the large house.

"I'll go bring her back!" Benjamin volunteered.

"It's not necessary," said Mark. "Her answer now wouldn't be reliable. She's not sure and is eager to eat. She might make up something only to make us leave her alone. Benjamin, please stay close to her and pay attention if she mentions any information about Tortoise or the Archbishop."

"Will I be rewarded?" Benjamin asked.

"If we find Tortoise and he's proven guilty of the murders, then maybe," answered Mark.

The two detectives turned and walked away from Benjamin, making their way back to the car. Behind them, the Archbishop's men struggled to clear the path for the van, which was heading towards the exit from Aurora Street. They mercilessly beat any homeless individuals who came in their way.

Chapter 17

Eleven o'clock at night, Mark was seated at his dining table. Once again, he examined the photos he had found the previous night. They were spread out before him, occupying the entire table.

In the solitude of his apartment, the detective's thoughts were consumed by his recent dreams and the peculiar conversation he had with the stranger the previous night. He opened a cupboard beside him, took out a sheet of paper and a pen, and placed them on the table. In large letters, he wrote: "LINTSA."

Mark wasn't entirely sure that he spelled the name correctly. "It's an unusual name," he pondered. "Maybe the 't' should be silent or replaced with a 'd,' but it looks better and more familiar this way." He gazed at the letters, feeling as though he was looking at Lintsa's very own image. He took off his reading glasses to wipe the sweat from his forehead.

The detective decided to take some rest. He took a quick shower, changed into sleepwear, turned off the bedroom light, and climbed into bed. Pulling the blanket up to his neck, he closed his eyes. Rapidly, the image of Lintsa returned to his mind. He envisioned himself walking alongside her through a vast green field. Together, they walked up a hill and beheld a city beyond the mountains. Lintsa said something, but her words eluded Mark's understanding. He yearned to touch the woman, to feel the texture and the scent of her skin.

For over thirty minutes, Mark tossed and turned in bed, trying to fall asleep. But his mind refused to relax, and his eyelids remained closed for mere seconds. The blanket covering his body felt like it was burning his skin. After two hours of frustration, he threw the blanket off the bed.

The situation became clear—his desire for Lintsa was consuming him. And perhaps, at that moment, there was only one individual he could talk to about the woman.

The detective decided to rise from bed. He changed his clothes once more, picked up his car keys, and left the apartment.

It was past midnight when Mark arrived at the Café and Grill restaurant. Upon entering, he got not surprised to find the striking figure of Delasher, with an erect posture and his ivory suit, seated at the same table where they had met the previous night.
As soon as the waitress noticed the detective entering the establishment, she approached him.
"Good evening, sir! Will you be dining tonight, or will you run away once again?"
Mark looked at the young woman, feeling embarrassed.
"Apologies for yesterday, miss. Please prepare the same meal, and you can charge for both orders. I insist on paying."
Mark walked slowly and hesitantly to the corner of the restaurant. Delasher gazed at him serenely. The detective took a seat in front of the stranger, who offered a friendly smile.
"I knew you would return, Mark Randall," said Delasher. "Do you have a strong motivation for being here, haven't you?"
Mark locked eyes with Delasher and said, "Let me make sure I understand this correctly: Yesterday, you claimed that I, Mark Randall, am actually an individual from another universe called Zalthor Acri. This Zalthor guy is one million years old. He is an immortal being who had an accident and was buried for thousands of years. As a result, he created a world inside his mind to live in. This world is where we currently exist. "
"Exactly, Mark Randall. I'm glad that you've grasped this," Delasher responded. "It's a sign of intelligence on your part."
The detective attempted to disregard any hint of mockery in Delasher's last statement and continued, "What

about Lintsa? Tell me, who is Lintsa? Why can't I stop thinking about her? It feels like I've known her forever. I've never felt anything like this in my life. In my youth, I thought I had fallen in love with some girls from high school, but nothing I've experienced before compares to what I'm feeling now."

"This was expected. Lintsa is an extraordinary woman. She is an immortal Hubbian like you. Lintsa was your wife for hundreds of thousands of Hubbian years. Be cautious, Mark Randall! Perhaps your mind in this world is not prepared for the emotions you will have to deal in the coming days."

"How long does a Hubbian year last exactly?" Mark inquired.

"Ah, my apologies. Fortunately, today I managed to gather some information about your world, and I can confirm that a Hubbian year is almost equivalent to a year in your world. That makes complete sense, after all, when constructing a new world, it's most convenient to adopt units of measurement that you were already familiar with."

Mark's eyes widened.

"So, Lintsa has been with me for an incredibly long time. Am I still married to her?"

"Yes. Since your disappearance ten thousand years ago, Lintsa has been searching for your whereabouts."

Mark pondered for a moment, performing mental calculations, and raised his arms.

"Are you telling me that when writing was still to be invented in my world, there was already a woman seeking me out ten thousand years before I was born?"

"Exactly."

"I don't understand. You're saying I've been missing for ten thousand years, but my universe is demonstrably billions of years old. Are you suggesting that it's not true, and the Holy Book was right. How could my world have been created only a few thousand years ago?"

"Currently, the pace of time in your birth world and in the world you created is synchronized, Mark Randall. However, when you got stranded ten thousand years ago, you couldn't wait for the Universe you created to mature before living in it. Prior to beginning your first life here, the relative pace of time between the two dimensions was quite different. In ancient times, when the world you created was inhabited by primitive beings, millions of years passed within mere days in your birth world. As your consciousness guided the evolution of the world you were constructing, you witnessed the beginning and end of numerous ages in just a few weeks. However, when the first individuals began forming the early civilizations, you decided it was time to join these people and live as if you were one of them. At that point, the pace of time in this world became synchronized with that of Zalthor's reality."

Delasher scrutinized Mark's expression and concluded that his listener hadn't understood a single word he had uttered.

"To simplify, let's say you sped up the tape until it reached the part that interested you," the stranger summarized.

Seeming to have grasped Delasher's last statement, Mark raised his eyebrows. He took a deep breath and reminded the stranger of the purpose that brought him there.

"In my last dream, I heard that I will be set free from that recovery tank in two days. Will I find Lintsa?"

"Yes, it's a highly anticipated meeting. That's why Lintsa sent the rescue ship to the B-23 moon. However, this meeting won't take place in two days; it's scheduled for tomorrow night."

Mark's eyes widened once again. The news intensified his anxiety. He thought for a moment, then recalled another individual he had heard about.

"And what about Doctor Axlow? Who is he?"

"Doctor Axlow is your oldest friend. You met him during your childhood when you both were still mortal Hubbians. Doctor Axlow developed the Conversion Process, which granted Hubbians immortality. You played a significant role in this achievement and were the first Hubbian to undergo the conversion into immortality. Doctor Axlow was the second."

"Let me make sure I understand. Are you saying that Zalthor Acri wasn't always immortal? He... better said, I became immortal after this so-called Conversion Process. Is that what you're saying?"

"Yes, you and Doctor Axlow worked together on the planet Hubberia's underground for decades and constructed the Converter Chamber—a large facility capable of converting Hubbians into immortal beings. The process was carried out near the planet's core, the only location where pressure and temperature conditions allowed for the necessary energy to be directed to the reactor of the Converter."

"And Lintsa? How did I meet her?"

"You met Lintsa after she had been abducted by a Tautorian spaceship, a few millennia after the conclusion of the great Zort Interstellar Wars."

"Zort Interstellar Wars?"

"It was a great war where the Hubbians defeated the biggest power in the galaxy. The Zorts were exterminated, but the Tautorian, a former ally of theirs, remained and continued committing terrorist acts even thousands of years after the wars. After they kidnapped Lintsa, you infiltrated their vessel and rescued her. Subsequently, the two of you fell in love and got married."

"Do we have children?"

"No, converted Hubbians are unable to conceive children. It was the only side effect of the Conversion Process."

At that moment, the waitress approached the table and interrupted the conversation. She brought Mark's order.

To the girl's surprise, as soon as she finished serving the meal on the table, the detective grabbed her arm.

"Miss, wait a moment. I need a favor from you."

"Yes, sir. How may I help you?" responded the girl, a little scared.

"Listen! I know it might sound like a bizarre question. It's just that I've been under a lot of stress lately, and I'm afraid I might be imagining things. So, I need to ask you this: Is there another man sitting at this table in front of me? A tall man wearing light-colored clothes."

Mark released the girl's arm, and she took a step back.

"Well, sir. Unless I'm going insane too, I see a tall, elegant man sitting in the chair across from you. He is looking at you right now."

Delasher smiled at the waitress.

"Tell him my name, miss. Let him hear that my name is Delasher."

Startled by the strange conversation, the waitress complied with the request.

"His name is Delasher, sir. I don't know why he asked me to tell you that."

"Alright, miss. You can go. Thank you very much," said Mark.

"If you need anything, just call me," said the waitress, walking away from the table.

Mark gazed at the meal and chuckled.

"You have no idea how crazy all of this sounds, do you? Immortal beings, interstellar wars. Me, the Creator of the Universe! It's an overwhelming amount of fantastical information for my mind to digest in such a short time. It feels like I've been transported into a science fiction movie, one of those produced forty years ago, and not a particularly good one."

"Yes, I understand, Mark Randall. In my research about your world, I learned that your people have difficulty accepting what is different or contradicts their beliefs. You seem to be a skeptical one. You don't believe in anything that cannot be scientifically proven. I am well aware that accepting my words is not easy for you."

Mark pushed his plate of food toward Delasher.

"Would you like to eat this? I ordered this meal solely to avoid any interruptions while we talk."

"I'm merely a projection, Mark Randall. I can interact with your world but cannot experience any sensations here. It's a shame because this meal looks delicious."

"Yes, the food here is not bad," said Mark, picking up a small portion of fries. "But you're right about me, my friend. I don't believe anything you are saying. In fact, I'm fully aware that I'm going completely insane and nothing more. However, I choose to embrace this madness. I want to see how far it will lead me."

"Because you believe it will lead you to Lintsa, don't you? So, it doesn't matter whether it's true or not."

"At this stage of my life, if I have a chance to find a woman like Lintsa, I don't care if she isn't real. I just want to be with her. When I think of her, everything else fades away. Right now, I'm paying attention to you solely because of Lintsa. I should be saddened by the fact that I can already envision a future in a mental institution or something similar."

"The waitress confirmed my presence here. Doesn't that mean anything to you?"

"Who can prove to me that the waitress isn't also a hallucination? Perhaps I'm still in my bed right now, or even sitting on the floor of an abandoned building, talking to the walls. You must accept one thing, my friend: the odds of me being crazy are statistically much higher than those of your story being true."

The expression on Delasher's face hardened in a way Mark hadn't seen before.

" You completely missed the point of what is unfolding, don't you, Mark Randall? In less than twenty-four hours, you will arrive at Doctor Axlow's Planet, awake as Zalthor Acri, and meet Lintsa."

Mark wiped his mouth with a napkin and smiled.

"This Zalthor seems to be quite an impressive guy, doesn't he? He was the first immortal Hubbian, married one of the most stunning women in the galaxy, and possesses an entire planet, doesn't he? He must also be remarkably good-looking. When I emerge from the recovery tank, I believe I will be pleased with my reflection in the mirror, won't I? Are you carrying a picture of Zalthor and one of Lintsa with you? I'd love to see them right now."

"Listen, Mark Randall! What do you think will happen to this world when you awaken? What happens to a dream when someone wakes up?"

"If the story you recounted is true, yourself just stated that this world I inhabit is nothing more than a dream. So why should I concern myself with that? Tomorrow, I'll awaken next to the most beautiful woman I've ever seen, and I'll leave behind this wretched existence I endure here. Where's the bad news?"

"This world we're in now, Mark Randall, is not a dream. It's a real world. The individuals here are genuine beings residing in this dimension. Your mind built this reality to provide you with a place to live, and these people were inadvertently born here, coexisting by your side, even if you don't like it. You bear responsibility for everyone who lives in this universe, and the destiny of all of them hinges on the decision you will make in the coming days."

Mark stretched his neck and rose from his seat.

"Listen closely, Delasher: You shouldn't even be here. You infiltrated my mind covertly. You're a stowaway, and now you have the audacity to dictate what I should do? Who are you to tell me what to do with my world?" Mark turned toward the counter and called out to the waitress. "Ma'am, please bring me the bill."

The detective placed some banknotes on the table and walked briskly toward the exit door.

"I'm here to prevent you from making a huge mistake, Marcos Randall, one that you'll regret for all eternity," Delasher warned.

But the detective didn't listen to the stranger. He left the restaurant, heading towards his car.

Chapter 18

The following day, Mark awakened around seven o'clock in the morning. He opened his eyes but didn't immediately rise from the bed. For almost half an hour, he gazed at the ceiling of his bedroom. He didn't have any dreams last night, yet his mind felt foggy, as if he'd been lost in a jumble of thoughts for hours. Unclear flashes of Lintsa persistently emerged in his mind, as if his brain struggled to remember the woman. He envisioned fragments of places and moments: a smile, a fleeting glance, an embrace. However, he couldn't piece together a complete memory.

Every time Mark started thinking about Lintsa, his heart raced uncontrollably, compelling him to consciously shift his thoughts away from the woman. He feared that thinking too much about her could even lead to a heart attack. The solution was to divert his mind to other topics of interest. This prompted him to refocus on the Sinclair family.

"Where could Carol Sinclair be now?"

Thus far, there were no leads concerning the kidnapped girl's whereabouts. Mark was eager to question the Mayor's son, Paul Andraus, as soon as possible. However, he lacked sufficient grounds to implicate the young man in the crime. Without direct evidence, obtaining a court order from a judge seemed unlikely.

Mark got out of bed and headed toward the only individual who might provide new information about the case.

At nine o'clock in the morning, Mark arrived once again at the Archbishop's official residence. He pressed the doorbell and, while waiting for an answer, examined the surroundings. A thought crossed his mind, wondering where Delasher might be at that moment. The stranger could be nearby, observing his every move.

The doorbell emitted a quick crackling sound, and Sister Anne's voice came through the speaker.

"May I help you, Detective? Do you have an appointment?"

Mark looked up and noticed the surveillance camera pointed at him.

"Good morning, Sister. This is an unplanned visit," he responded. "I apologize for the inconvenience, but please inform the Archbishop that I need to speak with him urgently. If Euzebius doesn't want to see me, I'll leave without further insistence."

The doorbell speaker fell silent for a moment.

Once more, Mark waited. He gazed at the street in front of the residence. It was a sunny day, albeit a bit windy. The street was almost deserted. Only a couple of elderly women were walking near the house, dressed in vibrant and expensive sportswear, indicating they were residents of the wealthy neighborhood taking their morning stroll. Mark greeted the women, but they didn't respond. Instead, they looked away, as if purposefully avoiding him.

This behavior infuriated the detective, yet he wasn't surprised. The wealthiest individuals in the city always behaved in this manner, maintaining distance from anyone who didn't appear to be in the same privileged class. Mark's old and worn-out car parked by the curb, as well as the quality and condition of his clothing, immediately revealed his social status.

Even without receiving a response to the doorbell, the small gate in front of Mark opened, and Sister Anne appeared.

"The Archbishop is having breakfast. He has invited you to join him."

Mark followed Sister Anne until they found the Archbishop in a large dining room, seated at the head of a long table made of sturdy, noble wood, surrounded by twenty imposing chairs.

Euzebius noticed the detective's presence and greeted.

"Good morning, Detective Mark Randall! Please, have a seat and help yourself. It's not every day that breakfast is served at this hour, but I had to work late yesterday."

Mark pulled a chair next to Euzebius and sat down.

"I hope I'm not interrupting you, Your Grace. My apologies for this unexpected visit."

"I was certain you would come to me, Detective. Sister Anne informed me that she saw you on Aurora Street yesterday. However, I didn't expect your visit to be so early. Nevertheless, I understand the urgency and importance of the matter."

The detective curiously observed the meal laid out on the table. Around the Archbishop, a splendid array of pâtés, freshly baked loaves of bread, and exquisitely presented fruits caught his attention, rare delicacies that one could only find in the most expensive grocery stores in the city. Mark recognized a small glass jar containing expensive fresh fish roe.

"Sister Anne, please bring a plate and serve our visitor with some bread," the Archbishop requested.

Sister Anne handed Mark an elegant porcelain plate. Before serving himself, the detective marveled at the variety of food in front of him. He cut a loaf of bread in half and spread some roe.

The Archbishop resumed the conversation.

"Sister Anne informed me that she saw you on Aurora Street yesterday. If you're looking for a suspect, you'll find many there.

"We received a lead about a man who might be involved in the Sinclair family case, Your Grace. He has been missing since the day of the crime. He is a well-known figure in the community, a former martial arts fighter."

"You're referring to Joseph Assis, also known as Tortoise, correct? Poor man. He had a promising life ahead of him. Married with three children, he was on the rise in his fighting career but made mistakes and paid a heavy price for them. I feel great sadness for him, especially for his children. Innocent children who now depend on charity for their survival."

"So, you know him well, I assume?"

"I am an instrument of the Lord, Detective. My mission is to be close to the souls most in need of help. I meet individuals whom you may fear being a hundred yards away from, even as a police officer. But I trust that the Lord will always protect me from harm, so I fear nothing."

Mark regarded the Archbishop with a serious expression.

"Tell me, Your Grace, what do you know about Tortoise, or rather, Joseph Assis?"

"He is now a lost soul, like all those who live on Aurora Street."

The detective took a bite of the bread slice with roe, savoring it. Impressed, he exclaimed, "Wow, this is delicious!" He examined the small jar and inquired, "How much does one of these cost?"

"I must confess, Detective, that I no longer keep track of the prices of things. Since I became archbishop, my assistants handle everything for me. Honestly, I wouldn't even know how to cook rice without them."

"It seems they take good care of you, Your Grace," remarked Mark, wiping his mouth with a white napkin. "But let's talk about Tortoise. You've had conversations with him, haven't you?"

"I have spoken with everyone on that street, Detective."

"Has he ever mentioned anything about his activities?"

"Do you think he confessed his crimes to me?"

"Well, as a priest, people often confess their sins to you, don't they?"

"The Sacramental Seal is inviolable, Detective. If Joseph were to confess his crimes, I couldn't disclose them. However, the truth is, it's been over two decades since I last heard a confession. My time as a priest was relatively short."

"I understand, Your Grace. I came here because I regard you as a person of great wisdom. I thought that if anyone had noticed something about Tortoise, it would be you."

Maintaining his calm demeanor, the Archbishop replied, "Or perhaps you want to know if Tortoise has any connection to my nephew, Paul? You suspect him, don't you?"

"Well, so far, I haven't found any evidence linking your nephew to Tortoise. But since you brought it up, tell me: has Paul Andraus ever been on that street?

The Archbishop sensed the detective's intentions.

"My nephew wouldn't go near that street even in an armored vehicle, Detective, I assure you."

Mark fell silent, contemplating, while Euzebius continued his meal undisturbed.

After a moment, the detective let out a long sigh and broke the silence.

"I apologize for my next question, Your Grace, but what kind of world is this where we are sitting here comfortably, talking and enjoying the finest food, while a young girl is out there, possibly suffering unbearable pain after her entire family has been brutally murdered? As a philosopher and theologian, what are your thoughts on this?"

"The Lord has different plans for each of his children, Detective. We cannot comprehend his plan for young Carol Sinclair."

Mark looked around and noticed that Sister Anne had left the room. He was now alone with the Archbishop. Taking a deep breath, he looked up, searching for inspiration to continue the conversation.

"I need to share a personal story with you, Your Grace. Would you allow me to tell it now?" asked Mark.

"Feel free to speak, Detective."

Taking another deep breath, Mark begun: "I had a daughter, a beautiful girl named Luana. Sadly, she passed away in a domestic accident when she was only three years old. After this tragedy, my marriage started to crumble. I blamed my wife for being distracted and letting our daughter fall into the pool while I was at work, and she blamed me for not installing a safety cover or a fence that could have prevented the accident. From that day on, our communication at home became almost nonexistent. It seemed like we both wanted the same thing: to be far apart from each other. I expected Deborah to be the first to give up and file for divorce. Every day, when I returned home, I hoped her car wouldn't be in the garage anymore. I envisioned myself opening the wardrobe doors and finding them empty. The mere thought brought me some relief. Each day, as I saw her slumped on the living room sofa, her spirit seemingly gone, I hoped for her to rise and announce that she was leaving me. But all she ever managed to do was utter a cold 'good night,' barely acknowledging my presence. She then focused on the television, acting as if I didn't exist."

Mark swallowed, feeling the trapped saliva in his throat, and continued, "I truly did my best to make her file for divorce. I treated her coldly, ignoring her occasional attempts to engage in conversation, even if it was about trivial subjects. All I wanted was for her to leave that house. We lived in that agonizing state for seven painfully long years."

The Archbishop silently observed Mark. Noticing that Sister Anne was about to enter the room, he discreetly signaled her to walk back, and the detective remained unaware of this minor incident.

With his head lowered, Mark continued speaking, "Then, on a day like any other, I arrived home exhausted and in a bad mood, as usual. I carelessly placed my gun on the table and went to take a shower, hoping to find some respite under the warm water. As I was in the shower, trying to relax, I was suddenly startled by the sound of a gunshot."

Euzebius remained silent, his gaze fixed on Mark. The detective's expression shifted from profound sadness to restrained anger.

"Since that moment, I've always asked myself: what did I truly desire when I left that gun on the table? I drove my wife to her demise! I killed her slowly every day with my resentment, my indifference. And I left that gun there, right in front of the sofa where she sat day after day, hoping for her to pick it up. But..." Mark's voice cracks. "I'm certain of one thing: that bullet that pierced her head... It wasn't meant for her. She should have fired a different target. She should have fired..."

The detective reached for a glass of water and took a long sip.

"Now, I make this question to you, Your Grace: what was God's plan in my own ordeal?"

Mark gazed at the Archbishop, certain that he had asked a difficult question to answer. However, the priest smiled, displaying his customary tranquility.

"The Lord devises his plans to safeguard us, Detective. He always shows us the right path, but we fail to hear him when our hearts are flooded with anger, vanity, ambition, or even laziness. Unfortunately, we often choose to follow these toxic emotions and end up disregarding the gentle voice of the Lord. When we do this, unfortunate events occur. It is not God who falters in his plans, but rather men who falter when they refuse to heed the Lord's guidance."

Mark reflected upon everything Delasher had recounted to him the previous night. Now, Euzebius' words appeared to be a great irony. The detective couldn't resist and left out a light chuckle. He noticed a sudden change in the Archbishop's expression and feared that he had offended the clergyman.

"I apologized, Your Grace. I'm not laughing at your words, but at my own ignorance. I wish I possessed a fraction of your faith."

"You can't change what has already happened, Detective, but you can change the way you perceive the past.

If you view these events as moments of trial rather than just tragedies, they can make you a better person."

Mark smiled, amazed by the gracious manner in which Euzebius treated him. The clergyman had every reason to scorn the skeptical police officer who was attempting to implicate his nephew and challenging his faith, yet he treated him as an old friend.

The detective took a bite of the remaining bread in his hands and exclaimed, "This is one of the tastiest things I have ever tasted!"

Sister Anne entered the dining room. However, this time, the Archbishop did not halt her.

"I apologize for the interruption, Your Grace, but there is an important call waiting in the office," the sister informed.

"Very well. I was just about to leave," said Mark, rising from his seat. He extended his hand to the Archbishop. "It was a pleasure speaking with you once again, Euzebius. Thank you for your words and for lending me an ear."

"The pleasure was entirely mine, Detective. I hope you locate the poor Joseph. He is now a tormented soul, much like everyone else on Aurora Street. However, if he has indeed committed such a heinous crime, he must face the consequences." The Archbishop glanced at the nun. "Accompany the detective to the door, Sister."

Mark smiled and departed, escorted by Sister Anne.

Chapter 19

In the late afternoon, Mark was seated at his desk in the Civil Police Station. Beside him, Andrew absentmindedly worked at his workstation. The floor was almost deserted, with only a few individuals in the distance, and most of the lights were already switched off.

Using a small headphone, Mark perused local news on his computer while simultaneously listening to music, attempting to calm his mind. Suddenly, his attention was drawn to a figure standing directly in front of his desk. He raised his gaze and saw Oswald wearing an expression of displeasure. Mark removed his headphone and greeted the chief, while Andrew observed the scene.

"Answer me, Mark Randall: is it true that you visited the Archbishop's residence this morning without prior permission?" Oswald questioned sternly.

Mark pushed his chair away from the desk but remained seated. He replied, "Listen, boss, I know I should have made arrangements in advance. However, I was on the way to this station when I decided to pay a visit to the Archbishop. I didn't insist on entering his residence. He informed me that he was already expecting my arrival. One of the nuns on Aurora Street recognized me yesterday, and the Archbishop had already deduced that we would return with further questions."

"Yes, and you questioned the Archbishop about whether he or his nephew had any connection to Tortoise, didn't you? I expected more tact from someone of your experience," Oswald asserted.

"Or perhaps someone with my experience would be capable of posing the question without arousing rage, don't you think?" Mark responded. He leaned back, clasped his hands behind his head, and stretched, displaying little concern for the chief's words. "Listen, boss! I am well aware of the complex situation we find ourselves in. I understand your desire to solve this case without antagonizing influential figures in town. However, with such individuals linked to the Sinclair family, uncovering the truth will be challenging without stirring up a hornet's nest."

"Pay close attention, Mark Randall. I am not asking you to neglect your duties. That would be a grave failure on my part." Oswald made eye contact with Andrew as he uttered this final sentence, then turned back to Mark. "I know you very well, and the Archbishop holds immense power in this city. From what I've heard, he has exercised remarkable patience with you. But let me warn you: if you dare set foot in the Archbishop's residence once more, you'll spend the rest of your career confined to the basement of this police station."

Mark pondered for a moment; his previous apathy had now faded away.

Before the detective could respond, Oswald interjected, "Answer me one more thing: is it true that you fainted and fell into the Archbishop's swimming pool?"

At that instant, Andrew glanced at his colleague. The young detective's eyes widened in surprise.

"I had a sudden loss of senses, boss," Mark replied. "I think it was just dehydration, but nothing too serious. And I didn't fall into the pool. I fell beside it and didn't even get wet."

"May I know why you didn't inform us about it?"

"It's quite simple: because it's irrelevant to the case," the detective replied harshly. "Listen, boss: my conversation with the Archbishop was amicable. We even discussed personal topics, including religion. Contrary to what you may be thinking, it was a calm and rational discussion. Euzebius is a wise man, not an arrogant fool like his brother-in-law. I'm confident our meetings won't jeopardize your position at the police department."

"I truly hope so, Mark Randall. If I receive the slightest complaint from the Archbishop, you'll be out of this station."

Oswald turned and headed toward the department's exit; his heavy footsteps audible as he descended the stairs leading to the ground floor.

Once Mark was certain that the boss wouldn't return, he started closing the programs on his computer.

Andrew pulled his chair closer to his partner's.

"Did you faint while talking to the Archbishop at the official residence?"

"No, I was alone when it happened," Mark replied, turning off the computer. "I apologize for not informing you, Andrew, but, as I told the boss, it's irrelevant to the case."

"It matters to me, Mark. I don't want my partner passing out when I need him. Is it related to the noise you heard on Wednesday?"

"Don't worry about it. It won't happen again. I'm heading home now. It's Friday. I'll take the weekend to rest. By Monday, I'll be rejuvenated. Trust me."

Mark stood up and put on a light coat.

"Are you planning to rest the entire weekend!? I thought you were concerned about the girl," Andrew questioned.

"At this moment, there's nothing we can do for Carol Sinclair unless you want to hit the streets and question prostitutes and drug dealers. But I wouldn't recommend it. It usually ends badly. What we need now is rest."

"Do you think Carol Sinclair's kidnappers will stop harming her just because it's the weekend?"

"Don't lose sleep over this, Andrew. There's nothing we can do now. I'm going home. Maybe once I'm rested, I can think about the case with a fresh perspective."

Mark realized he was so focused on what was expected tonight that he was being insensitive regarding Carol Sinclair. However, if Delasher was telling the truth, Zalthor's body would finally be removed from the recovery tank in a few hours, and Mark would reunite with Lintsa. He couldn't wait to get home and sleep now.

"Have a good weekend, Andrew. Call me if anything new arises," Mark said, turning toward the department's exit.

Chapter 20

Back in his apartment, seated at the center of the living room couch, Mark was dressed in cotton shorts and a sleeveless T-shirt. In front of him, the television played a documentary about wild birds.

According to Delasher's words, Zalthor would awaken any moment. Earlier, the detective had even contemplated searching for the stranger again but opted to leave work and head straight home. The last conversation with Delasher had not ended well, and Mark also reflected on the incident at the Archbishop's residence when he passed out beside the pool. If a similar episode were to occur while driving, for instance, it could have resulted in major problems. However, experiencing a sudden loss of consciousness on the couch at home wouldn't cause any harm.

In the documentary displayed on the television screen, Mark observed a fabulous sight of a large starling murmuration soaring above a beautiful lake, complemented by a stunning sunset backdrop. Thousands of birds came together in a densely packed formation, appearing as a singular immense giant being amidst the clouds when viewed from afar. The documentary's narrator suggested that such phenomena might have inspired legends of giant dragons traversing the sky.

Yet before Mark could fully contemplate the scene, he heard a female voice.

"Wake up, Mr. Zalthor!"

It wasn't Lintsa's or Fhastina's voice; it belonged to another female, possibly another assistant of Lintsa.

Calmly, Mark reclined on the couch, finding a position that would allow him to remain still for an extended duration without discomfort. He patiently awaited the fading of his senses. In just a few moments, he would awaken in another world, where he was no longer Mark Randall, the detective, but rather Zalthor Acri, the owner of Planet Dolmen, an immortal Hubbian. Most importantly, he would finally reunite with Lintsa.

Everything gradually faded into darkness.

Part 2

Zalthor

Chapter 21

Mark opened his eyes and found himself lying in a spacious, comfortable bed. Soft, light sheets covered his body, and the air was filled with a pleasant floral fragrance. As he stretched, it felt as though he was awakening from a long and deep sleep. He looked upward, gazing at a ceiling adorned with softly colored frescoes depicting unfamiliar themes that escaped his understanding.

In his peripheral vision, Mark caught sight of someone standing beside the bed. He turned his head and saw a humanoid figure possessing a female body but with a feline head featuring upturned ears, wide yellow eyes, and vertical pupils. The female was dressed in light-colored attire and wore a gentle expression.

Startled, Mark sat up and leaned against the headboard of the bed.

"Greetings, Mr. Zalthor. I'm pleased to see you awake. How are you feeling?" asked the female. She was the same voice Mark heard moments ago while still in his apartment's living room.

Mark glanced at his bare chest, now revealed as he sat up, and realized that he was naked beneath the sheets.

"I feel fine, thank you for asking," he replied. "But who are you, and where am I?"

"I am Kiasra. My purpose here is to welcome you, Mr. Zalthor. You are on Doctor Axlow's Planet. The Doctor awaits you on the terrace of the social hall," Kiasra explained.

For a brief moment, Mark tried to comprehend Kiasra's words. Then he recalled what Delasher had told him. Doctor Axlow was his former friend. However, his main interest resurfaced.

"And where can I find Lintsa?"

"Doctor Axlow will answer all your inquiries, Mr. Zalthor. My current duty is solely to guide you to him." Kiasra pointed toward a set of mirrors positioned before the bed and continued, "Those mirrors also are doors. Behind them, you will find clothing options. Select the attire that suits your preference. I will be waiting outside this room. When you are ready, proceed through this pathway," Kiasra instructed, gesturing toward a hallway behind her.

The female withdrew, gently closing the door at the end of the hallway. Still seated on the bed, Mark examined the physical form he now inhabited. He studied Zalthor's hands. They were large and strong, yet smooth and flawless. His gaze shifted to his arms, admiring their length and strength, reminiscent of a professional fighter. Continuing to explore his new body, a smile formed on his face as he observed his newly acquired six-pack abs.

Standing up, Mark was taken aback by the height of his new body, nearly stumbling over his own legs. When he looked down at the floor, it felt as though he was towering over a chair. Still adjusting to his unfamiliar physique, he made his way toward the mirrors and, for the first time, gazed upon Zalthor's face.

When the detective caught sight of his reflection in the mirrors, the first thought that sprung to his mind was, "So this is the visage of a god." Zalthor's face bore resemblances to Mark's countenance in his world, yet the features were far more harmonious and symmetrical, exhibiting smooth skin and elegantly straight lines interrupted by sharp curves. It was an imposing appearance indeed.

"So, God created mankind in his own image!" Mark uttered, captivated by the reflection of Zalthor's face.

He noticed a small button at the corner of the mirror. Pressing the device, the mirror bent until it completely retracted, revealing a spacious closet behind. The detective examined the assortment of clothes and opted for a set comprising a blue shirt and matching pants. The futuristic and minimalist aesthetics of the attire pleased him, yet there was only a lone pair of shoes: two sturdy gray boots. Lastly, he selected a refined black jacket.

Fully attired, Mark proceeded to the hallway. Outside the room, he found Kiasra patiently awaiting his presence. Observing the female, he noticed the fur around her head standing on end as a sign of excitement, but he chose not to comment on it. Additionally, he observed the significant height difference between his new body and Kiasra's.

"If you are ready, Mr. Zalthor, I shall lead you to Doctor Axlow," the female suggested.

Mark nodded in agreement, and Kiasra took the lead. He followed the female in unsteady steps, struggling to adjust to Zalthor's towering stature.

"I can arrange for a wheelchair if you so desire, Mr. Zalthor," Kiasra offered.

"No, thank you. I am perfectly fine. I am simply acquainting myself with these long legs," the detective responded.

Mark and Kiasra traversed several corridors until they reached a vast open courtyard bustling with numerous individuals. Although humanoid in shape, their faces exhibited an array of animal-like features reminiscent of creatures Mark recognized from his world—bears, horses, even insects. Some possessed fur or feathers adorning their skin, while others boasted snouts or beaks.

The attention directed toward the detective by the onlookers did not escape his notice. Unsure of how to proceed, Mark waved his hand to greet the spectators, who remained motionless, their expressions filled with curiosity and wonder.

"Don't be afraid of their wide eyes and opened mouths," Kiasra reassured him. "This was anticipated."

"Why are they gazing at me in such a manner?" Mark inquired. "Is there a particular reason?"

"You, Mr. Zalthor, are a legend. To them, meeting you in person is akin to encountering a notorious celebrity."

"Is it because I was the first immortal Hubbian? Delasher informed me of this."

"Delasher?" Kiasra exclaimed, turning toward Mark.

Remembering that Delasher entered his mind without Lintsa's knowledge, Mark realized that he had not thought before he spoke, and mentioning the stranger's name could lead to trouble.

"Do you know him?" the detective asked.

"I've heard about this Delasher. Doctor Axlow knows him better."

Kiasra and Mark reached a huge gate that opened automatically as they approached. Two other humanoid beings with coyote-like heads emerged from behind the structure. One of them addressed Kiasra, saying, "Proceed ahead. Doctor Axlow awaits Mr. Zalthor."

Kiasra and Mark walked toward a towering structure. They entered the building and stepped into a glass booth. It closed and began to ascend. The detective realized that they were inside a panoramic elevator.

Through the glass walls of the elevator, Mark saw a huge city appearing in front of him. He could see hundreds of skyscrapers, and a bluish sun was emerging from a reddish sky on the horizon.

"So, this is Doctor Axlow's Planet? What is it called?"

"This planet where we are is named Axlow 3, but most of the Galaxy's population calls it Doctor Axlow's Planet because it is where the glorious Doctor lives and has his headquarters: these facilities where we are."

"Is Doctor Axlow the owner of this planet? And two others as well?"

"Actually, the Doctor's system has a total of seven inhabited and economically active planets. Axlow 3 is the biggest and most developed of them all. The others are mainly occupied by farms and mineral extraction fields. Most of the resources extracted from these places end up here, where they are manufactured and then exported to other systems. Doctor Axlow's Planet has large cities, renowned universities, and is one of the most vibrant cultural centers in the Galaxy."

The detective looked up and spotted various dots moving in the planet's sky. He watched more carefully and realized that they were hundreds of aircraft of different sizes and shapes.

The elevator stopped, and the door opened. Mark and Kiasra continued their walk, passing through a long corridor, and then crossing a large hall with an immense table in the center. Finally, they entered a portal leading to a terrace the size of a sports court. Immediately, Mark's attention was drawn to a small table and two chairs installed near the terrace railing. Seated in one of the chairs was a being similar to Zalthor, although smaller and with less sophisticated features. Mark presumed that he was Doctor Axlow.

The Doctor noticed the arrival of the pair and rose.

"Ten thousand years, old friend! Ten thousand years!" The Doctor exclaimed. He approached with quick steps and gave Mark a strong hug. The detective remained motionless, unsure of how to react.

Doctor Axlow continued, "We thought we had lost you forever, Zalthor. We feared that you might have been trapped inside a neutron star or swallowed by a black hole, making it impossible to rescue you. Luckily, you merely collided with a small moon."

Mark gazed at the Doctor.

"You're Doctor Axlow, right? I've heard we were close friends, but I must admit I don't remember you, Doctor. I hope you're not offended."

Doctor Axlow took a step back and carefully observed Mark.

"Don't worry, my old friend. Your amnesia was anticipated. Come, sit beside me. We have much to discuss. I understand that your current situation must be quite bewildering. Awakening from a ten-thousand-year slumber is not an everyday occurrence, is it?"

Kiasra stepped forward, interrupting their conversation.

"Doctor, I need to inform you: there has been an invasion."

Doctor Axlow's expression turned grave.

"An invasion?"

"Yes. Mr. Zalthor mentioned the name Delasher."

The Doctor clenched his fist tightly.

"Accursed deniers! They always manage to infiltrate stealthily. How did they gain access to Zalthor's mind? Nobody knew he was on that rescue ship. There must have been a traitor among the crew! Do you have any information about this, Zalthor?" Doctor Axlow inquired, turning to Mark.

The detective was aware that Delasher entered his mind with Fhastina's assistance. He concluded that Delasher and the Doctor were on opposing sides. However, he was unsure whom to trust and believed that revealing Fhastina's involvement might not be the wisest move at the moment.

"No, Doctor. I didn't witness anything. A strange man suddenly appeared in my world and foretold what would happen. He mentioned that I would awaken on this planet."

"Ah, yes! They must have infiltrated while you were sedated," Doctor Axlow concluded. He pondered for a moment, glanced at Kiasra, and said, "But let's not dwell on it for now. This is a time for celebration. Kiasra, please instruct the assistants to bring us some drinks and a delicious meal for our guest."

The Doctor gestured toward the two chairs and the table next to the railing.

"Zalthor, let's have a seat over there. We have much to discuss, and I'm sure you're bursting with questions."

As Kiasra stepped back, Mark and the Doctor took their seats. The detective marveled at the city view from the terrace. The bluish sun had risen higher, and he could even catch a glimpse of what appeared to be a sea in the distance.

"Who is this Delasher?" Mark inquired as he settled in. "Do you know him?"

Doctor Axlow sighed.

"He's a member of a group known as the 'immortality deniers.' While you were trapped and isolated beneath the surface of moon B-23, your mind created a kind of dream, a simulacrum to keep your brain active until you were rescued. Delasher's associates claim that you now possess what they refer to as a 'parallel universe' within your mind. They believe that while you were buried on that moon, you built a real world inside your own consciousness."

"Yes, Delasher mentioned it to me."

"These individuals are quite presumptuous to venture into your mind at such an early stage. I've met many Hubbians in your situation. I understand that at this moment, you hold the opposite perspective. You believe this world where you are now with me is just a dream, while the simulacrum created by your mind is perceived as the real world. Am I correct?"

"Exactly, Doctor. I must admit that I am seriously considering the possibility that you and everything around me are nothing more than a product of my imagination. And while we speak, I am merely asleep in my apartment."

"This is an expected response, Zalthor. The only vivid memories in your mind presently stem from the dream you generated while trapped beneath the surface of moon B-23. You undoubtedly believe that you were born and raised as a mortal being in a primitive world. When someone has lived their entire existence within a dream, they will question the reality presented to them. Only time will help you grasp that your true life resides here, in this world where you exist as Zalthor Acri, an immortal and invincible Hubbian, not as the limited mortal creature you still perceive yourself to be."

"Doctor, allow me to ask you one thing: if I am truly awake now, what happened to the world I originated from? Did it vanish when I awakened?"

"Firstly, please stop referring to me as Doctor. We are childhood friends, Zalthor. We have known each other for a million years. I understand that you do not remember me at this moment, but soon you will comprehend how deep our friendship is."

"I apologized, Doctor, or rather, Axlow, but you didn't answer my question. Will I never see the world I came from again?"

"A dream that endured for thousands of years does not abruptly finish upon waking. It continues to reside within your mind for a while longer. This dream took root and dominated a significant portion of your brain, occupying spaces that were once filled with genuine memories. In a few hours, you will return to slumber, not for another ten thousand years, of course, but according to the regular sleep intervals of a Hubbian. When that occurs, you will once again encounter your imaginary world. However, there is no need to worry. In a few days, this dream will disintegrate, and all that will remain for you will be the real world—the world you see now—the world of Zalthor Acri."

"What do you mean by 'disintegrating'?" Mark asked, displaying some concern. "How will this occur?"

The Doctor changed the subject of the conversation.

"Tell me, Zalthor, did you like the life you lived before you awoke?"

Mark reflected for a few seconds.

"Well, I have to admit I wasn't living in paradise."

Doctor Axlow laughed.

"I must tell you something, old friend. It doesn't matter what life you think you had before waking up. I'm sure you won't be eager to return when you discover the wonders that await you here, in the real world."

Discreetly, two humanoid beings arrived, carrying some domed serving trays. They placed the objects on the small table.

When the lids were removed, some colorful and delicately decorated snacks appeared.

"Taste these appetizers, Zalthor. They were made by one of the top cooks in my system, using the finest ingredients we could find in the Galaxy."

Mark looked at the table in amazement but soon remembered Lintsa.

"Tell me something, Axlow. When you talk about what awaits me in this world, are you referring to a Hubbian woman named Lintsa? I saw her when I was submerged in the recovery tank. I noticed the way she was looking at me. Delasher told me about her. He said Lintsa was the wife of... I mean, my wife. If that's true, shouldn't she be here right now?"

The Doctor raised his arms as if he had remembered something very important.

"Yes, Lintsa! I can imagine how eager you must be to meet her. You are a very lucky Hubbian, Zalthor. Lintsa is one of the most desired women in the Galaxy, not only for her physical beauty but also for her intelligence and personality. She is truly amazing. Don't worry about Lintsa. She would love to be here now, but things have gotten a little complicated. The news of your rescue reached the planet Dolmen, and it has caused significant turbulence there."

"What's happening on planet Dolmen? I heard I own this planet. So why am I not there now?"

"Before you went missing, you were the owner of the planet, and you never had any problems exercising your authority. In your absence, the command naturally passed to Lintsa. However, two thousand years after your accident, another Hubbian—an unpleasant individual named Pheldon—organized a movement that threatened the peace of the planet, and Lintsa concluded that engaging in a war against him could bring great suffering to the population of Dolmen. She chose to avert a direct confrontation with Pheldon and relinquished her power while you were away."

As Doctor Axlow spoke, Mark decided to taste one of the snacks before him. He served himself a pink rice ball covered with blue mushrooms. As soon as he put one in his mouth, he jumped so high that he almost fell off his chair.

"Wow! This food is wonderful!" Mark realized he interrupted Doctor Axlow. "Sorry about that, Doctor, I mean, Axlow. I didn't mean to cut you off."

"It's all right! I can imagine the pleasure you must be feeling right now. After all, you certainly haven't experienced anything like this for thousands of years, not in the imaginary world that you created in your mind."

Mark wiped his mouth with a handkerchief.

"Yes, today I was in the house of someone very wealthy in my world, and I had the opportunity to try some of the finest foods available there, but I must admit that nothing in my world compares to the taste of these appetizers."

"You have just tasted some exceptional rice, Zalthor. It is harvested from the swamps of a very remote planet. An algae that only grows there gives it this unique flavor. As for these mushrooms, they only grow on the towering walls of the mountains on one of the most dangerous moons of the galaxy. They are a precious delicacy."

"But please, continue, Doctor. What is happening in planet Dolmen now?"

"Ever since news of your rescue reached Dolmen, the planet has been on the brink of civil war. Pheldon has issued special commands to capture you. Knowing this, we sent a second rescue shuttle to Dolmen, creating the impression that you were on board. Meanwhile, Lintsa traveled to the Flershar system. She is assembling a group of converted Hubbians to help you reconquer the planet."

"Reconquer the planet? How will that happen?" Zalthor asked. "Are you talking about war? Will Lintsa fight against Pheldon?"

"No, Zalthor. You will fight against Pheldon."

At that moment, Mark noticed a humanoid being descending from the sky. The being possessed wings and the head of an owl. The figure landed gracefully on the terrace near the table, catching Dr. Axlow's attention.

"Hello, Volsler. I was expecting you."

The humanoid folded its wings, hiding them inside his costume.

"Your ship is ready, Doctor. You can depart whenever you're ready," Volsler announced.

Doctor Axlow turned to Mark.

"It's time to go, Zalthor."

"Where are we going?" asked Mark.

"Let's take a quick tour around Axlow 3," the Doctor said, rising from his seat. He pointed to Mark's chest. "I'll take you for a brief training session with this body. We'll see if the being inside this head is ready to go to Dolmen, fight Pheldon, and reclaim the planet."

Before getting up, Mark grabbed some snacks from the table, filling his hands. As he enjoyed the assortment he had gathered, he followed the doctor to the same courtyard he had walked through with Kiasra a few minutes ago.

Now, at the very center of the courtyard, there was a gleaming aircraft about the size of a railroad car. Mark and Doctor Axlow boarded the ship, which took off promptly.

Chapter 22

Through a large, slanted window at the back of the ship, Mark beheld the city of Doctor Axlow, who noticed the detective's admiring gaze.

"It's a spectacular city, isn't it, Zalthor? I am very proud of what I have built here. When I acquired this planetary system, it was one of the most inhospitable in this region of the Galaxy, with a star emitting radiation levels that were harmful to almost all living beings unless they were converted immortal Hubbians. But after tens of thousands of years, we managed to build dense magnetic fields for all planets in the Axlow system, allowing us to welcome inhabitants of other races," explained the Doctor. "Currently, Axlow 3 has nearly a billion residents and stands as one of the most prosperous planets in this area of the galaxy."

Mark noticed that the ship had departed from the city's airspace and was now soaring over the sea.

"I don't understand. How could someone own a planet with nearly a billion people? Kiasra mentioned that you possessed six more. How is this possible?"

"Many prosperous Hubbians own planets nowadays. It's an achievable goal when you are an immortal being. Firstly, you have a very large amount of time to accumulate substantial wealth, which enables you to finance such endeavors. Secondly, managing a planet provides an excellent way to occupy oneself when eternity lies ahead. You and Lintsa are the owners of the planet Dolmen. Though it may not be as densely populated as Axlow 3, it boasts breathtaking beauty, with boundless forests adorned in trees of every imaginable color. Dolmen is also home to some of the most majestic and exquisite waterfalls in the Galaxy, particularly the renowned Lyria Falls. You and Lintsa are privileged to possess such a planet."

"So, we are going to reclaim this planet Dolmen from this guy named Pheldon, right? I'm still not entirely clear about what I am supposed to do."

"Don't concern yourself with that for now, Zalthor. Lintsa is taking care of the matter. You have much to learn or rather relearn. Unfortunately, your mind is still confined to the limitations of the mortal being you believe yourself to be. This entity owns only a fraction of the intelligence and abilities that Zalthor possessed before his disappearance. However, your skills should resurface swiftly."

"I understand," Mark responded. He observed that they were now traversing a vast plain. The detective pondered for a moment and inquired, "But... what about our birth world, the planet Hubberia? How is it today?"

Doctor Axlow's expression shifted from excitement to melancholy. He took two steps back and settled into a chair, his gaze fixated downwards as he spoke.

"Unfortunately, our beloved planet Hubberia was destroyed long ago. When we discovered the secret of immortality, our people were still enslaved by the Zorts, the dominant race that governed the Galaxy a million years ago. We managed to conceal our discovery for a time, but it was inevitable that the Zorts would uncover the Converter Chamber. Once they learned of our discovery, they realized that an army of immortal converted Hubbians would eventually pose a threat to their dominion. In their desperation, the Zorts made the fateful decision to destroy our planet. Unfortunately, at the time of the attack, only two million Hubbians living on the planet had undergone the process of immortality conversion. The other two billion perished in the planet's explosion."

Mark remained silent, showing respect for the Doctor's sorrow.

Continuing, Doctor Axlow said, "Actually, the Zorts were justified in their fears. The surviving converted Hubbians managed to regroup and, within a few thousand years, overthrow the Zort Empire. You were the leader of this uprising, Zalthor. You became a legendary figure in the Galaxy, known as Zalthor, the Liberator of the Galaxy."

"Me, leading an insurrection to free an entire galaxy? I can't envision myself doing such a thing. I've never been good at leadership in my life."

"You must understand, Zalthor, the insignificant being that you now think you are may does not know how to lead, but you possess great leadership qualities. Thanks to you, thousands of planetary systems can now live in peace."

"They started to descend. Mark looked through the window's glass and noticed a large and white surface beneath the ship."

"This place looks like a massive salt flat. We have similar locations in my world," Mark observed.

"Everything in your imaginary world is inspired by what you saw and experienced here, Zalthor, in the real world. Dreams are built based on memories, nothing more than that," explained the Doctor.

The ship landed, and Mark and Doctor Axlow disembarked. Mark walked over the salt surface while the Doctor followed him on a small flying platform.

The Doctor pointed to Mark's boots and explained, "These boots you're wearing are designed to withstand intense friction and extreme temperatures. They are also incredibly comfortable, allowing you to move at high speeds for extended periods without feeling any discomfort."

Mark raised his hand to protect his eyes from the light reflected by the bright surface surrounding them. As he gazed at the horizon, he saw only the distant peaks of mountains.

"How fast do you think I can run?" Mark asked the Doctor. "In my world, places like this are used to test vehicles powered by jet engines, not for people on foot."

"Why don't you start running and find out for yourself?" suggested the Doctor.

Mark hesitated to begin running, seeming insecure.

"What's the problem?" asked the Doctor.

"I haven't run for a long time. In my world, I have a knee injury. Walking is painful, and running is impossible for me."

"Just start walking briskly and gradually increase your speed, Zalthor. Your mind may not be accustomed to running at high speeds, but your new body is capable of anything."

Following the Doctor's advice, Mark began walking and gradually sped up. He gained confidence that his knee wouldn't cause any pain, and his strides became longer, resembling the characteristic movements of running.

The platform carrying Doctor Axlow accelerated, and Axlow kept pace with Mark, staying beside him.

"How fast am I?" asked the detective.

"You can run much faster if you wish," responded the Doctor.

Mark started running at a high speed, feeling like he must be as fast as a car on a highway in his world. He gazed at the horizon and was consumed by curiosity to discover the limits of his new body.

"Be careful, Zalthor. You are going too fast now," warned the Doctor.

"You didn't tell me the maximum speed I can reach."

Mark accelerated further. The wind hit his face forcefully. In his old body, the detective wouldn't be able to keep his eyes open at this speed, but Zalthor's eyes seemed to be shielded. He should also be having difficulty breathing with the strong wind blowing directly in his face, but Zalthor's body didn't seem to require any breathing.

The detective began to hear a ringing sound in his ears, which intensified as he sped up. He noticed that Doctor Axlow was falling behind. His flying platform was no longer able to keep up with Mark. However, the detective believed he was still far from reaching the limits of Zalthor's body and accelerated even more.

Suddenly, Mark heard a loud crash and felt as though he had collided with an invisible wall. This strange sensation caused him to lose focus and stumble. He fell and rolled across the salty surface for nearly half a mile before finally coming to a stop.

Mark was aware that if he were still in his old body, Doctor Axlow would be picking up the pieces of him scattered across the salt. But in Zalthor's body, despite the pain, he managed to rise as if nothing happened.

Doctor Axlow, on his platform, caught up with Mark.

"I warned you not to go so fast."

Axlow noticed that Mark was laughing.

"That was amazing!" exclaimed the detective. "I think I surpassed the speed of sound. I feel like I have superpowers in this body. I'm like a superhero! Can I fly too?"

"No, but you can leap to great heights. Why don't you give it a try?"

Mark pointed to the platform beneath Doctor Axlow's feet.

"You're a converted Hubbian too, Axlow. So why are you using this device to accompany me? What makes me different from you?"

Doctor Axlow wore a sad expression as he responded, "The Conversion Process didn't yield the same results for everyone, Zalthor. Variations in each individual's genetic code influenced the speed, endurance, strength, and even mental abilities of each Hubbian in diverse ways. You were the first to undergo the conversion. When you entered the Converter Chamber, you were on the brink of death, afflicted by tumors throughout your body. Yet, when you emerged from the Converter, you had the appearance you possess now—much taller and stronger than when you were a young mortal Hubbian. I was the second to enter the Converter Chamber. While the process made me considerably younger and stronger, I must admit that my transformation paled in comparison to what you achieved."

"Are there Hubbians who became faster and stronger than me?"

"Yes, there are Hubbians more powerful than you, although they are rare. Lintsa, for instance, is perhaps nearly as strong and skilled as you are."

Suddenly, Mark and Doctor Axlow heard a loud noise from above. They glanced up and saw a luminous aircraft descending beside them.

"It's her!" announced the Doctor. "Lintsa has arrived."

As the ship touched the ground, a side door opened, and Zalthor's wife emerged. The Hubbian woman rushed toward Mark, who watched her in awe.

"Brace yourself for impact," warned Doctor Axlow.

Lintsa leaped into Mark's arms with such velocity that the two rolled for several dozen yards. Finally coming to a halt, the couple lay on the ground, covered in salt. Lintsa rested atop Mark with her face pressed against his.

"I can't believe you're finally here, my love!"

Lintsa embraced Mark tightly and gave the detective a passionate kiss. Mark felt his hands trembling, and he sensed Lintsa must be aware of his anxiety, yet she didn't seem to mind. The detective did not resist and reciprocated the embrace, holding Lintsa tightly and returning her kiss.

After a few minutes, Mark took held Lintsa's shoulders and gazed into her Hubbian eyes.

"Listen: I understand that you're Lintsa, and we were married for thousands of years, but you know that I don't remember you, don't you?"

"I do, Zalthor," Lintsa replied. "But I couldn't resist. Ten thousand years is far too long to be apart from you."

Mark smiled.

"Even though I don't recall our past, my heart raced the moment I first saw you when I was still in that recovery tank. It must be because we shared so much time together, right? And you are the most beautiful woman I've ever laid eyes upon. I needed to say that."

Lintsa responded by resuming her passionate kisses with Mark.

After finishing their kiss, Lintsa and Mark stood up. The woman turned to Doctor Axlow and said, "We need to depart immediately, Axlow. Our support in the Flershar system is already on its way to Dolmen. If we hurry, we can join them before they reach the planet."

"Who is leading the Flershar group?" asked Axlow.

"Ranson is personally in charge. He has gathered another twenty converted Hubbians and at least a hundred Flershians," replied Lintsa. "With this addition, we now have almost thirty Hubbians and two hundred warriors from other races." She smiled and gazed at Mark. "I knew that an old friend like Ranson would not abandon you at a critical moment like this."

Doctor Axlow stepped off his platform and walked toward Lintsa.

"Do you really think you can regain control of Dolmen with a group of this size? Pheldon has at least twenty thousand soldiers on his side."

"Pheldon has fewer converted Hubbians. And, more importantly, if we manage to reach the Capital gates, the population will support us," explained Lintsa.

"What if the population takes different sides?" asked the Doctor. "There could be a violent conflict in Dolmen, and that's not what you want."

"That won't happen, Axlow. Not with Zalthor by our side," Lintsa asserted. She turned to Mark. "Are you ready to travel to Dolmen, my love? Are you prepared to reclaim our planet?"

Doctor Axlow gave Lintsa a disapproving look.

"Don't you think it's too early for that? Zalthor just woke up a few hours ago. He has no memory of our world. It's not even Zalthor's consciousness inside this body right now, but some primitive mind that believes it's living in a dream created by Zalthor. Do you honestly believe this limited intelligence can defeat Pheldon?"

Mark's patience with Doctor Axlow's derogatory comments began to wane, but he tried hard not to show his displeasure.

"It will take us nearly twelve hours to reach Dolmen. Zalthor will have time to prepare and be briefed on the mission details," Lintsa replied. She turned to Mark, speaking tenderly, "Actually, it's up to you, my dear. How do you feel? If you're afraid of going to Dolmen, we'll understand."

Mark contemplated for a few moments and looked at Doctor Axlow with determination.

"Listen, Axlow: I believe the people of Dolmen don't expect a great leader like Zalthor to hide here like a frightened puppy while they fight to liberate the planet. I know I'm not the same Zalthor I used to be, not yet. But that won't stop me from going out there and retaking Dolmen from this Pheldon."

As soon as Mark finished his statement, he noticed the admiring gaze from Lintsa. He firmly grasped the woman's hand and declared, "We must depart now!"

Chapter 23

A few hours later, Mark was alone inside a private room on Lintsa's spaceship. Standing before a large glass window, he gazed upon the myriads of stars and nebulae in the galaxy they were traversing.

The detective contemplated the events that unfolded on Planet Axlow and how confident he felt when he asserted that he should go to Dolmen. It was unusual for him to demonstrate such self-assurance when making decisions. Within Zalthor's body, he felt not only the strength of the Hubbian physical form but also the power of his mind.

Lintsa entered the room and grabbed Mark's arm. He smiled warmly at her and pointed to the window.

"I gazed upon the night sky of my world on several occasions. Sometimes, I drove to remote areas far from the glare of city lights. In those places, I could catch a glimpse of the galactic center, albeit faint and devoid of color. It took some time for my eyes to adapt to the darkness and perceive the faint details in the brightest regions of the sky. But now, here I am, beholding these vibrant and luminous nebulae. They seem exactly like the images I used to see in magazine photographs in my world. But those images were the result of long exposure shots, impossible for normal eyes."

"Many Hubbians gained remarkable light sensitivity following the Conversion Process, my dear. You always spoke of seeing the full spectrum of colors in the Galaxy. Unfortunately, this was not a skill I acquired. My vision did not improve significantly after the conversion."

Mark looked thoughtfully at his hands.

"I must admit that I didn't fully comprehend this so-called Conversion Process, which bestowed immortality and immense power upon the Hubbians. They say I was involved in the project, became immortal, fought against the Zorts, and ended up becoming the Liberator of the Galaxy. Now, I find myself aboard this spaceship, on a mission to reclaim a planet that is rightfully mine." He gazed at Lintsa. "I am also married to the most beautiful woman I have ever laid my eyes upon. What other incredible feats have I achieved in this world? How many diseases have I managed to cure?" he asked, a faint smile gracing his face.

"You haven't discovered a cure for any diseases, my dear, but you have saved more lives than you can imagine," replied Lintsa.

Releasing Mark's arm, Lintsa approached the window and lightly touched the glass with her fingertips.

"I am aware that, after such a prolonged slumber, converted Hubbians create worlds within their minds," she said. "You were living a different life before your rescue, weren't you? What was it like?"

Mark's expression turned somber at this question. He stood beside Lintsa and responded, "It wasn't a remarkable life, Lintsa. In my world, I was an ordinary person. I was neither famous nor wealthy. I lacked any exceptional skills or talents. I lived a rather mundane existence."

"But what did you do? What was your occupation?"

"I sought out missing individuals, but more often than not, I failed to save them. They perished before I could locate them."

"Before disappearing in B-23, you also failed to save everyone you tried, Zalthor. We are never able to save everyone we want to."

"Doctor Axlow claims that this world inside my mind is just a dream and that it will disappear now that I have awakened. But there are people in your world who think differently, right? They believe that there is a genuine universe within my mind, and that other people are living here," Mark said, touching his forehead. "What are your thoughts on this topic?"

Lintsa approached her partner.

"Extensive research has been conducted on cases of converted Hubbians who were imprisoned for prolonged periods and the worlds they built in their minds. Technically, there is no way to prove whether this world in your mind is a real parallel universe or merely a projection generated by your brain, akin to a dream. Ultimately, it depends on what you choose to believe."

"So, if I believe that this world inside my mind is a genuine universe, in order for it to endure, I will have to bury myself in a hole again and remain there for eternity?"

Lintsa didn't answer. She simply gazed at Mark.

"Does that mean I would have to relinquish being Zalthor Acri? And give up being with you as well?" the detective inquired.

The sound of a loud siren reverberated throughout the ship. Mark looked out the window and spotted another spacecraft approaching. One of Lintsa's assistants entered the room.

"Mrs. Lintsa, Ranson has arrived."

Lintsa glanced at Mark, displaying a smile that exuded immense joy upon receiving the news.

Mark and Lintsa proceeded to the ship's main hall, where a small, stout man stood at the forefront of twenty individuals. Mark recognized them all as Hubbians, as their humanoid bodies and resemblances to Zalthor and Lintsa were evident.

"The Hubbian in front is Ranson," Lintsa informed. "He is a dear friend of yours from the time of your conversion."

As soon as Ranson caught sight of Mark, he exclaimed, "Finally! The great Zalthor Acri, the Liberator of the Galaxy, has been resurrected! It's a pleasure to meet you again, my dear friend."

Mark scrutinized Ranson for a few seconds, contemplating what to say.

"The pleasure is all mine, Mr. Ranson. I don't know how to express my gratitude for your assistance."

"No need for thanks, Zalthor. To me, you are much more than a friend, and it will be a delight to oust Pheldon from the planet Dolmen. I never liked him anyway."

Ranson placed his hands on Mark's shoulders and examined him closely. The detective noticed that the Hubbian's eyes were watery.

"Seeing you in such good shape, Zalthor, renews my hope of finding another Hubbian who went missing a long time ago."

Mark didn't know how to respond and simply smiled.

Ranson turned to Lintsa.

"I heard that Zalthor woke up only a few hours ago. Are you sure he is ready to confront Pheldon?"

Lintsa stepped forward.

"We need to launch the attack now, Ranson. We cannot afford to give Pheldon time to organize his resistance. He is attempting to gather all his troops in the Capital. If he succeeds, it will be quite challenging to capture the city without resorting to violence."

Lintsa's assistant interrupted the conversation.

"Mrs. Lintsa, we are approaching the Dolmen system. The jumps will commence in a few minutes."

Lintsa surveyed her surroundings and spoke aloud, "Comrades, let's prepare ourselves. Zalthor, come with me."

"What are the jumps?" Mark asked, but Lintsa didn't hear him.

Chapter 24

In a spacious cargo compartment at the rear of the spaceship, Lintsa, Zalthor, Ranson, and twenty other Hubbians equipped themselves for the imminent battle. Lintsa prepared herself next to a large table while Mark examined the available equipment. What particularly caught his attention was a blue-bladed sword with a hilt crafted from dark metal.

"Is that sword for me?" Mark inquired, looking at Lintsa.

"Yes, dear. This sword is known as The Hubbian Heart. It was presented to you by the Hubbian War Council shortly after its establishment during the Zort Wars. I thought you might like to use it in today's battle," Lintsa responded.

"How effective would a sword be? I see the other Hubbians arming themselves with laser guns and explosive weapons. Can this sword penetrate the skin of an immortal converted Hubbian?" Mark questioned.

"Nothing can penetrate the skin of a converted Hubbian, dear, but laser shots don't harm a Hubbian either. This sword is capable of unleashing powerful energy waves, but activating this feature requires great skill, and you were one of the few able to do this."

Mark took hold of the sword and raised it, executing a few moves, slicing through the air with the blade.

Lintsa grabbed a small device from the table, resembling the compass that Delasher carried when he entered the Café and Grill restaurant.

"Take this," Lintsa said, handing the device to Mark.

Simultaneously, a strap materialized, automatically securing the detective's arm and attaching the gadget to his body.

"What does it do?" Mark inquired.

"This will enable us to locate you on the planet Dolmen in case you land too far away from us."

"That won't work," Ranson interjected, approaching Lintsa and Mark. "Pheldon must have deployed signal blockers throughout the Capital."

Mark turned to Ranson and inquired, "Will we be able to identify these blockers? It might be possible to destroy them."

"Yes. The blockers are quite apparent, with a vivid and luminous sign that says 'signal blockers'," Ranson responded.

"I know you're teasing me, Ranson," Mark reacted.

Ranson chuckled lightly.

"Many soldiers of Pheldon carry them, these soldiers have slightly larger backpacks compared to others. However, they will be scattered all over the place. Take this." Ranson handed Mark a pistol with a short barrel. "The trusty old flare gun. It may be ancient technology, but it's immune to any blockers. This particular flare is blue. It's the only one of this color. When you fire it, we'll know your location."

At the end of the cargo compartment, a large ramp started descending, revealing the opening of Lintsa's spaceship. Mark could now observe outer space without the need for glass windows. The surface of a planet, adorned with shades of blue and green, became visible beneath the ramp.

"We are in orbit around Dolmen," announced Ranson. "It's time to jump."

"But we are still in orbit above the planet," Mark observed. "Are we going to jump from here?"

Lintsa nodded.

The detective scanned the surroundings and noticed that everyone on the ship was completing their preparations. He turned back to Lintsa.

"Listen, Lintsa, shouldn't we descend to the surface using a spacecraft?"

"Ships are easily detectable, dear. The stealthiest way to reach Dolmen is by jumping from here. Do you see the jetpack on the table?" Lintsa pointed toward a rigid, gold backpack. "It will control your descent and reduce the speed as you approach the ground."

Mark observed that all the Hubbians were equipping themselves with similar gear. He picked up the one Lintsa indicated and did the same.

Lintsa also strapped on a jetpack and walked to the edge of the ramp, with Mark following. The surface of Dolmen dominated the view. They were flying over a lush green region with numerous lakes and rivers.

"Are you ready to jump?" Lintsa asked, looking at Mark.

"Do we have to jump right now?"

"If we jump now, we will land in a secure location near the Capital, amidst the dense Forest of Loot," explained Lintsa, pointing to a prominent green area on the planet's surface. "Pheldon's troops won't easily find us there. Do you have everything you need?"

"But... what exactly do I need?"

Lintsa pointed to the Heart of Hubbian in Mark's right hand.

"You already have everything you need."

Lintsa turned forward, crouched, and jumped off the ramp.

"Wait!" Mark shouted. But it was too late. The Hubbian woman had already departed.

Mark gazed downwards. He knew the ship was moving at a very high speed. If he took too long to jump, he would be far away from Lintsa's landing site.

Other Hubbians also began jumping. Ranson handed the sheath of the Heart of Hubbian to the detective.

"Take care of that sword," advised Ranson. "It's very precious."

Ranson jumped.

Mark sheathed the sword and fastened it around his waist. He then adjusted the jetpack on his back, tightening the chest straps. With his arms extended backwards, he searched for a button or lever to activate the equipment.

"But how do I operate this thing?"

Mark surveyed the platform. The place was now empty, with all the Hubbians having already jumped. Time was running out. He looked down and saw the surface of the planet Dolmen, two hundred miles below.

"Damn it!" Mark exclaimed.

He closed his eyes, clenched his fists, and jumped.

Chapter 25

Lying at the bottom of a small crater, Mark felt his entire body aching. He made an effort and moved his arms, lifting his back and sitting up. He looked around and comprehended what happened. The crater was formed by the impact of his body against the ground. He had jumped out of Lintsa's spaceship and, not knowing how to operate the jetpack on his back, fell until reaching the surface of the planet Dolmen. He must have been unconscious for a few minutes after hitting the ground.

His clothes were dirty, but they survived the entry into the planet's atmosphere. The garments were still hot, especially the boots.

Mark got up, left the crater, and searched for the Heart of Hubbian, finding the sword a few yards away from the crash site. He removed the sheath and got relieved to discover that the sword's blade was still intact.

After surveying the surroundings, the detective realized he was in the middle of a dense forest. This seemed to be the Forest of Loot. All he saw around were tall trees with thick foliage.

Mark remembered that Doctor Axlow claimed that Zalthor's body could jump to high altitudes. So, he decided to take a mighty leap to test this ability. He bent his legs and catapulted his body upward. In a few seconds, the detective reached almost three hundred feet in height. From the top of his leap, he could see a large urban settlement a few miles ahead.

When Mark landed on the ground again, he braced his legs to stay upright, but the force of the impact caused his body to be thrown forward, and he hit his face on the ground.

"Maybe Doctor Axlow was right. I should have trained more," Mark thought. He got up and patted his chest, trying to remove some of the dirt that had gotten into his clothes.

The detective held the Heart of Hubbian in one hand and the flare pistol in the other but decided not firing the signal at that moment. He preferred to walk toward the urban settlement.

As Mark made his way through the forest, he heard distant explosions coming from all directions. He continued walking until the trees gave way to a grassy field, and he saw a river just ahead.

The detective decided to take a quick dip to clean his clothes and improve his current appearance.

When Mark emerged from the water, he noticed humanoid beings on the opposite bank of the river, observing him. None of them resembled a Hubbian. They had heads that resembled rabbits.

"It seems that every animal in my world is a humanoid race in this place," Mark pondered.

The beings looked at the Hubbian with great curiosity but remained silent. The detective noticed their keen interest in his presence.

"Hello there!" Mark greeted in a voice loud enough to be heard on the other side of the river.

The beings took a startled step back.

"Listen, all of you!" the detective exclaimed. "Do you know who I am?"

One of the beings, a younger-looking one, stepped forward from the group and responded. "Yes, we know you, Mr. Zalthor."

Another individual stood beside the first and asked, "Are you heading to the Capital?"

"I saw a large city a few miles ahead. That's the Capital, right?"

"Yes!" some of the individuals answered.

Mark smiled and declared, "I'm going there. It seems I'll be taking a Hubbian named Pheldon out of the government. So, tell me, what do you think about that?"

The beings remained silent for a few seconds until a female, visibly enthusiastic, stepped forward and asked, "Can we go with you?"

Mark didn't know how to respond. Now he was the one who was silent. More humanoid beings arrived, and the group quickly turned into a small crowd.

"I don't think it's safe for you to be by my side at the moment. It could be dangerous," the detective cautioned. "But you must spread the news that Zalthor Acri is in Dolmen and heading to the Capital."

When Mark finished speaking, he leaped into the sky at great speed, disappearing from sight. During the flight, he looked ahead and spotted a massive rock protruding above the forest canopy. He decided to reach it. Upon landing, the detective extended his legs in front of his body to avoid rolling on the ground. He leaped again and landed on top of the rock. Mark then took out the flare gun and fired it into the sky, creating a brilliant blue light that spread in all directions.

Waiting at the top of the rock, Mark had the opportunity to take a closer look at the surrounding area. Small explosions were happening all around, but toward the Capital, the situation seemed relatively calm. He also noticed numerous small aircraft crossing the sky, engaged in aerial combat, but he couldn't discern which ones were on his side and which ones were fighting for Pheldon.

Suddenly, the detective spotted some dots moving among the clouds and approaching him. He tightened his grip on the Heart of Hubbian sword, preparing for a potential attack. However, despite being distant, Mark recognized one of the dots as Lintsa, traversing the sky after a high-altitude leap.

Zalthor's wife landed on the rock just a few yards away from Mark. The impact caused her feet to sink a few inches into the stone. A few seconds later, another dozen Hubbians also landed on the rock, including Ranson.

Lintsa approached Mark.

"It's such a relief to see that you're okay, dear. I was worried that Pheldon had captured you."

"Why did it take you so long to use the flare?" Ranson asked. "We were getting worried about you."

"I blacked out for a few minutes after the fall, but I'm fine now. I think my jetpack is faulty," explained Mark, concealing the fact that he didn't know how to operate the equipment. "What do we do next?"

Lintsa pointed toward the city.

"Let's head to the entrance of the Capital. Pheldon is waiting for us. He wants to talk."

"This could be a trap," Mark cautioned.

"He wants to confront you," Lintsa replied.

"Will we be fighting each other?"

"Not exactly."

Chapter 26

Standing on a tall and imposing wall just above the grand gate of the Capital, Pheldon evaluated the situation. Alongside him, hundreds of armed soldiers assumed combat positions. Around the entrance, a few hundred more gathered at the base of the wall.

Thousands of civilians closely observed the scene, eagerly awaiting what would unfold next. This crowd encircled a colossal statue of Pheldon, positioned about a hundred yards in front of the Capital's entrance.

Suddenly, a distinct group of civilians began to chant the name of Zalthor Acri. Mostly young individuals hailing from the Dolmen countryside, they were dressed in simple attire.

A soldier standing next to Pheldon, noticing the commotion, approached his leader and asked, "Sir, should we take any action?"

"Open the gate," Pheldon responded.

The soldier reached for a small communication device strapped to his chest and ordered the entrance to be unlocked. The massive gate opened slowly, allowing hundreds of individuals clad in sophisticated or even luxurious clothes to emerge from behind the wall. They merged into the crowd outside, passionately shouting Pheldon's name and drowning out the cries for Zalthor.

"Much better now!" Pheldon remarked to the soldier beside him.

Pheldon gazed at the blue sky ahead of the wall and spotted some dots moving amidst the clouds.

"They're approaching!" he warned.

Two dozen Hubbians landed atop the towering statue of Pheldon. Zalthor and Lintsa perched on the statue's right hand, at the pinnacle of the monument. The couple stood directly in front of the enemy leader, who fixated his gaze on them.

The crowd erupted in cheers upon the arrival of the group of Hubbians, and the chants for Zalthor resonated throughout the area.

Mark scrutinized his adversary. Pheldon possessed a taller and slimmer physique compared to Zalthor but was very athletic. His attire, a golden armor embedded with gemstones, revealed a lot about his character.

"What do we do now?" Mark inquired of Lintsa.

"Let's wait and hear what he has to say," Lintsa responded.

"Shouldn't we prevent letting him take control over the situation? Why should we allow him to speak first?" Mark questioned.

"Because I already know what he's going to say," Lintsa replied.

Several Pheldon soldiers blew horns, and everyone fell silent, watching intently. Pheldon pressed a button on his armor, and his voice reverberated through powerful sound amplifiers installed atop the wall.

"Hello, my old friend Lintsa. I'm delighted to see your return to Dolmen. It has been week since we last met. Tell me, what brings you here on this splendid day?" Pheldon's voice resonated across the area.

Lintsa raised her head and replied, "Zalthor has come to reclaim what rightfully belongs to him, Pheldon. He is the true owner of the planet Dolmen, and you are well aware of this." Her voice lacked the assistance of amplification, yet it carried enough strength to permeate the silence, allowing everyone to hear her.

"But where is Zalthor, Lintsa? I don't see him," Pheldon retorted. "There is a Hubbian by your side. He may resemble Zalthor, but we both know he is not the one you claim. The real Zalthor Acri was left buried on that moon at the edge of the Galaxy. The one standing beside you is nothing more than an ignorant soul who barely comprehends what's going on here. Or am I mistaken?"

The part of the crowd closest to the gate started screaming Pheldon's name. Mark watched him and concluded that his opponent's posture displayed a familiar arrogance.

"Listen, everyone! I would gladly return Dolmen to Zalthor. He was a great friend and aided me during tough times. However, Zalthor no longer exists," claimed Pheldon. "Lintsa is misguided. The beautiful face that once belonged to Zalthor deceives her. The one who lurks behind Lintsa is not the former owner of this planet. He is merely the consciousness of an inferior life form, occupying the body that once belonged to the great Zalthor Acri. It is solely out of respect for my old friend's memory that I refuse to surrender Dolmen to this impostor."

The cheers for Pheldon intensified, causing vibrations on the statue Mark and Linda were hanging. The group in favor of Zalthor seemed to be retreating.

Mark observed Lintsa and noticed the worry on her face. He also glanced at Ranson and the other Hubbians, who looked unsure about what to do. Pheldon, on the other hand, looked confident, surrounded by soldiers shouting his name with raised clenched fists.

Witnessing all this, the detective began to feel a heat in his chest, as if some kind of energy was building up inside him. This sensation continued to rise until, to the astonishment of the crowd, he launched into a long leap, directing his flight to land a few steps ahead of Pheldon. Upon touching the ground, Mark bent his body to cushion the impact and prevent the embarrassment of falling in front of his opponent.

The landing was successful, and Mark firmly touched the ground, silencing everyone.

"Hello, Pheldon!" greeted Mark as he stood up.

Pheldon now looked frightened. Nobody expected such a response from the new Zalthor. Even Mark himself was surprised to have achieved such a feat.

"I don't need anyone to speak on my behalf, Pheldon. I'm right here in front of you," stated the detective.

Pheldon hesitated but managed to speak.

"What do you know about Dolmen, stranger? What do you know about Hubbian? Do you even remember the date of The Liberation Day?"

"What is The Liberation Day?" asked Mark.

The pro-Pheldon crowd roared once more. The detective realized that he made a mistake by asking that last question.

Pheldon burst into laughter.

"The Liberation Day was when the Hubbian army finally liberated the Galaxy from the Zort Empire. It was the day the great Zalthor Acri executed Torlox, the King Zort. The real Zalthor would never forget such an event, yet you have no idea what it is. I stood beside Zalthor when he raised the Heart of Hubbian before King Zort and put an end to his empire. But clearly, you don't remember any of that. You're no longer Zalthor. You're not even Hubbian!" exclaimed Pheldon.

More cries in support of Pheldon echoed through the crowd. Mark realized that his opponent's confidence had returned. He glanced back and spotted Lintsa and her allies perched atop the colossal statue. The group looked worried.

However, to the surprise of the Hubbians clinging to the monument, Mark smiled and turned to Pheldon.

"You're right, Pheldon. I no longer possess my old memories. I've been away for a long time and have forgotten many things, I admit it. But there's one thing I haven't forgotten."

Mark raised the Heart of Hubbian, a gesture that caught Pheldon and his allies by surprise, causing them to take a step back. The detective tightly gripped the sword's hilt and felt a tremendous power flowing from his body to the weapon. Mark applied more pressure, compressing the hilt until the blue blade started to glow, then he turned his gaze toward Lintsa. The Hubbian woman immediately understood what was happening and shouted to her comrades. Everyone jumped off the Pheldon statue.

With all his strength, Mark firmly grasped the hilt of the Heart of Hubbian and swung the sword through the air. It would be a strike into emptiness, but a surge of immense energy erupted from the blade and raced toward the giant statue. Upon impact, the monument's head shattered into thousands of pieces.

Mark turned to face Pheldon, pointing the blade of the sword at his opponent.

"I am Zalthor Acri, Pheldon. I may not possess Zalthor's memories, but I am him. And you know how I know that? Because I know that if I want to, I can kick your ass out of the atmosphere of this planet."

Suddenly, both sides of the crowd around the wall erupted in cheers, now united in calling out for the same name.

Chapter 27

A grand procession moved through the capital of the planet Dolmen, accompanied by hundreds of vehicles trailing a large transport platform hovering a few meters above the ground. On the platform, Zalthor, Lintsa, and a dozen other allies waved to the surrounding crowd.

The procession moved along a wide avenue that cut through the center of the capital. The road was paved with golden stones and flanked by towering buildings. The sidewalks were packed with people, and every window along the facades was filled with onlookers. Many cheered and chanted Zalthor's name, waving enthusiastically. Confetti rained down from the building windows, and the sound of fireworks echoed from all directions.

At the avenue's end, several miles ahead, stood a colossal rock formation that reached almost half a mile in height. Perched atop the rock was a sprawling and intricate castle, boasting two dozen towers, some of which were as tall as the rock itself. Mark realized that the procession was making its way toward this magnificent structure.

The detective raised his arms, clutching the Heart of Hubbian in one hand, provoking euphoric screams from the surrounding crowd. Lintsa stood by his side, holding his hand, as they greeted the people.

Mark lowered his arms, signaling that he needed some rest. Lintsa gazed at him intently.

"Zalthor, how did you manage to remember how to wield the Heart of Hubbian? No one expected you to exhibit such skill with the sword in such a short time."

"Well, I'm not entirely sure what happened," Mark replied. "It was as if the sword was communicating with me. I felt an immense surge of energy inside my body, yearning to be unleashed upon Pheldon. The sword acted as a catalyst. Now I understand why you entrusted it to me instead of a gun."

While speaking, Mark noticed Lintsa's intense gaze, which almost embarrassed him. Her eyes were wide and vibrant, their irises surrounded by a radiant white glow that seemed to emanate light of its own.

Mark leaned in for a lingering kiss with Lintsa, igniting the crowd's applause and cheers. When the kiss finished, Lintsa pointed ahead, and Mark noticed that they had arrived at the colossal rock at the end of the avenue. Suddenly, the platform began to ascend, rising toward the castle's entrance.

Minutes later, Mark and Lintsa were in a vast hall inside the castle. They walked together on a grand red carpet, surrounded by over five hundred individuals. The carpet led them to an oversized chair at the far end of the place, adorned with gold and an abundance of precious stones.

Mark noticed the ornate seat.

"Is that chair a throne?" he asked.

From Mark's expression, Lintsa deduced his discomfort with the ostentation.

"Yes, honey, it is. But don't worry. That was an addition made by Pheldon when he seized control of the planet. That throne didn't exist during your time. I'll arrange to have it removed today."

"Yes, please do. I'd feel ridiculous sitting in it."

Lintsa smiled, sensing a touch of the old Zalthor in Mark's words. She affectionately squeezed his hand.

Suddenly, the entire room erupted in applause, celebrating the presence of the couple.

"Who are all these people?" asked Mark. "Did I know them all?"

"The majority on the right side are former allies of Pheldon. They hope to gain forgiveness and maintain their positions after their former leader's downfall. On the left side, you'll recognize several Hubbians and other soldiers who fought alongside us to reclaim Dolmen. Look! There's Fhastina and Physter. They were the ones who rescued you on the B-23 moon and took care of you until you reached Doctor Axlow's Planet. Let's go say hello to them."

Following Lintsa's direction, Mark saw the two humanoid beings with eagle-like faces. He and Lintsa approached the couple, and Mark noticed the tension in the female's eyes.

"Fhastina! Physter! It's great to see you here!" exclaimed Lintsa, embracing Fhastina. "I thought Pheldon's allies had captured you."

"Our spaceship was briefly held by Pheldon's soldiers," Fhastina explained. "They believed Zalthor was still inside, but they released us soon after. I think that's when Pheldon surrendered."

"I'm relieved to hear that everything went well here in Dolmen," said Physter. "I was informed that there were minimal casualties during the power takeover. I'm certain it would have been much more difficult without Zalthor's presence."

As Lintsa and Physter engaged in a friendly conversation about Pheldon's reaction when his monument's head was pulverized by the Heart of Hubbian, Mark fixated his gaze on Fhastina. He noticed that the female was embarrassed, yet she didn't avert her eyes, maintaining a steady stare at him.

"She must know that I didn't report her! Otherwise, she wouldn't be here," the detective pondered.

At that moment, Physter turned and extended his hand to Mark.

"It is a great honor to have been part of your rescue, Mr. Zalthor. If even half of the legends about you are true, you are a hero of galactic proportions. Allow me the pleasure of shaking your hand."

Mark smiled at Physter and obliged, shaking hands with Fhastina's companion. However, as their hands touched, the detective felt a faint surge of energy coursing through his body, traveling from his arm to his head. He also sensed a slight tingling behind his right eye. It raised Mark's suspicions, and he stared intently at Physter, who released his hand and turned to Lintsa.

"If you ever need us, Mrs. Lintsa, we'll be ready," said Physter, smiling at the Hubbian woman.

"Thank you for everything," Lintsa responded. "Take some rest. You deserve it. We all do."

"Thank you, Madam."

Physter and Fhastina swiftly departed, vanishing into the bustling crowd.

Mark examined his hand, attempting to comprehend what had just happened.

Night fell over the capital of Dolmen. In the castle's grandest suite, Mark enjoyed a refreshing shower. The first day on the planet had been long. He had been awake for over twenty-four hours, attending various ceremonies, meeting countless acquaintances of Zalthor, receiving flattery from numerous individuals, and pleas for forgiveness from former allies of Pheldon. To his surprise, he didn't feel tired.

Emerging from the bathroom, clad only in a towel, Mark's attention was drawn to a massive double bed at the center of the suite. He noticed Lintsa standing next to it. The look exchanged between them revealed their desires, and Lintsa understood perfectly well what the detective was thinking. However, to Mark's surprise, Lintsa took a small device from her pocket and brought it close to her mouth.

"Is my ship ready?" she inquired.

"Yes, madam," a voice responded from the tiny device. "We have it prepared on the main terrace."

Lintsa smiled and returned the device to one of her pockets. She then looked at Mark.

"Put on something comfortable, honey," she instructed, walking toward a large glass door that led to a footbridge outside the suite. "We're going out."

Observing the golden sheets adorning the bed in front of him, Mark's expression displayed a tinge of disappointment. Nevertheless, Lintsa was already outside, leaving him with no choice but to search through the wardrobes and find something suitable to wear.

Five minutes later, on the main terrace of the castle, Mark stood beside Lintsa. He gazed at her spaceship, but it looked cleaner and smaller, as if only the front half remained.

"What happened to your ship?" Mark asked. "Looks like a big chunk is gone."

"It's without the interstellar compartment. We won't need it where we're going. Come!" Lintsa called, ascending the access ramp to the ship.

Minutes later, Lintsa's ship hovered mid-air, approximately three hundred feet above an immense collection of waterfalls. Over thirty grand cascades, each towering around six hundred feet in height, encircled a large circular crater with a captivating blue lake at its center.

A wide door on the side of the ship opened, with a ramp extending outward. Mark and Lintsa stood on the structure.

"These must be the Lyria Falls, right?" the detective asked. "Doctor Axlow mentioned them."

"Yes," Lintsa confirmed. "They are the largest waterfalls on this side of the galaxy."

Mark gazed down in awe.

"They're amazing. They remind me of a cluster of waterfalls back home, but these ones are way bigger."

Suddenly, Lintsa began to undress.

"What are you doing? Someone might see us here," Mark exclaimed.

"Don't worry, honey. The park's airspace has been closed off. No one will see us."

Lintsa boldly jumped naked into the lake at the base of the falls. Mark hurriedly removed his clothes as well, struggling a bit with a few pieces, and looked down. The sight momentarily startled him, but after having jumped from a space platform just hours ago, such a descent no longer seemed as frightening. He jumped in as well.

During the descent, Mark felt the refreshing chill of water droplets splashing against his face. Upon hitting the water's surface, he sank nearly one hundred feet. Lintsa's arms embraced him, and he sensed her lips against his. The two Hubbians engaged in a passionate kiss.

Two hours later, Mark and Lintsa were perched on a large rock, granting them a breathtaking view of the waterfalls. They lay down, holding each other closely. The detective gazed at the Hubbian woman's face with passion, and she responded with a warm smile.

Mark closed his eyes, wishing he could remain there beside Lintsa forever.

Chapter 28

Mark opened his eyes and found himself back in his apartment, lying on the living room couch. The light from outside came in through a forgotten open window, and the sun's rays illuminated her legs. His body was sweaty, stuck to the fabric of the sofa. As he shifted his back, a sharp muscle pain coursed through him, causing him to groan. He attempted to rise, but the pain intensified, as if his nerves were on the verge of tearing.

"I should have gone to sleep on the bed instead of the couch," Mark thought to himself.

After finally managing to position himself in a sitting position, the detective detected a strong odor of urine. Glancing down, he noticed that the shorts he had worn before sleeping were wet.

Stretching his arm, Mark picked up his cell phone, activated the screen, and checked the time. It was ten in the morning, significantly later than his usual waking time, even on a Saturday. A small number overlapped the missed calls icon in the corner of the phone's screen, indicating seventeen ignored calls. It was unusual for Mark to receive so many calls in a single night unless something extremely serious had occurred. When he noticed that most of the calls were from his boss, he promptly returned.

"What happened?" Mark asked as soon as Oswald answered.

"Where in God's name have you been? I've been trying to reach you since Friday night. I was on the verge of sending a patrol to your apartment with instructions to break down your door."

"Today is Saturday, Chief. It's normal to wake up later on a Saturday. But tell me, what's happened?"

"Firstly, today is not Saturday. Now go to the police station, or rather, head to the coroner's office. I'll call Andrew and instruct him to meet you there."

"Did they find the girl's body?"

"Meet Andrew at the entrance of the coroner's office. He will provide you with the details."

"Now is not the time for riddles, boss. What happened to the girl? How is the body?"

"Go to the coroner's office and see for yourself."

"Okay. I'll just take a quick shower before that. I really need it," Mark said, looking at his wet legs. "But let me ask you something: what do you mean by 'today is not Saturday'? I remember working yesterday and getting back home late. Are you going mad?"

"You're the one going mad, Mark Randall. Today is Sunday. You must have taken too many drugs to sleep and spent the entire Saturday high! I bet that's the reason you didn't answer the phone. Meet Andrew at the coroner's office in forty minutes."

"Understood, boss," Mark replied, ending the call. He gazed at the cell phone screen and verified that it was indeed Sunday.

Oswald spoke the truth when he said that the detective had slept for two consecutive nights. This explained the pain coursing through his body and the fact that he wet his own pants.

Mark stood up and stretched, feeling his spine crack and the pain in his back subside. He headed to the bathroom, undressed, stepped into the shower, and turned on the water.

As the warm water ran down his body, Mark recalled the adventures he had just experienced: the descent into the planet Dolmen, the freefall from space without a parachute, the duel against Pheldon, the resounding cheers of the crowd chanting Zalthor's name, and the passionate night spent with Lintsa by the Lyria Falls. He yearned to go back to sleep and forget about the Sinclair family and the missing girl. However, he was wide awake now, making it difficult to lie down and rest. Maybe leaving the apartment and keeping his mind busy until the end of the day would be the best thing to do.

Forty minutes later, Mark and Andrew entered in the refrigerated chamber of the coroner's office. They stood next to an open morgue drawer, inside which laid a body wrapped in a black bag. A young coroner began to unzip the bag.

"It's too big to be the girl's body," Mark observed.

"You're right," agreed Andrew.

As the corpse was unveiled, Mark realized it belonged to a tall, muscular man, but he could not immediately identify who he was due to the crushed face. After analyzing the body for a few seconds, he noticed a prominent tattoo on the chest, depicting martial arts. Mark pointed to the tattoo.

"This is Tortoise's body, isn't it?" he asked.

"Yes," confirmed Andrew.

"Where was he found?" inquired Mark.

"He was found in a rural district on the outskirts of town, buried under a disposal area. Some garbage collectors were digging through the trash when they stumbled across a human hand beneath a pile of debris and promptly alerted the police."

Andrew turned to the coroner.

"Show him."

The coroner took a transparent plastic envelope from a nearby table and displayed it to Mark, revealing an old hammer inside.

"This hammer was found next to the body and contains traces of blood. DNA tests confirmed that the blood belongs to the Sinclair family and Joseph Assis himself," reported Andrew.

Mark looked at the coroner.

"Thank you for your assistance, Coroner. You may close the drawer." He then turned to his partner. "Let's continue our conversation outside."

Outside the coroner's office, in the parking lot, the two detectives discussed next to Mark's car.

"And what about Carol Sinclair? Any leads on her whereabouts?" asked Mark.

"No, no leads yet," responded Andrew.

"So, it's clear that Joseph Assis, aka Tortoise, was one of the murderers, but someone else killed him later, and the girl is still missing."

"Probably the other intruder who broke into the house is responsible," Andrew suggested.

"Yes. It's possible that the person who strangled the mother is the same one who killed Tortoise using the hammer. That's why the weapon was left with his body," deduced Mark. "Where exactly is this disposal area located? Is there anything in the neighborhood that could give us a lead?"

"On one side of the area, there's a gated community called Paradise Ranch Houses. It's a large complex with about five hundred lots," Andrew responded.

Mark observed his partner's face and noticed a certain agitation in Andrew's expression.

"What do we have on the other side?" Mark inquired.

"There is a large rural property called Leticia Andraus Farm," Andrew replied.

"Leticia Andraus? That's the name of the Mayor's wife. The property belongs to him, right?" Mark questioned.

"Exactly," Andrew confirmed.

Mark displayed a sly smile.

"Have you discussed this with the boss?"

"Yes. Just yesterday, Oswald got in touch with Judge Robert Brown. I believe the judge is going to grant a court order to question the Mayor's son," Andrew informed.

Mark looked at Andrew with an expression of anger and declared, "Carol Sinclair's body must be buried somewhere on the Mayor's farm. We need authorization to search the place as soon as possible. We also must question the employees. They might have valuable information, more than the Mayor and his son. The employees might be aware of any unusual events that have occurred on the property in the past few days. If they feel intimidated, one of them will eventually speak up.

Andrew reflected for a few seconds. Mark noticed his partner's apparent doubt.

"Tell me what's bothering you, Andrew."

"Don't you think it would be too foolish for the Mayor and his son to bury Tortoise's body under a pile of rubble next to their farm? I saw the area. The place has many scavengers digging through everything. It would only be a matter of time before someone stumbled across the body. Since the crime occurred, everyone has been talking about the girl's connection to the Mayor. And now, Tortoise's body appears right beside their farm?"

"Do you think someone could have deliberately placed the body near the Mayor's farm to frame him?"

"Well, I see it as a possibility."

"This type of mistake is not uncommon, Andrew. In numerous cases, murderers end up being arrested because they fail to dispose of their victims' bodies cleverly. I've witnessed cunning psychopaths being caught because the cleaning lady found body parts in plastic bowls left inside their refrigerators. Paul Andraus wouldn't be the first killer to carelessly dispose of a body. If we're fortunate, they hid Carol with the same lack of diligence as they did with Tortoise."

"You speak as if you're sure the girl is on the farm," Andrew observed.

Mark took his cellphone from his pocket and checked the time.

"We need to pay another visit to that woman on Aurora Street. Do you recall her name?" Mark questioned.

"Her name is Marisa. Do you want to talk to her right now?"

Mark took a step toward his car.

"It's Sunday, isn't it? And I don't have anything better to do. What about you?"

"I need to go home. My fiancée is waiting for me. I've promised to have lunch with her parents today."

"If Marisa already knows about Tortoise's death, she may be frightened. We'll be fortunate if we can still locate her. Perhaps Tortoise approached her and mentioned someone significant before he was killed."

Mark took his car key from his pocket and pressed the button to unlock the doors. The vehicle's horn beeped twice.

"Are you joining me?"

"I can't. My fiancée will get extremely upset. I risk becoming single again if I don't show up at her parents' house within half an hour."

"Alright, you don't need to come with me. Honestly, I know I'll likely be wasting my time, but I feel compelled to meet Marisa now. It's better than going home."

"Are you heading to Aurora Street alone? I believe you should at least contact an armed agent to protect you."

"Don't worry. I'll be fine."

"You could at least take a gun. Do you want to borrow mine?"

"You know I don't carry guns, Andrew. Don't worry about me. Go meet your fiancée's parents and secure your wedding plans. I'll locate Tortoise's girlfriend."

Chapter 29

Mark arrived at a block near Aurora Street. The area where he parked was practically deserted, which was expected for a Sunday afternoon in a region close to downtown.

The detective stepped out of the car and walked along the empty sidewalk. A few dozen yards before reaching the usual gathering point on Aurora Street, he spotted a tall, thin young man leaning against the closed roller door of a shop. The youth carried a small backpack, attempting to conceal it under his arm. He looked at the approaching middle-aged man with suspicion.

Mark stopped in front of the young man and scanned the surroundings to ensure there was no one else nearby. Once he was sure they were alone, the detective took out his wallet from his pocket and displayed some banknotes to the youth.

"Listen, kid: what do you have that would knock me out?"

The young man lifted his head, glancing over the detective's shoulder. He wanted to make sure the stranger was alone. Then he opened his bag and took out a small, transparent bottle containing approximately fifty white pills.

"How much is it?" Mark inquired.

Ten minutes later, Mark was standing on the sidewalk of Aurora Street. The street seemed different from his last visit. It was cleaner now, and the homeless individuals were no longer scattered on the ground but organized in a long line that bent multiple times.

Mark walked past the homeless people, who seemed indifferent to his presence. He headed toward the house where he found Marisa three days ago but didn't find her there. The residence was empty. It seemed that at that moment, everyone on Aurora Street was in the line.

The detective decided to investigate what was happening. He searched for the start of the line and found the same white van from three days ago. Five nuns were outside the vehicle, handling five large pots on a long table. Mark also noticed that people leaving the line carried a plate of food in their hands after passing by the table. He comprehended the situation. The clergy were once again providing food for the homeless, but this time, they had brought a larger quantity.

"Perhaps to prevent a repeat of the brawl from the other day," Mark pondered.

The detective scanned the line for Marisa but failed to locate her. To his surprise, he found another woman he recognized. She noticed his presence and quickly turned away, embarrassed.

Mark hurriedly approached the woman and exclaimed, "Millie! What are you doing here?"

The woman remained silent, taking a step forward, following the movement of the line.

"What happened to you, girl? You shouldn't be here," he insisted. "Where is your son?"

Millie glanced at Mark.

"He's fine. He's with his grandmother. And since when do you care about that?" she retorted, turning her gaze forward again.

"Listen, Millie, you know what will happen if you stay on this street. Let's leave this place. I'll take you home. I'm going to buy some medicine to help you quit smoking these stones."

"Leave me alone!" the girl shouted.

Mark seized Millie's arm.

"I can't leave you here. Please come with me!"

"Go away!" Millie yelled.

The girl's scream caught the attention of others nearby. Several menacing men now surrounded Mark.

"Take it easy, guys! I just want to help her," Mark explained, releasing his grip on Millie's arm. "I don't want any trouble." He raised his hands and took a step back.

One of the men approached, standing in front of the detective. He had a shaved head and numerous tattoos on his arm, which accentuated his intimidating appearance.

"What's a fancy guy like you doing here?" the man snarled. "Looking for trouble, I bet!" He clenched his fists and assumed a fighting stance.

Mark felt his heart racing, his arteries pulsating in his neck. He scanned his surroundings, considering which direction to escape. However, at that moment, a burly elderly man in clean white clothing emerged from among the homeless.

"Gentlemen, gentlemen! Let's calm down. We have enough food for everyone. There's no need to fight," the man stated.

Mark immediately recognized the man in white. It was Euzebius, the Archbishop.

The man with the shaved head lowered his hands.

"I apologize, Father." He didn't attempt to justify himself. Instead, he walked away, accompanied by his companions.

The detective redirected his attention to the line. Millie was no longer there. But before he could set off in pursuit of the woman, the Archbishop approached him.

"What brings you here, Detective? Did you come looking for Joseph? Unfortunately, I must inform you that it's too late. The poor man is no longer with us."

"I'm aware of that, Your Grace. Just an hour ago, I saw Tortoise in a body bag. I came to search for his alleged girlfriend, a woman named Marisa. She's blonde, with curly hair. Have you seen her?"

"I know who you're talking about. Poor soul! I've heard she was an excellent doctor in the past. She's not the type of person you'd expect to find in a place like this. But this drug is horrendous, isn't it? No matter how intelligent or resilient you are, once you smoke one of these stones, it completely enslaves your soul. I hope you're not using them either."

"No, of course not, Your Grace. I would never smoke one of those things. I'm well aware of the effects they have on people. But what about Marisa? Have you seen her today?"

"I must admit, I also searched for her," the Archbishop replied. "Like you, Joseph's death intrigued me as well. I wanted to speak with Marisa and make sure everything is okay with her."

As the Archbishop spoke, he walked over to the table and positioned himself alongside one of the pots. With a wooden spoon in hand, Euzebius scooped out white rice from a cooking vessel and deposited it onto the plate of each person passing in front of him.

"Do you have any leads on who might have eliminated the poor Joseph, Detective?" questioned the Archbishop.

"I believe it was the same person who ordered the murder of the Sinclair family, Your Grace. Probably a witness elimination. Tortoise had a reputation for being a talker. Unfortunately, with his death, it becomes much more difficult to uncover the mastermind behind the crime," explained Mark. "And our chances of finding Carol Sinclair diminish a lot."

"Don't worry, Detective. The Lord will aid you in finding your girl. You will locate her when the time is right. Trust me."

Mark scrutinized the condition of the people waiting in line. Their clothes were tattered, their skin coated in filth. Many of their hair resembled the debris extracted from a vacuum cleaner's dirt bag.

"I apologize, Your Grace, but do you truly believe in this God even when you're surrounded by this place?"

The Archbishop set down the spoon and grabbed a towel to wipe his hands, while a nun took his place at the table. Euzebius approached Mark, held his arm, and began walking with the detective at his side.

" I believe that the Lord wishes for the happiness of all living beings, Detective. He safeguards us continuously. The Lord speaks to our hearts, guiding us toward the path of happiness. Unfortunately, the people here have chosen to ignore the voice of the Lord, and they are now facing the consequences of their misguided decisions. Of course, the Lord observes the pain in this place and suffers with it. He cares about everyone."

Mark released his arm from the Archbishop and stepped away.

"But then, if this God is so concerned and if He is the almighty entity depicted in your Holy Book, why does He limit Himself to providing ambiguous guidance? Why doesn't He actually do something to fix this world?"

The Archbishop responded solemnly, "The Lord will eradicate all evil when the time is appropriate, Detective."

Mark stared at Euzebius and took a step back, his voice growing more intense.

"It's all a huge scam, Euzebius. Religious leaders make up fantasies and assert the veracity of these tales. They concoct tales that solely benefit their Church and sustain the lavish lives of authorities like yourself. Then you come to places like this, appeasing your guilt by distributing cheap food to these people, instead of taking real actions to help them break free from this miserable existence. Look at this place! Every day, more addicts flock here."

Euzebius observed Mark's trembling hands.

"You don't understand the reality of this situation, Detective. There's no hope left for these people. They have forsaken the voice of the Lord. They are lost souls."

"We all are, Euzebius. There's nothing in this world worth fighting for. Unhappy souls have nothing but to walk alone, through darkness, witnessing their very beings crumble under the weight of pain and guilt, with no one to offer real assistance. Until they can no longer endure their suffering and resort to consuming those damned stones!"

Mark was now screaming, drawing the attention of those in line and the nearby nuns. The Archbishop's expression showed concern, but Euzebius attempted to maintain composure. He approached the detective as if to offer support, his hand reaching for Mark's shoulder.

"Do not touch me!" Mark roared.

Suddenly, a deafening bang reverberated from all directions. Mark felt as if the ground beneath him had vanished. Gravity momentarily disappeared. The street's asphalt collapsed, only to rise abruptly, causing everyone on Aurora Street to topple over. With his palms pressed against the scorching asphalt, the detective questioned his own sanity, yet he saw the Archbishop before him. Euzebius was also lying on the ground, a frightened expression etched on his face.

The street jolted once more, this time with even greater force, throwing everyone into the air. The Archbishop was flung toward the pavement, and his head hit the curb.

As if that wasn't enough, the ground continued to convulse for another thirty seconds. Anyone who tried to climb was promptly thwarted and repeatedly knocked down. Mark remained lying on the asphalt, his elbows supporting his torso, struggling to comprehend the chaos unfolding around him.

Finally, as the ground stopped moving, screams and pleas for help permeated the street. The Archbishop sat on the pavement, placing a hand on his forehead. The detective observed a deep gash on the priest's head, blood cascading down his body, staining his white shirt. Two nuns hastened to his aid, but Euzebius dismissed them, insisting they tend to others.

Mark stood up. Euzebius stared at him, a blend of terror and disbelief etched on the clergyman's face. However, the Archbishop remained silent.

Then, a loud crash resonated. But this time, it was not the ground jolting. One of the houses on the street, the very one where the detective found Marisa for the first time, collapsed in a heap. The sound startled everyone, and a cloud of dust billowed from the rubble.

Mark turned, sprinting toward his car, disappearing into the chaos.

Chapter 30

Mark drove his car hastily. Through the vehicle's windows, he realized that the chaos he witnessed while arguing with the Archbishop extended beyond Aurora Street. Everyone on the streets was gripped by terror, running and screaming. On the horizon, a dark cloud of dust loomed, advancing over the city.

The streets were strewn with fallen trees, debris from construction sites, and wrecked cars. The detective steered through the wreckage, determined to keep moving. He reached for his cell phone and called Andrew, but his partner didn't answer, and neither did his boss, Oswald.

The car crossed the city's main avenue and passed in front of the city hall. Mark looked at the imposing building. It had huge cracks and broken windows, but the structure remained standing.

Fear filled the detective's mind as he contemplated his thoughts. Determined to find answers, he steered the car, ignoring traffic lights and signs. In that chaos, no one would care about a vehicle running red lights. Most of the lights weren't functioning anyway. Mark wasn't concerned about getting a fine either. At that moment, he had far more urgent matters to worry about.

As Mark arrived at the Café and Grill restaurant, his car was speeding. Despite slamming the brakes, the vehicle collided with a lamppost near the entrance, crumpling the bumper. Ignoring the damage, the detective hastily left the car and headed straight for the restaurant's door.

The restaurant was closed, its glass windows and doors shielded by metal barriers. The building appeared relatively undamaged, and the surrounding area was calm, showing few remnants of the seismic event that occurred half an hour ago. However, the vast cloud of dust was approaching, carried by the wind, darkening the sky above the restaurant.

Mark scanned the street in front of the establishment and noticed a tall man walking toward him. The man waved, and the detective immediately recognized him—it was Delasher, precisely the person he was looking for.

Delasher approached, and when he was four yards away from Mark, he stopped and silently stared at the detective.

With rapid breaths, Mark spoke, "Listen, Delasher! Until half an hour ago, I believed that everything happening in these past few days—Zalthor Acri, Lintsa, even you— everything was a creation of my mind. Yes, I know. The waitress affirmed she could see you too, which should prove your existence. But in a state of madness, we can conjure up anything, right? I felt like I was losing my grip on reality, but it was a delightful insanity. I was the owner of an entire planet, married to the most stunning woman in the Galaxy. Moreover, I was young, invincible, and immortal. Who wouldn't desire such a thing, even if it were an illusion? I didn't feel remorse for departing from reality and residing in that fictitious world. Actually, I was glad that something like that could happen to me."

Mark fell silent for a few seconds, gazing at the sky before continuing, "But now, this is happening. I witnessed the fear in the Archbishop's eyes, the panic on Aurora Street, and the chaos engulfing this entire city. So I drove here because somehow I knew you would be in this place, waiting for me."

Delasher surveyed the closed restaurant and headed toward a bench on the corner of the block. Mark followed suit.

The bench sat at the edge of a slope, offering a panoramic view of the city. Delasher calmly took a seat and observed the landscape. The looming dust cloud started to dissipate, becoming lighter.

Mark positioned himself in front of the stranger, remaining standing.

"What will happen now?" the detective asked.

"Nothing for now," Delasher replied. "But you will return to sleep, find Lintsa, and become Zalthor Acri once again. You will relish the pleasures of being an immortal converted Hubbian and will have no desire to come back here. Your mind will begin erasing this place, making room for the new memories Zalthor will acquire."

Mark turned his gaze toward the city below. He witnessed the bustling movement of people in the streets, as well as the flashing lights of ambulances and police cars.

"What will happen with these people? What awaits them?"

"They will cease to exist. All of them," Delasher responded sternly, almost insensitively.

"You mean they will die?"

"Mark Randall, why is it so difficult for you to understand? Every person, every living being in this universe is linked to you. If you choose to carry on with your life as Zalthor Acri, in a matter of days, this place will face what many here refer to as 'The Doomsday.'"

Nausea overtook the detective, and he took a seat beside Delasher.

The stranger continued, "During our time apart, I have taken the opportunity to learn more about your world, Mark Randall. I must admit, it is a fascinating place. The multitude of people and languages here is remarkable. I have never seen a Hubbian create a world with such cultural richness and complexity. You should be proud of your creation."

Mark pondered for a moment, lowering his head.

"I have nothing to be proud of, Delasher. I don't even remember building this world. I simply exist here, like everyone else. How can I be the Creator of this universe?"

"Because Zalthor Acri has awakened," Delasher replied. "And when he awakens, it is you, and no one else in this world, who inhabits his body."

Suddenly, the small device in Delasher's pocket emitted a warning sound. The stranger stood up and took out the gadget, noticing a strong red light flashing on the device.

"Unfortunately, it seems he has found me. My time in your world has come to an end," Delasher stated.

Mark also rose and scanned the parking lot, searching for other individuals, but found no one in sight.

"Who found you? What are you talking about?"

"Doctor Axlow. He has found me!" The stranger looked upward, as if anticipating something to descend upon him.

Mark observed Delasher's appearance changing, becoming increasingly indistinct and blurry.

"You must understand your true identity, Mark Randall. You must comprehend who Zalthor Acri truly is. Only then can your world be saved."

"But what am I supposed to do?" Mark inquired.

"You know where to seek the answer, but you must have the desire to find it!" Delasher responded.

Delasher's body began to emit an intense glow, intensifying gradually, as if on the verge of an explosion.

"Find Dana, Mark Randall! She holds the answer!" These were Delasher's final words before transforming into a beam of light and disappearing.

"Who is Dana?" the detective questioned, but Delasher was no longer present.

Mark now was alone.

Chapter 31

Mark was back in his apartment, seated at the dining table, wearing pajamas and a pair of old slippers. From his chair, he could see the time displayed on the clock hanging on the living room wall. It was almost ten o'clock at night.

In front of Mark rested a plate of pasta. He attempted to start eating the meal, but despite barely eating anything all day, he had no appetite.

In the living room, the television broadcasted a daily news segment, revealing that the earlier seismic event was felt worldwide. Major cities had reported landslides and significant casualties. Many areas were now isolated without access to water or power. Governments across the globe urged the population to remain calm, while the world's leading scientists worked tirelessly to uncover an explanation for an event of such magnitude.

Mark tried to understand how such a planetary occurrence could be linked to his own emotions. He was merely an ordinary public servant with no leadership role, stationed at a dilapidated police station, an unremarkable citizen lacking exceptional talent. How could someone so average be the supreme being responsible for creating the entire universe? And now, the whole world was in peril simply because he preferred to live elsewhere?

Mark's thoughts were abruptly interrupted by the sound of the apartment's doorbell. He quickly rose and rushed to the intercom. The detective heard a female voice speaking in a highly formal manner.

"Good evening, Mr. Randall. The Archbishop kindly requests your permission to ascend to your residence."

The detective was taken aback by the unexpected request, leaving him feeling unable to refuse. Without hesitation, he granted Euzebius authorization to come up.

Mark quickly ran to the apartment window and looked down at the street in front of his building. He saw a large black car accompanied by a smaller vehicle parked directly behind it. A man in a black suit emerged from the smaller car and opened the door of the larger one. Although the man tried to assist the Archbishop in exiting the car, Euzebius motioned for him to step aside. The priest donned his customary white attire, but there was also a large bandage covering the entirety of his forehead. With slow, careful steps and leaning on a wooden cane, the clergyman made his way toward the building's entrance.

The detective hurried to his bedroom and exchanged his pajamas for more formal attire. He put on a clean T-shirt but had difficulty in locating suitable pants. Once he finally managed to put on the only pair he could find, someone knocked on the door of the apartment. Mark remembered that he didn't have time to comb his hair and rubbed a hand over his head, attempting to tame the unruly strands.

When Mark opened the door, he saw Euzebius standing alone in the middle of the corridor. The Archbishop cast a serious gaze upon the detective. There was something different about the clergyman's face, but Mark could not comprehend what it might be. He noticed a red bloodstain on the large bandage covering Euzebius' forehead.

"Good evening, Your Grace. I didn't expect you here at this hour," Mark greeted.

The Archbishop raised his head and tried to look inside the apartment over Mark's shoulder, as if searching for something or someone.

"May I come in?" Euzebius asked humbly.

"Of course. It is an honor to have you here, Your Grace." Mark took a step back and, holding the doorknob, gestured toward the apartment's interior. "Please, make yourself at home."

Walking slowly, the Archbishop entered, inspecting the small apartment. There was nothing special about the property, only details that showed the resident's neglect for his home: dusty furniture, old magazines on the living room rug, a towel hanging from the back of a chair, and, what caught the Archbishop's attention the most, a small bottle of white pills resting on the dinner table, next to a plate with pasta.

"I apologize if I interrupted your dinner," said the Archbishop.

"Don't worry about it, Your Grace," Mark responded. "I had already given up eating. I'm not hungry."

The clergyman sat on the couch in the living room.

Mark peeked out of the apartment door to check if anyone else was in the corridor. Then, he closed the door, went to the dinner table, pulled out a chair, and sat across from Euzebius.

"Are you okay?" asked Mark, pointing to the bandage on the Archbishop's head.

Euzebius placed his hand over the wound.

"I am fine. It was a minor injury, a long but shallow cut. Nothing that a few stitches couldn't fix."

"How are the people on Aurora Street? I didn't see what happened afterward."

"Yes, I saw how quickly you left the scene. But don't worry about the people on the street. Fortunately, there was no one inside the collapsed house. Some individuals were injured and have been hospitalized, but everyone will be fine."

"I apologize for leaving that way, Your Grace. Now I see I should have stayed and helped the people there, including you, who were hurt. Maybe I got more scared than I should have."

"Your reaction is perfectly justified, Detective. Our city, or even our world, has never experienced a seismic event like this."

Mark pointed to the kitchen.

"May I offer you a glass of water or another drink? I can make coffee in five minutes."

"Thank you, Detective. I don't want to trouble you," replied the Archbishop.

"But tell me, Your Grace, what brings you here?"

Mark noticed that the Archbishop's posture seemed more hunched than usual, and the priest avoided making direct eye contact.

"Is it something related to the case of the missing girl? Is it about Tortoise?" asked Mark.

The Archbishop looked up, but instead of answering the question, he gazed at the walls around him.

"I see no pictures in this apartment, Detective, neither on the walls nor on the furniture," remarked the Archbishop.

Mark looked at the wall behind Euzebius and only saw the clock hanging in the center.

"You know I don't have good memories, Euzebius. I told you about what happened to my family."

"Yes, I remember, and I'm sorry for your pain, Detective."

The Archbishop fell silent for a few seconds. Then, he took a deep breath and faced the detective.

"Tell me, who are you, Mark Randall?"

The detective raised his eyebrows, displaying surprise.

"What do you mean, who am I?"

"Listen, Mark Randall. I witnessed what took place on Aurora Street. I observed your rage. There was something about it that I had never felt before. And the way the ground shook, it seemed as if all that energy was emanating from you."

Mark chuckled lightly and looked around. "That was just a coincidence, Your Grace. A colossal coincidence. You don't believe that this humble police officer before you could have anything to do with an event like this afternoon, do you?"

"That would be absurd of me, wouldn't it, Mr. Randall?" responded the Archbishop, with a hint of mockery.

"No, not at all, Your Grace. It would just... I don't know how to put it."

Euzebius took another deep breath.

"After the incident on Aurora Street, I was taken to my house. My assistants wanted to take me to a hospital because of this," he said, pointing to the bandage on his head. "But I insisted on staying home, and Sister Anne stitched my forehead."

"I'm relieved to hear that you're doing well, Your Grace."

Euzebius continued, "When everyone finally left my room, I had a chance to reflect on what I had witnessed on Aurora Street, particularly what I had felt this afternoon. I must confess: I can't recall the last time my bedroom felt so dark and silent. It was during that moment, Mr. Randall, while still awake, that I experienced a vision. And it was because of that vision that I came here."

Mark remained silent, gazing at the Archbishop.

"Do you know what I saw, Mr. Randall?"

"No, Your Grace, I don't know." The detective shook his head.

"I saw the ground opening beneath my residence and then underneath this entire city. I saw thousands of women and children being swallowed by deep abysses, great mountains crumbling, and the seas boiling until they transformed into a massive cloud of toxic gas. The sky was ablaze, and in every direction across the heavens, stars were exploding like mere fireworks. Above all of this, high up among the stars, I beheld the Creator of the Universe. He was looking down upon us, witnessing our destruction with an expression of complete indifference, Mr. Randall." The Archbishop tightly gripped his cane and struck the floor. His eyes were bloodshot, and his hands trembled.

He repeated with more vigor, "With complete indifference, Mr. Randall!"

"And why did you come here, Your Grace?" Mark asked, sighing. "How is this related to me?"

"Because I saw the face of the Creator, and it was the same face I'm looking at now, Mr. Randall."

That last sentence hit Mark like a punch to the stomach. The living room of the apartment became so quiet that he could hear the ticking of the clock on the wall.

"Who are you, Mr. Randall?" insisted the Archbishop.

Mark stood up and tried to appear composed.

"You know who I am, Your Grace. I am Mark Randall, a police detective. I am nobody. I believe you might have been deeply affected by what happened on Aurora Street. As you mentioned, such a catastrophic event has never taken place in our city before. Your Grace is a person of unwavering faith. Individuals like yourself often associate natural events with divine manifestations. I apologize if my words seem harsh, but that's my perspective."

The Archbishop's gaze shifted, revealing a hint of impatience with the detective's words.

Mark walked over to the window, gazed outside, and observed the numerous scattered lights across the cityscape. Some emanated from buildings still engulfed in flames, while others came from helicopters or ambulances. For a few moments, he contemplated the conversations he and Euzebius had in the last few days. He also reflected on the city he called home and all the events that had unfolded there in recent years.

Suddenly, Mark turned toward the Archbishop. As soon as his eyes met Euzebius', the clergyman lowered his gaze. Mark finally grasped the change in Euzebius' posture: the Archbishop appeared to be afraid—afraid of him.

The detective smiled slightly and changed his tone, exuding a newfound confidence.

"Tell me, Euzebius. On Aurora Street, I asked you why God does not intervene to fix this world, didn't I?"

"Yes, I recall it vividly."

"So, you must also recall the response you provided."

Euzebius remained silent, simply locking eyes with Mark.

"What happened this afternoon and the vision you experienced, perhaps they are signs," posited Mark.

"Signs of what, Mr. Randall?"

"Your very own Holy Book talks about it, doesn't it? I remember how often I heard those words in school as a young boy. 'He shall descend from heaven to announce the end of time.' The nuns frequently recited this verse, relishing in the fear it instilled within us. Maybe God is moving closer to proclaiming the end of all evil in this world."

The Archbishop fell silent. He leaned forward, struggling to stand. Euzebius looked pale and feeble. Observing the clergyman's difficulty, Mark approached and lent a helping hand.

Euzebius grasped Mark's shoulder.

"I apologize for burdening you with my nonsensical thoughts, Mr. Randall. I must be losing my sanity. I should not have come here."

Mark remained silent. He walked beside the Archbishop toward the apartment's exit. These were silent steps that stretched out as if time had slowed down.

Upon reaching the door, Euzebius turned to the detective.

"Answer me one last thing, Mr. Randall. I shouldn't insist on this subject any longer, but I need to ask you this question."

Mark opened the door and looked at Euzebius, who released his shoulder.

"If I can answer, Your Grace," Mark said.

Euzebius examined Mark once more, as if he was trying to find something in the detective that he missed.

"What is your connection with this world, Mr. Randall?" the Archbishop asked.

"What do you mean, Your Grace? I haven't understood the question."

"What ties you to this world? Do you have any friends? Are any close family members still alive?"

"I am an only child, Your Grace. My parents passed away shortly after my marriage, and I don't have friends, only acquaintances and co-workers."

"Do you have something in this world that you still care about, Mr. Randall?"

Mark pondered for a few seconds.

"Well, there's the girl, the daughter of the Sinclairs. I want very much to find her. Finding out what happened to her has been pushing me out of bed when I wake up in the morning."

"Yes, the girl. Do you think you'll find her alive?" asked the Archbishop.

"Although I have a lot of reasons to believe not, Your Grace, I must keep looking for her. After all, this is my job. That's what I do in this world."

Euzebius nodded and turned to the bodyguard, who was now waiting for him at the end of the hallway.

"Have a good night, Mr. Randall."

Euzebius stepped slowly toward the bodyguard, but before the clergyman entered the elevator, Mark interrupted him.

"Listen, Euzebius: let me tell you something."

The Archbishop halted and turned to Mark. He didn't say anything, just stared at the detective while the bodyguard supported him by the arm.

"You are the most powerful person in this city, and you know it," Mark spoke. "You command the police and court system. You lead your family. And I know the Cacellas wouldn't dare to attack you. So why don't you use this power?"

"What do you want me to do, Mr. Randall?"

"You can do much more for this city than just donating food and reading stories to those people on Aurora Street, Euzebius. You can do something that truly makes a difference to everyone around you."

Mark waved to the Archbishop and took a step back. He closed the apartment door as Euzebius remained still, staring off into space, with the bodyguard waiting for the boss to inform him when to leave.

Ten minutes later, Mark laid on his bed, holding a glass of water in one hand and two pills in the other. Lintsa came to his mind: her passionate expression, the scent of her skin, the way she walked, displaying firmness without losing the sweetness in her steps. The detective also recalled the details of everything that happened when he was on the planet Dolmen: the people of the Capital calling his name, hailing him as if he were a great hero, making him feel important like never before in his life.

Suddenly, the Archbishop's terrified face flashed into his mind. How could a man like Euzebius, the highest authority in town, look at him in that way?

The Archbishop was someone Mark recognized as a personality far above him or anyone else in that city. Now, that sovereign man looked helpless and scared.

But that reaction was not entirely unexpected. As someone who dedicated his whole life to worshiping the Creator of this universe and studying Him, it was not surprising that it was precisely Euzebius who could sense what was happening now. After all, the Archbishop woke up, ate, and slept thinking about this Creator. Euzebius may have developed a heightened sensitivity, especially in a moment like this.

The detective looked at the pills in his hand, wondering if it was time to swallow them. However, before he could do that, he heard a voice, one he immediately recognized: it was Doctor Axlow.

"Zalthor, wake up," said the voice. "Let's go! Wake up."

Mark looked around and didn't see anyone. The voice seemed to come from behind the walls. The detective looked at the pills and realized he no longer needed to take them. His vision blurred. The glass fell from his hand, hitting the floor and shattering, splashing water and shards beside the bed. He quickly lost consciousness, lying awkwardly on the bed, with his head resting between the headboard and a pillow.

Chapter 32

When Mark opened his eyes, he was once again inhabiting the body of Zalthor Acri, reclining on an armchair. He raised his back, sitting upright, and noticed he was in a well-illuminated room. Adjacent to the armchair, he saw a collection of devices resembling those found in a hospital setting. On the opposite side, Doctor Axlow sat on a small stool, attentively observing the data displayed on a screen before him.

Mark sensed a hair cap tightly fitted around his head and examined it, detecting slender wires connecting to the apparatus.

The Doctor noticed Mark's awakening and offered a smile.

"Zalthor, you have conjured an incredibly impressive dream within your mind. I must admit, you have crafted stunning landscapes: intricate geological formations and vibrant forests, teeming with diverse flora and fauna. However, the race of dominant living beings appears to lack a sense of purpose or direction."

Doctor Axlow rose, approached the device adjacent to the chair, and pressed a series of buttons. Suddenly, the larger screen of the equipment displayed Mark in his own world. It showed a sequence of images recorded a few hours ago, capturing the detective's purchase of the pill bottle from the young man near Aurora Street. As Mark watched the recording, he felt a pang of embarrassment, observing his nervous demeanor during the transaction—constantly glancing around, anxious about being recognized by someone he knew.

"So, is this the life you lead within your imaginary world? I surmise you must be relieved to have returned to being Zalthor Acri, rather than remaining this pitiable creature," stated the Doctor. "Observing this Mark Randall, as you named yourself in this dream, one can only see a traumatized, aged, neglected individual—a friendless man abandoned by the very universe he created. I am certain that when you initially beheld your reflection as Zalthor and stood beside Lintsa, you marveled at the fortunate escape from your former existence."

Mark removed the cap from his head, got up, and walked to the window situated at the corner of the room. Gazing upon the landscape, he realized he had returned to the capital of the planet Dolmen, inside Zalthor's Castle.

The detective turned to the Doctor and approached the Hubbian.

"You attacked Delasher, didn't you?" Mark inquired. "You erased him from my mind."

"I apologize for this intrusion into your privacy, Zalthor, but I could not allow that unwanted projection to roam freely. Delasher would wield a negative influence over you. He belongs to a group of individuals who aim to convince you that this dream within your mind is a genuine world. They might succeed in persuading you to return to the abyss from which we rescued you, forsaking your magnificent life as Zalthor Acri and opting to exist solely within an obscure dream. Such an abomination cannot be permitted. You deserve far more than that, my dear friend."

Mark approached one of the devices near the armchair and looked at its screen. He witnessed himself at the very moment he confronted the Archbishop on Aurora Street, followed by the ensuing seismic event, where people were flung into the air and tumbled along the ground.

"How can I rewind this recording?" Mark inquired.

The Doctor pointed to a red controller positioned above the device's screen.

"Turn this knob backward and adjust the speed as you desire."

Mark carefully manipulated the controller as instructed by the Doctor. The recording moved back and forth a few times until the detective comprehended the sensitivity of the mechanism.

The video paused just moments before the strong tremor takes place. The screen exhibited a close-up of Mark's body, with clenched fists raised in front of his chest, and a furious expression on his face.

"What is that?" the detective asked, pointing to a yellow glow surrounding his body on the screen.

The Doctor approached the device and examined the image.

"It seems to be some kind of aura. It originates from your dream. I cannot provide a precise explanation. It might be a form of energy that you emitted."

"Can I navigate around the image?"

"Utilize this small joystick beneath the screen. It will enable you to explore the surroundings."

Using the controller indicated by Doctor Axlow, Mark navigated through the frozen scenery of Aurora Street. He caught sight of the Archbishop's face, wide-eyed and filled with fear as he gazed at the detective. The brightness of Mark's aura illuminated Euzebius' face.

"Why is this of such interest to you?" Doctor Axlow questioned.

Mark looked at the Doctor and spoke with authority in his voice.

"Listen, Axlow. Where are Fhastina and Physter? I need to speak with them."

The Doctor turned off the device's screen and replied, "Are you referring to the Zarconians who rescued you in B-23? They were apprehended a few hours ago. We have determined that they were responsible for invading your mind."

"Can I see them? Are they present in this castle?"

"Unfortunately, I have not been informed of their whereabouts. It is possible that they are no longer on this planet."

Doctor Axlow proceeded to the corner of the room, picked up a coat hanging on a coat rack, and put it on. Mark observed his actions attentively, sensing that Axlow might not have been entirely truthful about his knowledge of Fhastina and Physter's location. However, the detective decided not to confront the Doctor at that moment.

"I need to return to my own planet, Zalthor. Lintsa awaits you on the main terrace of the castle. She wishes to take you to a place that will provide insights into your past. I shall return in two days to monitor your recovery."

Doctor Axlow pressed a button beside the room's exit, and the door quickly opened, allowing him to leave.

"Axlow, who is Dana?" Mark inquired, causing the Doctor to interrupt his departure.

For a few prolonged seconds, Axlow remained silent. Mark discerned that the question has angered the Doctor. It was evident from his clenched fists.

"She is a criminal, Zalthor, a wanted criminal. Dana has been manipulating the minds of Hubbians for countless millennia, persuading them to forsake immortality and bury themselves in deep holes in the pursuit of upholding the allegedly authentic worlds she espouses. Therefore, if I may offer you a single piece of advice: stay away from this woman. She will lead you to a choice you will regret forever."

Doctor Axlow withdrew, walking with purposeful steps until he disappeared into the hallway outside the room.

Chapter 33

On the main terrace of the castle, Lintsa awaited Mark inside a compact transport vehicle, deftly operating a few buttons on its dashboard. She noticed her companion approaching and immediately discerned a sense of concern in his demeanor.

Mark walked with a lowered head, taking slow and measured steps, as if carrying a burden on his shoulders. However, a smile graced his face upon seeing the Hubbian woman.

"Is everything okay?" Lintsa inquired, stepping out of the vehicle.

The detective pondered whether he should disclose his recent conversation with Dr. Axlow. However, suspecting that Lintsa might be aligned with the doctor's perspective, he chose not to broach the subject.

"Yes, I'm fine. Just reflecting on matters from my world, you know? The one that still exists within here," Mark responded, lightly tapping his index finger against his forehead.

Lintsa smiled and embraced her companion.

"Do not fret about the troubles of this world, my dear. You are with me now."

The two Hubbians exchanged an affectionate kiss, and Mark pointed toward the vehicle.

"Where are we going next?"

"Lintsa took hold of the detective's hand and guided him into the transport vehicle.

"We are going to a place that will help you recall your former life."

A short while later, the transport vehicle descended onto a vast square, facing a colossal building. The edifice stood approximately eighty feet tall, divided into four expansive levels, spanning nearly half a mile in width. Sturdy columns encircled the entire external wall of the façade. Directly in front of the entrance staircase, a monumental fountain commanded attention, adorned by imposing stone statues.

Mark and Lintsa disembarked from the vehicle. Despite their prominence and importance on the planet, there were no bodyguards present to protect the couple. The detective presumed that such measures were likely unnecessary, as no individual in the vicinity possessed the capability to threaten two immortal and converted Hubbians so powerful. Nevertheless, the couple was surrounded by a throng of onlookers eager to catch a glimpse of and greet the leaders of Dolmen. The people exuded elation at the return of the legendary Zalthor Acri. Mark noticed Lintsa moving away, now standing beside the fountain, her eyes fixed on the bustling crowd, a smile adorning her face.

As the commotion gradually subsided and the crowd dispersed, Mark managed to approach the Hubbian woman. He studied the fountain more closely, observing the towering sculptures that embellished the ornate structure. The two most prominent statues, positioned at the center, depicted Zalthor and Lintsa. Zalthor's physique was portrayed as even more muscular and athletic than what Mark observed in his own reflection. The statue of the Hubbian woman featured curves that were more accentuated than her actual form. From Mark's perspective, it was an artistic exaggeration that failed to capture the true beauty of the genuine Lintsa.

The detective also examined the smaller statues. He recognized a depiction of Doctor Axlow, seated in front of Zalthor's image. Another sculpture, positioned to their right, depicted Pheldon, the adversary Mark defeated to reclaim the planet.

On the left side of the statues, two other Hubbians were portrayed. Mark immediately identified one of them as Ranson, the stout Hubbian who stood by his side during the retaking of Dolmen. However, he didn't recognize the curly-haired Hubbian with one hand resting on Ranson's shoulder. Despite his smooth facial features, his physical stature suggested he was almost as formidable as Zalthor himself.

"Who is the one with Ranson? The curly-haired one," Mark asked, gently gripping Lintsa's arm and pointing to the sculpture. "I don't recall seeing him among the Hubbians I've encountered so far."

Lintsa gazed sadly at the sculpture.

"His name is Juscieh. He disappeared a few millennia before you did. That's why he didn't come to Dolmen."

"So, he went through the same thing as me. Are you and Ranson also looking for him?"

"Yes. Since Juscieh vanished, Ranson has been tirelessly searching for him. But we haven't found any leads regarding his whereabouts."

"He's the missing friend Ranson mentioned when we first met, isn't he?"

"To Ranson, Juscieh was more than a friend; he was a companion. However, Ranson chose to interrupt his search and come here to aid you in retaking the planet Dolmen," the Hubbian woman replied.

"It's a shame," Mark commented. "This Juscieh must have been really important for us to be portrayed in this sculpture."

"You and Juscieh fought together in all the major battles of the Zort Wars," Lintsa revealed.

"Did Pheldon also fight alongside me?"

"You and Pheldon were close friends for the majority of your lives, Zalthor. That's why Pheldon resided in Dolmen when you disappeared, despite you occasionally mentioning some negative aspects of his behavior to me."

Mark listened to Lintsa's account but wasn't inclined to discuss Zalthor's friendship with Pheldon. The Hubbian couple ascended the stairs leading to the entrance of the building, but the detective noticed that the place was closed.

Before Mark could inquire further, Lintsa spoke, "This is the Historical Museum of Dolmen. It has been closed by Pheldon's order for the past few millennia, but it will reopen in a few days. I thought it would be a good idea for us to visit the museum before its official opening. Today, we can explore it undisturbed. Here, you will learn about your past. Perhaps it will aid in recalling your former life as Zalthor."

"It's a pretty big museum, isn't it?" Mark spoke, contemplating the façade of the building. "How long will we stay there?"

"It contains hundreds of thousands of years of history, honey," Lintsa replied. "But do not worry. We are not going to visit the entire museum. This would take weeks long."

Lintsa smiled and held Mark's hand, pulling his companion into the building.

The first section of the Historical Museum of Dolmen that Mark and Lintsa visited was filled with thousands of disparate objects. There was a lack of harmony or contextualization in the exhibits, giving the impression of sprawling and haphazard collections.

"For hundreds of thousands of years, the planet Dolmen has been a member of the Galactic Confederation," narrated Lintsa. "The Confederation replaced the old Galactic Council. While the Council aimed only to destroy the Zort Empire, the Confederation has a much more comprehensive mission. It has been actively preventing dictators from seizing power in developing planetary systems and preventing militarized civilizations from oppressing weaker populations. Whenever the Confederation assists a planet or civilization, it receives gifts from the leaders of these peoples. These gifts can range from large precious metal statues to rustic handcrafted objects. The nature of the gifts depends on the economic conditions, culture, or technological advancement of the nation that received the aid. You had requested that an entire floor of that museum be dedicated to storing the gifts donated to the Confederation as a way to honor those peoples."

Lintsa and Mark walked through the exhibits calmly, observing the objects. However, as they passed in front of one of the displays, the expression on the face of the Hubbian woman changed, becoming more serious.

"Unfortunately, many of these nations had already vanished. Some went silent for hundreds of thousands of years, and when we revisited them, they were no longer in existence. They had been replaced by civilizations that, at the time of their last contact, were insignificant or even non-existent. Many objects on this floor serve as unique examples of extinct cultures. This section was highly sought after by researchers and students from all over the Galaxy."

The two Hubbians reached a tall, wide staircase situated in the center of the building and proceeded to climb up to the next floor.

"The second floor is dedicated to our former planet, Hubberia," explained Lintsa. "Our birth planet was destroyed by a Zort-built ray cannon. The Zorts were the dominant civilization in the Galaxy during the time when Doctor Axlow developed the

Converter Chamber. They fired a concentrated beam of energy against Hubberia, penetrating its lower layers and reaching the planet's core, causing it to explode and scattering debris throughout the system. For thousands of years, a group of Hubbians tirelessly scoured the area, searching for any recognizable fragments. Despite the planet's destruction and the survival of only the immortal converted Hubbians, hundreds of thousands of objects were salvaged."

Mark and Lintsa walked past a collection of vehicles that bore a striking resemblance to the automobiles in Mark's world.

"This section is one of the most remarkable," Lintsa continued. "Hubbians always had a fondness for this type of land transport. When the Zorts first arrived on our planet, our people had not yet developed efficient flying vehicles, and everyone enjoyed these models that ran on wheels and used liquid fuel. It was primitive but enjoyable."

Lintsa stopped in front of a large red sport utility vehicle. It featured a sleek body with four wide wooden-paneled doors and elongated rear windows, indicating a roomy trunk. The Hubbian woman gazed at the vehicle and let out a sigh. Mark noticed that her eyes were watery.

"My father used to drive a transport vehicle like this," Lintsa reminisced. "I remember it vividly! When I was seven or eight years old, he would use it to take the whole family on vacation trips. My parents would fill the trunk with bags and belongings. During the journey, my siblings and I would move everything to the backseat, and eventually, we would end up in the trunk. We loved keeping our faces pressed against the rear window, watching the road fall behind us. When Dad found out what we had done, he scolded us but didn't take any further action. I saw his face in the rear-view mirror and noticed that he was smiling, simply because we were happy."

Mark pondered how the vehicle resembled the old models in his world, not the modern cars filled with electronic gadgets and plastic components that are commonly available today, but rather the cars he traveled in during his childhood. For a few seconds, he envisioned himself in the trunk of that vehicle, peering out the window at the road, and memories of his own childhood resurfaced.

The tour continued, and the couple now stopped in front of a large glass wall. Behind it, there was a depiction of what appeared to be the interior of a middle-class family home.

"This is a replica of a typical middle-class Hubbian residence from the time when our birth planet still existed," explained Lintsa.

Mark carefully examined the representation before him. Life-sized sculptures depicted a family that bore a striking resemblance to typical middle-class individuals in his own world. The furniture in the living room even reminded him of his own home, not the somber apartment he currently occupies but the dwelling he shared with his wife and daughter years ago.

The two Hubbians continued walking, and Lintsa pointed out a depiction of a garden with a large swimming pool in the background.

"I'd rather not see this. Let's proceed straight ahead," Mark requested.

"You're acting like Doctor Axlow. He doesn't enjoy visiting this floor either. He always says it makes him feel uncomfortable. But perhaps it's a positive sign. Maybe this visit is rekindling memories from before your disappearance," Lintsa remarked.

"Not exactly," Mark responded. "Let's head to the stairs."

Mark and Lintsa ascended to the third floor of the museum. The detective immediately noticed a change in the lighting ambiance. Warm tones now replaced the cool colors of the previous floors.

The third floor primarily consisted of spectacular depictions of battles. There were several statues of Zalthor himself. In these reproductions, he always appeared at the highest point, holding the Heart of Hubbian sword. Pheldon and Juscieh were consistently shown by his side, facing enemies or protecting their allies. In many representations, Zalthor's allies were seen shooting or slashing their enemies. However, he was never shown fighting. Zalthor was always depicted with his sword raised, as if just displaying it rather than using it to harm anyone.

"You ordered that you should never be portrayed attacking an opponent," Lintsa reported. "That's why you always struck this pose in the depictions."

Lintsa and Mark approached a representation of an event that seemed to have been very important. They were now in the center of the floor.

"This is the moment when you finally met the King of Zorts, Torlox. He is the one kneeling in front of you."

The detective observed the enormous representation. Zalthor and Torlox were at the top of a staircase, in front of the Zort King's throne. The Hubbian pointed his sword at the king, who knelt before him. Several other Hubbians stood around the scene, including Pheldon and Juscieh, while numerous Zort soldiers appeared to have surrendered.

It was the first time Mark saw what the so-called Zorts looked like. The ancient enemies of the Hubbians were humanoid, but their bodies were covered in reptile scales. They had elongated snouts, and many had large teeth, while others had long necks or horns. Indeed, the Zorts had an appearance reminiscent of the colossal beings that once dominated Mark's world tens of millions of years ago and went extinct after a massive meteor's fall.

The couple continued walking and found various other depictions, but now, instead of battle scenes, they witnessed moments of camaraderie. In these scenes, Zalthor was often depicted receiving gifts. Lintsa was now also shown in the depictions.

"This was a new phase of your life after we met. These people were liberated or assisted and were paying tribute to us before we left their planets," explained Lintsa. "These are the gifts you saw on the first floor."

In one of the depictions, there was a large banner behind a group of humanoid foxes thanking Zalthor. It was written in bold letters: 'Zalthor, the Galaxy Liberator.'

Finally, the couple reached the top floor of the building.

"This floor is entirely dedicated to your life, honey. Here we have objects and depictions from your childhood to moments shortly before you disappeared," explained Lintsa.

The two paused before an imposing painting. The image dominated the entrance to the floor. The immense picture depicted portraits of a Hubbian man and woman. The man had strong, prominent features, while the woman had a softer, more gentle appearance.

"These were your parents, Doltrod and Menfita," informed Lintsa.

"I can clearly see that I took after my mother," Mark observed. "What happened to my parents? Didn't they become immortal like us?"

"You were already very old when you were converted, dear. Unfortunately, your parents had passed away many years before the Converter Chamber started to work."

Zalthor and Lintsa walked toward a representation of a scene resembling a living room.

"Two floors below, we saw something similar to this, didn't we?" asked Mark. "But this house seems to be more modest."

"Yes, you're right," Lintsa replied. "That was a typical room in a Hubbian house, but this one here reproduces the house where you spent your childhood, a million years ago."

In the representation, there was a tube television, with a sofa and a humble rug in front. Sitting on the couch were two adults, whom Mark immediately recognized as the Hubbians portrayed in the painting, Doltrod and Menfita—Zalthor's parents. On the rug in front of them, there were two boys who bore a strong resemblance to each other, but one seemed to be older.

"Which one of these boys am I?" asked Mark.

"You are the smaller one," Lintsa replied. "The bigger one was your older brother. His name was Chiron."

"So, I had a brother! But what happened to him? Did he also pass away before he could be converted?"

Mark noticed a saddened look on Lintsa's face.

"Unfortunately, Chiron lost his life at a young age. He spent three years as a prisoner in a Zort concentration camp."

"A Zort concentration camp?! Did these Zorts have concentration camps?"

"Yes, Chiron was taken to the home planet of the Zorts, Troctalia. Your brother was accused of participating in an attack against the Zort Ambassador on the planet Hubberia."

"It seems to me that these Zorts were a big problem for the Hubbians for a long time, right?"

"When the Zorts arrived on Hubberia, they seemed friendly. They claimed to be a peaceful people, aiming to bring development to less advanced civilizations in the Galaxy. In exchange, they wanted a few natural resources that were rare in their planetary system. At first, they provided us with some technology and seemed to want to build a fair relationship with the Hubbians. However, as the Zorts took control of the main Hubbian institutions, they started to impose harsh and unfair rules on our people. They exploited our ancestral planet for about sixty years before the Conversion Processes began."

As the couple continued walking through the representations, Mark saw many images of himself alongside his brother.

"It seems that my brother and I were very close," he observed.

"Yes, you always spoke to me about your brother with great admiration. Before you went missing, you always named your personal spaceships 'Chiron.' I remember that your last ship, the one that crashed into moon B-23, was called 'Chiron 137.' You said it made you feel like your brother was still accompanying you."

Suddenly, in one of the representations, a very short and thin boy appeared. He wore oversized glasses and had a prominent nose.

"This is Doctor Axlow when he was still a boy," Lintsa informed. "You met him when you were eight years old. Axlow was a small and frail child, but his intellect set him apart from other boys his age. The Doctor always said that your friendship saved him many years of therapy. You protected Axlow numerous times, even ending up in the hospital after confronting three bullies who tried to attack him. You both ended up getting the worst of the fight, but it forged a lifelong friendship and, above all, a bond that changed the entire destiny of our people."

Lintsa gently took hold of Zalthor's arm and led him down another corridor.

"Come, I'm going to show you something you'll enjoy."

The two Hubbians reached the depiction of a forest with vibrant crawling plants and trees with elongated trunks.

"This was one of your most renowned adventures. It took place several thousand years before your disappearance. You,

Ranson, and Juscieh crash-landed on a wild and unknown planet called Valiana. After the crash, your ship was reduced to ashes, leaving you isolated without any means of communication. Perhaps you would have remained there until the present time if you hadn't built a nuclear reactor practically from scratch."

"I built a nuclear reactor? That's impressive!" Mark exclaimed, recalling that, in his world, he wouldn't be capable of constructing an electricity-powered engine.

"That wasn't your judgment at the time. You always regretted not being able to build a warp engine, which would have allowed you to escape the nebula surrounding the planet Valiana in significantly less time."

"What's a warp engine?" Mark asked, recollecting having heard the term in some television program in his world.

"It's an engine capable of traveling faster than light," Lintsa replied. "It enables us to traverse the Galaxy in a matter of days instead of thousands of years."

"So, after that incident, I learned how to build this warp engine, right?"

Lintsa burst into laughter.

"Actually, I have to tell you: that's something you put off until the day you went missing."

"How lazy of me!" exclaimed the detective, breaking into a wide smile. His eyes revealed a desire for Lintsa, and she sensed his intentions. Mark decided that he had heard enough about Zalthor's life. He pulled Lintsa closer, embracing her waist, and shared a long kiss with the Hubbian woman.

Chapter 34

In the main suite of the castle, Mark and Lintsa rested under a thin sheet. They lay on the large bed positioned at the center of the room. Lintsa slept lightly, her face gently resting on Mark's chest.

Mark carefully pushed the sheet aside, gently placed a pillow under Lintsa's head, and rose from the bed. He slipped on a pair of pants and walked toward the spacious balcony connected to the room. The daylight still illuminated the surroundings, allowing Mark to observe the entire city laid out before him. Dolmen's capital buzzed with activity as thousands of flying ships, in various shapes and sizes, traversed the sky above the castle.

Lintsa joined Mark, her arms tenderly embracing his waist as she spoke, "What are you thinking, honey?"

"It's fascinating how this city seems to have returned to its normal rhythm after everything that occurred yesterday," Mark observed.

"This is the outcome of centuries of hard work, honey," Lintsa explained. "Thanks to your efforts, Dolmen possesses robust institutions that sustained the planet's prosperity even during Pheldon's reign. Our strategy was to make Pheldon believe he had control over the planet. I suspect he cared more about his own ego and privileges within the castle than about his authority over the planet's economy and infrastructure."

Mark smiled appreciatively but kept his gaze fixed on the capital. After a few moments of contemplation, he shifted his attention to Lintsa and raised a new topic.

"Listen, Lintsa, I heard about someone who might help me uncover my true identity. A woman named Dana. Do you know her?"

Lintsa released her embrace and turned her gaze to the landscape. "Yes, I heard of her. Dana is a well-known figure among the Hubbians."

"Doctor Axlow considers her a criminal and advised me to stay away from her. Do you share the same thought?" Mark inquired.

"Who told you that?" Lintsa's expression shifted to a disapproving surprise.

"Tell me, Lintsa, was it you who ordered Fhastina and Physter's apprehension, or was it Doctor Axlow?" Mark's question carried a hint of suspicion.

Stepping back, Lintsa's expression became stern. "Zalthor Acri, do you see me as a high school teenager? Do you believe I would conspire to keep you from meeting anyone you wish? Do you think I would implore you to abandon the world you've constructed in your mind? You are free to go and pursue whatever path you desire, my dear," Lintsa responded sharply. "I am a million years old. I believe that is enough time to mature and accept that your future choices may not include me, even if it pains me."

Mark was taken aback. For the first time, inhabiting Zalthor's body, he felt embarrassed. "I apologize, Lintsa. I didn't mean to offend you. We spent a million years together. Would you let me go so easily? In my world, people take aggressive actions toward breakups in much shorter relationships."

Lintsa forced a smile. "Come with me. I will show you something."

Mark and Lintsa entered a small room, which appeared to be a storage space for small tech equipment, with cabinets and drawers lining the walls.

Lintsa opened one of the drawers, took out a metal bracelet, and showed it to Mark. "Do you recognize this?" asked the Hubbian woman.

The detective examined the object. "I had one of these on my wrist when I was rescued from that moon, but I must confess, I'm not sure what it is."

"This is a plutonium-beam bracelet, Zalthor. It was the one on your arm when Fhastina and Physter rescued you. When your spaceship crashed into the surface of Moon B-23, everything on board was destroyed except for your body and this bracelet. It was designed to be almost indestructible and emitted long-range signals, helping us locate Hubbians who experienced accidents like yours. Without this device, we might never have found you. Doctor Axlow developed it shortly after you, Ranson, and Juscieh went missing on Valiana. It sends out a special kind of signal that could have penetrated even the nebula surrounding that planet."

Mark reached out to Lintsa and took the bracelet. "But... if I had this attached to me, why did you take so long to find me?"

"Because the bracelet only started sending signals a week ago. Prior to that, we believed it had malfunctioned. It wouldn't have been the first time. As I mentioned, it's 'almost' indestructible. These bracelets don't always continue functioning after impacts like the one you experienced. When we received the signal, I thought you had repaired it or replicated its frequency using some other device you had constructed. However, upon finding you, we realized you were too weak to have done something like that."

Mark remained silent, sensing sadness in Lintsa's voice. Continuing, the Hubbian woman said, "After we rescued you, I asked the ship's computer to analyze the bracelet's internal mechanism. It reported that the mechanism was in perfect working order, but the computer also provided an operating log, revealing that the bracelet had been programmed a few hours before your disappearance. It was set to remain silent for ten thousand years and only resume sending signals last week."

Lintsa looked at Mark with teary eyes. "Do you understand what this means, Zalthor?"

Mark pondered for a moment and said, "It means that Zalthor, or rather, I, had already planned to be trapped on that moon for a specific period of time. So my collision with Moon B-23 was not an accident."

Mark returned the bracelet to Lintsa, noticing a tear rolling down her cheek. Lintsa wiped her eyes. "I must admit, at first, it wasn't easy to know that you had intentionally left me behind. That's why I didn't stay by your side until you arrived on Doctor Axlow's Planet. I needed time to process what I had discovered. You see, I'm not as insensitive as you may think."

Mark gently held Lintsa's shoulders, his voice filled with concern. "Why would I do that? Why would I abandon a fabulous woman like you and the life I had here, just to be alone, buried miles beneath a desert moon?"

Lintsa's expression reflected her own confusion. "That's the question I've been facing since I discovered the bracelet was programmed."

Lintsa released herself from Mark's grasp, returning the bracelet to the same drawer from which she had taken it. "This woman named Dana," Lintsa sighed, her voice tinged with uncertainty. "Perhaps she holds the answers you seek."

"Will you lead me to her?" Mark asked, holding Lintsa's hand.

"I don't know where this Dana is, my dear. I'm sure her allies wouldn't permit me to approach her, especially not now. However, I do know someone who can guide you to her."

Chapter 35

Mark entered a dark and silent underground corridor in the castle. He walked slowly, carefully surveying his surroundings. The area was lined with multiple doors, each bearing a large number on top. Eventually, he located the door with the number Lintsa had provided: forty-two.

Beside the door, there was a hand-shaped reader sensor. Mark placed his hand on the device, and the mechanism recognized him as Zalthor Acri. The door quickly ascended, revealing the entrance.

Beyond the opened door, Mark found a modest room. Adjacent to a narrow bed, there was a small refrigerator, and a television mounted high on the wall played some sort of planet Dolmen program. It was a comfortable room, for a prison.

A humanoid being was sitting on the bed. It had an eagle-like head. Upon noticing Zalthor's presence, the shiny beak of the humanoid formed a wide smile.

"Hello, Mark Randall," greeted the humanoid.

"Hi, Physter," Mark replied, a smirk forming on his face. "Or should I call you Delasher?"

"Call me Physter, Mark Randall. Delasher was merely an avatar I used to visit your world, disguising myself as one of your people. I couldn't reveal my true form. This Zarconian face would scare your people," Physter responded, pointing to his eagle beak.

Mark stepped into the cell.

"In my world, your avatar instructed me to find someone named Dana. Can you guide me to her?"

Physter rose from the bed. He seemed energized.

"We must act swiftly then. If Doctor Axlow discovers that you have freed me, he might go as far as attempting to kill me to prevent you from finding Dana."

"Do you believe the Doctor would go to such lengths?"

"I wouldn't put it past him. But tell me, how did you manage to locate me here?"

"Lintsa informed me of your whereabouts. She won't let Doctor Axlow harm you."

"Has Lintsa accepted the fact that you are going to meet Dana?"

"Not only has she accepted it, but she has also made her ship and a pilot available to transport us to Dana."

"We cannot travel to Dana's Planet on Lintsa's ship, Mark Randall. That would expose our location to Doctor Axlow. He might attempt to intercept you before you can speak with Dana. Do you comprehend?"

"Yes, I comprehend."

"We will travel on my ship."

A short while later, Mark and Physter were aboard the Zarconian's spaceship. The vessel was smaller and less equipped compared to Lintsa's ship, but it provided ample space and sufficient structure for its two occupants.

Mark was situated in a small yet cozy chamber that resembled a living room. A sizable window lay ahead, offering a view of the planet Dolmen gradually receding. He heard the reverberation of a high-pitched sound, and Physter's voice emanated from a loudspeaker installed in the ceiling.

"I advise you to brace yourself, Mark Randall. The ship is about to accelerate a lot."

Mark noticed several colored bars positioned around him and grabbed one of them.

The high-pitched sound intensified, and the disk of the planet Dolmen vanished from the window. Mark felt his body being propelled backward but maintained a firm grip on the colored bar. The spaceship tilted until it reached a position where the entire acceleration force acted as gravity, allowing the detective to release the bar.

A door in front of Mark opened, revealing Physter. The Zarconian carried two glasses and a bottle containing a clear liquid. He placed one of the glasses in front of Mark and proceeded to pour the drink.

"We have initiated a warp journey. Our speed will enable us to traverse a star system within minutes. However, the galaxy is vast, and Dana's Planet lies many star systems away. It will take us a full day to reach the planet."

"What about the world within my mind? Will it experience any further seismic events or catastrophes during this time?" Mark inquired.

"Not significantly if you return to sleep, Mark Randall. This will ensure the preservation of your world until we meet Dana."

"I don't feel particularly sleepy at the moment, Physter. With so much on my mind, I'm unsure if I'll be able to sleep. Do you have any medication that can help me fall asleep?"

"Immortal converted Hubbians like you are unaffected by medication, Mark Randall. However, this spaceship is equipped with a room specifically designed for situations like yours. Inside that room, you will receive a combination of light and sound frequencies that will help you fall asleep within minutes. But first, have a drink with me. We have a few minutes."

Mark took a sip from the drink presented by Physter. The liquid had a sweet taste with a subtle hint of cherry. Tiny gas bubbles danced along Mark's throat as he drank.

"What about Fhastina? What has the Doctor done to her?" Physter inquired.

"Lintsa informed me that she would release Fhastina as soon as you and I departed Dolmen. However, Fhastina is forbidden from leaving the planet. Lintsa asked me to choose between the two of you, and I had already deduced that you and Delasher were the same individual." The detective gazed at his own hand. "It was because of what I felt when we shook hands in the castle hall. You did something to me there, didn't you?"

"You must be referring to the small pulse of energy you felt when I shook your hand. It's impressive how perceptive you are! I made an effort to ensure you didn't feel anything unusual in that moment," Physter explained, taking a sip of his drink. "When Delasher was inside you, he wasn't me. He was merely a copy of my mind manifested as one of your kind. While he was in your world, my mind and Delasher's mind remained completely separate. However, when I squeezed your hand, Delasher was able to establish a connection with me. In those few seconds, everything he had witnessed and discussed with you was transferred to my mind, becoming my memories as well."

"So, you know about my world?"

"I could see everything Delasher saw up until that handshake. Unfortunately, Doctor Axlow erased him from your world, and I no longer have visibility into what took place afterward. That's why I need to know: has your perspective changed since our second conversation at the restaurant?"

"After you shook my hand, we had one more brief conversation. It occurred following a devastating seismic event in my world. Many lives were lost in that event, and Delasher claimed it was my fault. The magnitude of the tragedy made me realize that this world we are currently in, the world of Zalthor Acri, is not a mere figment of my imagination but something real. Furthermore, it became apparent that my world, the world of Mark Randall, is in genuine peril."

"What are your thoughts on the matter? Are you willing to let an entire universe perish just to exist here as Zalthor Acri?"

Mark remained silent for a moment, avoiding eye contact with Physter. His gesture revealed his discomfort in providing an answer.

"That's precisely why you need to meet Dana, Mark Randall."

"Do you believe this woman can change my final decision?"

"I believe the future of an entire universe rests on Dana's ability to persuade you to make the right choice. I'm certain she will put forth great effort to accomplish that."

Mark looked up at Physter.

"Tell me, who exactly is this Dana? Why would she have the power to alter my beliefs?"

"Because she is like you."

"What do you mean by that?"

"She is a Hubbian, like you, and she was also a Constructor."

"So, what became of the world she constructed? Was she able to preserve it while living here?"

"It is impossible to sustain an entire universe within your mind and remain conscious, Mark Randall. Some Hubbians have attempted to spend most of their time asleep in a bid to preserve their worlds, but this only prolonged the suffering of the civilizations within their minds, with calamities and dreadful plagues gradually extinguishing billions of lives. There is no way out! You must decide which universe you will inhabit."

"So, Dana made her choice then?"

"That's correct."

"And now she wants to convince me to do the opposite of what she did?"

"Exactly."

"But why should I trust her, considering she allowed her world to be destroyed?"

"Because she possesses knowledge far beyond what you can imagine. Believe me, after you talk to Dana, no matter who you choose to be in the future, whether it's Mark Randall or Zalthor Acri, you'll never be the same."

Mark remained silent, and Physter took the cue to rise from his seat.

"But don't dwell on it now, Mark Randall. Let's proceed to your room. I will lull you to sleep again before there's no longer a world within your mind left to save."

Chapter 36

On Monday at 7 o'clock in the morning, the Leticia Andraus Farm witnessed a group of eight workers gathered around a barn that was at risk of collapsing. The structure was leaning to one side but had withstood the previous day's seismic event. The men were securing ropes to the roof in an attempt to prevent the building from toppling over.

The farm manager, a middle-aged strong man named Edward, carefully assessed the construction. Although he was not an engineer, he had extensive experience as a carpenter, and the barn was made of wood. He examined the areas that required repair or reinforcement. His workers tugged on the ropes with force, striving to restore the structure to its original position.

"Take it easy, guys. If you pull too hard, it might lean in the opposite direction," Edward advised.

Suddenly, a young man standing beside Edward tapped him on the shoulder.

"Boss, take a look at that!"

Edward turned his gaze toward the entrance of the farm and noticed a cloud of dust billowing up. It originated approximately two miles away, on the gravel road leading to the farm. His initial thought was that the farm owner might be arriving to inspect the damage caused by yesterday's seismic event. However, the significant amount of dust suggested a large number of vehicles approaching.

"Hold on a moment!" Edward shouted to the workers. He turned to the young man beside him. "Keep an eye on the men. I need to see what's going on."

Edward mounted a horse and headed toward the farm's entrance. As he reached the gate, he saw ten police cars parked in a row, forming an arch in front of the property.

A gentle breeze brushed against the manager's face, providing a brief moment of pleasure. It was the first positive sensation he had experienced that day, but the arrival of the police cars indicated it might be the last.

The rear doors of a vehicle at the center of the row swung open, and Mark and Andrew stepped out of the car.

Mark held a sheet of paper and raised it so that Edward could see.

"My name is Mark Randall," he spoke up. "I'm a detective from the police department. This document in my hands is a search warrant issued by Judge Robert Brown."

"What are you searching for?" Edward asked, remaining on his horse.

"We are looking for a girl named Carol Sinclair or any evidence related to her, alive or deceased," the detective replied.

"Hold on, let me talk to my men," the manager reacted.

"I don't think you understand, my friend. We are going in now, and you will remain right where you are!" Mark ordered.

Armed police officers started to emerge from all the vehicles.

Half an hour later, on a large terrace at the top of the farm's main house, Mark leaned against the railing and surveyed the surroundings with a pair of binoculars. He searched for any signs of a place where someone could be held captive or traces on the ground indicating a possible burial site.

The detective spotted a large utility vehicle approaching from the same road that he and the other officers arrived on. It was a big luxury SUV, likely armored.

Andrew appeared at the entrance to the terrace and joined Mark.

"I've dispatched a team to search the plantation field. We have ten men walking in a line, meticulously combing every inch of land. But it's a vast property, and it could take them hours. The rest of the team is inspecting the main house and other buildings," the young detective reported.

"We need to keep a close watch on all the farm employees. Nobody should leave this property until we're finished," Mark asserted.

"The farm employees seem quite tense. Something is definitely troubling them," Andrew deduced. "I'm keeping an eye on the manager, the guy who welcomed us. He's trembling like a leaf. He claims it's due to the cold since we arrived, but I suspect there's more to it."

"He wouldn't be so nervous without a good reason. It must be the same concern that drew them here," Mark observed, gesturing toward the utility vehicle, which was now parking directly in front of the main house.

Andrew noticed Mark's intense gaze fixed on the car.

"Is it the Mayor?" the young detective asked.

"Or perhaps his son," Mark replied.

Simultaneously, all four doors of the vehicle swung open. Two enormous, stern-faced men in dark suits emerged from the front seats. Charles Andraus and his son, Paul Andraus, stepped out from the back seat. The Mayor's son swiftly entered the house, berating two police officers stationed by the door. Charles, on the other hand, walked without haste. Along the way, he looked up at the terrace and spotted the presence of the two detectives. The Mayor waved at them.

"It seems we've managed to irk the Mayor's family," Andrew commented. "Let's hope this doesn't cause any complications for us."

Mark overheard Paul shouting at the officer near the entrance of the house, but he couldn't discern the Mayor's son's words.

"Go downstairs and calm the young man down before any incident occurs between him and the guards. I'll stay here. I'm certain Charles is heading this way," Mark instructed Andrew.

"First, I need to pick up a coat from the car. This cold weather is really getting to me," Andrew replied, departing from the terrace.

Mark resumed surveying the surroundings. The farm was truly vast. Despite the land being exceptionally flat and the main house situated at a high point, he couldn't see the boundaries of the property.

The detective examined his bare arms, covered only by the thin fabric of his shirt. He realized that he didn't feel the cold that bothered Andrew. The trees in front of the main house swayed in the wind, and Mark raised his hands, attempting to sense the breeze passing through his fingers, but he couldn't perceive even the slightest movement of the air.

At the entrance to the terrace, Mayor Charles Andraus appeared. He stood still, facing Mark from a distance. The Mayor was the same age as the detective. However, despite being much wealthier, he appeared to be about ten years older. Sparse gray hair only covered the sides and back of his head. Large bags of fat under his eyes were evidence of excessive alcohol consumption and brought out wrinkles on his face.

"Hello, Big Ear! It's been a long time since I last saw you. How are things at the police station?" asked the Mayor. "Have you been arresting many pickpockets?"

When Mark heard Charles' voice, he felt his blood heat up. The fact that the Mayor called him by his old school derogatory nickname only increased his anger.

Charles walked toward the railing and inquired, "May I know the reason for this invasion of my property?"

The detective puffed out his chest and answered with authority.

"The body of Joseph Assis was found in a disposal area attached to this farm. You know who I'm talking about, don't you?"

"The fighter suspected of having participated in the murder of the Sinclair family, am I right?"

"That's right. Joseph's body had marks of aggression. We believe that his murder was a witness elimination."

"And what are you looking for here? May I know?"

"If we find a body outside this farm, there might be another inside. Humbert Sinclair's eldest daughter is still missing."

Charles stood in front of Mark. He observed the detective and examined his attire, noticing how old and worn his clothes were. Mark also looked thinner and paler than the last time the Mayor saw him, at the burial of the detective's wife.

"Do you think if I had murdered someone, I would have been such a fool to dump the body beside my farm?" asked the Mayor.

"That's what we came to discover," Mark answered with a slightly mocking tone.

"Or is it because you are eager to find something here? I know you would love to find any evidence that incriminates me. It doesn't have to be a body you know isn't here. It could be an envelope with money or some illegal product. I know that would make you happy. You've finally found a way to harm me, haven't you, Big Ear? How can I be sure that it wasn't the police themselves who threw a body next to my fence just to get a court order to invade my property?"

"This is a very serious accusation, Mr. Mayor. I advise against making it without proper evidence. The judge who signed the order may not appreciate what you just said."

"A judge associated with the Cacellas. I am well aware of who he is."

"You can tell him yourself. Your statement will definitely be taken into consideration."

Charles let out a light laugh.

"Look around, Big Ear! See our city on the horizon, the rising columns of smoke. Many houses are still ablaze from yesterday's tragedy. And it's not just here. This event has struck the entire planet. We have tsunamis flooding cities and volcanoes erupting all over the globe. The world is in chaos. Hundreds of thousands of people perished yesterday. Stores are being looted, and criminals are invading homes. Yet, the police department deploys ten vehicles and thirty of its men to come here, to my farm, in the hope of finding a body."

"A heinous crime like the one that occurred last week justifies even more vigorous action, Mr. Mayor. It doesn't matter what other problems are unfolding. I apologize for the inconvenience we are causing, but it is our duty."

"This is not your duty, Big Ear! This is personal. I am well aware of that. You have never gotten over the past, and now you are here seeking revenge. For something that happened over thirty years ago when we were still boys."

"Although every step I take reminds me of what you did to me, Mr. Mayor, I am not here for revenge."

The Mayor smiled.

"I know very well what your problem is, Big Ear. I know why you cannot forget me. It is because you know I was always right about you and your lack of faith. That's why God hasn't been kind to you, and so many misfortunes have befallen you. Why don't you come to my church tomorrow? Why don't you try speaking to the Lord for a while instead of denying Him, as you used to do in school? Perhaps good things will start happening to you, just as they did to me."

Mark remained silent, and Charles Andraus realized that the detective was contemplating a response.

The Mayor continued, "I understand that you despise me, Big Ear, and I know I have harmed you irreversibly. But look: was I ever punished for what I did? No! Do you know why? Because I have always been a person of faith. I have always attended religious services. I say my prayers every night before bed, and now I am the mayor of a large city. I am one of the wealthiest individuals in this town. Look at this property! See everything the Lord has bestowed upon me. And what about you? What have you gained from your blasphemies? How have you been rewarded?"

Mark took a step toward the Mayor, and the two drew close to each other, almost touching.

"Forgive me, Mr. Mayor, but I do not see legitimacy in a faith that seeks material possessions and social advancement. The first followers of your Church had true faith. They pledged allegiance to your God even when they knew it would lead to torture and death. Those men understood the true meaning of your Messiah's teachings," said Mark. "Furthermore, everyone in this town knows that you are in your position solely because you married the granddaughter of George Andraus."

"If my marriage was a good one, it was because God ordained it, Big Ear. He aided me and also wanted me to serve this town as the exemplary mayor that I am."

Mark's gaze shifted into an expression of sorrow, and his voice took on a somber tone.

"I did some research on this property, Mr. Mayor. The lands of this farm and the neighboring gated community were once a reservation. They belonged to a small group of indigenous people, a tribe comprising approximately thirty individuals. Over the course of three years, this very group experienced two suspicious fires in their village and several unexplained deaths among their members. Eventually, the half-dozen survivors sold everything to George Andraus for a mere fraction of its true value. That is the origin of the property you proudly boast about."

"Listen, Big Ear: old George was a straight man. Otherwise, there wouldn't be a thirty-foot-tall statue honoring him in the main square of our city."

"I heard that statue collapsed yesterday," Mark observed.

"That statue was very old. I'll order the construction of another one, twice its size, and this time it will be crafted from bronze."

Mark fell silent, and Charles also calmed down. Both of them inhaled deeply, as if seeking energy, but in truth, they were searching for arguments to assail each other.

Suddenly, Mark's gaze changed. He straightened his posture, puffing out his chest as he confronted the Mayor.

"Answer me this, Charles: when was there ever a global seismic event like yesterday's? Such a huge tremor that reverberated throughout the entire world?"

The Mayor was taken aback by his rival's posture, displaying a newfound confidence.

"What do you mean by that?" Charles inquired.

"Has it ever occurred to you that yesterday's event might be a sign from your God?"

"And what would that sign mean?"

Mark smiled, narrowing his eyes slightly.

"Perhaps it means that your God is on the verge of bringing it all to an end. Maybe He has grown weary of a world where good men are crushed by murderers and swindlers, where authorities sacrifice humble individuals and innocent children merely to secure their power and influence."

Charles remained silent, and the detective continued.

"How would you feel if you discovered that the Creator is on the brink of obliterating this world, Charles? Ending it all? Simply because He has grown tired of looking down and seeing individuals like you in positions of authority."

The Mayor pondered for a moment, but his expression of surprise quickly faded, replaced by a suspicious gaze.

"Listen, Big Ear: are you now attempting to make people believe that you are God?"

"I have no idea what you're talking about," Mark retorted, caught off guard.

"I encountered my brother-in-law before coming here. He wasn't well. The staff at the official residence informed me that you were arguing with Euzebius during yesterday's seismic event, and he was greatly affected by what happened. I also heard that you visited his residence twice last week and had lengthy conversations. He came to your house last night and broke down in tears afterward. He claimed to have spoken with our Lord."

The Mayor's words left Mark momentarily speechless.

"It seems my brother-in-law has convinced himself that a loser like you could be the Creator of the entire Universe. I don't know how you managed to accomplish this, but you've deceived the smartest person I know." The Mayor's expression transitioned into one of thoughtfulness. "No! You couldn't be that cunning. It must be an absurd chain of coincidences that led Euzebius to embrace this nonsense. It wouldn't be the first case of insanity in the Andraus family. Even George Andraus himself spent his final days in a psychiatric clinic."

At that moment, Andrew appeared at the terrace entrance, interrupting the quarrel between the two opponents.

"Mark, I need to talk to you. Alone," Andrew requested.

Mark's colleague's face bore an expression of anxiety. The older detective smiled at the Mayor and walked over to Andrew.

"Did you find the body?" Mark asked in a whisper, leaning in close to his partner's face.

"No, there's no sign of the girl, but we discovered something else, something very serious!"

The Mayor observed the conversation between the two detectives, but they spoke in hushed tones, preventing Charles from discerning the content of their conversation.

As Mark listened to his partner's information, he noticed from the corner of his eye that Charles Andraus looked nervous. When Andrew finished speaking, Mark raised his head and turned to the tense figure standing next to the railing.

"Well, Mr. Mayor. Let's delve further into the topics of faith and personal gain. By the way, you are under arrest!"

Chapter 37

Late afternoon in Oswald's office. Mark slumped in the armchair beside the chief's desk while Andrew sat in one of the chairs facing the boss, resting his elbows on the desk.

Oswald looked through some sheets of paper in his hand and put on his reading glasses.

"According to this report, two hundred and fifty pounds of raw material for illegal drugs were found on Leticia Andraus Farm, along with over five thousand envelopes containing processed stones ready for sale. All the materials were discovered inside the farm's barn, concealed in hay bales. The barn also housed a drug manufacturing laboratory in its basement."

"This is the same narcotic used on Aurora Street. With the number of envelopes we found, we now know who the supplier of these drugs is," Andrew pointed out.

"The same family that serves soup to the homeless every Sunday," added Mark.

"Are you suggesting that the Archbishop is involved in this operation?" Oswald asked Mark, giving him a stern look.

"I'm not suggesting anything, boss. I'm just reminding you that the Archbishop and the Mayor are from the same family, and Euzebius regularly visits that street. It's a fact," Mark replied. "But I can only speculate about their relationship."

"Be cautious with your speculations, Detective," Oswald warned, his tone firm. "They can lead you into big trouble."

Before Mark could respond, Andrew interrupted the discussion.

"The media will undoubtedly comment on the Archbishop's connection to Charles Andraus. I'm certain of it," he turned to the chief. "Do you think this discovery could harm the Archbishop's position?"

"I've heard rumors that Euzebius isn't doing well. They say his conversations with your colleague here have affected him. Oswald looked at Mark. "What kind of discussion could have such an impact on a man like the Archbishop?"

"The Archbishop's condition has nothing to do with me," Mark clarified. "It was the seismic event yesterday that affected his mind. I was with Euzebius on Aurora Street when it happened. I think he was struck by the fact that the event occurred while he was discussing the Sinclair family case with me. In the evening, he came to my apartment and spoke about a vision he had. He claimed to have seen the end of the world or something like that."

"Do you think his behavior could be a sign of guilt regarding the murder of the Sinclair family?" Andrew inquired. "Perhaps he's feeling pressured to reveal something."

Mark adjusted himself in his chair and responded, "I don't believe so. I didn't get the impression that Euzebius knew anything about the family's murder. His concerns seemed to revolve solely around religious matters. He hit his head on the curb during the event."

"Yeah. I saw an image of the Archbishop earlier this morning. He was wearing a large bandage on his head," Oswald recounted.

At that moment, the landline on the boss' desk rang. Oswald picked up the phone.

"Chief Oswald, good afternoon. Who am I speaking to?... Yes... I see... What time was that?... Who issued it?... But what's the reason behind all this?" Oswald spent nearly five minutes listening intently. He ran his hand over his head multiple times. Sweat started to form on his forehead as he listened to the voice on the other end.

"Alright, I will comply with the order," the chief replied, placing the phone back on the hook. His expression reflected a mix of sadness and anger.

"Who were you talking to?" Andrew asked.

"It was the Appellate Judge. He informed me that a protective order was issued in favor of Mayor Charles Andraus and his son, Paul. They were released fifteen minutes ago."

"What do you mean by 'released'?" Andrew exclaimed. "They were caught with five thousand envelopes of drugs!"

"The farm manager took responsibility for all the illegal substances found in the barn. He stated that the Mayor and his son had no knowledge of what was happening there."

"And this was taking place in a barn just fifty meters from their farmhouse, and they were completely unaware of it?" Andrew questioned.

Mark remained silent, seated in his armchair, observing the unfolding events.

"The other farm employees corroborated the manager's version. Without any evidence contradicting their statements, there's little we can do," the boss replied.

"You must be joking!" Andrew shouted. "This guy works for the Mayor on his farm. There's no way Charles Andraus and his son aren't involved."

"That statement is merely an assumption, Andrew. We can't arrest someone when witnesses claim their innocence, especially if our accusations are based on assumptions."

"Do you honestly believe the Mayor would have rushed to the farm if he didn't have a good reason to believe we were on the right track?" Andrew argued.

"Would you need a good reason to hurry home if you knew that, at this very moment, the police invaded it and is searching for incriminating evidence?" Oswald retorted.

"Are you by any chance defending the Mayor?" Andrew reacted.

"I'm simply analyzing the facts," the chief answered. "And I have one more piece of bad news: both of you are suspended!"

Andrew gasped in astonishment, while Mark turned to the boss and gave him a subtle smirk.

"You two are being accused of harassing the Mayor and his family," explained Oswald. "Listen carefully, Andrew: the charges primarily target Mark, but they also implicate you as an accomplice in his actions. According to the charge presented to the appellate judge, Mark harbors long-standing resentment against Charles Andraus dating back to their elementary school days. Additionally, Mark is accused of disturbing the Archbishop and causing harm to Euzebius' mental state." Oswald pointed toward the older detective. "You will probably be summoned to explain yourself."

"But these accusations have no basis. It's all nonsense!" Andrew exclaimed, causing the chief to lean back slightly, wary of his subordinate's temper.

"The chief is aware of that," Mark interrupted. He stood up, reached into his pocket, and took out his wallet. "But it doesn't matter now, Andrew. They have records of me entering the

Archbishop's residence. They will use whatever they can against us. I'm sorry for involving you in this."

Mark removed his police officer's ID from his wallet and placed it on the boss' desk.

"I was expecting this," he stated, turning toward the exit of the office.

"But... what about the girl?" Andrew exclaimed, looking at Oswald. "What about Carol Sinclair?"

"You searched the entire farm and found no trace of her, right? Carol Sinclair was not on the Mayor's property. Unless further leads emerge, there's nothing we can do about her," replied the chief.

"But the Mayor's family owns many other properties. We should search those as well."

"Do you really think we can investigate all of the Mayor's properties without ruining our careers, Andrew?" Oswald questioned.

"I believed that after what we discovered today... I thought it would be the next step."

"In a perfect world, perhaps it would," responded the boss. "But in the real world, you two will be lucky if you can keep your jobs. Andrew, you might have a chance." The chief gazed sternly at Mark and declared, "But you, I'm certain your career is over."

Mark looked at his boss indifferently.

"Are you done?"

Before Oswald could answer, Mark left the office.

Oswald got up, walked over to Andrew, and placed his hand on the young man's shoulder.

"I'm sorry about all of this, Andrew. You still have much to learn. It seems I made a mistake assigning you as Mark's partner. Once this situation is resolved, we will assign you a new colleague—someone who isn't trying to destroy himself."

Andrew also took out his police ID from his wallet and handed it to Oswald. He opened his coat, unbuckled his holster belt, and placed his gun on the chief's desk.

"No, boss. He's not trying to destroy himself," Andrew responded. "He's only doing his job. The consequences are simply stemming from that."

Andrew turned and exited the room. Oswald remained silent.

Chapter 38

The two detectives were next to Mark's car in the police station parking lot. Andrew displayed his anger, talking loudly as he paced in circles and hugged himself in an attempt to withstand the freezing wind outside the station.

"I can't believe this happened. It's surreal. We should have been promoted, not suspended. It can't be happening! The boss is acting like he's on the same side as the Mayor," Andrew exclaimed.

Mark sat on the car hood, three yards away from his partner. His face showed no signs of anger as he responded, "The chief is a cunning guy, Andrew. He knows that confronting the Andraus could lead to the end of his career. By suspending us, he made a statement that the police department won't bother the Mayor again."

"We had a search warrant signed by a judge. We didn't do anything wrong. The Mayor had a drug lab operating on his farm, and we were punished for finding it. That's not fair!" Andrew protested.

"Everyone knows that, Andrew," Mark affirmed calmly. "Everyone in this town knows that the Mayor is a dangerous criminal. The Andraus family has always been a house of lawbreakers, but they are the lawbreakers who control this city. Many important people owe them. Thousands of workers depend on them, and all these people would be affected if the Mayor were arrested for drug trafficking. That's why we are outside the police station now."

"What about the Cacellas? Aren't they going to do anything about it? Will they let their rivals get away with this?" Andrew asked.

Mark stood up and patted his pants to remove the dust from the hood.

"A drug trafficking operation of this size is always linked to many other sorts of crimes, such as money laundering and corruption. A major investigation, especially if carried out by the National Police, would also implicate the Cacellas. Cacellas and Andraus are rivals, but they are both part of the same system that commands this city. An enterprise of this size would not collapse without dragging many other families into the grasp of Justice. The Cacellas are not going to act against the Andraus. Not in this case."

"You knew all of this before entering the farm, didn't you? You knew this was going to happen! You're smarter than you look, Mark Randall. In the end, Oswald might be right. You're just trying to destroy yourself, and you're taking me with you," Andrew accused.

Mark raised his finger, pointing in Andrew's direction.

"Listen to me, my friend: if we had discovered that the Mayor's son went mad and brutally slaughtered an entire family due to his mental illness, it would be advantageous for the Cacellas and all the criminals and corrupt individuals in this city. They would eagerly seize the opportunity presented by the Andraus family. The Sinclair family's murder would be seen as a crime of passion, an isolated act of madness, which would tarnish the Andraus' public reputation and leave them alone to face ruin," explained Mark. "But remember: we went to the farm in search of a body. It was you who stumbled upon a drug lab. Your discovery is what led us into this mess. If only you had focused solely on what we were looking for, we wouldn't be arguing now."

"Are you joking? Did you expect me to turn a blind eye to a drug lab?"

Mark sighed and adopted a softer tone.

"Absolutely not. We did what we had to do. It's you who fails to comprehend the underlying mechanics of what's happening and blames me for the inevitable."

Andrew fell silent and felt defeated. He remained motionless, intensifying the sensation of cold. He noticed that Mark was wearing only a light coat and yet appeared unaffected by the low temperature.

Mark continued, "This city will sweep everything they witnessed today under the rug because a collapse in the Mayor's family business would benefit no one. At least not those who profit from these illicit dealings, and there are many."

Mark observed that his partner was trembling uncontrollably.

"Let's get in the car. I'll drive you home." The older detective removed his coat and draped it over Andrew's shoulders.

With quivering lips, Andrew asked, "Aren't you feeling cold?"

"No," Mark replied.

"You must be ill!"

Mark opened the door on the right side of the car and assisted his partner in getting inside.

"I'm fine, Andrew. I just feel...," he paused and gazed up at the sky as his partner settled into the passenger seat.

"...as if I'm no longer connected to this world," Mark whispered, but Andrew could not hear him.

Chapter 39

Mark's car moved unhurriedly through streets with hardly any traffic, yet still covered in dirt left behind by the previous day's seismic event. Andrew shivered from the cold, placing his hands near the air vents as the vehicle's heating was set to the maximum.

"Do you remember ever being this cold in this city?" Andrew asked.

Lost in thought, Mark remained silent. He switched on the radio and tuned it to a news station.

In a formal tone, a broadcaster delivered the breaking news about the weather: "Numerous international authorities have expressed deep concern regarding this devastating cold wave. The phenomenon occurs just one day after a major seismic event caused widespread damage across the globe. Reports are coming in of snowfalls in coastal cities located in normally hot zones of the planet. Northern cities, typically experiencing warm weather at this time of year, are facing temperatures akin to their harshest winters. The most alarming situation is unfolding in regions naturally cold during this season. In some southern capitals, temperatures are approaching those of the remote polar regions. Representatives of international organizations estimate that if temperatures continue to drop, we may witness hundreds of thousands of freezing-related deaths before the upcoming weekend."

"Experts from international universities are currently investigating any potential connection between this sudden temperature drop and the seismic event that struck the world yesterday. The cold wave has severely disrupted rescue operations for those trapped under landslides. Thousands of injured individuals are now buried beneath rubble, awaiting assistance while enduring freezing conditions. Tragically, many will perish before help can reach them."

Andrew rubbed his hands together.

"That's terrifying! What's going on with our world? It's like God decided to wipe us out," he exclaimed.

"Don't talk nonsense, Andrew," Mark reacted.

"I know you don't believe in these things, Mark, but just look around! It feels like doomsday has arrived. I wouldn't be surprised if tomorrow angels descended from the sky, playing harps and proclaiming the end of everything. Well! I'm sure you'd be more surprised than me," Andrew added, injecting a hint of mockery into his comment. He quickly regretted his words, fearing he might have irritated his colleague, but Mark remained unresponsive and continued driving.

The two detectives maintained silence for a few minutes as the vehicle traversed the city's deserted streets. Suddenly, Andrew turned to his partner.

"I noticed how you stared at the Mayor as he walked toward the house. You truly despise him, don't you?"

Mark halted the car at a red traffic light. Even though there was no visible movement in the streets, he patiently waited for the light to turn green.

"What has Charles Andraus done to you?" Andrew asked. "You risked your job for a chance to get revenge on him."

Mark stole a quick glance at his partner and switched off the radio.

"Do you genuinely want to know?" Mark inquired.

"Ever since I noticed your rage toward him," Andrew responded.

With the air of someone preparing a meticulously crafted presentation, searching for the ideal starting point, Mark pondered for a few seconds before beginning his narrative.

"I was attending elementary school when my parents enrolled me in a prestigious institution affiliated with the Traditionalist Church. Up until that point, my parents hadn't engaged in discussions about religion with me. They were fairly apathetic toward such matters, and television was rarely on in our household. However, when I was introduced to tales of an all-powerful and ever-present being known as the Creator or God, the advent of the Messiah, along with the miracles he performed and the message of love he espoused, my curiosity was piqued."

The traffic light turned green. Mark released the brake pedal, gently pressed on the accelerator, and set the vehicle in motion once more.

He continued, "I became increasingly intrigued by the subject, longing to delve deeper into the nature of God. Yet, the more I studied, the more doubts crept into my mind, leading me to pose questions daily to the priest who taught religious studies. Perhaps I overwhelmed him with the number of questions I asked. One day, the priest got really mad and chewed me out in front of the whole class, telling me to stop interrupting the lesson with stupid questions."

"Undoubtedly, he was an unprepared priest, Mark. His behavior was uncalled for," Andrew remarked.

"After that scolding, I resolved to avoid further complications, deciding to remain silent henceforth. I began seeking answers to my doubts solely within the confines of the school library. I remember refraining from asking a single question in class for several months, assuming that everyone had forgotten about it. It turns out that young Charles was in the same class as me and witnessed everything that happened. Then, one day, after class had ended, as I was making my way home, four boys intercepted me, with Charles leading the group. Without warning, two of the boys forcefully threw me to the ground, while another stayed at a nearby street corner, keeping a vigilant eye out for any potential onlookers. Charles positioned himself before me, brandishing an iron bar. I can still vividly recall the sheer terror emanating from that darkened piece of metal. He swung it with a sense of pride, parading it before me while his two accomplices pinned me down, their knees pressing into my arms. Charles approached and uttered, 'It is inscribed in the Holy Book: Discipline your son, for there is hope. Consider this a lesson for you to cease your nonsensical questioning where it is unwelcome, Big Ear.' It was the first time I heard him refer to me in that manner."

Mark inhaled deeply, swallowing hard.

"He threw a single blow that hit my left knee so hard I could hear the bones in my leg breaking. I must have screamed so loudly that I attracted the attention of people who were far away. I don't know what else Charles would have done to me if the boy on the corner hadn't warned him that some people were approaching. Charles and his colleagues ran away. They denied any participation in the aggression and were not punished. The school did not want to admit this kind of behavior among its students and stated that I was attacked by homeless people. I couldn't walk without the help of crutches for two years, and I know that, for the rest of my life, I won't spend a day without remembering what Mayor Charles Andraus did to me. It's not only because of the pain in my knee, but also because I've never been able to stop asking myself why he did this to me. Why did simple questions generate so much hatred against a boy?" Mark let out a light laugh. "As you can see, my problems with religion began very early."

Andrew pondered for a few seconds, digesting the story he had just heard. Then he stated, "Charles didn't attack you because of religion, Mark. He just wanted to hurt someone and found an empty excuse in your questions."

Mark let out a slight sigh.

"I think it's the nature of people, isn't it?"

"What?" Andrew asked. "What is the nature of people?"

"Using empty excuses to harm others."

"Perhaps the true origin of evil is something they don't have the strength to face," Andrew concluded.

Mark glanced at his partner and turned his face forward. Those last words made him thoughtful, and the oldest detective drove in silence.

The vehicle parked next to the gate of Andrew's residence.

"Is your fiancée at home?" asked Mark, parking the car beside the curb.

"Yes," Andrew answered. "Would you like to come inside? I think she would be glad to meet you."

Mark turned off the car.

"I'd like to give you some advice, Andrew. I know you will find what I am about to say strange, but listen carefully: enjoy tonight as if it were your last. Make love to your fiancée, feel every part of her body as intensely as your senses allow, and then prepare the best meal you can. If there are other people you love, phone them and let them know how you feel. If there's anyone you'd like to apologize to, call them and ask for their forgiveness. And when you go to bed, sleep holding your fiancée in your arms."

"What is all this conversation, Mark? Are you really thinking the world is going to end?"

"You said a few minutes ago that you wouldn't be surprised if angels come down from the sky tomorrow, didn't you?"

Mark extended his right arm toward the door beside his colleague and opened it.

Andrew looked at his partner.

"Don't you think it's better to come and spend this night here with us? You sound weird. Spending a night like this, alone in your apartment, might not be the best for you."

Mark displayed a complacent smile.

"This is a perfect night to be alone, Andrew. Now get inside your home. I need to go."

With a confused expression, Andrew took off the coat Mark lent him and got out of the car. He quickly entered his house, hugging his body to withstand the cold.

The gate to Andrew's house closed, and Mark scanned his surroundings. There was no one on the street in front of the residence. With the cold weather, everyone should be indoors by now.

Despite the low temperature, it was a beautiful evening, with a clear blue sky and gentle clouds. Mark decided to leave the car and walk to his apartment. He glanced at the coat left by his partner on the passenger seat but decided not to put it on.

The neighborhood where Andrew lived, with its deserted streets, exuded a bucolic charm. Tree-lined sidewalks and vibrant walls enclosed the blocks. It was regrettable that the imposing walls, topped with razor wires, served as a reminder of how dangerous the city had become in recent years.

As Mark walked, his thoughts drifted to Carol Sinclair. Where could the girl be now? He failed to find her, just like many other young women before her. But perhaps she was in a better state now. Maybe she was resting in a shallow grave, blissfully unaware of the happenings in this unpleasant world.

Or perhaps not. Carol might still be alive, enduring not only the cold but also the torment and abuse inflicted by despicable criminals, yearning for release from this world.

In that moment, a dark thought struck Mark's mind. He held the key to ending Carol's suffering, as well as the suffering of countless others freezing in their homes or buried beneath the rubble left by yesterday's seismic event. Now he possessed the power to end the agony endured by families in impoverished and forsaken places, oppressed by violent and heartless individuals. He could finish the hunger that plagued children scavenging for food amidst garbage heaps and dismantle the hypocrisy of religious figures like Euzebius Andraus, donning silk robes, seated on thrones adorned with gold pieces, nestled in grand marble temples, reciting prayers to offer solace and strike fear into the hearts of the humble. Tonight, all he had to do was make a choice, and pain and injustice would cease to exist in this world.

As Mark continued his walk, he neared the city's Traditionalist Cathedral. Two more blocks and he arrived at the main avenue, where the entrance to the imposing temple stood.

Despite the Cathedral's doors being closed, the detective heard a sound emanating from inside the structure: an indistinct chorus of voices. Mark contemplated entering the temple and observing the people inside, but he hesitated, considering the possibility of Euzebius being among them. If the Archbishop spotted him, it could lead to panic. Perhaps the clergyman would utter something desperate, prompting his followers to attack Mark.

The detective halted in front of the Cathedral steps. The singing grew louder. He closed his eyes and extended both hands before his chest, attempting to tune in to people's prayers and absorb the energy emanating from the place. After all, if they were singing to the Creator of this world and if Mark was truly that divine entity, he might be able to sense people's faith. The collective prayers could touch his heart.

But the Creator of the Universe felt nothing. Neither the cold of the late afternoon nor any kind of empathy for the inhabitants of that world. Nothing seemed able to reach him now. He decided to resume his walk.

"There is nothing else for me in this place. It's time to find that woman named Dana and put an end to all of this," Mark concluded.

Part 3

Dana

Chapter 40

When Mark opened his eyes, he realized he was wearing a cap with strings attached to his head again. It became clear to him that while Zalthor's body was sleeping, Physter had been monitoring his thoughts.

"It seems to be a common practice in this world to disregard the privacy of others' minds," grumbled the detective, noticing the presence of the Zarconian seated in a nearby chair.

"I apologize for that, Mark Randall. I needed to assess the state of your mind," Physter explained.

Mark sat up and removed the cap from his head without much care, displaying his displeasure.

"What did you see?" he asked.

"I observed that Dana will have a tough job ahead," Physter replied wistfully. "She needs to convince you, and trust me, Dana won't give up easily."

"Suddenly, the sound of a siren filled the room, prompting the Zarconian to stand up.

"Come with me, Mark Randall. Let's head to the ship's cockpit," Physter instructed.

Mark followed Physter to the spaceship's cockpit, where he noticed two seats in the front and one in the back. Physter occupied one of the front seats, and Mark chose to settle in the back. Prominently displayed in front of Physter were a sparsely equipped dashboard, a joystick, a large information screen, and a vast panoramic window.

Through the window, Mark spotted a dark sphere gradually growing in size.

"That's the planet of Dana," Physter announced. "You're witnessing one of the most secretive places in the galaxy. Prior to our arrival, we traversed countless uninhabited planetary systems. This planet isn't part of any system and lacks the illumination of a sun. The limited light that reaches its surface originates from the galaxy itself. It's perpetual night here, and the heat is sustained by a mechanism of radioactive decay deep within the planet. Dana herself developed this system, spending hundreds of years excavating until she reached the planet's core. Before her intervention, the planet was a colossal icy sphere. Now, it's a vast ocean."

"Did you assist her with the excavation?" Mark inquired.

"I'm not an immortal Hubbian, Mark Randall. When she migrated here, Zarconians were still living in caves," Physter explained.

Mark raised his head to gain a better view through the window and examined the planet.

"I don't see any land, only water. Where are we going to land?"

A red light flashed on the screen in front of Physter, and he grabbed the joystick.

"Buckle your seatbelt and hold on tight, Mark Randall. You're about to find out," Physter said.

Mark watched through the cockpit's window as the front of the spaceship started emitting a red glow, indicating its entry into the planet's atmosphere.

The ship momentarily wobbled but quickly stabilized, maintaining a horizontal position. From the detective's seat, he could see the vast expanse of ocean waves below them, extending as far as the eye could see.

After a few minutes, Mark noticed a small dot on the planet's surface. As the ship approached, it gradually grew larger, revealing itself to be a small rectangular platform surrounded by water.

"This is the only solid surface on the entire planet," Physter remarked.

The ship circled around the platform, preparing to land. In Mark's world, the area of this place would be equivalent to that of a small city block. Positioned at the center was a wooden house, encircled by a bountiful vegetable garden and numerous fruit-bearing trees. In one corner of the platform, there was a circular landing area where the ship was heading.

Mark's attention was drawn to a tall lighthouse situated at the opposite corner of the platform. Although it towered over any trees nearby, it was unlit, blending into the darkness.

Physter safely landed the ship and put on a sealed helmet made of a glass-like material.

"The air here is too thin for the Zarconians, but you won't have any problems," he reassured.

Physter rose from his seat, headed toward a hallway behind the cockpit, and grabbed some plastic bags from a compartment in the wall. He handed two bags to Mark and carried two himself.

"What is that? "the detective inquired, examining the bags.

"They are groceries that Dana asked me to bring from the planet Dolmen. She enjoys cooking, and Dolmen produces some of the finest ingredients in the Galaxy. Whenever I come here, I bring her supplies. After all, the nearest grocery store is over two hundred light years away."

"That makes sense," Mark concluded.

The ship's access ramp descended, and both Physter and the detective disembarked. However, there was no one waiting for them.

"She must be inside the house," Physter explained. "Let's go there."

The two headed towards the cottage's entrance. Mark took in his surroundings, looking around in awe. He gazed upward, and his eyes widened.

Physter noticed the detective's fascination.

"It's impressive, isn't it, Mark Randall?"

Above them, the sky revealed a breathtaking sight of hundreds of red and blue nebulae converging into a magnificent and radiant stellar cloud. The sheer number of stars was overwhelming, impossible to distinguish individually. At the center, a luminous whirlpool of light captivated the eye.

"What is that?" Mark asked, pointing toward the whirlpool. "Is it the center of the Galaxy?"

"Exactly. It's a supermassive black hole. It holds the entire Galaxy together, rotating around it. It's a remarkable spectacle, isn't it?"

"Yes, it's the most magnificent sky I've ever seen."

"As you can see, this property may not have many stores nearby, but the view is worth it. From here, you can see practically the entire Galaxy, and better yet, it's visible at all times."

The pair continued walking until they reached the entrance of the house—a door installed beneath a small porch. The residence, although rustic, appeared to be quite sturdy with its wooden construction.

"Take off your shoes. Dana doesn't appreciate dirty shoes inside her home," warned Physter.

Mark placed the bags on the floor and, following Physter's gesture, removed his shoes.

The Zarconian lightly knocked on the door, but received no response. He turned a small round knob, and the entrance opened. The two entered the house, finding a cozy atmosphere inside.

At the entrance, there was a spacious living room adorned with a brown rug and furnished with a set of antique-looking couches. Behind one of the sofas, there was a large device, almost five feet tall, adorned with lights and small controls. It resembled a record player, a type of equipment that ceased production long ago in Mark's world. Toward the back of the room, there was a spiral staircase leading to a second floor, although the detective did not recall seeing an upper floor from outside the house.

"Leave these items here, and let's go upstairs," called Physter. The two dropped their bags by a wall and ascended the stairs.

On the upper level of the house, there was a terrace the size of a living room. In the center of the terrace, a Hubbian woman sat cross-legged in what appeared to be a meditative state. Mark remained silent, observing her as she kept her eyes closed.

"Hi, Physter," the woman greeted. "Did you bring my peppers from the Loot Forest?"

"Hi, Dana. Yes, I did. They're downstairs," Physter replied.

"You're such a sweetheart, dear. I don't know what I would do without you," Dana expressed her gratitude.

"It's always an honor to serve you, Dana. You know that," Physter responded.

Mark stood by, towering over Physter with his tall Zalthor body, while the Zarconian's height barely reached the Hubbian's chest.

With her eyes still closed and facing away from the visitors, Dana asked, "And what about this handsome Hubbian by your side? Is he the famous Zalthor Acri?"

"Yes, Dana. He came to see you," Physter confirmed.

Dana rose and turned to face the visitors. She was a statuesque woman, appearing even taller than Zalthor. Mark was taken aback, having never encountered such a physically imposing woman. Despite her size, she possessed a beautiful face accentuated by a genuine smile upon seeing him for the first time.

Dana approached Mark.

"But you're not Zalthor, are you? You know yourself by another name. What is your true name?"

"My name is Mark Randall, ma'am. I was born in another world as an ordinary person. I grew up and lived as a mortal being with a modest life until a few days ago when I was awakened in this current world. Here, I am known as Zalthor Acri, an immortal Hubbian and the owner of the planet Dolmen. After being rescued, your friend here appeared in my world as someone called Delasher, claiming that I am the Creator of the entire universe in which I reside."

Dana carefully examined Mark's face, studying him intently.

"I can only imagine how confusing all of this must be for you."

"I'm not sure if 'confusing' is the right term, ma'am. I would say it's complicated. I was curious to meet you. It seems to me that Physter had a strong desire for that to happen."

Dana smiled warmly.

"Physter is a dear friend, Mark. He only wants what's best for you and all the inhabitants of the world within your mind." The woman turned her attention to Physter. "Thank you for everything, honey. Once I'm finished here, I'll turn on the lighthouse."

Physter smiled, nodded, and departed, descending the stairs.

Dana sat back down on the floor and patted the space beside her, gesturing for Mark to join her. He did as instructed.

For a while, Dana remained silent. In the meantime, Mark observed Physter below them as the Zarconian walked away from the cottage toward his spaceship.

"Where is he going?" the detective asked.

"He will stay in orbit around this planet at a low altitude. He will be able to see when I turn on the lighthouse lamp and will return to retrieve you."

"The lighthouse lamp? But don't you have a radio or some other communication system? Wouldn't that be an easier way to contact him? I saw a device downstairs that resembled a large radio."

"That equipment doesn't serve the purpose you think, Mark. It has a very specific function."

Mark scanned the surroundings.

"I also noticed that there are no other spaceships here, Dana. What do you do if you need to leave this planet?"

"I never leave this planet, Mark."

"But... what if something happens to Physter? Don't you have a ship or some other means of communication?"

"Don't worry about me, Mark. I'll be fine."

The detective watched as Physter's ship took off, ascending into the sky and disappearing among pale clouds that drifted over the ocean.

Mark gazed at Dana, who had her eyes closed.

"Who exactly are you, Dana? Why did you bring me here?"

"I am like you, Mark. I am a Hubbian. I was the converted number one thousand five hundred thirty-two. I was already very old on the day of my conversion, but after leaving Doctor Axlow's chamber, I looked as you see me now."

A moment of silence enveloped the two Hubbians. Mark listened to the rhythmic crashing of the waves against the stone barrier surrounding the platform. The sound brought him a sense of tranquility.

Dana continued, "Being a Hubbian is not the only thing we have in common, Mark. I was once in the same situation as you are now. I, too, was a Constructor."

"Yes, Physter mentioned it to me. So, you were also trapped like me, and you created a world within your mind, didn't you?"

"Yes, I created my own world too."

"And what happened to it?"

"Like you, I was rescued, but unfortunately, I made the wrong choice. Now I live here, exiled on this planet."

"Why do you think you made the wrong choice? What's wrong with becoming immortal? Embracing who you truly are?"

Dana stood up and walked forward, leaning against the railing that surrounded the terrace. She gazed out at the ocean.

"I witnessed the destruction of my world, Mark. I saw everyone I loved perish before my eyes, crying out for their

Creator's help, begging for forgiveness. And I knew that their suffering was my responsibility."

Mark remained seated, lowering his head.

"Listen, Dana: the people I loved in my world..." he spoke in a somber tone, "...they're gone. They're gone because of me. I don't think there's anything else left to suffer for if I choose to live here, as Zalthor Acri, alongside Lintsa."

"I once wished it could be that simple, Mark. When I decided to leave the world I had created, I thought I didn't care about anyone. I felt lost and lonely in that place. The idea of living as an immortal being with exceptional strength and intelligence seemed like a perfect way out. But then, I heard the cries for help from the people in my world. I looked into their eyes and saw the pain they suffered, abandoned by a Creator who no longer needed their company. That's when I realized how much they meant to me. Can you fathom what I feel now?"

Mark remained silent, waiting for her to continue.

"How many beings like you inhabit your world today, Mark?"

"Too many, Dana. Several billion."

"Do you not care about eliminating them all?"

Mark rose and walked over to the railing, standing beside Dana.

"I need to tell you something, Dana, and listen carefully." He gripped the metal fence tightly in his hands, exerting enough force to bend it. "I despise everything that walks or crawls in my world, but most of all, I despise myself, Mark Randall. I led my daughter and wife to their deaths due to my negligence and selfishness. The people in my world, they are all like me—selfish and indifferent. I don't know how your world was in your mind, but I would welcome seeing my planet being destroyed. I would welcome witnessing the annihilation of Mark Randall."

Dana looked at Mark and placed a hand on his shoulder. "The world I constructed, Mark, was no different from yours. That's how worlds are. There is always good and evil; there is always life and death. It is the conflict within them that propels them forward. Look at this world we are in now! There is strife in this galaxy as well. While we speak, enslavement and genocide are taking place on numerous planets. Your world is neither worse nor better than this one; it is simply another world, and like all worlds, it deserves to be preserved."

"Listen, Dana. I don't even know if what's inside my mind is real. Maybe it's just a dream, as Doctor Axlow claims. Is it worth burying myself in a hole again, just to live inside a dream? Look at who I am here! I'm important. You say there are people suffering now. Tell me where they are, and I'll call other Hubbians to rescue these people tomorrow! If genocides are taking place on some planet, we will go there and put an end to the killings. In my world, I don't make any difference. I can't even find a missing girl. Almost every time I locate them, they are already dead. I'm tired of it."

"This world you're in now, Zalthor's world, is more complex than you can imagine, Mark. You know very little about the true identity of the Hubbian whose body you currently inhabit. You have limited knowledge of who Zalthor Acri truly is."

"I know that Zalthor Acri is the king of the planet Dolmen. He is immortal, handsome, and invincible. He is confident, skilled, and married to the most stunning woman I have ever seen. Zalthor is recognized and respected by all as the Liberator of the Galaxy. This is the life I want to live. I'm tired of being who I am in my world. And in the end, what difference does it make? In a few years, Mark will be dead. Within a hundred more years, all the people who are now alive inside my mind will be dead. What difference will it make to them if they are alive today? They are all ephemeral."

Dana released Mark's shoulder and gazed up at the sky.

"You are right that in a hundred years, all the people currently alive on your world will be free of their physical forms, Mark. But do you want to deny all these souls the right to exist, to create their own life stories, just because you want to be the immortal king of Dolmen?"

"I will prevent the vast majority from being massacred, raped, and abused by selfish scoundrels who exploit the world I created solely for their pleasure, inflicting pain and suffering on people who truly deserve happiness. I don't care if this is what always happens in all worlds. I want to stay here. I want to be with Lintsa. I want to live with her for all eternity. I want to be Zalthor Acri forever and not live another meaningless life as Mark Randall."

Dana moved away from Mark and walked toward the staircase. She looked at him intently and asked, "Is this your final choice?"

The detective remained silent, his gaze fixated on the floor. Dana realized that he was feeling troubled within.

"Come with me, Mark Randall. I'll show you something that might change your mind," Dana stated.

Chapter 41

Five minutes later, Mark and Dana were in the living room below the terrace. The Hubbian woman pointed to the couch beside the large device, the same one Mark had seen when he entered the house.

"Sit there," she requested.

The detective sat on the couch, feeling comfortable. Dana took a small stool and positioned herself directly in front of Mark.

"Give me your hands."

"What are you going to do?" Mark asked.

"I want to see what's inside your mind, to understand the world you've constructed."

"Won't you connect any wires to my head, like Physter and Doctor Axlow did?"

"I don't need mechanisms to read your mind. Just let me hold your hands."

The detective extended his hands to Dana. When she touched him, he felt a wave of nostalgia, as if he had returned to his childhood.

"Close your eyes, relax, and let me delve into your mind."

Dana remained silent for about a minute. Mark felt a gentle touch on his head, even though she was holding his hands.

"You can open your eyes now."

The detective gazed at Dana, who wore a serious expression.

"I've seen what is happening in your world right now. We don't have much time. The people within your mind are scared and feeling hopeless. I saw you as well, Mark Randall. I observed your memories—how you embraced your daughter and told her bedtime stories. I saw the love she had for you, considering you the center of her world. I also witnessed you kissing your wife, caressing her tenderly on a night of passion. The three of you laughed while giving each other hugs. You experienced moments of joy. You simply choose not to acknowledge them in the present."

"Why are you telling me this?" Mark inquired, releasing Dana's hands. "You're right! These are memories I don't want to remember."

"These are beautiful memories from your life, Mark. Just because they cannot be revived doesn't mean they cease to exist."

"The same applies to the painful moments," the detective replied. "But in the end, these are the moments that leave wounds and make us want to forget even the happiest times."

Dana stood up and walked around the couch toward the large device. The equipment had a transparent lid at the same height as the Hubbian woman's chest. She lifted the lid and manipulated some controls on the device. Mark observed her actions but could not comprehend their purpose.

"Let's make this clear," Dana said. "You despise your world, and you despise yourself. Overwhelming guilt consumes you, and you believe you should punish yourself for what happened to your family. Digging into your mind, I've also noticed that you can't stand how people refer to God in your world, as you now consider yourself to be God."

"Am I not?" Mark asked. "The God of my world?"

"For the people within your world, Mark, God is someone who constantly cares for them, protects them, and offers guidance. You are not this entity."

"People hold diverse beliefs about who God is in my world," Mark explained. "But they all agree on one thing: God is the one who created the place they inhabit."

"Yes, people in your world refer to it as the Creator. That would be a more accurate term for you, although I prefer the terminology we use here. To us, you are 'The' Constructor, or rather, 'A' Constructor. While you may be unique in your world, right now, there are thousands of other Hubbians missing who are in a situation similar to yours. They too reside in worlds they have constructed, unaware of their role as the Constructors of their respective universes. Some live happily, while others do not. It all depends on the circumstances they find themselves in at the present time."

"Yes, I am aware of that," Mark acknowledged.

Dana continued, "Who can guarantee that the world we are now in is not the result of a Constructor above us? In the end, we might be just a part of a vast network of interconnected universes, all linked through the minds of superior Constructors. At the apex resides the entity that everyone considers to be the real God of all universes. The truth is, we may never know the answer. This supreme being is beyond our reach, even to us, immortal converted Hubbians."

Mark remained silent as Dana continued adjusting the device. Some lights on the equipment turned on, and she kept speaking.

"I noticed that you incorporated certain myths into your world to strengthen your connection with its inhabitants. One of these myths was undoubtedly inspired by the tale that served as the foundation of the ancient Hubbian civilization," Dana explained. "It revolved around a humble man who existed during the time of the Hubbian Empire. Amid an era characterized by violence and slavery, which seemed to be the only means of maintaining unity in our civilization, this man emerged in a small village. He preached about love and compassion like no one else ever had. However, the myth you created within your mind introduced a new element to the Hubbian legend. It suggests that this preacher would return one day, in a different form, and that righteous individuals would be rewarded with a place beside him. That would be the end of everything. This addition reveals something significant about your world."

"What?" Mark asked. "What does it reveal?"

"It reveals that you embedded an apocalypse into your myth—a warning that your world has a limited existence, right? Physter informed me about the plutonium-beam bracelet and its schedule."

Dana closed the transparent lid on top of the device and looked at the detective.

"Lie down, Mark! We are about to begin."

Mark remained seated, listening to a soft piece of music emanating from the device in front of the Hubbian woman.

"What do you intend to do with me, Dana? What will this device reveal?"

She walked toward the house's door and replied, "Even without the aid of machines, I can perceive what's on your mind simply by touching you. However, what we are about to do is far more complex, and I require the assistance of this equipment. It is a powerful computer programmed to unveil the memories associated with the creation of your world," Dana explained, flicking a few switches next to the front door, causing some lights to dim, enveloping the room in darkness. "It will emit a melody at a specific frequency that will help you uncover deeply buried memories within your brain."

"Will I remember Zalthor Acri's past?"

"Yes, but only the past that matters. Now, please lie down."

As Dana returned to her small stool, Mark reclined on the couch.

"Now, close your eyes, Mark Randall. Let the music flow through your mind. It will unlock your memories, and you will finally discover the true identity of Zalthor Acri. You will understand who you truly are."

Mark felt a sensation of weightlessness, as if his body was becoming less dense. He closed his eyes and saw beams of light swirling around him. Suddenly, he felt a surge of gravity, and his body began to descend into an infinite void. He observed a deep abyss rapidly approaching below him, and he was drawn into its depths. Mark plummeted rapidly through a lengthy tunnel—a tunnel into the past...

...a million years into the past.

Chapter 42

It was a nice afternoon in the park. On a large concrete court, four young boys played with an old rubber ball. In the center of the area stood a ten-foot-high pole with a metal hoop at the top. The boys dashed around it. On one side were Zalthor, a tall and robust boy, and Axlow, a pale and short child. On the other side were two kids slightly smaller than Zalthor. They were Pheldon and Juscieh.

In the distance beyond the park, the imposing skyscrapers of downtown Hobbes, the capital of the planet Hubberia, seemed like a great wall on the horizon.

Zalthor and Axlow had the ball. The two positioned themselves facing Pheldon and Juscieh.

Zalthor instructed his partner, "Pay attention, Axlow: I'll pass by Juscieh's right side. You go by Pheldon's left side and distract him, alright?"

"I don't want to do this, Zalthor. Pheldon is going to kick my leg. He always does that. Just the thought of it makes my body ache."

"Don't worry about Pheldon. I know him well. He'll try to keep an eye on both of us and won't follow you. He won't resist the urge and will end up chasing me because I have the ball. When I throw the ball to you, you'll be at a safe distance from him."

Zalthor bounced the ball on the ground and sprinted to the right side of the court. Pheldon and Juscieh headed toward him while Axlow ran to the left. Pheldon returned to catch Axlow but hesitated upon seeing Zalthor approaching, leaving the smaller kid free.

Zalthor made a swift move and evaded Juscieh. He shouted at Axlow, who was right behind Pheldon, and threw the ball to his teammate. Axlow caught the ball but tripped over his own legs and fell, releasing the ball right next to Pheldon, who seized it and ran toward the pole. Zalthor tried to intercept Pheldon, but the boy passed the ball to Juscieh, who was already positioned under the metal hoop. Pheldon's teammate hurled the ball over the hoop, but it fell far from the target.

"Damn you, Juscieh!" Pheldon shouted. "You ruined all my effort."

Zalthor approached his teammate, who was sitting on the ground.

"Are you alright, Axlow?" he asked, noticing blood on his friend's knee.

"What a dumb game!" Axlow grumbled. "I knew this would happen."

"Well, actually, you said that Pheldon would kick you. He didn't even touch you," Zalthor responded with a smile. "You tripped all by yourself."

"I want to go home, Zalthor," Axlow requested as he got up.

"But it's still early, Axlow. It's good for you to breathe fresh air and get some exercise. You always spend the whole day in front of that computer."

"I'm working on something very important: a software for identifying chemical elements through spectroscopy. I'm wasting my time here."

"Exercising improves the oxygenation of this big brain inside your head, my friend. Let's play for another fifteen minutes. Then I'll come with you to your house, and you can show me your software. How's your leg?"

Awkwardly, Axlow took a few steps.

"My leg is fine, but my software isn't. Every time I try to set a more complex calculation, a strange message appears, telling me that it is impossible to compile. I looked for a solution on the world network, but I didn't find much."

"When we get to your house, show me this message. Maybe I find the solution."

"You won't understand the programming language, Zalthor. I am writing in a very advanced code."

"Don't underestimate me, Axlow. I understand more about programming than you think."

"I'm not underestimating you. You might know a lot about programming, but you don't know more than I do. I'm just being realistic."

At that moment, Pheldon, carrying the ball with him, interrupted the two.

"What's up, guys? Are you going to play or not? Zalthor, you should find a better partner. You'll never beat us if you keep playing with this weakling." Pheldon threw the ball to Juscieh.

Axlow whispered to Zalthor. "Don't tell them what I'm doing. The idiot Pheldon might want to go to my house and use my computer to play combat games."

"Don't worry about it," Zalthor said, smiling. "I never talk to them about your world domination projects."

The two friends approached Pheldon and Juscieh.

"I need Axlow, Pheldon. He may be small, but he's the brain of the team," Zalthor told them. "He plans all our moves."

Axlow knew Zalthor was lying, but he liked what his friend said and didn't deny it.

Zalthor observed that Pheldon and Juscieh suddenly changed their expressions. They looked perplexed, gazing up at the sky. Pheldon's body was shaking, and Juscieh dropped the ball.

"What happened to them?" asked Axlow.

Unable to speak, Pheldon pointed straight ahead, in the opposite direction of where Zalthor and Axlow were looking. The two friends turned, and their jaws dropped.

A gigantic red spaceship hovered above the skyscrapers behind the park. It was larger than anything the four friends had seen before. It looked like an entire city was flying above the other.

Zalthor looked around and saw many panic-stricken people running to their vehicles, while others, like his friends, were astonished, just staring in the direction of the huge ship.

Later at home, Zalthor sat on the carpet in the middle of the living room. Beside him was his older brother Chiron. On the sofa behind them were their parents, Doltrod and Menfita. Everyone looked intently at the television set.

On the screen, a news anchor appeared to be very tense.

"The Minister of State has urged the population of Hubberia to remain calm. At least ten supermarkets in the capital have been looted. Heavy traffic jams have been reported on the roads leading to the countryside in major urban centers. However, according to the government, there is no reason to panic."

The image changed to another news anchor who continued, "Just a few minutes ago, a small transport vehicle left the large spaceship flying over the capital. It landed in front of the Central Government Palace. Simultaneously, over a hundred police vehicles surrounded the vehicle, creating a tense situation around the Government Palace. Fortunately, thanks to the actions of the Minister of State, the military forces remained calm and did not open fire on the visitors."

The image returned to the previous news anchor.

"The area where the alien vehicle landed is currently isolated, but we have obtained unauthorized images of the visitors leaving the transport and being greeted by Hubbian authorities. The Minister of State himself was among them."

The image changed to blurry footage captured by an amateur using inferior equipment. In the recording, it was possible to see five humanoid creatures exiting the alien vehicle.

"They look very ugly!" exclaimed Zalthor. "They must not be good."

"Dear, don't talk like that!" warned Menfita. "You must not judge them based on their appearance."

"They resemble giant lizards," said Chiron. "I bet they eat people."

"Don't talk nonsense! You're scaring your brother," complained Doltrod.

The television image changed to a close-up of an elderly Hubbian surrounded by microphones.

"This is a historic day for all of us. Today, it was revealed that we are not alone in the universe. An enormous door has opened for the Hubbian civilization, a door leading to the knowledge of the deepest mysteries of the cosmos. We still know very little about these visitors, but they have announced that they come in peace and are willing to provide us with the knowledge to guide our people toward an unprecedented age of discovery," spoke the Minister of State.

"But what will they want in return?" Doltrod asked.

No one in the room answered. They simply remained perplexed, following the news of this historic event.

Seven years later, Zalthor was a teenager. Chiron, who had become a young adult, was with him in their shared bedroom. The older brother presented a hologram to the younger one, displaying an image simulating the galaxy they inhabited.

"Here is the planet Hubberia, situated in the middle arm of the Galaxy," Chiron pointed to a blue dot in a section of the galactic disk between the center and the edge. "And here is Troctalia, the birth planet of the Zorts and where their capital is located." He pointed to a red dot near the galactic center.

As Chiron spoke, he traced his finger from the red point to the blue one.

"The Zorts expanded their territory by a radius of twenty thousand light-years until they reached our planet. Along the way, they conquered ten thousand planetary systems. Do you understand what that implies, brother?"

"That they possess immense power," Zalthor replied.

"Yes. The Hubbians are insignificant compared to the might of the Zorts. However, it also signifies that the Zorts are an imperialistic civilization. They conquered the systems they discovered."

"Do you think they can harm us?" the younger brother asked.

"They are already harming us, Zalthor. This is the reality that the people of Hubberia refuse to accept. Look at what is happening on our planet. We already have five Zort military bases established here, one on each continent. These bases possess enough firepower to decimate the Hubbian army in just one day. It's crystal clear who's calling the shots on this planet now. Have you seen the new Minister of State? He may be young and charismatic, but he is merely a puppet of the Zorts."

Chiron closed the image of the galaxy, and the holographic device started displaying photos and graphics that floated around the room.

"Did you take a quick look at Hubbian's trade balance with Troctalia? Look at what we are exporting to them: food and mineral products. In merely seven years, the Zorts have acquired four out of Hubbian's seven largest mining companies. Furthermore, they already own one-third of the arable land on our planet. Have you observed the skyrocketing prices of food in supermarkets? They have nearly doubled since the arrival of the Zorts. Do you know why this is happening? Our local producers are prioritizing the exportation of their products to planetary systems where the majority of the Zort population resides, neglecting our local market. I have a colleague at the university who traveled to a planet in the Zort system last month. He told me that the fruits being sold there bore the Hubbian label. He claimed he had never seen such magnificent vegetables. When he got back to Hubberia, he found out that the ones sold here are puny, less juicy, and not as tasty. Can you believe it? They select the finest products for the aliens and leave us with the inferior ones."

The holographic device began to malfunction, and the image started flickering.

"And what are we purchasing from them? Crappy stuff like this device, which never works properly. We're getting technology that is generations behind what is available in the Zort Capital—scrapped and outdated."

Chiron pulled a small rectangular device from his pocket and pressed a button. The screen, covering the entire face of the device, lit up, displaying images of Hubbian individuals.

"But worst of all is this piece of crap here, a personal assistant that takes photos, records videos, and lets you connect to those social networks. This thing is ruining Hubbian society. Our people have forgotten healthy habits like reading books and playing sports, opting to spend the whole day indulging in short and silly posts on these devices. The Zorts are turning the new generation of Hubbians into lazy slobs, incapable of deep thoughts. The aliens control all the content generated by these gadgets. They use them to spread fake news and shame any Hubbian who questions their dominance. Thanks to those damn devices, our people are just sitting around while the Zorts pillage our planet."

Zalthor, who had been listening to his brother's little lecture, decided to speak.

"But if the Zorts are so powerful, ruling over thousands of systems, with weapons and technology far superior to ours, how can we even fight them?"

"If the Hubbians wake up and react against the Zorts, if there's an event so big that it can't be hidden by the newspapers or the Zorts' censorship, our people might wake up and rebel against their rule."

"But what good would that do? The Zort Army would crush us."

"You're wrong! My colleague visited other planets. He told me that in places where there's more resistance, the Zorts tend to be more tolerant. They're afraid of news spreading across the Galaxy about uprisings, and they'll do anything to suppress them."

"And what are you planning to do, brother?"

"What am I planning? I'm not planning anything! But listen to me: one day, something will happen. Someone on Hubberia will rise up against the Zorts. I just hope it won't be too late."

A few years later, Zalthor walked out of a large building, holding a cardboard tube in his hands. He descended a wide staircase and spotted Axlow, Pheldon, and Juscieh waiting for him next to a modest yellow vehicle. All of them had grown into adults, except for Axlow, who still looked like a teenager with his youthful appearance and old-fashioned haircut.

Juscieh asked eagerly, "How were the tests? Did you graduate?"

Zalthor raised his arms in triumph and exclaimed, "You're looking at the newest naval officer of Hubbian!"

The friends congratulated Zalthor with hugs, and then Zalthor turned to Pheldon and asked about his application.

Pheldon shook his head sadly and replied, "I didn't make it this time. But don't worry, Zalthor, I'll try again next year."

Zalthor consoled him, saying, "Don't lose hope, Pheldon. You'll make it, I'm sure."

Pheldon nodded and added, "Yeah, I might not graduate as quickly as the 'weakling' here," pointing at Axlow, "but I'll get there eventually."

Juscieh interrupted the conversation and suggested, "Let's put our worries aside for now and go out to celebrate Zalthor's conquest. Pheldon, take this opportunity to have a night of drinking. Tomorrow is a new day."

The four friends got into the yellow vehicle, with Juscieh taking the driver's seat, and they drove away.

Two hours later, Zalthor, Pheldon, Juscieh, and Axlow were sitting around a table full of empty bottles. Pheldon's eyes were bloodshot, and he was sweating profusely. He raised his voice to be heard over the loud music, his speech slurred from excessive drinking.

"This is all a waste of time! We all know it," Pheldon exclaimed. "Hubbians are being trained for important positions in the government and army, but it's pointless. We're just going to be puppets for the Zorts. Your brother is right, Zalthor. These aliens are destroying our people."

Juscieh leaned forward and whispered, "Keep your voice down, Pheldon. You know the government is cracking down on anyone involved in resistance activities."

Pheldon ignored the warning and continued loudly, "Look around, my friends! Look at our capital. Ten years ago, Hobbes was thriving. There was no poverty, no violence. Now the streets are filled with criminals, beggars, and drunkards!"

Axlow interjected, "I see a drunkard right in front of me."

"Shut up, weakling! All you know is how to crunch numbers. You don't understand the real world," retorted Pheldon. "I'm telling you, the future of Hubberia is grim."

Zalthor gripped Pheldon's arm tightly and pleaded, "We all know that, Pheldon. Please, just keep your mouth shut, or we'll have to silence you ourselves."

Pheldon tried to free himself from Zalthor's grip and glared at his friend with anger in his eyes.

"Go ahead, 'naval officer'! I dare you to try it!" The words were filled with challenge and bitterness.

Suddenly, the music in the venue abruptly stopped. A bartender behind the counter turned up the volume on a television set. The screen displayed a street strewn with rubble, a large pile of ashes dominating the view. Smoldering debris completed the scene of destruction.

A voice in the background narrated the events.

"This afternoon, a massive explosion obliterated the official vehicle of the Troctalia Ambassador in Hubberia. Fortunately, Ambassador Zort was not present at the time of the attack. However, a Hubbian driver and a Zort security guard lost their lives. Numerous metal plates were found at the scene, bearing the inscription 'Go home, Zorts! Hubberia belongs to the Hubbians!'"

The television image revealed two covered bodies lying motionless.

The voice continued, "In response to the outrage, the Minister of State has just decreed a state of siege in the capital, Hobbes. All residents are instructed to return home immediately. Army troops are conducting extensive searches across the capital to apprehend any suspects. Furthermore, the government has announced substantial rewards and special citizen status for anyone aiding in the apprehension of those responsible for this act of brutality."

The bartender switched off the television.

"Well, folks, you heard it. It's time to call it a night."

The four friends tossed some banknotes into an empty glass on the table and rose from their seats.

Juscieh grabbed Zalthor's arm and whispered to him. "Zalthor, what about your brother? Is he still living with your family?"

"No. Chiron left home two years ago. We haven't had much contact since then."

"Do you think he could be involved in this attack?"

"I hope not." Zalthor wiped his sweaty forehead. "I truly hope not."

Chapter 43

It was late afternoon. Zalthor walked along the pavement, carrying a paper bag filled with groceries. The surrounding neighborhood appeared neglected, with streets strewn with rubbish and derelict houses.

Zalthor now exhibited a more pronounced adult appearance. He sported a neatly trimmed beard and slightly tousled long hair. His build was stronger, with a broad chest and muscular arms, but a noticeable belly suggested a lack of concern for a healthy diet.

As he arrived at the block where he lived, Zalthor noticed a police car parked on the street corner. Inside the vehicle, a well-dressed Zort official and a Hubbian policeman observed the street's activity. Zalthor regarded them with concern. When he caught the Zort policeman's gaze in his direction, he quickly averted his face, pretending not to be bothered by the presence of the vehicle.

Zalthor reached his house, unlatched the small wooden fence gate in front of the property, crossed the garden, took a key from his pocket, and hastily opened the door to the interior of the residence.

Closing the door behind him, Zalthor dropped the groceries and glanced through a peephole mounted in the door. He observed the vehicle outside. Upon seeing that the car was still parked in front of his house, he lifted his head, took a deep breath, pulled a handkerchief from his pocket, and wiped the sweat from his face.

Looking through the peephole again, the police car was no longer there. Zalthor decided to step outside the house and scan the activity around the property. The street now appeared empty. He let out a deep sigh, relieved.

Suddenly, a loud whirring echoed, and a strong gust of wind swept through his garden. Zalthor took three steps back, gazed upward, and saw a flying transport vehicle descending toward the street, right in front of his house. He thought about running away, but a feeling of curiosity kept him rooted in place. He shielded his eyes with his hands, protecting them from the dust particles that assailed his face.

The transport vehicle landed, and a door opened, revealing Axlow stepping out with a wide smile upon seeing his old friend.

"Hi, Zalthor! It's been ages! You have no idea how hard it was to track you down."

"What brings you to this impoverished part of Hobbes, Axlow?" Zalthor asked. "I thought people of your stature were afraid to venture into this area."

Two burly Hubbians exited the vehicle and positioned themselves beside Axlow, acting as bodyguards.

Axlow briefly glanced at his guards and signaled for them to stay by the transport vehicle. Turning back to Zalthor, he assumed a formal tone and said, "Would you mind inviting me inside your house? I have an important matter to discuss with you. I assure you, it's in your best interest."

Zalthor gazed suspiciously at all this commotion, trying to understand what was happening. He contemplated for a few seconds and spoke up, "So, you work for the Zorts now, don't you? This ship of yours is an official Zort vehicle."

"I have been your friend since our childhood, Zalthor. I've always looked up to you as a hero. You know I would never do anything to harm you. Tell me, have you learned to make that hot drink your parents used to offer me when I visited you?"

"Yes, I've learned."

"Could you prepare a mug for me while we talk?"

Minutes later, Zalthor and Axlow were inside the residence. Zalthor strained a dark drink in an old kettle heating on a stove.

Axlow walked through the interior of the house, closing all the windows and curtains he found. Zalthor carefully observed his friend's peculiar behavior but pretended to ignore it and instead updated Axlow about his family.

"As soon as the attack on Ambassador Zort took place, the Hubbian police went to my family's house. They were looking for my brother, Chiron, but they didn't find him. They said our entire family would be included on the Contestable List. At the time, we didn't understand what that meant, but two days later, I was informed that my position as a naval officer had been revoked. After two weeks, my father lost his job at the Hobbes power plant. He also noticed that the neighbors were avoiding us, so he decided we should go back to living in the countryside. He ended up accepting an invitation to work on my uncle's farm. But as you can see, I've stayed here in the capital. I got a job as a docker at the harbor. It wasn't all bad. At least I've gained strong arms," Zalthor said, flexing his arm to show Axlow, who ignored the gesture.

After ensuring that all the curtains and windows in the house were closed, Axlow finally took a seat on a chair in front of a table near Zalthor. He took a small red disk out of his pocket and pressed some buttons on the device.

"What about your brother?" Axlow asked. "What happened to Chiron? I never heard about what the Zorts did to him."

"I know you haven't heard. Nobody has heard. He was located and captured three days after the attack on the Ambassador. Despite swearing his innocence, Chiron was taken to a prison on the planet Troctalia. He was denied the right to a trial in any official court and remained in the Zort system for two years until finally my parents were informed that he would be released and return to our planet. My parents were so happy with this news that, for the first time since they had moved to the country, they came to Hobbes to welcome Chiron upon his return."

Zalthor opened the door of a cupboard beside the stove and took out two crockery mugs. He continued, "I was with my parents when Chiron came out of the Zort spaceship. But what we got back wasn't my brother. It was just a lifeless body, maintained alive by electric devices. The devices worked for a month until their battery ran out. They were not compatible with any Hubbian technology and couldn't be replaced or recharged. Chiron died two hours later. Since he returned home, he didn't say a word or make a single gesture."

Zalthor took the kettle and poured a dark liquid into the two mugs. He held one in each hand and sat on a chair, facing his friend.

"I'm sorry, Zalthor," Axlow lamented with a saddened tone.

Zalthor handed one of the mugs to his friend.

"I vividly remember every scar and mark of torture on my brother's body. I tried to imagine the suffering Chiron endured at the hands of the Zorts until his spirit gave up. Well, at least he returned home. At least he could be laid to rest with dignity instead of ending up in some ditch on Troctalia."

"I wanted to get in touch, Zalthor, but I knew it would be risky."

"That would certainly hurt your career, wouldn't it, 'Doctor Axlow'? I've heard about you. Juscieh kept me updated. Unlike you and Pheldon, he didn't stop talking to me once I became 'contestable'."

Zalthor took a big sip of his drink as Axlow placed the small disk on the table.

"I know it may have seemed heartless of me to stop contacting you, Zalthor, but you know how calculating I can be. I had to weigh the future and what would be safer for all of us. A call at that time would have had dire consequences for me in the short term, but even worse for you in the long run. If I hadn't advanced in my career over the past years, I wouldn't be in a position to offer you the invitation I'm here for."

"Invitation? What do you mean?"

"A proposal to work with me in the Hubbian Army Forces Science lab."

Zalthor placed the empty mug on the table.

"Work with you? In the most important Hubbian laboratory? Look at me, Axlow. I'm just a docker now. Why would you want a contestable citizen working alongside you?"

Axlow pressed a button in the center of the small disk placed on the table. The device started glowing, and a red force field enveloped the two friends.

"Because you're the only Hubbian I trust," he replied. "I know how much you despise the Zorts, and you're a skilled engineer. You can assist me in what I'm building. You're the only one who can."

"What are you building?" Zalthor asked as Axlow took a sip of his drink.

"A weapon to defeat the Zorts," the Doctor answered.

Zalthor remained silent for a few seconds, his eyes displaying surprise. After ensuring he comprehended Axlow's last statement, he asked, "What kind of weapon could possibly defeat an empire that controls ten thousand planetary systems? I've heard that the Zorts even possess a cannon capable of obliterating an entire planet with a single shot. How can we stand against such a powerful enemy?"

"The Hubbians will be that weapon. I will make Hubbians immortal, more than that, indestructible! We will build an army capable of defeating any empire in the Galaxy."

Zalthor gazed at the force field surrounding him.

"What is this thing around us?" he asked.

"It's a sound and electromagnetic wave blocker. Nothing we say here will be heard or recorded by any devices outside this field."

Zalthor ran a hand over his face as he pondered.

"I know the Zorts now control the Hubbian Army, including the Army Science lab. Are you constructing a weapon to defeat the Zorts within an institution they oversee?"

"They think I'm just working on some fancy energy capturing device from our planet's core. They have no clue about my real project. The Zorts think the Hubbians are too obedient to be a menace. We can thank our Minister of State for that."

"And what kind of project are you building?"

Doctor Axlow took out two little rocks from his pocket and placed them on the table. One was all dark and rough, while the other was a shiny, transparent crystal.

"Look at these two rocks. The dark one is fragile and rough, but the bright one is beautiful and super tough. This stone can last forever and withstand almost anything, even the heat of a star's core. These two rocks are made of the same stuff; their molecules are just arranged differently. That's what I intend to do. I'm going to rearrange every Hubbian's genetic code to perfection. The result will be like this." He held up the bright crystal, gazing at it. "Indestructible beings, gorgeous and eternal, just like this stone. The only problem is that the process requires tons of energy, so I will build the Converter Chamber in the heart of our planet. It will be powered by a massive reactor that will soak up the energy generated by the planet's core heat and pressure, enough to make the conversions. It will take several decades to build, and I must carry out this task without arousing suspicion from the Zorts."

"Will your Converter Chamber make all Hubbians born from it immortal?"

"Even better! It will make any living Hubbian immortal, but they must be alive for it to work. The Conversion Process won't work on deceased Hubbians."

"Do you really think you will be able to fool the Zorts for that long?"

"If they don't suspect they're in danger, yeah. Look around, Zalthor, and see what those Zorts did to our planet. Over half of the Hubbian population lives in poverty now. They crushed our people's spirit. They shut down nearly all of our museums. They turned our forests into pastures. So, if there's even a slim chance to take down those Zorts and free our planet from those bastards, we have to give it a shot."

Zalthor rubbed his face, lost in thought. He walked up to Axlow and gripped his friend's shoulder firmly.

"No need to explain what those Zorts did. Not to me, Axlow. I'll do whatever it takes to liberate our people from those scumbags, even if it means risking my life. If you want to take down the Zorts, I'm with you. I'm with you 'til the bitter end."

A few decades later, Zalthor and Axlow worked together in a large laboratory. Zalthor's aged physique was frail, and he carried a bag fastened to his abdomen. Axlow, also significantly older but in better health, sat before a computer, focused on the screen.

Zalthor looked fatigued, his gaze distant as he spoke to his friend.

"Axlow, it's time to rest. it's getting late. We won't solve the reactor instability issue today."

"I'm on the verge of completing the energy flow sequence, Zalthor. There's very little left to be done."

"I analyzed the computer data, Axlow. It indicates that instability will arise when we activate the Converter."

"The reactor will inevitably exhibit some level of instability, regardless of our efforts, Zalthor. It will receive millions of gigawatts per second from the planet's core. What we need to achieve is a secure energy transfer sequence between the core and the reactor, while maintaining efficient execution of the conversions. If we reach that threshold and carry out the conversions at the appropriate pace, there will be no risk."

Zalthor started coughing, struggling so much that he almost fell out of his chair.

"Are you okay, Zalthor?" Axlow asked. "Should I call a nurse?"

"Just give me a sec," Zalthor replied, speaking with difficulty. He continued coughing for another minute until he finally recovered and used a handkerchief to wipe the sweat from his face.

Axlow got up and headed toward a water purifier nearby. Pressing a button, he filled a glass and handed it to Zalthor.

"I don't think there will be enough time for me, my friend," Zalthor said. "I'll be gone before the Converter Chamber became operational."

"Don't talk like that, Zalthor. You still have at least another ten years to live," Axlow insisted.

"I won't last another two months, Axlow. The illness is spreading within me. I can feel it coursing through my muscles, gradually eroding what's left of my life."

Axlow returned to his seat before his computer.

"I know the answer is somewhere here, Zalthor. The sequence we seek lies within these thousands of lines of code. I've tried computer-based calculations, but no software has provided the correct solution. It must be accomplished by my own mind. Hold on a little while longer, my friend, and I will uncover those values. From now on, I'll spend each day here in this laboratory. I won't rest until I find the answer."

Zalthor rose, struggling as he walked toward a table adorned with personal belongings. He looked at a picture frame holding a photograph of himself, his brother, and parents during their younger years. They stood in front of a wooden cabin.

"There's only one way to buy more time for me. I need to rest. I'll retreat to a cabin that has been in my family since my grandparents resided on the southern islands. The property is semi-abandoned but still habitable. I will live there until my body no longer has the strength to breathe."

"You should go to a hospital, Zalthor. With medical care, you may be able to prolong your life," Axlow suggested.

"I don't want to spend my last days stuck in a hospital. Honestly, I don't think there's a right way to fix the reactor instability. Maybe your super-Hubbian project is just a wild idea, like stories told to kids."

"Don't be so pessimistic, Zalthor. The solution to our predicament is right here before me, begging to be discovered, and I will find it. I am the only one capable of doing so."

Zalthor approached Axlow and placed a hand on his shoulder.

"Dont hurry because of me, my friend. You still have many years ahead of you. There'll be plenty of time to find the answer."

"Listen, Zalthor, if I'm feeling urgent, it's not because of you. Have you seen the reports about the insurgency in the northern continent? Each day, thousands of Hubbians are losing their lives at the hands of the Zort counter-revolutionary forces. With a small group of just a hundred immortal converted Hubbians, we would have the power to expel the Zort Army from our planet."

Zalthor released Axlow's shoulder and took a step back.

"Do what you believe to be best, my friend. I am heading to the southern islands. If you need to locate me, I'll have my personal electronic assistant's tracking enabled."

Zalthor left, closing the laboratory door behind him. Axlow remained motionless for nearly a minute, lost in thought, his gaze fixed on the screen. He returned to his work on his computer.

Chapter 44

Sitting in a wheelchair, Zalthor awaited the moment of his conversion. His complexion was pallid, and his eyes were covered by bandages. He was in the center of an expansive empty chamber, towering hundreds of feet in width and height. Positioned high on the wall, a small glass window allowed Doctor Axlow and his new assistant, a young Hubbian named Jwinxs, to observe Zalthor.

Speaking through a speaker, Axlow addressed his friend. His voice reverberated throughout the chamber.

"The entire procedure will last approximately half an hour, my friend. You won't experience any discomfort. You'll feel relaxed, almost like you're sleeping."

Zalthor inhaled deeply, struggling to speak. Despite the faintness of his voice, the chamber's acoustics and quietness allowed Axlow to hear him.

"Don't you think we should test it on another individual first, Axlow? Perhaps on a pet?"

"I'm confident that everything will proceed as anticipated, Zalthor. The new computer simulations are remarkably faithful to reality itself. My calculations are precise, and there is no risk of failure. I'll commence with a light load, gradually increasing it until we reach the maximum level. This will be sufficient to transform every cell in your body into a state of pure perfection."

The doctor continued, "After your transformation, we'll have two billion Hubbian citizens to convert, Zalthor. You are fortunate to have the Converter Chamber at your exclusive disposal for such an extended period. This will ensure utmost efficiency in genetic recombination. Now, relax and embrace this moment. Today, you will become part of the galaxy's history."

Zalthor took another deep breath, mustering the strength to speak.

"Axlow, promise me this: if anything should go awry, do not give up on the Converter. Continue with the work and free Hubberia from the clutches of the Zorts. Do it for me. Do it for Chiron."

"Rest assured, my friend. In a few days, you will lead the troops that will liberate the Hubbian people." Axlow turned to his assistant. "Jwinxs, initiate the reactor power-up process. Increase the output by five points per minute until I instruct you to cease."

The following day, silence and emptiness filled the interior of the Converter Chamber. The tranquility was broken by the sound emanating from a small hatch near the floor. The entrance to the chamber opened, and Zalthor emerged. His appearance now was the same as what Mark initially glimpsed in the mirrors: youthful, tall, and athletically built. Even his facial features, once ordinary in their beauty, had been enhanced by the Converter.

Zalthor stepped inside the chamber, followed by Doctor Axlow, who now appeared identical to his first encounter with Mark. Pheldon, Juscieh, and another Hubbian joined them, their appearance betraying advanced age.

"Gentlemen, this is the Converter Chamber," declared Axlow. "Zalthor ensured that you would be the next Hubbians to undergo conversion. We'll start this morning. First, we are going to proceed with your transformations, and then we will initiate the mass processing."

Pheldon examined the chamber, wearing a suspicious expression as he turned to the Doctor. "How many Hubbians do you intend to convert, Axlow?"

"All of them," replied the Doctor.

"How long does the Conversion Process take?"

"Well, with the current machine, it takes about ten to thirty minutes to achieve a thorough conversion."

Pheldon calculated silently in his mind and spoke, "So, it will take nearly forty thousand years to convert all the Hubbians, assuming the Zorts don't discover what you're doing here before then."

"Within two days, a troop of one hundred converted Hubbians will depart from these facilities and oust the Zorts from our planet. We won't require more than that to drive their entire army off the planet. The Zorts won't even know what hit them!" responded Axlow.

"Yes, but within a few weeks, a fleet of a thousand Zort ships will breach our planet's atmosphere and destroy everything in their path," Pheldon noted.

"In a few weeks, we'll have thousands of converted Hubbians. We are preparing the reactor to carry out multiple simultaneous conversions," explained Axlow. "These Hubbians will board the Zort ships and dismantle them from the inside."

Juscieh decided to interject into the discussion. "I stand by your side, friends. I'm ready to rid our planet of the Zorts."

"That's what we wanted to hear, Juscieh!" exclaimed Zalthor, smiling at his friend.

"I'm in too! Nobody would want to miss out on this opportunity," said Pheldon. "But just answer me one more thing: why is Zalthor so much taller and more athletic, whereas the 'Weakling' is almost the same as he was when he was thirty years old?"

Axlow emitted an almost inaudible grunt before responding.

"The Conversion Process manage to recombine the genetic material of each organism in the most optimal manner, but it functions uniquely for each Hubbian. The final outcome depends on the genes available for recombination in each individual. However, I can assure you that the result will always surpass what you were before. You will become stronger and more attractive than ever."

Pheldon nodded, indicating that he understood. At that moment, Juscieh touched Zalthor's shoulder and spoke in a gentle tone, "Zalthor, I need a favor from you. This Hubbian beside me is Ranson, my partner," announced Juscieh, pointing to a stocky individual who stood shyly behind him.

Zalthor looked surprised at his friend and exclaimed with a smile, "You have a new partner, Juscieh? Congratulations. I'm happy for you."

Zalthor noticed that both Juscieh and Ranson seemed embarrassed. Nevertheless, he continued, "Keep an eye on him, Ranson. "Juscieh has always been a charming guy. If I were you, I'd be extra vigilant now that he's going to be young again!" Zalthor warned playfully.

"Listen, Zalthor. That's precisely why I need a favor from you," said Juscieh. "Ranson isn't on the first lists to be converted. Since he's twenty years younger than me, his conversion may take a while. I know you have the authority to include him in the Converter Chamber today, alongside me and Pheldon."

Zalthor looked at Doctor Axlow. "What do you think, Doctor? Can we make an exception for Ranson?"

"If it's for Juscieh's partner, yes, we can make an exception," answered Doctor Axlow, glancing at Pheldon as he spoke.

Pheldon's dissatisfaction with the Doctor's tone prompted him to turn to Zalthor. "What about my family, Zalthor? I have three children and seven grandchildren. Why can Juscieh's partner be converted today while my direct descendants have to wait?"

Before Zalthor could respond, Axlow interjected, "Juscieh's companion is in the early conversion group age range, Pheldon. Your children and grandchildren are young and can afford to wait many years before being converted. The priority now lies with the eldest individuals."

Pheldon glared at Axlow and retorted, "Tell me, Axlow: if tomorrow my entire family is on board a plane that crashes, what will you do? Resurrect them?"

"Accidental death prior to The Conversion Process is a risk that all Hubbians will face. If you're concerned about your descendants' safety, tell them to be more cautious from now on." Axlow advised. "If you are eager for their conversion, let us not waste time with this futile discussion and proceed with today's conversions. You must understand, Pheldon, that you are here today solely because of Zalthor's insistence. If it were up to me, I would place you at the end of the conversion waiting list."

"You scoundrel!" Pheldon exclaimed, lunging toward Axlow but being effortlessly restrained by a converted Zalthor.

"Calm down, Pheldon. Axlow is in charge here. If you provoke him, you might lose your chance of being converted today," Zalthor warned.

Pheldon pondered for a moment and took a step back, resigning himself to the situation.

Chapter 45

Fifteen years later, Zalthor was inside a grand hall situated atop an imposing skyscraper in downtown Hobbes. A vast glass window behind him offered a panoramic view of the capital city of the planet Hubberia, bathing the room in natural light. Standing in front of Zalthor were twenty converted Hubbians, including Juscieh and Pheldon. Clad in combat attire, they exuded youth and strength.

One of the Hubbians in front addressed Zalthor, "General Zalthor Acri, our spies have confirmed the presence of a Zort fleet in a neighboring planetary system. It consists of ten thousand spaceships, the largest gathering of Zort ships ever witnessed. They are on their way to Hubberia. Our informants also reported the existence of a colossal Zort cruiser, triangular in shape and comparable in size to a small moon. It is believed that the King Zort himself is aboard."

Zalthor gazed at the assembled group and spoke with commanding authority, "Gentlemen, an attack of this magnitude only reveals the desperation of the Zort Empire. Over the last fifteen years, since the Conversion Process began, the Zorts have suffered successive defeats in their attempts to regain dominion over our planet. Now, they fear that our newfound power poses a threat to their empire. But let it be known to all planetary systems that the Zorts are no longer the most powerful force in the galaxy."

Another Hubbian, standing beside Pheldon, stepped forward. "General, we have witnessed increasing unrest due to the slow pace of conversions. Two million Hubbians have been converted, yet there are a thousand times that number awaiting the chance for immortality. At the current rate, less than one percent of the Hubbian population will have the opportunity to be converted before their demise."

Zalthor observed Pheldon becoming tense upon hearing these words.

"Gentlemen, I understand your concerns," he replied. "Many of you here have children and grandchildren eagerly awaiting their turn for conversion. Don't worry. In the coming years, we will initiate the construction of numerous new conversion chambers, strategically placed within the cores of other planets. These additional chambers will enable the conversion of the entire Hubbian population alive today."

Juscieh stepped forward and interjected, "General, considering the imminent Zort attack, I suggest reinforcing the defense line surrounding Hubberia."

"You are correct, Colonel. We cannot allow a battle of this magnitude to unfold upon the surface of our planet. We will dispatch a force of ten thousand trained and converted Hubbians to each neighboring planetary system. I believe this will make it extremely difficult for the Zorts to approach our system."

"Yes, General, understood," responded Juscieh.

Suddenly, a reddish hue permeated the room as the lighting from the glass window behind Zalthor changed. The expressions of all the Hubbians present shifted from confidence to sheer terror.

A shiver ran through Zalthor's entire body as he turned around. A colossal red sphere loomed on the horizon of Hobbes, rapidly expanding. Within moments, it dominated the sky above the capital city of the planet Hubberia.

"But... what is that?" Juscieh asked, his voice trembling.

Immediately, the majority of the Hubbians in the room comprehended what was unfolding.

"My family!" Pheldon screamed. "My sons!"

In a matter of seconds, the Hubbians witnessed to the annihilation of their planet's capital. Zalthor closed his eyes, feeling a shockwave of unparalleled intensity surge through his converted body. Even throughout the fifteen years of battling against the Zort dominion, he had never experienced such a devastating impact.

Gradually, Zalthor opened his eyes, only to be greeted by absolute silence. He found himself floating aimlessly in the void. His body, even his so-called indestructible Hubbian immortal body, bore bruises and injuries.

Attempting to comprehend the situation, Zalthor realized he was adrift in outer space. Surrounding him were numerous asteroids, entangled in a chaotic web of debris and wreckage. Passing before his eyes were the lifeless bodies of unconverted Hubbians, torn apart and ravaged. Office artifacts, articles of clothing, and even a mangled bicycle wheel drifted alongside him. Everything appeared broken and distorted.

A pair of lights approached, illuminating the darkness. Zalthor recognized them as the powerful headlights of a spaceship navigating through the wreckage. It was a Hubbian transport freighter, similar to those used to transport converted Hubbians into battle against the Zorts. The ship halted near Zalthor and deployed its hatch, revealing a converted Hubbian who was instantly recognizable—Ranson, Juscieh's partner. Using a jetpack, Ranson reached Zalthor and pulled him into the ship.

Inside the ship, Zalthor gripped Ranson's arm and inquired, "What happened? What is this chaos unfolding outside?"

Ranson gazed at Zalthor sorrowfully and responded, "The Zorts did it. They unleashed a colossal beam that traversed our system and struck the planet Hubberia, obliterating it entirely."

"When did this occur? How long was I unconscious?"

"Our planet was decimated two months ago," Ranson revealed. "Countless neighboring systems came to our aid to rescue the converted Hubbians. Unfortunately, many remain adrift in space."

"Where are Juscieh, Pheldon, and Axlow?"

"We encountered Pheldon and Juscieh last week. As for Doctor Axlow, he was near the planet's core when the explosion occurred. Locating him will require more time."

"Is there an estimate of the casualties? How many Hubbians lost their lives?"

"The planet was utterly obliterated, Zalthor. It has disintegrated into fragments. We fear that no unconverted Hubbians have survived."

Zalthor bowed his head, falling silent for a few moments as he grappled with the information. Then, he lifted his gaze, his voice resonating with fury, "We need to gather as many converted Hubbians as possible. We will seek retribution for this heinous act. Every Hubbian must participate in the counterattack. The enemy may have destroyed our planet, but they will not stand a chance against two million immortal soldiers. We will annihilate the Zort Fleet and then proceed to Troctalia, where we shall demonstrate the consequences for those who dare to commit such a crime against a race of invincible warriors."

Chapter 46

Thousands of years later, Zalthor descended into the atmosphere of a colossal planet. He used a jetpack to control his entry. Accompanied by hundreds of Hubbians, they faced a barrage of fire from thousands of Zort battleships below. When they were hit, the Hubbians were thrown hundreds of yards away, but they promptly turned on their jetpacks and swiftly got back to their combat positions.

Armed with mighty swords, the Hubbians sliced through enemy ships, creating openings and sending the helpless crew plummeting to their death. Under the aerial battle, a sprawling city came into view, engulfed in fires and explosions. Countless civilian ships could be seen in the distance, desperately fleeing the planet.

The Hubbians had arrived in Troctalia, the capital of the Zort Empire.

Directly ahead, a colossal pyramid-shaped structure loomed. Zalthor adjusted his jetpack and steered his descent toward the massive building, accompanied by a group of a dozen Hubbians, including Pheldon and Juscieh.

The group of immortal warriors landed in a courtyard at the pinnacle of the immense pyramid. Without delay, two hundred Zort warriors appeared before them, clad in radiant armor.

"It's the King's Guard," Zalthor informed his comrades.

The Zorts unleashed a barrage of heavy ammunition against the Hubbians. However, the enemy's fierce arsenal proved to be their own downfall. Many of them succumbed to the impact and heat generated by their own weapons. The explosions that followed caused the collapse of the courtyard, resulting in the death of all remaining Zorts. In contrast, Zalthor's companions rose and proceeded deeper into the structure.

Gripping their swords tightly, the Hubbians followed Zalthor's lead as he carried the Heart of Hubbian in his hand. Raising the sword, he asserted, "This way. Three floors up, and we'll reach the throne room. Torlox awaits us."

Pheldon questioned Zalthor's certainty.

"How can you be so sure?"

Zalthor didn't respond, and they continued their ascent without encountering any resistance. Scaling three grand flights of stairs, they arrived at an expansive garden, facing an immense golden gate. However, a huge group of Zort soldiers gathered between them and the gate.

Standing a few yards from the enemy soldiers, the Hubbians exuded confidence, while the Zort soldiers looked paralyzed with fear. Many trembled in the face of the impending confrontation.

"Look how young they are," Juscieh observed.

"It's what's left of the Zort Army," Zalthor informed.

Pheldon approached his leader.

"We'll take a long time to finish them. This might give Torlox time to escape."

Zalthor gazed ahead and raised his sword.

"Let me handle this."

The Hubbian leader took a few steps toward the Zort platoon, isolating himself between the two groups of warriors.

The Zort soldiers looked terrified at Zalthor. They raised their weapons and aimed at the Hubbian leader, but their fear prevented them from firing.

Zalthor swung the Heart of Hubbian and tightly gripped the sword's hilt. Its blue blade began to glow.

"This is for every Hubbian who perished in the destruction of our birth planet and for everything the Zorts did to my family. We will never forget!" he shouted.

Zalthor slashed the air with the sword and pointed its blade at the Zort platoon. A gigantic burst of energy struck the soldiers, causing them to burn. They let out deafening screams but quickly fell silent. The troop of Zort soldiers became a dense cloud of dust, and the Hubbians made their way to the gate.

Shortly after, the group entered a large hall. The place was adorned with statues of ancient Zort kings and crossed by a huge blue carpet that led to the base of a staircase.

Seated on a golden throne at the top of the stairs was a long-necked, aged-looking humanoid lizard. In his trembling hands, he held a cedar decorated with glittering stones.

The Hubbians slowly walked toward Torlox, the King Zort.

"Watch out! It might be a trap," warned Pheldon.

"There are no traps," Zalthor replied. "It's over."

When Zalthor reached the bottom of the stairs, in front of Torlox's throne, the Hubbian raised a hand, signaling his comrades to stop. He wielded his glowing sword in the other hand, displaying it to the king.

"So, this is the famous Hubbian Heart!" said Torlox. "My grandfather used to tell me stories about this sword. It was once called the Pearl of Zhosg, named after the star system where its blade was forged. For thousands of years, this sword belonged to the Zort Empire until the Hubbians stole it from us and gave it a new name."

Zalthor stopped on the first step of the stairs.

"This is the end, Torlox! Your armies have been decimated. Troctalia has been captured. Only a few systems on the Galaxy's periphery still resist the Hubbian advance. Surrendering is your only option."

"You know that won't happen, Hubbian. Not after everything your race has done. There's nothing left for Zorts in this world. We shall accept our extinction."

Zalthor climbed a few steps and pointed the Hubbian Heart at King Zort.

"So, you know what I must do now, Torlox."

Even with hatred in his eyes, the king smiled.

"I know what you're going to do, Zalthor Acri. It's all you Hubbians have been doing for the last thousand years. Killing and destroying everything in your path since your race discovered immortality. Now, your people consider yourselves the liberators of the Galaxy, but you fail to realize that you have become barbarians. You are not liberators of anything! You have become animals!" shouted Torlox. "Wild animals, thirsty for blood!"

Zalthor raised his sword toward the king.

"Shut up, Torlox. It was the Zorts who invaded the planet Hubberia. We weren't even aware of your civilization's existence when you appeared and enslaved my people. And, feeling threatened, you didn't hesitate to destroy our planet."

Zalthor climbed a few more steps. The King Zort remained seated, motionless, glaring at the Hubbian.

"Stop talking nonsense, Hubbian. The Zorts didn't blow up your world. If that happened, where is the powerful weapon capable of obliterating an entire planet with a single shot? You never found it, did you?"

Zalthor stood beside Torlox, who offered his neck to the Hubbian.

"All the horror out there, Torlox, could have been avoided if your people hadn't done what you did. We didn't want this war. We just wanted to free our world from slavery. This conflict is your race's fault. In your final moments, have the dignity to admit your mistakes."

Torlox smiled and looked smugly at Zalthor.

"Admit my mistakes?" exclaimed the king. "My greatest consolation in my final moments is knowing that you will have eternity to regret your faults, Zalthor Acri."

Unaffected by Torlox's words, Zalthor raised the Hubbian's Heart and slashed the antagonist's long neck with his sword. The king's head dropped, rolling down the steps in front of his throne.

Chapter 47

Inside the cockpit of a gleaming spaceship, Zalthor sat comfortably in the command chair with his legs resting on the dashboard. Painted on the fuselage, a beautiful inscription read "Chiron 7." The Hubbian heard Juscieh's voice coming from a small speaker installed on the cockpit ceiling.

"...the target is a Tautorian transport ship. The Tautorians are an ancient race. They were allies of the Zorts. You must remember them. Since the end of the Zort Wars, these people have been committing terrorist acts on the outskirts of the galaxy."

"What are they doing in this region, Juscieh? What do they want here?"

"These Tautorians became aware of the presence of a Hubbian woman named Lintsa in this system. She usually visits planets whose populations are facing precarious conditions and helps their people build important infrastructure projects or even rebuild entire cities destroyed by wars. Lintsa spends generations on a planet, teaching about technologies that help underdeveloped civilizations produce more food or energy. These Tautorians decided to kidnap Lintsa to use her as a hostage. They hope to charge the Hubbian War Council a high price for the ransom."

Zalthor watched a small dot of light appear in the window. It quickly got brighter.

"How many Tautorians are inside the spaceship?" he asked.

"According to witnesses of Lintsa's kidnapping, there are about twenty Tautorians on this ship," Juscieh replied.

"It's a small contingent," Zalthor analyzed. "Nothing to be worried about."

"Take care, Zalthor. From my research, this Lintsa is one of the strongest known converted Hubbians. Such a small number of Tautorians shouldn't have been able to overpower her. I suspect that this group has some kind of special weapon and that they have used it against Lintsa. If you see something pointed at you, don't wait to find out what will happen. It could be a dangerous shot."

"I understand," Zalthor replied. "As soon as I'm back at Chiron 7 with this Hubbian woman, I'll get back in touch with you."

"Oh, there's one more thing, Zalthor. I haven't found any pictures of this Lintsa, but reports say she's the most beautiful Hubbian ever. So watch out for this girl. Anyone who knows her says it's impossible to look at her and not fall in love."

"You didn't warn me that this mission would be so dangerous!" Zalthor protested, smiling. "You know I've been alone for many centuries. I'm not prepared for that kind of threat."

"No one is, my friend. Be very careful. It is also said that she is unbearably intelligent. You don't want to get involved with someone like that."

Zalthor laughed and pressed a red button on the dashboard, ending Juscieh's call. For a few seconds, the cockpit was silent.

He then muttered, "This mission is going to be more dangerous than expected!"

Minutes later, Zalthor was inside the Tautorian ship. He grabbed a metal door and pulled it back, causing it to fold like a large sheet of cardboard. Behind him lay the bodies of three Tautorians who were knocked down a minute ago.

He entered the compartment where Lintsa was supposed to be imprisoned. It was a spacious hall with several cells distributed along the sides, of which only four were currently occupied. In one of the cells, Zalthor spotted a Hubbian woman lying with her back turned to the bars. She appeared to be sleeping.

Zalthor noticed two Tautorian guards rushing toward him. They opened fire, reminding him of Juscieh's warning, but the shots had no effect. Zalthor unsheathed the Heart of Hubbian and pointed it at the enemies, causing them to disintegrate under the beam of light emitted by the sword.

The screams of the disintegrating Tautorians awakened Lintsa. She turned around and noticed Zalthor's presence. The sight of the Hubbian woman, despite the prior warning, struck Zalthor like a blow to the chest. He lifted his head, straightened his back, aiming to look even taller than he already was, all while trying not to reveal his admiration for the woman in front of him.

"You are Lintsa, aren't you? I'm Zalthor Acri, and I've come to rescue you," he proudly announced, returning his sword to its sheath.

For a few seconds, Lintsa scrutinized Zalthor. She then rose and approached the bars of her cell, gripping the metal bars and bending them as if they were fragile flower stems.

"I know very well who you are, Zalthor Acri," Lintsa said as she left the cell. "You're an idiot! What do you think you're doing?"

"What am I doing?" he responded, bewildered. "I'm here to save you. These Tautorians despise Hubbians. They would have ended up throwing you into a black hole."

Lintsa proceeded to the other occupied cells and one by one, freed all the prisoners, tearing off the bars with her bare hands.

"Go away!" she commanded the prisoners. "There are escape pods at the rear of this spaceship. Set them to land on the planet Halifax. There, you will find help."

The prisoners expressed their gratitude to Lintsa and left the hall. She turned and walked toward a nearby table, opened a drawer, and retrieved some personal belongings. She then sat down and put on a pair of boots.

Zalthor, staring on Lintsa, said, "So, I can conclude that you allowed yourself to be captured by these Tautorians! Do you have any idea of the risk you were taking?"

"And you killed the entire crew of this ship, didn't you? Do you have any idea how foolish your actions were?"

"I came here to save you, Lintsa. These Tautorians are an enemy race. They are space terrorists who hijack ships allied with the Hubbians."

"The Tautorians were once one of the most advanced races in the Galaxy until you, Zalthor Acri, and your allies excluded them from all trade agreements. Then you devastated their three primary planetary systems and relegated them to a single inhospitable planet. If they have become hostile toward the Hubbians, it is solely due to the brutality they have endured at the hands of people like you."

"Listen here, lady! The Tautorians were allies of the Zorts. I don't know if you still remember, but the Zorts destroyed our planet."

"And when there were no more Zorts for you to seek revenge on, what did you do? You redirected your anger toward the Tautorians, didn't you? You subjected them to hunger and fear.

And now, when they retaliate, you label them as terrorists. Yes, I allowed myself to be captured, and I was being taken to their planet. There, I could assist them in many ways."

"You're aware that this would be considered treason against the Hubbian War Council, aren't you?"

"You think this council is quite important, don't you, Zalthor Acri? But it's nothing more than an entity created to institutionalize revenge in this galaxy. Since you and your comrades established it, converted Hubbians have become a bigger problem than the Zorts themselves were in the past."

"Listen, Lintsa: we were compelled to do everything we did. When news spread across the Galaxy that Hubbians had discovered a way to attain immortality, many systems turned against us. We had to fight against everyone, especially the Zorts. I understand there was immense destruction, but it occurred because we were at war."

Lintsa rose from her seat. In that moment, Zalthor observed the gracefulness of her movements. He felt his chest tighten but tried to conceal any signs of attraction toward the impertinent woman.

She spoke, "Now, the Hubbians govern the Galaxy and possess the power to bring peace to all planetary systems. But what do you do? You continue to seek out races to designate as enemies, believing it to be the path to maintaining peace."

"We don't do it because we desire to, Lintsa, but because we believe it is necessary. We soil our hands with blood so that other civilizations in the Galaxy can rest with a clear conscience. This is what the Hubbians have become—protectors of peace in the Galaxy. The fear of our strength keeps aggressive civilizations quiet on their home planets."

"Exerting control over others through violence is not strength, Zalthor. It is merely an admission of incompetence. As long as violent incompetents rule the Galaxy, it will remain a wretched place to live."

"Why are you talking such nonsense? What do you hope to achieve by it?" Do you believe you will save this galaxy?" exclaimed Zalthor, his impatience starting to show.

"I cannot save the Galaxy, Zalthor, but you possess that power. You can save the Galaxy."

"That's precisely what I'm doing here, right now. That's why I came to rescue you."

"But you're saving the Galaxy from the wrong villain, Zalthor. This is your mistake."

"So, tell me: who is that villain?"

"That villain is you, Zalthor Acri!"

The Hubbian man fell silent, unable to comprehend or believe what he has just heard.

"It is the anger that you and other Hubbians have been nurturing for thousands of years that is causing suffering in this world now," Lintsa continued. "To restore true peace to the Galaxy, you must let go of your desire for revenge. It still resides within you, even after the Zorts have vanished. As the most respected member of the Hubbian War Council, if you declare the wars are over and the time has come to rebuild the Galaxy, the council members will listen. No one wields as much influence as you do today."

"Listen, Lintsa: if we do this, soon all the other races in the Galaxy will attack the Hubbians. We are merely two million individuals. Converted Hubbians are unable to procreate, and there are no more unconverted Hubbians. The only way we can remain safe now is through the fear that everyone holds toward us."

"You perceive fear as the sole means to maintain peace, Zalthor, but there is another way—respect. Fear will make you the king of a galaxy in ruins, but respect will make you the leader of a prosperous galaxy. That is the kind of place I desire to live in, and there is only one way to earn this respect: by replacing violence for assistance, evil for good. Come with me! Let's aid the remaining Tautorians. Come and see that there is an alternative path to the one you are currently following, where the pain in your chest will finally fade away."

Zalthor emitted an indistinct grunt and turned away, making his way toward the exit with brisk steps.

"Where are you going?" asked Lintsa.

"I am leaving. I am weary of hearing so much nonsense."

"Wait, I'll accompany you!" exclaimed Lintsa. "I need a ride back to my system."

"Then follow your own advice. You seem to be a champ at that," Zalthor retorts. "Use an escape pod and go to Halifax. I can't stand another minute in your presence."

Two weeks later, as suggested by Zalthor, Lintsa was on the planet Halifax. The planet was not highly developed, but it possessed a charming natural beauty and was inhabited by peaceful people. The prisoners released from the Tautorian ship had arrived before her and had been recounting to the locals how she assisted them in escaping.

It was late afternoon. Lintsa stood in a square, surrounded by young students from Halifax. Most of them were thrilled to see a Hubbian up close for the first time. Some, more enthusiastic, requested her to demonstrate her strength as a converted Hubbian. They handed her a thick metal bar and asked her to bend it. Some local police officers asked the crowd to stop bothering the visitor, but Lintsa attended to all the requests with patience and kindness.

Suddenly, someone in the middle of the crowd shouted.

"Look! There's another Hubbian here!"

Everyone turned their eyes toward the source of the exclamation and saw a local young man pointing at a tall individual whose features indicated he was a Hubbian. The visitor had been there for a few minutes, observing the commotion around Lintsa, but only now did the crowd take notice of him.

"He's Zalthor Acri!" exclaimed another resident of Halifax. "He's a very famous Hubbian."

Lintsa looked at Zalthor and smiled. He felt embarrassed but returned the gesture.

Thousands of years later, a magnificent transport spaceship glided through outer space. Adorning its exterior was a prominent inscription: Chiron 62. Ahead of the ship loomed an orange planet. However, the ship was not bound for the planet but rather a small space station orbiting the celestial body at a low altitude. The station featured a spaceport on its side, where Zalthor docked Chiron 62. Accompanied by a Hubbian woman, he disembarked.

A humanoid female with a flamingo-like head emerged. She wore a delicate glass helmet, enabling her to breathe at the orbital altitude they found themselves in.

"Greetings, Lintsa and Zalthor. I am Vitria. I have been expecting you," she welcomed.

Zalthor gazed toward the planet. Its orange hue dominated the entire landscape beneath the space station.

"Is this XB-17? It looks larger than I envisioned," he remarked.

"Isn't it breathtaking?" Vitria exclaimed. "It's nearly the size of your ancestral planet, Hubberia, and boasts three major continents. The atmosphere is mainly composed of methane, which gives it its orange hue, but the oceans contain pure liquid water, and multicellular organisms already thrive in its depths."

Lintsa, alongside her companion, evaluates:

"With an extensive plantation of blue algae and methane extractors, this planet will be as lush as Hubberia was thousands of years ago. Maybe even more," she stated.

Vitria pointed to a mountain formation passing beneath the space station.

"Observe those waterfalls! They are named Lyria Falls. Witness the splendor of these cascades. Envision how they will look when forests blanket this terrain."

"How much are the owners of the planet asking for it?" inquired Lintsa.

"They are requesting seven trillion spheres from the Galactic Confederation," replied Vitria.

"That's a tremendous amount of spheres!" exclaimed Zalthor. "Who owns the planet?"

"It's owned by the Volcon Federation, one of the neighboring systems. They maintain a base on the largest continent solely for possession purposes. There is no economic activity taking place here."

"The Volconians are amicable people," Lintsa interjected, glancing at Zalthor. "We aided them when they encountered difficulties with an infestation of giant insects. Do you remember?"

"Yes, I remember it vividly. If we hadn't subdued the insect queens, half of Planet Volcon would have been decimated by colossal wasps. Perhaps the Volconians will offer us a substantial discount for the planet. At the very least, we may be able to arrange a lengthy installment plan, spanning several thousand years," reflected the Hubbian man.

"I lament not possessing immortality like you Hubbians," sighed Vitria. "I would relish witnessing this planet adorned with forests and magnificent cities. Have you already chosen a name for it?"

"Yes, we shall name it Dolmen, planet Dolmen," Zalthor replied, his gaze fixed upon Lintsa. "In honor of my parents, Doltrot and Menfita."

Zalthor's wife nodded in agreement.

Chapter 48

On top of a hill, Zalthor gazed upon a massive construction site. Right in front of him, there were thousands of humanoid beings hustling and bustling, engaged in various tasks. Some carried construction tools and materials, while others vigorously hammered and sawed wood or metal pieces. Heavy machinery dug the ground, spread cement, or transported large wooden and concrete beams. Amidst all this activity, two broad pathways were lined with young trees. These paths led to a gigantic rock where the outline of a castle began to emerge.

The Hubbian meticulously unrolled a sheet of paper, colored in a deep shade of blue, and attentively studied the printed drawing. Then, he looked ahead, comparing the ongoing work with the blueprint in his hands.

"It's becoming really impressive. Lintsa will be thrilled," he concluded, wearing a smile.

Suddenly, a humming sound caught the attention of Zalthor. He looked up and saw an aged, spherical spaceship descending nearby. The Hubbian immediately recognized the ship and knew exactly who was aboard.

The spaceship's hatch opened, and Pheldon stepped out. He regarded Zalthor with a serious expression, clutching a small white cylinder, scarcely larger than a drinking glass. He approached his friend.

When they were just a few yards apart, Zalthor greeted him, "Hi, Pheldon! Is everything okay?"

"Hi, Zalthor," Pheldon replied, his demeanor less friendly than usual.

"I wasn't expecting any visitors today. You should have given me a heads-up. Lintsa and I could have prepared a proper reception. Things are quite hectic here, and Lintsa is currently overseeing the construction of a wind farm on the other side of the planet. It's going to power our future capital in the east."

Pheldon glanced at the construction site behind Zalthor. He spotted the imposing structure taking shape at the end of the two wide lanes.

"What's that building over there, on that rock at the end of the avenue?" Pheldon inquired, showing some curiosity.

"That will be the government headquarters of Dolmen—a magnificent castle where Lintsa and I will reside once the construction is completed. She designed it herself," Zalthor explained.

"A castle! That's something I like," Pheldon commented, looking at the construction site. He turned to Zalthor. "I heard rumors that you are offering shelter to refugees on this planet. Is it true?"

"Yes, indeed. That's going to be the primary purpose of the planet Dolmen. Unfortunately, even though countless millennia have passed since the Zort Wars ended, the Galaxy remains a hotbed of conflicts. Dolmen is becoming a sanctuary for those in need. Most of the individuals you see working here come from worlds devastated by natural disasters or are members of races persecuted by others," Zalthor explained. "And what about you? What have you been up to for the past thousand years?"

"Nothing too exciting, just wandering around the Galaxy. I should have my own planet too, like you and Lintsa. It must be a fantastic way to pass the time for those who have eternity ahead, right? Unfortunately, every time I manage to accumulate a substantial amount of wealth, someone comes along and steals everything from me," the friend justified.

"What about your gambling habit? How's that going?"

Pheldon didn't respond. He raised the small cylinder in front of his chest.

"I need to show you something, Zalthor. Is there a place where we can have a private conversation? Somewhere with walls around us."

Zalthor pointed to an elevation just behind Pheldon. "Yes, there's a building beyond this hill. It serves as the administrative hub for the construction. Let's go to my office."

The two Hubbians entered a small room. Inside, there was a table, several chairs, and a couch. Behind the table, there was a larger, taller chair, where Zalthor would typically sit. However, he now opted to rest on the couch while Pheldon took a seat on one of the smaller chairs in front of the table. He placed the small cylinder on the corner of the table and pressed a few buttons.

"What is this device?" Zalthor asked, eyeing the cylinder curiously.

"Well, you see, after the destruction of Hubberia, many items that were lost amidst the rubble were snatched up by treasure hunters. Most of these objects ended up on the black market. Most are practically worthless, while a few might fetch a hefty sum of Galactic spheres. A couple of days ago, a descendant of the Tautorians, a highly discreet individual, approached me and presented what he claimed to be a holographic recording. He found it amidst the wreckage near the former core of our ancestral planet, close to the facility where the conversions took place. This Tautorian watched the content and asserted it was something truly, let's say, revealing," Pheldon explained. "He demanded twelve million spheres for this cylinder and swore there was no other copy."

"Why did he ask for such a high price for a mere recording? What makes it so important?" Zalthor inquired with a serious expression.

"It shows a conversation between two Hubbians. A conversation that occurred minutes before the explosion of Hubberia," Pheldon revealed.

Zalthor leaned forward, displaying his anxiety.

"Show me!" he demanded, his expression filled with urgency.

Pheldon pressed a button on top of the cylinder, and the object illuminated in blue. Suddenly, in front of them, a life-size hologram of Doctor Axlow materialized in the middle of the room. The Doctor was seated, gazing at a computer screen. Standing behind him was Jwinxs, his young assistant, whose projection was partially outside the recording field.

They engaged in conversation.

"Doctor, the reactor pressure and temperature seem to be stable."

"That's good news, Jwinxs. We'll be able to carry out numerous conversions by the end of the day. How many have we completed thus far?" Doctor Axlow asked.

"Approximately five thousand conversions," the assistant replied.

"Five thousand! That's an impressive number."

"Yes, Doctor. We have been utilizing the reactor's maximum capacity, and it has been functioning exceptionally well for the past few weeks, allowing us to operate with minimal interruptions."

"Then let's include fifteen hundred Hubbians in the next session. With five more sessions, we will surpass our record by the end of the day. Afterward, we should give the reactor a few hours of rest."

"Yes, Doctor."

The recording displayed Jwinxs instructing other assistants to bring more Hubbians to the Converter Chamber for the next session.

"Initiating the Conversion Process," announced Jwinxs.

For nearly five minutes, the Doctor and Jwinxs remained almost motionless, fixated on the screens surrounding them.

"Doctor, the reactor temperature and pressure are increasing rapidly," reported Jwinxs. "Should I take any action?"

Doctor Axlow glanced at his screen for a moment and replied, "These values are not good. Increase the power of the chillers."

"The power of the chillers has been raised to seventy percent, Doctor. The reactor's temperature is now decreasing, and the pressure is stable."

"That's better, Jwinxs. Decrease the conversion rate. It's better to prolong this session rather than risk destabilizing the reactor."

Suddenly, the assistant alerted, "Temperature is rising again, Doctor, and it's increasing at a faster rate!"

Observing the scene, Zalthor noticed that the young Hubbian looked quite nervous.

"How could it have escalated this quickly, Jwinxs?" asked the Doctor, looking at his screen. "Set the coolers to full power. Put the reactor into sleep mode. We'll have a batch of subpar converted Hubbians today. I apologize, but it's a matter of security."

"Reactor in hibernation mode," informed Jwinxs, who fell silent.

Doctor Axlow gazed at his assistant. The young Hubbian had sweat running down his forehead.

"What's the current situation?" asked the Doctor.

"Temperature and pressure are still rising! They have reached critical levels," Jwinxs replied, stuttering.

"This is impossible!" shouted Axlow. "All indicators were supposed to be decreasing. We shut down the reactor!"

The room where the Doctor and his assistant were situated began to shake. Zalthor and Pheldon heard the distant screams of hundreds of individuals.

"These screams are coming from the Converter Chamber," explained Pheldon.

"What's happening, Doctor? What's going on?" Jwinxs asked, screaming.

"The reactor is going to blow up, Jwinxs! I don't understand what caused this. It wasn't supposed to happen. All the calculations were supposed to be correct. There must have been an error in the measurements or..." The Doctor's voice trailed off. "...we made a terrible mistake!"

The shaking in the image intensified, causing Jwinxs and Doctor Axlow to struggle to remain in their seats. Fragments of the ceiling lining started to fall off, and the screams from the Converter grew louder. Jwinxs looked at the screen before him and then turned to Doctor Axlow.

"Doctor, what are we going to do? I haven't been converted yet. I don't want to die!"

"I'm so sorry, Jwinxs!" exclaimed Doctor Axlow, his hands covering his face.

Suddenly, a tremendous red glow engulfed the recording, bringing it to an abrupt end.

Zalthor remained silent, lost in his thoughts. His trembling hands moved aimlessly as he rose from the couch. He walked toward the large chair behind the table and sat down.

"The recording ends precisely at the moment of the planet's explosion," Pheldon informed him.

Zalthor took the cylinder and examined it closely.

"Who else has seen this, Pheldon?" he asked in a hushed voice.

"I also showed it to Juscieh."

"How can we be sure that this isn't a fake recording? You know how easily such things can be fabricated."

"You know Axlow better than anyone, Zalthor. You aided him in constructing the Converter Chamber. You were aware of the risks as much as Axlow was. You must have considered this possibility before. You knew the peril in harnessing the planet's core to power the reactor. After the explosion, we searched for the elusive Zort super cannon for millennia but never found it. Not a single blueprint or document about this alleged weapon has ever surfaced."

Zalthor stood up. With unsteady legs, he walked toward Pheldon and raised the cylinder in front of his visitor.

"Why did you bring this to me? Why did you want Juscieh and me to watch it? Why didn't you simply destroy it and forget about it?"

"If I had to watch this recording, so did you, Zalthor. I didn't single-handedly exterminate all those Zorts or Tautorians. You and Juscieh stood with me. You led us. Is it fair that I should bear all the guilt alone for everything that was done?"

"You've always harbored resentment toward Axlow, Pheldon. It's because he didn't prioritize your family members on the conversion waiting list, isn't it?"

Pheldon also stood up.

"Understand this, Zalthor Acri. Axlow is not just accountable for the death of my heirs. He caused the demise of two billion Hubbians. Axlow brought about the destruction of our birth planet and silently watched as we ravaged countless planetary systems in pursuit of revenge for what he knew was a falsehood."

"Listen, Pheldon: Axlow wasn't the only one responsible for what happened with our planet. He was under immense pressure to convert as many Hubbians as possible."

"Please! Do as you wish, Zalthor. If you're angry with me, you can hurl me into a black hole, but don't defend that bastard!" Pheldon's eyes displayed a fury that Zalthor could not recall ever seeing in his friend before, at least not directed toward him.

Zalthor remained silent for a while, processing those words, then asked, "What will you do next?"

"I won't do anything," Pheldon replied. "There's nothing else to be done. No one else needs to witness this. We already bear the burden of guilt. We don't need the shame."

Zalthor handed the recorder back to Pheldon and walked toward the exit door. He opened it and pointed down the hallway.

"So, there's nothing more for us to discuss."

Pheldon headed toward the exit. Before he could leave, Zalthor grabbed his arm.

"What about the Tautorian who sold you this recording? What did you do to him?"

Pheldon said nothing, but his silence spoke volumes. Zalthor understood its meaning.

Chapter 49

Zalthor was seated on a fallen log. Behind him, there was a small wooden cabin and a partially dismantled spaceship under construction. The surroundings were of a wild planet, specifically Valiana, the planet Mark saw depicted in the Dolmen Historical Museum alongside Lintsa.

A short distance away, another Hubbian, Juscieh, stirred some stones at the bottom of a burning fire using a wooden stick. Over the flames, a native animal was being roasted.

"When do you think Ranson will return, Juscieh?" Zalthor inquired.

"Well, I believe he'll be out for another two weeks. Ranson firmly believes he can find materials to fuel the new engine on that mountain," Juscieh responded.

"Do you understand that even with a nuclear-powered engine, it will take at least five hundred years to reach the nearest planetary system?" Zalthor questioned.

"So it's fortunate that we're immortal. Otherwise, all this work would be in vain. Maybe someone will find us before then, Zalthor. Your tracker is still functional, right?"

"It's working, but I don't think the tracker will be of much use here. There's a massive radioactive nebula between us and the rest of the Galaxy. It blocks any transmissions we send. Lintsa and Axlow won't be able to find us on this planet. We can only send them our location when we reach the first system outside this nebula," Zalthor explained.

Juscieh remained silent for a few minutes, gazing at fire and admiring the slowly browning meat. He cut a piece of the meal and placed it on a small plate, which he handed to his friend.

"Zalthor, you woke up screaming again last night. It's becoming more frequent," Juscieh remarked.

"I apologize, my friend. It's the usual nightmares. They're becoming worse."

"Have you been dreaming about the Zorts again?"

"Yes, always the same dream. I see the desperate Zort soldiers screaming before turning to dust. When I wake up, their cries linger as if they were still present."

Juscieh joined Zalthor, sitting next to him, and gazed up at the colorful and luminous sky, illuminated by the giant nebula surrounding the planet.

"I think we're cursed, Zalthor. I also dream about Zorts and Tautorians every night. In my dreams, they grab my legs, drag me into a sea of bodies, and pull me beneath the surface. When I wake up, I can still feel their hands squeezing my body, as if they refuse to let go, even after I open my eyes."

"We'll spend eternity haunted by these dreams. Axlow explained to me what's happening to us. The memories of converted Hubbians never fade. This remorse will accompany us forever. We'll always remember our actions in the Zort Wars as if it occurred yesterday. We'll carry this guilt and endure nightmares until the end of the Universe."

"If only that stupid Pheldon hadn't shown us that recording. If we still thought there was any good reason for what we did to the Zorts. Maybe we wouldn't be eaten up with this guilt like we are now."

"Don't blame Pheldon for his actions, my friend. Deep down, we all suspected that the Converter's reactor caused the destruction of our planet, yet we continued attacking the Zorts until they were extinct. We were blinded by the pain we inflicted upon ourselves and made a huge mistake. Pheldon merely lifted the veil and revealed the truth we refused to see."

Juscieh remained silent for a moment, contemplating Zalthor's words. Then he spoke, "I should have listened to Ranson. He begged me not to join the war against the Zorts, and I ignored him. Whenever I see him sleeping peacefully, I envy the tranquility he experiences. Ranson did the right thing by not joining us in that madness."

Juscieh lowered his head, reflected for a moment, and then looked back at Zalthor. "You never confronted Axlow about what truly happened to our planet, did you?" he asked.

"No, and you?"

"I'm not as close to Axlow as you are, Zalthor. I have no right to do it before you."

"Well, I believe Axlow knows very well what happened to our planet. Telling him that we are aware the reactor caused the explosion will only make him feel worse. Nobody would gain anything from it. It sounds like something Pheldon would do, not us," explained Zalthor.

Juscieh rose, walked back to the firepit, and poured water from a pitcher over the stones, extinguishing the fire.

Zalthor continued, "Every day, before I go to sleep, the first image I see after closing my eyes is the face of Torlox, the former king of the Zorts. He always looks at me the same way he did when I executed him, as if he knew what was going to happen. But there's no way to bring him back to life. There's no way to resurrect the dead Zorts and Tautorians. There's no way to forget," said Zalthor with a sorrowful expression. "Now I understand why, before the Converter Chamber, all beings in this universe were created with a limited lifespan. Everyone, at some point, needs rest, to heal the pain and regrets of the past, to cleanse the soul from the wounds accumulated in life, and start anew with an empty and innocent mind. When Hubbians became immortal, a fundamental rule of the Universe was broken. Now, all we can do is accept our curse."

Juscieh sat next to the firepit, and both Hubbians fell silent, lost in thought.

Eventually, the silence was broken.

"Actually, there is a way," Juscieh spoke up.

"A way for what?" asked Zalthor.

"A way to forget everything. A way to end this remorse. There's a way to do it. Another Hubbian told me about it a while ago."

"What did he tell you?"

Juscieh moved closer to Zalthor and sat down beside him once again.

"He told me that if you find a place that is completely isolated and dark, like a deep tomb... If you bury yourself there for thousands of years, at some point, your mind will shatter, but after that, it will reassemble and create a world inside your head, a place where you can live other lives as if you were born again. If you spend enough time living in this world, when you wake up, your Hubbian memories will be erased. You'll become a new individual, free from trauma and remorse. You can start your life anew as an immortal being."

"This is nonsense, Juscieh. I've heard these rumors."

"The Hubbian who told me this story said it happened to him. He buried himself in the depths of a great mountain on a remote planet for thousands of years until someone found him. After that, he claimed to have no memories from before he was buried."

Zalthor fell silent, reflecting on what he had just heard.

"I'm going to do it, Zalthor," Juscieh declared.

"What are you going to do?"

"I'm going to bury myself in a deep hole. I'll crash my ship into an asteroid and stay there for thousands of years. I'll hide where no one can find me. The Hubbians don't like to talk about it. It's like a taboo in our community, but many converted Hubbians have already done it."

"Are you going to leave Ranson? Have you discussed this with your partner?"

Juscieh didn't answer. Zalthor realized that the question had upset his friend.

Chapter 50

In a small office inside his castle on the planet Dolmen, Zalthor was seated at a desk. In front of him rested a letterhead sheet with his and Lintsa's names written at the top. He picked up a fancy gold pen and began to write:

"To my dearest love, Lintsa,

I know that what you are about to read might not be easy to accept. By the time this letter reaches you, I'll be already on my way to an isolated planetary system far away in the Galaxy. Unfortunately, I cannot disclose the specific location. Please do not attempt to search for me, and if someone unintentionally discovers me, they must leave me there.

I intend to remain absent for ten thousand years, believing it to be sufficient time for my mind to undergo a process I have learned about. I hope you can find it in your heart to forgive me for what I am about to do. Even for immortal beings like ourselves, ten thousand years is a very long span. Many civilizations do not endure for such an extended period.

According to what I have been told, when we meet again, I will not remember you, and we will have to start anew. Should you still desire it, of course. However, even as memories fade, I will always be Zalthor Acri, and you will have the opportunity to teach me about our world. I am confident that I will have the best teacher by my side.

Please be patient, my love. Continue to govern our cherished planet and keep a watchful eye on Pheldon. Since his arrival in Dolmen, he has shown a lot of interest in everything here. If he causes you any trouble, tell him that we will have a serious conversation upon my return.

I understand that I should have shared the burden I have been carrying. You see, when I awaken in the middle of the night, covered in sweat and screaming, I have always attributed it to a childhood problem I had prior to the Conversion Process. But that is not the truth. The cause of these nightmares lies in the guilt I carry for everything that occurred during the Zort Wars. I allowed the pain inflicted by the Zorts upon our people, especially my brother Chiron, to transform into hatred. This hatred blinded me to the true fate of our world. It was we Hubbians alone who destroyed our ancestral planet in our fervor to convert as many Hubbians as possible.

After the wars, you showed me the path of kindness and charity. Regrettably, by the time I comprehended the truth, it was too late. Now, every night, I carry this remorse within me, even when lying beside you. This feeling haunts me, causing me to wake up startled in the middle of the night. And if I do not take action to bring it to an end, I will...

Before finishing writing, Zalthor heard the sound of a spaceship's engines. A gust of wind blew through the office window, and he spotted a trapezoidal spacecraft landing in the courtyard outside. Zalthor recognized the ship and left the office to greet the unexpected visitor.

As the vehicle's access ramp lowered, Ranson emerged with tears streaming down his face. Zalthor noticed his friend's distress and embraced him.

"Hello, Ranson. What brings you here at this late hour? Is everything alright?"

Ranson clung tightly to Zalthor and sobbed, "He's gone, Zalthor! He abandoned me!"

Confused, Zalthor asked, "Who abandoned you, Ranson? What are you talking about?"

"Juscieh. He abandoned me! He said he would be away for thousands of years and asked me not to look for him."

Zalthor released Ranson but continued to hold his shoulders firmly.

"Did Juscieh explain why he chose to do this?"

"He said he needed to forget certain things, that it was the only way. He told me he might not remember me when he returns. He abandoned me, Zalthor. Completely abandoned me."

"Calm down, Ranson. It won't be forever. He will come back, and I'm certain he will still love you when he returns. You must be patient."

"When he comes back, he will be someone else. A stranger who won't even remember my name. And he made that choice." Ranson broke down in a loud sob and added, "He chose to forget me!"

"You need to stay strong, Ranson. Juscieh would be devastated if he saw you like this. You both have a planet to take care of. Without Juscieh, it's up to you to look after your home. The people there need you," Zalthor said firmly. "Listen to me, my friend: go back to your planet and try to rest. Focus on your responsibilities. It will take time but you will become accustomed to Juscieh's absence."

Ranson wiped away his tears with his hand, trying to regain composure.

"Everything feels so strange without him. The world is not the same anymore. There's no joy left. I don't know if I can handle this. Sometimes, I wish I could disappear into the nearest black hole."

"Don't speak like that, Ranson! You are a resilient Hubbian, even stronger than Juscieh and me. Here's what we'll do: I will talk to Lintsa now, and we will stay with you on your planet for a few months. We'll take care of things until you recover. Go to the main hall of the castle. Lintsa is there. I'll finish up some work in the office and join you in five minutes."

Ranson hugged Zalthor once again.

"Thank you, my friend. I don't think I could face this moment without you and Lintsa."

Zalthor released from Ranson and returned to the office. He noticed a communicator on the table and considered informing Lintsa about their friend's arrival. However, his gaze fell upon the unfinished letter on the desk. He glanced out the window and saw Ranson standing motionless, unable to move toward the main hall. Ranson's pale and lifeless appearance reminded Zalthor of how Lintsa would suffer upon his departure. A pang of pain shot through his chest, echoing Ranson's words: "He chose to forget me!"

Zalthor took the letter and tore it into pieces, discarding them in a trash can.

Chapter 51

Alone in the cockpit of a gleaming spaceship, Zalthor clutched the same plutonium beam bracelet that Lintsa would later show Mark ten thousand years in the future. The Hubbian gazed at the device contemplatively. A meticulously painted image on the spacecraft's fuselage revealed its name: Chiron 137.

A soft beep resonated within the cockpit, accompanied by a flashing yellow light on the dashboard. Zalthor reached out and pressed a button next to the pulsating light, causing Lintsa's image to appear on a screen before him.

"Hello, my love. I'm sending this video message because I'm worried about you. Doctor Axlow informed me that you hadn't arrived at his planet yet. He has been awaiting your arrival since last week. Also, here in Dolmen, we haven't received any transmissions from your ship's communicator. Shortly after you departed the system, the signals from Chiron 137 ceased."

Lintsa continued, "I hope everything is well with you. Please, respond to this message as soon as you can. We've already dispatched a search fleet to scour the entire route between Dolmen and the Doctor's planet. If you can hear me but are unable to reply, know that I loved you and eagerly hope for your return."

Zalthor pressed a button on the cockpit panel, causing Lintsa's image to fade away. He placed the bracelet on his left wrist and adjusted its fit by twiddling a small knob attached to the device.

Taking a key from his pocket, the Hubbian used it to unlock a crimson cover at the center of the panel. Beneath the cover, a small lever was revealed. Zalthor pushed it forward.

In an instant, all the lights on Chiron 137 extinguished, revealing the expanse of starry space surrounding the spaceship.

The ship was navigating through the outermost arm of the Galaxy, a sparsely populated region with no planetary systems capable of sustaining life. Zalthor knew that no advanced civilizations would emerge in the coming millennia.

Up ahead, in the direction aligned with the ship's nose, a small moon came into view. Zalthor was unaware of its name, but in the future, Mark Randall would know this celestial body as moon B-23.

The small lunar disk expanded rapidly, filling the ship's entire forward field of view within seconds.

The spaceship Chiron 137 collided with the moon's surface, disintegrating upon impact, and Zalthor's body penetrated tens of miles through the rocky crust.

Everything faded into darkness.

Chapter 52

Mark opened his eyes, finding himself back in Dana's living room, lying on the couch. The Hubbian woman watched him closely from the small stool in the middle of the room. Slowly, Mark lifted his body and took a seated position, placing his bare feet on the floor. He looked down, feeling nauseous. Tears streamed down his face.

"Is everything okay, Mark?" Dana asked.

Taking a deep breath, the detective looked straight ahead, facing the Hubbian woman.

"So, Dana, is this really all that my world is? A refuge built by a murderous creator, trying to forget his crimes?"

Dana got up, sat next to Mark, and held his hands.

"Zalthor Acri was not a murderer, Mark. He was someone driven by uncontrollable circumstances and emotions, which led him to make terrible mistakes. He regretted those mistakes for countless millennia. The burden of remorse consumed him, and creating your world, Mark Randall, was where he finally found peace."

Anger flashed across Mark's face.

"Tell me, Dana: why did you show me all of this? If Zalthor built a world to erase the past, why reveal to me what he wished to forget?"

"Because you needed to understand your true situation, Mark. You needed to see how Zalthor couldn't escape the remorse for his actions. If you leave your world, even if you have a wonderful life as an immortal being ahead of you, you will carry the regret for the destruction of an entire civilization. In the end, you will subject yourself to the same pain that led to the creation of the world you destroyed. Now you understand that you cannot bear this feeling and won't make the same mistake I did."

Mark lowered his head, feeling weak and unable to respond.

Dana continued, "Happiness goes beyond beauty and power, Mark. No amount of wealth or power matters if the mind lacks peace. Zalthor Acri understood this, and that's why he created your world. He sought peace for his mind and willingly abandoned everything in exchange for it. However, he couldn't foresee the consequences: the immense responsibility that came with this new world, a responsibility he cannot abdicate."

Mark remained silent, digesting Dana's words. He felt too feeble to argue.

"Understand, Mark: when great beings are young and intelligent, they are brave and confident. Everyone, at some point, with their strong bodies and brilliant minds, makes mistakes they will regret for their entire existence. But in the future, most of them will strive to find the one thing that gives their existence meaning."

"What would that be?" Mark asked with a weak voice.

"Redemption, Mark," Dana replied with a warm smile. "Zalthor Acri deliberately crashed into that moon, thinking he was seeking oblivion, but what he truly desired was redemption."

Mark remained quiet, reflecting on Dana's words.

She continued, "Only when you comprehend the connection you have with the people inside your mind, Mark Randall, will you transcend being a mere Constructor. The true greatness of a God is not measured by power, wealth, or the number of worshippers but by their strength to renounce everything for the sake of those under their care. Only a true God can understand this."

Dana rose and walked to the entrance of the cottage. She opened the door and stepped onto the porch, gazing at the vast ocean before them. She understood that Mark needed a moment alone.

After a few minutes, the sound of engines filled the cottage. The curtain on an open window fluttered, and a gust of wind rushed through the door. Mark walked to the porch and stood beside Dana, observing a large spaceship descending onto the same circular area where Physter had landed with him hours ago.

"It's Doctor Axlow's ship!" the detective exclaimed in surprise. He quickly put his shoes back on and asked, "What is he doing here? How did he find us?"

At that moment, Doctor Axlow's ship touched the ground and powered down its engines. The side door of the ship opened, revealing the figures of the Doctor and Lintsa. As they descended the access ramp, Mark noticed Physter's partner, Fhastina, following closely behind the Hubbians.

Perplexed, Mark turned to Dana and asked, "Did she lead them here? But why?"

"They've come to say goodbye to you," Dana announced.

Silence engulfed Mark's being.

Sensing the detective's emotions, Dana continued, "Your world doesn't have time for you to return to the planet Dolmen. So I decided it would be best if Fhastina brought them here." She took Mark's hand. "Are you ready to go?"

Mark gazed at Lintsa. The beautiful Hubbian woman walked beside Doctor Axlow, holding his arm. The detective's lips quivered. He wiped away the tears streaming down his face once again and looked resolutely at Dana.

"Yes. I'm ready."

Doctor Axlow released Lintsa and approached Dana with hurried steps.

"So, you're the one they call Dana!" the Doctor exclaimed. "This woman is a criminal, Zalthor! We must apprehend her. She should be cast into a black hole immediately, to prevent her from persuading Hubbians to forsake the gift of immortality."

Mark positioned himself between Dana and the Doctor.

"Don't talk nonsense, Axlow. She only called me here to help."

"To help? Help with what? To bury yourself in an eternal abyss? Is that what you desire, even though you know of all the wonders you can experience here? She has manipulated your mind, like so many others."

The Doctor glared fiercely at Dana.

"Damn you, Dana! You have brought ruin to the Hubbian civilization by influencing countless Hubbians to reject the gift I bestowed upon them. They forsake immortality under your influence, living wretched lives in dreams you claim are real." The Doctor turned to Mark. "Is that what you want, Zalthor?"

Ignoring the Doctor's words, the detective walked past him and approached Lintsa. He took hold of the Hubbian woman's hands and gazed into her eyes.

"Listen, Lintsa: thanks to you, Zalthor discovered a new path—the path of charity and love for others. However, the memories of his past mistakes were tormenting him to an unbearable extent. He had to find a way to attain peace, and that's why he left." Mark lowered his head and spoke as Zalthor now, "I shouldn't have left you the way I did, but when I saw how devastated Ranson was when Juscieh left him, I thought it would cause you less suffering if you believed I had departed by accident, not by choice. I caused you too much pain for so many years. I beg for your forgiveness."

Lintsa embraced Zalthor.

"It wasn't your fault, my love. I understand the immense suffering you had to endure to reach this point. You didn't leave because you wanted to, but because you had to when you believed it was the only way out. It was the same for Juscieh and many other Hubbians."

Mark raised his head and gazed into Lintsa's eyes.

"Listen, Lintsa: you're not just the most beautiful woman I've ever met, you're also the smartest, and you possess a strength far greater than mine. I'm confident that you will understand what I must do now."

The Doctor approached Mark and spoke with urgency, "What do you need to do now, Zalthor? Are you truly planning to leave this world? Will you renounce immortality? And for what?"

Mark released Lintsa and turned to face the Doctor.

"I apologize for this, Axlow. I know how proud you are of bestowing such power upon our people and how deeply offended you feel when Hubbians choose to relinquish this privilege."

The Doctor raised his finger in the air, and tears began to stream down his face.

"Offended? Do you think I feel offended? Listen, Zalthor, or whoever resides within this body: two billion Hubbians perished so that you could be immortal! Our ancestral planet has been reduced to ruins. That is the price we paid for what you now reject."

Zalthor's expression changed, and his gaze hardened.

"You should have told me that the Zorts were not responsible for the destruction of Hubberia, Axlow. Why did you never reveal that the core of our planet exploded due to the Converter? I assisted you in designing the reactor. What happened was also my responsibility."

Lintsa displayed a look of surprise, but she chose not to say anything during this difficult moment for the two friends. Mark noticed that Axlow's body began to tremble as if he was about to collapse.

Mark approached the Doctor and embraced him tightly. Axlow sobbed uncontrollably, his face buried in his friend's chest.

"Listen, Axlow. We achieved immortality, and many paid a heavy price for it. Our ancestral planet was destroyed, and entire civilizations were devastated, but the surviving Hubbians gained more than just immortality. They were bestowed with the gift of creating new worlds. These worlds became our redemption. My world is my redemption. I am now responsible for billions of lives. Lives that, thanks to you, I was able to create. I need to return there, even if it means abandoning everything I have here, even if it means leaving you and Lintsa behind."

Mark looked at Lintsa. She approached and placed her hand on his shoulder, gazing at him affectionately. The Doctor stepped away. His eyes were filled with tears, but now he appeared more resigned.

Axlow wiped away his tears and turned to Dana, but he remained silent. She simply nodded slightly, and the Doctor understood that there was nothing more to be told.

Mark embraced Lintsa once again.

She said, "Listen, my love. What matters to me is that you are safe. The past ten thousand years have been incredibly difficult because I didn't know what had happened to you. But if you need to return to your world and take responsibility for the existence of so many lives, it would be selfish of me to ask you to stay. We had our time. We spent nearly a million years together, and we have eternity ahead of us. Who is to say we wouldn't meet again? I have the privilege of patience, don't I?"

Mark cupped Lintsa's face in his hands and smiled at her. Then, gently, he pulled away. He could see that she was struggling to conceal her pain, and it weighed heavily on the detective's heart. Lintsa walked over to Doctor Axlow and took his arm, offering him support.

Dana stood beside Mark and declared, "You both need to leave now. The world created by Zalthor is running out of time. He must return immediately!"

Lintsa nodded at Mark, and he returned the gesture, while the Doctor turned away, his gaze cast down. The two Hubbians made their way back to the spaceship, their heads bowed, with Fhastina remaining by Dana's side.

Mark watched as the engines of Doctor Axlow's spaceship kicked up dust as it ascended into the air, disappearing amidst the stars above.

The detective took a deep breath and looked at Dana.

"What awaited me now? Where should I go?"

"You will stay right here, on this planet, Mark. Where nobody will disturb you," replied the Hubbian woman. "I'll activate the lighthouse, and Physter will return to give you a lift. He will take you somewhere over this ocean, where you can dive and sleep again. In the depths of these warm waters, your Hubbian body won't weaken as it did in B-23."

Mark gazed at the vast sea surrounding them. The waves gently lapped against the stone wall surrounding the platform. Suddenly, a thought occurred to him, and he took Dana's hand.

"Listen, Dana, before I depart, I have a favor to ask of you."

Dana was a little surprised.

"If it's within my power."

"In my world, there's a young girl who went missing and may be in danger. Could you delve into my mind once more and tell me where I can find her? Perhaps there's still time to save her life."

Dana pondered for a few seconds.

"Let's activate the lighthouse while we wait for Physter. Then, I'll see what I can do to help this young girl."

Dana turned to Fhastina.

"Fhastina, please wait inside the house. You deserve some rest."

Fhastina nodded and walked toward the cottage's entrance, while Dana headed in the opposite direction toward the towering lighthouse.

Mark followed her.

A few minutes later, Physter landed his spaceship. He stepped out of the vehicle and walked toward the lighthouse, which now illuminated the area. When the Zarconian reached the base of the structure, he saw Dana and Mark. The Hubbian woman had her hands touching the detective's head, and he kept his eyes closed. Physter remained silent, simply observing.

Dana released Mark's head and took two steps back.

"So, is this what you wanted to see?" she asked.

The detective opened his eyes and took a few seconds to gather his thoughts.

Finally, he looked at Dana and spoke, "Well... it's not what I expected. In fact, I must say I'm almost shocked. But now, I realize I should have at least suspected it. I was so convinced that someone else was the true culprit that I couldn't see the signs right in front of me."

Dana turned and greeted the newly arrived Zarconian. "He's ready, Physter." She then turned to the detective. "It's time to go, Mark Randall. Your world awaits the return of its Constructor."

Mark nodded and said, "Yes, you're right."

The detective approached Dana and took hold of her hands.

"Goodbye!" He lowered his head as a sign of respect. "And thank you for everything."

Mark walked over to Physter. Dana noticed a certain sadness in the detective's eyes. It was certainly not easy for him to leave Lintsa and everything Zalthor possessed in that world. But despite the pain in his chest, Mark knew he was doing the right thing.

Slowly, Dana walked toward the entrance of the cottage, keeping an eye on the Zarconian and the detective as they made their way to the spaceship.

Fhastina joined the duo, and the three visitors ascended the access ramp into the ship. Once inside, Mark turned to Dana, who was standing on the porch. He had to raise his voice to be heard.

"Listen, Dana. Answer me one last question: if you regret the loss of your world so much, why have you never considered building another one?"

"I've already done that, dear," replied the woman.

As the spaceship's ramp was raised, and the entry closed, Mark turned to Physter.

"Hold on! Now I understand. Dana is the..." Mark's voice broke. "... of this world!"

Physter smirked at Mark.

"If you already know the answer, Mark Randall, I don't need to say anything."

The ship's entrance closed, and it took off, soaring above the ocean.

Chapter 53

Lintsa returned to Dolmen. Her spaceship landed on the expansive terrace in front of the main suite of the castle. Stepping out of the vehicle, she made her way to her bedroom, where her gaze lingered upon the bed she had shared with Zalthor just the day before. Sitting down on the mattress, she tenderly ran her hand over the sheets.

In a sudden motion, Lintsa got up and headed toward the adjacent hallway. Upon entering a small room, she directed her attention to a drawer— the very same one she had opened in front of Zalthor two days prior. Peering inside, she discovered that a small item was missing.

"It's not here!" Lintsa whispered. "Zalthor took the plutonium beam bracelet."

Lost in thought, she gazed into the distance and declared, "Zalthor Acri, we will meet once more. It is inevitable!"

Part 4

Carol

Chapter 54

Mark opened his eyes and found himself back in his apartment, lying on his old mattress. After a brief stretch, he rose from bed, leaping out with a burst of energy. However, the sudden movement caused him to feel momentary dizziness.

Once the detective's balance stabilized, he grabbed his cell phone and saw that it was nearly eleven o'clock on Tuesday morning. Swiping through the contact list, he located an icon with a picture of Lauren, the police station secretary. Tapping on the image, he made a call, and Lauren answered.

"Hello Lauren, how are you this morning? It's me, Mark... Yes, Andrew and I were suspended, but I really need your help now. I need you to find the list of property owners in the Paradise Ranch Houses Community... That's correct. It's neighboring the Mayor's farm. Search for a land lot that belongs to a relative of the Sinclair family, even if it's a distant relative... No, don't inform Oswald about this. It's an unofficial operation... What do you mean you can't assist me? This is not just work. It's about saving someone... Dinner? You want me to go on a dinner date with you?... Alright, if the information you get helps us find Carol Sinclair, I'll go out with you... Yes, I promise. I won't break my word... As soon as you have the data I requested, please call me immediately."

Mark ended the call, placed the phone back on the bedside table, and connected it to a charging cable. His attention then shifted to a pill bottle containing nearly fifty small tablets, resting alongside the phone. It was left there before he went to sleep. Adjacent to the bottle, a glass of water was placed.

The detective took the pill bottle and headed to the bathroom. He poured all the tablets down the toilet and flushed them away. He proceeded to step into the shower stall and enjoyed a hot shower. Upon drying off and standing in front of the fogged mirror, he ran his hand over its glass surface, observing his own reflection.

There stood the aging Mark Randall, with gray hair, a receding hairline, two distinct wrinkles running down his eyes, thin arms, and a substantial layer of fat surrounding his abdomen.

He brushed his hand over his arms and thought to himself, "Well... I'm going to miss Zalthor Acri's biceps."

Just then, the cell phone rang, and Mark rushed to answer it. It was Lauren, returning his call. For a few moments, he listened intently to the secretary's words.

"Excellent! Good job!" exclaimed the detective. "Do you know the exact location of the lot with that number?... Can you send me a photo of the aerial map of the place?... Yes, please take a screenshot and send it to my cell phone as soon as possible."

Lauren ended the call. Mark opened Andrew's contact on his phone and dialed his partner's number.

"Good morning, Andrew. I apologize for canceling your lunch plans, but we have something very important to attend to right now. I know you gave your pistol to the boss, but could you get another gun?... We need to pay a visit... I'll inform you as soon as you arrive. That's right. Come to the entrance of my building in half an hour... Alright, I understand. Make it an hour then. There's one more thing. When you leave your house, you'll find my car blocking your gate... Yes, I left it there last night. The keys are inside. If no one has stolen the car, drive it here."

Mark ended the call. He would prefer to head straight to the ranch houses community, but his partner asked for more time to obtain the requested weapon.

The detective felt hungry, and with an important task ahead of him, he knew he needed to grab a good meal. So, he decided to take a walk down the street and have lunch at a nearby establishment.

Mark walked up to the window to check the weather. As he stood there, he noticed he could feel the breeze, and the icy chill from the night before had disappeared. Instead, he sensed a pleasant warmth in the air.

The detective walked two blocks down to a bakery near his building. Inside, he placed an order for a grilled cheese sandwich and a bottle of soda.

"Extra cheese, please!" he added.

The bakery employee, an elderly man with a humble appearance but a sturdy physique and vibrant eyes, served Mark with a smile.

"Isn't it amazing? What a nice day after yesterday's freezing weather," the employee remarked. "It's as if God has awakened in peace with the world today."

While waiting for his sandwich to be prepared, Mark gazed at a small television mounted high on the bakery wall. A cheerful reporter delivered the day's news.

"Scientists worldwide are striving to comprehend the events of the past two days. First, the significant seismic event felt across the globe on Sunday, followed by the dreadful freezing weather last night. Experts believe there must have been some sort of cyclic movement in the planet's core, giving rise to these phenomena. The seismic event caused a shift in the planet's rotation axis, impacting atmospheric circulation. These changes likely resulted in the widespread cold spell. Fortunately, as temperatures have returned to normal in recent hours, the major effects of the phenomenon are believed to have subsided."

Mark received his lunch and stepped outside the bakery. Taking a seat on an iron chair, he placed his sandwich and soda bottle on a small table. As he took a sip of the soda, the fizz tickled his nose, causing him to cough. He chuckled lightly at his own clumsiness.

As the detective finished his meal, his phone emitted a beep. He pulled it out of his pocket and glanced at the screen. A brief message from Andrew indicated that his partner was on his way.

Mark got up, handed a bill to the bakery employee, and headed back to his apartment.

Twenty minutes later, the two detectives were in Mark's car. The older detective assumed the driver's position while Andrew took the passenger seat, occupied with cleaning an old shotgun.

"Where did you get this antique piece?" Mark inquired.

"It belongs to my father-in-law. He used it for duck hunting," Andrew responded. "It may be old, but the old man keeps it well-maintained and recently tested it. It's just a bit dusty."

"Did your father-in-law inquire about its purpose?" Mark asked.

"I told him it's for a job, but assured him it wouldn't be a dangerous one. I hope I'm right," Andrew commented.

"Don't worry. Nobody at the location will be armed. We'll use it solely for intimidation," Mark reassured him.

"Do you really trust this informant? Why can't you tell me who they are?" Andrew inquired.

Mark chuckled softly, considering how ridiculous it would sound if he were to reveal the truth about the informant and the detailed explanation it would require.

"If I were to tell you, Andrew, you wouldn't believe it."

"The skeptic isn't me; it's you!" Andrew replied. "I believe in many things."

"I spoke with Lauren, and she confirmed the existence of a land lot owned by a cousin of Humbert Sinclair in the gated community neighboring the Mayor's farm. This suggests that the information is probably accurate."

"What does this cousin have to do with the murder of the Sinclair family?"

"It's not the cousin I expect to find at the location. The actual property owner resides out of state. Others are using the house."

"So, you hope to find Carol Sinclair there? Is she alive?" Andrew asked.

"You'll find out soon enough. We can't waste any more time. They could leave at any moment."

"It's like one of those old movies, you know?" Andrew remarked.

"Such as?" Mark inquired.

"This resembles a cliché from action movies. The police duo always solves the case after being suspended. That's what's happening to us now."

"Then brace yourself for the conclusion of this story because it might surprise you!" Mark asserted.

"What do you mean by that?" Andrew asked, intrigued.

Mark displayed a faint smile, quickly replaced by a serious expression. As they approached the gated community, he reduced the vehicle's speed. Andrew stared at the grand entrance to the complex, marked with the words: Paradise Ranch Houses.

To Andrew's surprise, instead of parking at the entrance, Mark continued driving slowly until he stopped the car at a remote spot where the wall receded, revealing a vast open field.

"Let's leave the car here. The property is located at the back of the community. We'll walk around the wall. On the rear side, the stone wall ends, and the lots are only protected by a wire fence. Our target house is there. Just conceal the shotgun. It might raise alarms if seen," Mark instructed.

"Understood," Andrew replied.

Chapter 55

Mark and Andrew proceeded along the community's wall, finding a narrow trail alongside it that allowed them to pass through. Andrew kept the shotgun concealed within a towel.

As anticipated by Mark, the wall eventually gave way to a dilapidated wire fence. Behind the fence, they caught sight of the houses situated at the rear of the community. These properties were noticeably modest, lacking paint or plaster on their exterior walls.

"Let's head up there," Mark suggested, pointing to a small hill ahead. "We can enter without being detected."

"Agreed," Andrew responded.

From their vantage point atop the hill, Mark and Andrew surveyed the final property within the community. It consisted of a small, overgrown plot of land with a modest house at the rear. The two detectives crouched low and took cover behind a rock.

"Can you see anything?" Mark inquired.

Andrew shielded his eyes from the sun with his hand and scanned the area. "I see a man outside the back of the house," he reported. "He's a sturdy-looking guy, right now he's busy getting clothes from a laundry sink."

Mark took out his cell phone and started typing a message.

"What are you doing?" Andrew asked.

"I'm informing the chief about our activities," Mark explained, sending Oswald their location.

"He's not going to be pleased. We're not supposed to be on duty," Andrew warned.

"Yeah. He's already cussing me out, but also said he's coming with backup."

"Shouldn't we wait for backup before entering the property?"

"No, we'll proceed now," Mark decided. "Let's approach that man." He pointed to the individual outside the house. "You go around him from behind, and I'll position myself on the side to cut off his escape. Keep the shotgun ready, but don't use it unless we have to. Understand?"

"Understood," Andrew responded.

The two detectives rose to their feet and advanced. Mark moved swiftly to one side of the house while Andrew unveiled the shotgun, holding it securely against his chest. He walked toward the back of the house, maintaining his focus on the man who remained unaware of their presence.

Andrew cautiously lowered himself to pass through the barbed wire strands of the aging fence, all the while keeping his firearm trained on the man who still had his back turned. Continuing his approach, Andrew remained vigilant, avoiding distractions and keeping his attention solely on the target. As he drew within ten yards of the house, he spotted Mark emerging from behind the side wall, positioned a mere three yards away from their unsuspecting subject.

Mark looked at the man.

"Good afternoon, John. Do you remember me?" The oldest detective spoke.

John Sinclair turned to the side and saw Mark, whom he recognized immediately. Humbert Sinclair's brother turned and tried to run away but found Andrew just ahead, with a shotgun pointed at his chest. John raised his arms and surrendered. He didn't say a word, displaying a mix of fear and frustration on his face.

"That's right, John, remain silent. Slowly lower yourself and lie down on the floor," ordered Mark.

Obediently, John lied down beside the back entrance of the house. Mark expected him to lie on his stomach, but to the detective's surprise, the middle-aged man lied on his side and curled up, hugging his own legs.

Andrew pulled a pair of handcuffs from his coat pocket and threw them to his partner, who proceeded to tie John to an iron bar attached to the house's wall.

"Do you know where the girl is?" Andrew asked Mark, whispering.

"I'll go inside the house and find her. Stay here and keep him as quiet as you can," replied Mark, pointing to John.

Andrew nodded, and Mark walked past him. The oldest detective carefully opened the door to the house.

Mark proceeded cautiously, making an effort not to make any noise. He walked through the kitchen and noticed two dirty plates in the sink and a still-hot pan on the stove. The detective entered a narrow hallway, looked around, and spotted an open door. He walked past the room and saw, on a single mattress, an old suitcase and some bags of clothes.

Suddenly, at the end of the hallway, a bathroom door opened. A girl appeared, distractedly tying her hair as she walked toward another room in the house. The girl wore a pair of cheap sandals and a T-shirt that was much bigger than her size, which looked like a shabby dress on her.

Before she entered the room, the girl heard a voice.

"Hi, Carol!" Mark greeted.

When Carol Sinclair turned around and saw a man who looked like a police officer, she didn't say anything. She just opened her mouth and widened her eyes in surprise.

"My name is Mark Randall. I'm from the Civil Police Department."

The girl looked over Mark's shoulder and noticed Andrew standing by the kitchen window, pointing the shotgun downwards.

"What did you do to my uncle?" asked Carol.

"He is fine. He's just lying on the floor. We didn't harm him."

Carol remained standing still, staring at the detective.

"Did you come to arrest me?"

"You killed your entire family, Carol. Why did you do that?"

"I didn't kill anyone. It was him." She pointed in John Sinclair's direction. "My uncle and that fighter killed my parents."

Mark reflected for a moment and said, "Listen, Carol. You will certainly be charged as an accomplice. I can see you're not a prisoner. You will have to explain yourself to the authorities."

There was a moment of silence. Carol looked at the floor as Mark watched her, waiting for her reaction.

Carol glared angrily at Mark. "My parents got what they deserved!" she spoke roughly.

"Don't say that, girl! Nobody deserves to have their face smashed with a hammer," Mark responded firmly.

The girl looked up, displaying a sarcastic smile and a strong sob, revealing her nervousness in a way that Mark could not fully understand.

"My father was broke. His company wouldn't last even two months. So he went to church and befriended the Mayor. Do you know how he did it, Officer?" she spoke, her tone bitter.

The detective remained silent, simply staring at Carol.

The girl continued, "My father threw me straight into the hands of Paul Andraus. That's how he and the Mayor became friends. My dad gifted me to a rapist! Do you know what the Mayor's son did to me and what he would have done to my sister when it was her turn? And all with my father's approval. My mother also knew what was happening and did nothing to stop it. She cared more about money than about her daughters. They deserved to die."

Mark's expression changed, showing confusion.

"But... what about your sister? Did she also deserve to die?" the detective questioned.

"I didn't want her dead. Joanna wasn't supposed to wake up, but she did. She was very scared, and that stupid fighter killed her before my uncle and I could do anything to stop him," Carol revealed.

"That was the reason your uncle killed Tortoise later, wasn't it?" Mark asked, connecting the pieces.

Carol didn't answer, but her silence was enough for the detective to understand what happened. She stared at the floor, refusing to show any emotion, though her trembling hands betrayed her impending collapse.

Taking two steps forward, Mark stood just one yard away from Carol, looking at her.

The girl lifted her head, met Mark's gaze, and said, "Tell me, Officer: what kind of world is this, where a father gives his daughter to be abused by a monster in exchange for financial favors? Is it worth living in a place like this?"

Mark looked at Carol, at a loss for words.

She continued, "Do you think God will forgive me? Is there forgiveness for what I've done?"

Mark and Carol began to hear the sound of sirens. Mark glanced out the window behind the girl, seeing the approaching lights of police cars. He then turned to look at Andrew, who raised his head, trying to see the vehicles.

Turning back to Carol, Mark said, "Listen, Carol: I'm not here to judge you. You were driven by terrible circumstances and emotions, which led you to make a huge mistake. You will surely face the consequences under the law, but I can see that you're already judging yourself. The greatest punishment lies within your own heart."

The girl glared at the detective.

"There are people who have nothing in their hearts, you know, Officer? They think they have the right to treat others like dirt. They never feel regret for what they do. Look at the Mayor's son."

Mark responded with a compassionate smile and said, "There is no evil without suffering, Carol. Trust me, the Mayor's son suffers just as much as you do, and he will never find peace. The more evil he commits, the more he will suffer, until he is consumed by his own madness. Do you want proof of this? Your suffering didn't diminish after your parents were killed, did it? In fact, it only intensified. I can feel it."

The sound of police cars burning rubber and the opening and closing of vehicle doors became audible. Loud voices of men could also be heard as they entered the property.

One of them shouted, "Head around to the back, and we'll go in through the front." Mark recognized this voice as Oswald.

Carol glanced back, anticipating the opening of the house door. She turned to Mark once again.

"Who are you?"

At that moment, Oswald and two more policemen entered the house, passing through the room.

Mark smiled at the young girl.

"I'm just someone who feels responsible for you."

Oswald emerged in the hallway wielding a pistol. When he saw Mark in front of a girl, the chief lowered his gun and approached his subordinate.

"Is everything okay, Mark?" the chief asked.

Mark simply nodded. Oswald turned to the girl. When Mark's boss recognized Sinclair's missing daughter, he let out a cry that echoed throughout the house.

"God Almighty!"

Chapter 56

On the street in front of the Paradise Ranch Houses Community, Mark and Andrew leaned against a wall, taking a rest beside the veteran's car. In front of them, the sun was about to set. The star was surrounded by yellow clouds, creating a striking contrast with the blue sky.

Andrew wrapped his father-in-law's shotgun back in the towel.

"The chief told me the town would be in an uproar when this story came out," said the young man. "The Mayor's family won't escape a scandal of this magnitude. A case involving sexual violence that culminates in the massacre of nearly an entire family cannot be ignored. Even if Paul didn't strike the Sinclairs with the hammer, he will face charges for the rape of a minor. That alone would be enough to ruin his life, and the public will inevitably associate the mayor's son with the murders. Just as you said, this is the story Charles Andraus' enemies have been waiting for. In the end, I believe you got your revenge against the Mayor."

Mark took out his cell phone from his pocket and pointed its camera at the sun. He smiled at Andrew.

"To be honest, I no longer care about what happens to Charles or his son." He took a picture of the sunset.

Andrew reacted, "I'll pretend I believe that! You've been waiting for this moment for over thirty years. You only say that because you're immensely happy right now. You've successfully found the Sinclair family murderers. The chief even mentioned that we'll be reinstated to the police force tomorrow. We might even be called for television interviews."

Mark looked at the screen of his cell phone, analyzing the photo he just took. "I won't be returning to the police, Andrew," he announced. "I'm resigning tomorrow."

"Are you resigning just like that? After solving such a case? You will become famous for what you accomplished today."

"Well, then it's the perfect time to leave. I'm forty-six years old. For the past twenty years, this job has exposed me to the worst of humanity. Such things are not doing me any good. I want to change my life. I want to travel, meet new people, broaden my horizons."

"You're talking like a hippie. How will you support yourself? Have you saved up any money? Will you receive retirement benefits after resigning?" asked Andrew.

Mark put his cell phone back in his pocket. "A week ago, I would have worried about those things. But now, I don't care."

"You're so different today! You sound like a completely distinct person. Tell me, apart from not seeming affected by the extreme cold yesterday, forgetting your car in front of my house, and not caring anymore about things that were tormenting you until yesterday, is there any other strange occurrence you want to share?

Mark remained silent, gazing at the horizon for a few moments. He took a deep breath and turned to his colleague.

"I'm about to share a secret with you, Andrew, but you have to promise to keep it between us. Can I trust you?"

"Sure. You know I don't talk to anyone else," Andrew replied.

Mark took another deep breath. "Yesterday, before I went to sleep, I had decided it would be my last night in this world. I've been contemplating this for many years, so it shouldn't come as a surprise. However, a few days ago, this desire intensified to the point where it manifested into something real. The thought of ending everything became seductive in a way I had never imagined. Leaving this life seemed like the solution to all my problems and pain. No more haunting memories or regrets, just a world beyond this one where I could be free and fulfill all my desires." Mark swallowed, feeling the saliva accumulate in his mouth, and continued, "Yesterday, before I went to sleep, there was a bottle of tranquilizers beside my bed. I planned to take all the pills and end my suffering once and for all."

Mark sighed and raised his eyes, gazing at the sky. "However, when I had made up my mind, a voice intervened. It made me reevaluate my entire life and all the tragedies that have tormented my soul. This voice showed me that leaving this world, leaving this body, would not resolve anything if I carried the same pain within me. The answer lies not in leaving, but in healing the wounds. And I need to do that right here."

The older detective looked ahead, observing the horizon. He watched as the orange disk of the sun hid behind the hill across the street.

He turned to Andrew. "Last night, I was on the brink of a precipice, Andrew, but just before I jumped, someone spoke to me, showing me another path to follow. I can't say what or who it was, but it was there." Mark's lips trembled. "Now I finally understand. There is something beyond what we can see, and it saved me."

In silence, Andrew approached his colleague and placed a hand on his shoulder. Mark noticed the tear-filled eyes of his partner. They hugged for the first time since they'd met. The detective felt like he had finally found peace within himself.

After a few seconds, Mark released Andrew and walked to the right side of the car.

"Do me a favor, Andrew. Drive the car back to town. I just want to gaze out the window."

The two detectives entered the vehicle. Calmly, Andrew adjusted the driver's seat position and the steering wheel's height. Mark sat beside him, resting his arm on the open window.

Mark looked at his partner. "I thought about it. This story about the Sinclair family and the Mayor's son, and all the negative attention it will bring upon the Andraus family. It will likely harm Archbishop Euzebius, won't it?"

"I don't think that will happen," Andrew responded, turning the ignition key. "I believed being Charles Andraus' brother-in-law will not harm Euzebius. Not after last night."

"Why do you say that?" Mark asked.

Andrew took his cell phone out of his pocket and opened a news website. "Listen to this: last night, Archbishop Euzebius Andraus took in more than five hundred people inside the city's Cathedral. They were mainly humble individuals who were left homeless after the major seismic event on Sunday, most of them from Aurora Street. The Archbishop's assistants turned on electric heaters and provided shelter for everyone inside the Cathedral until this morning when the temperature returned to normal." He looked at Mark. "They are saying that Euzebius' actions saved more than five hundred lives, including thirty children. He became a hero."

"Is that true?" Mark asked, surprised.

Andrew looked at his cell phone screen again and continued reading, "This morning, Euzebius made an announcement. He revealed plans to implement several changes in the archdiocese of our region. He plans to relocate his official residence to a more modest place and transform his current home into a treatment facility for drug addicts. Additionally, he stated that he intends to reduce luxury expenses and expensive meals provided to him by the church. He expressed his commitment to not only offer prayers and superficial favors to the people living on Aurora Street but to genuinely work toward saving everyone residing there."

"That's a big change in attitude," Mark said. "I'm really glad to hear that."

"There's more: Euzebius declared that he would now spare no effort in supporting the fight against drug trafficking in our city. He even expressed disagreement with the court's decision to release his brother-in-law and called for a thorough investigation by the Civil Police Department to uncover the truth about what was happening at the Leticia Andraus Farm." Andrew turned off the screen of his cell phone and put the device back in his pocket. "With even the Archbishop turning against Charles Andraus, it seems that the Mayor is truly in trouble now."

Mark remained silent, processing all the information he had received. Andrew gently pressed the accelerator, causing the car to start moving.

"You know, Mark? I've been thinking about your conversations with the Archbishop and the news of his existential crisis. Maybe you influenced this change," pondered Andrew. "Isn't that possible?"

"I didn't say anything important to the Archbishop, Andrew. There is nothing that a regular public servant like me could say to change the opinion of someone like Euzebius," Mark replied. He turned to the car window and felt the wind brushing against his face.

The detective observed the golden sunbeams filtering through the trees as the car moved. The sunlight seemed to dance among the branches.

"Unless he sees you as someone superior," Andrew insisted.

"What do you mean?"

"Euzebius revealed that he had a vision after the global seismic event. He claimed to have seen the Creator of the Universe and had a conversation with Him. The Lord conveyed that the Archbishop could do much more for this city. Some critics suggested that he might be delusional and that he suffered a head injury during the seismic event. However, Euzebius maintained that Sunday's event was a divine sign. Personally, I believed in the Archbishop. What about you? What did you make of all this? Still skeptical? Even after what happened to you last night? Even after everything that has taken place in recent days?"

Mark leaned back in his seat, feeling a sense of relaxation.

"Well, who am I to say I don't believe the Archbishop?" he replied.

Andrew smiled and remained silent, indicating that he had heard enough. He continued to drive.

The older detective redirected his gaze to the window beside him. He breathed in the fresh air of the late afternoon that filled the moving vehicle.

Mark Randall was happy, a feeling he hadn't experienced in a long time.

He was happy because he had chosen to remain in this world.

Printed in Great Britain
by Amazon